Dame Fiona Kidman OBE, Légion d'honneur, is one of New Zealand's foremost contemporary writers. A novelist, short story writer and poet, she is the author of more than 30 books. She has worked as a librarian, radio producer and critic, and as a scriptwriter for radio, television and film. She lives in Wellington.

PRAISE FOR *THIS MORTAL BOY*

'Kidman's prose is precise, detailed, lyric . . . The fluencies and hard-won command of a good writer bring out their own truth' *Irish Times*

'Magnetic . . . The ending of a life involves decisions made by many, Kidman reminds us, with opportunities for compassion that are regularly missed until it's too late' *New York Times*

'Kidman deftly sketches the personalities behind the headline story, along with the ambiguities and mitigating circumstances surrounding them . . . In the emotional catharsis experienced by the imprisoned Paddy Black, she demonstrates how redemption may be grasped even at the final hour of the darkest day' *Wall Street Journal*

'It's an amazing novel, this. It's compelling' Val McDermid

'Perfectly captures the life of a young immigrant while taking a sharp look at New Zealand's social history . . . Moving, compelling and ultimately tragic' Liz Nugent

'A haunting read. . . Blends events as they unfold, painting the bigger historical and social picture but it is in the sensitive characterisation of Paddy and his desperate mother, Kathleen, that Kidman excels' Jess Kidd

'Stays with you long after you've read it . . . It brings home what the death penalty really means for someone who wasn't bad, just young and misguided' Lesley Pearse

'Powerfully explores the ways that young men and women were demonised by politicians . . . a really moving book' @SamiraAhmed

'An essential read as a study of wrong choices, ambiguous motives, infinitely nuanced personalities and a grim complex tragedy of a loner . . . A tremendous novel' Arts Council of Northern Ireland

'A meticulously researched novel which holds up a dark part of our history to the light ... [Kidman] expertly brings readers into the lives of all those involved' *New Zealand Herald*

'A tale about violent acts that is infused with humanity and compassion' *New Zealand Listener*

PRAISE FOR *ALL DAY AT THE MOVIES*

'*All Day at the Movies* proves that Kidman is a masterful storyteller' *The Lady*

'A universal and honest book' San Francisco Book Review

'A truly gifted writer. She explores the subtleties of human interaction and family with a deft and insightful hand' Trip Fiction

PRAISE FOR *SONGS FROM THE VIOLET CAFÉ*

'Kidman, a poet, is a beautiful writer' *The Times*

'Readers are in good hands; like all Kidman's writing, it is engaging and captivating' *The Lady*

PRAISE FOR *THE INFINITE AIR*

'A sweeping saga of a fascinating life and an entertaining insight into the early days of aviation' Historical Novel Society

'A thrilling tale of adventure and heartbreak – Kidman has triumphantly brought this inspirational heroine to life' *The Lady*

'It's a given that Kidman couldn't produce a poor paragraph if she tried to and this is a narrative that – I have to say it – takes wing' *New Zealand Herald*

'A fascinating read' *Red Magazine*

'Gripping' *Woman's Own*

All the Way to Summer

STORIES OF LOVE AND LONGING

Fiona Kidman

GALLIC BOOKS

LONDON

A Gallic Book

Copyright © Fiona Kidman as per details on page 345

Fiona Kidman has asserted her moral right to be identified
as the author of the work.

First published by Penguin Random House New Zealand Ltd.
This edition published by arrangement with Penguin Random House New
Zealand Ltd.

First published in Great Britain in 2024 by Gallic Books,
12 Eccleston Street, London SW1W 9LT

A CIP record for this book is available from the British Library
ISBN 978-1-913-547-64-6

Typeset in Garamond by Gallic Books

Printed and bound by LSI

For Jennifer and Peter Beck
and life-long friendship

CONTENTS

PREFACE

How does one know what love really is? How many varieties of love are there? Does falling in love mean living happily ever after? Can we ever recover when love ends, or are we changed for all time? W.H. Auden, in his famous poem 'Tell Me the Truth about Love', from which I have shamelessly borrowed the title for one of the stories in this collection, wonders what it looks and smells and sounds like. It might howl like an Alsatian, or sing riotously at parties, or, more decorously, prefer only classical music. And, he muses, does it feel as prickly as a hedgehog, or as soft as an eiderdown? Some questions of my own: Does it ache like a tooth? Do hearts really break?

I can't answer these questions any more than the poet, but in the last lines of the poem Auden repeats the refrain, begging to be told the truth about love and asking if love will alter his life altogether. This last question seems central to these stories of mine. For the most part, they are about love that changes the lives of my characters, one way or another; love, long or short, and often dangerous, is never forgotten.

A number of the stories have appeared in my previous collections, written over some thirty years. The theme of love, between all manner of people, has been persistent. This year I turn eighty, and it seems like a good moment to gather up stories that reflect this preoccupation in my writing, but there are some new stories too. For those who have followed the earlier works, the stories are just the same in essence, although this volume has been an opportunity to refresh them, sharpen them up a bit. I am grateful to Harriet Allan for making this possible and for her constancy as my editor over many years of my writing life. The love of good friends matters too.

Some of these stories are written in the first person. If my readers think they recognise me in these, or the character of Jill in 'Stippled', they are probably close. We all have our own histories of love.

FIONA KIDMAN, 2020

1

CIRCLING

CIRCLING TO YOUR LEFT

Miracles, miracles. Alice was sitting at her desk preparing an interview when the phone call came. She works in a radio station, running a magazine programme about lifestyles. Alice is a personality in her own right, and people seek her views on all manner of issues. People say she is a powerful woman, and indeed she feels strong and vital, but she has also reached that more private age when her children worry about who will mow her lawns and what will become of her. The name of her caller is Kathryn Fox, Kathryn spelled with a K and a Y. She is phoning from Auckland, from an insurance company. Alice can see her behind the desk, cool and efficient, wearing a well-cut suit, a muted but pretty scarf arranged artfully at the throat of her plain cotton blouse. She can hear her asking claimants the correct spelling of their names, an instinctive precautionary gesture, which she carries into her own life – this is exactly who I am: Kathryn with a K and a Y. Mrs, she adds, Mrs Kathryn Fox.

'Yes, Mrs Fox?' Alice says, preparing to tell her either that she has more life insurance than she can afford, or that she can't spare an opinion on the subject this morning.

'It's about my father,' says Kathryn Fox, quickly. 'I believe you knew him when he was young, before he married my mother.

His name was Douglas McNaught.' Her voice has become less assured, dropping a note, as if she expects the rebuff Alice might be preparing. 'It was a surprise that you might know him.'

'How did you make the connection?' Alice asks, the interviewer at work. But she felt the flutter of her own pulse.

'Well,' Kathryn takes a deep breath. 'I heard you on the radio once, and you mentioned Fish Rock. You described a man you had known there, at work in his cowshed. When the cows got stroppy and wouldn't do what he wanted, he used to yell at them, "I might as well talk to Jesus".'

Alice puts down her pen. 'Niall McNaught.'

'My grandfather. Are you with me?'

'Yes,' says Alice. 'I am.'

'My father was dying and I had been sent to my grandparents' farm so that my mother would have more time to nurse him.' Kathryn's voice assumes a relentless quality now that she is underway. 'I was very small. I sat on the railing of the yard and listened to my grandfather say those words every evening one summer. "You might as well talk to Jesus," he said, and I knew he was talking to more than the cows. I've never heard anyone else say that since. Soon afterwards he died, and, not long after that, my father died too.'

'So your father didn't die on the farm?'

'He'd been overseas to fight in Malaya,' Kathryn says, 'you know, the one that's called Malaysia now.' Of course Alice already knows this, but she doesn't interrupt. 'When he came back, he had some jungle illness. He went back to the farm, but he was never able to work the way he had before, and he and my mother moved to town.'

This is something Alice doesn't know. 'Did he work again? In town?' Everyone in Fish Rock knew what you meant when you said 'town'. The place was to the north, not as big as a city, but it had hotels with starched linen tablecloths in the dining rooms, bookshops and a theatre, warehouses and stock and station agents. It was where you went if you needed the dentist.

'He went into the stock and station and worked there for as long as he could. You did know them, didn't you? I'm not wrong?'

'Yes, I did know them,' says Alice slowly. There is a silence between them while Alice asks herself whether or not she wants to help the woman at the other end of the call.

As if she senses her hesitation, Kathryn Fox steps in, assertive again. 'Just tell me what my father was like.' Not pleading, just matter of fact, and ready to give information of her own. 'My mother remarried, she couldn't see how much my father mattered to me. She was very happy with my stepfather, and he was good to my sister and me. "What is there to tell?" she used to say when I asked her about my father. "He was sick and he died." Whatever it was that she had fancied in him, she'd forgotten. Well, perhaps you wouldn't know about that, but just something, some of the things he might have said and done. Forgive me, perhaps you don't remember much about him at all.'

'He was a gay dog,' Alice says, instantly regretting it.

'Gay?' Kathryn says.

'Not like that. It's what we said back then. Language changes.' Alice recognises the distance between them, between Kathryn's age and her own, between knowing and not knowing her father. 'He did a fantastic set of Lancers. Well, we just did a set occasionally at the end of square dancing.'

'Let me get this straight, you're telling me my father square-danced?'

'Yes. But not only that. He was a knockout. I mean, he was very good looking.'

Kathryn says, 'I would never have imagined that. My mother didn't keep any photos. Nobody told me he was good looking.'

Alice thinks Kathryn may be sorry she has rung, that Alice is romancing an image for her, or that she doesn't remember him at all. 'Was your mother called Rhoda?' she asks.

'No.' Kathryn mentions the name of a woman Alice has never heard of, who, she says, her father had met in hospital soon after his return from the jungle. They had married almost straight away.

This is the miracle, a chunk of missing history, offered to Alice on a morning when the wind whistles between buildings and the traffic five storeys down is blocked by a blown water main and the tower block next door is being evacuated by a faulty alarm system.

Immediately after Alice left school, she went to work in the drapery store at Fish Rock. She pushed her way to the head of a queue of young women who thought it might be fun to work on the main (and only) street for a year or two while they got their glory boxes together. She had turned down the idea of going nursing or teaching. For other women, there was the burden of Catholic choice – to be a nun – but that was beyond the imagination of the Presbyterian circle of Fish Rock, a bizarre impenetrable mystery. Who, they asked themselves in hushed voices, would want to live amongst women?

'Why do you want to work in my drapery shop?'

Miss Macdonald, the proprietor, asked her. She was a tall, thin woman with hair escaping in wisps from a huge bun. She was proud that she had not cut her hair for twenty years, although no one had ever seen this massive accumulation let loose.

'I want to earn some money while I decide what to do next.'

'You mean, until someone comes along and offers to marry you? I don't want boys hanging around here,' said Miss Macdonald.

Alice thought it wiser not to tell her prospective employer that she had already been forsaken by Douglas McNaught, although, who knew, he could still turn up some day. Instead, she said, 'It'll be hard for my parents if I leave now, just when they're getting the farm going. I can still help out with the milking at the weekends.'

This appealed to Miss Macdonald, the notion of hard work and thrift, and also that she could hire Alice without committing herself to the long term. 'You can have a three-month trial, and then we can decide whether we like each other enough for you to stay on.'

This was how Alice came to stand behind the counter of the Fish Rock drapery shop, counting buttons, selling girdles and crêpe de Chine, ordering whirl bras spiral-stitched to pencil-sharp points, suggesting sewing patterns to young women beside whom, only a month before, she had sat in geography class, learning how to do rouleau button loops so she could demonstrate them to others, advising Miss Macdonald when they were low on three-ply in the knitting wool section, and all the while breathing in the steady crisp scent of new linen, which still reminds her of buttercups.

Miss Macdonald had hired Alice first and foremost to sweep out the shop and make cups of tea. All of which she did, but when Alice suggested they order cinch belts because she had heard that these were what the girls in town were wearing (and she yearned for one of her own), her employer gave her a long speculative look, ordered half a dozen and sold out the next day. After that, Miss Macdonald took time out to go to town on a buying expedition and left Alice in charge. When the new stock arrived, turnover increased, and so did Alice's wages.

Fish Rock is a string of shops divided by a main road. The post office has long closed. People go to town for their clothes, and the drapery shop has gone. A square white church stands beneath a spreading tree, a museum houses the unsmiling faces of the village ancestors, the community hall is showing its age, a monument to Fish Rock's war dead, surrounded by a heavy chain, stands sentinel beside the road. Douglas McNaught's name is not amongst the dead.

Douglas didn't fall in battle, and, besides, his war was a jungle skirmish, his going a young man's response to the unanswerable in his life, not to a call to arms sweeping a nation. His name is written on a headstone in a quiet cemetery near the sea, where sand lifts and falls in drifts against the tombs and dry grasses bend on windy days. Trooper Douglas McNaught, SAS, Malaya. No name of a wife appears. This much Alice knows.

Her parents' farm was next to the McNaughts. The McNaughts were an old, settled family, and the Emerys were newcomers, their land a fraction the size of their neighbours', neglected and overrun with gorse, except for three rich-green river paddocks. Her family had driven into the valley one afternoon in summer near milking time. Their cows were crammed in the back of trucks, their udders near bursting point. Gidday, said the men, standing on the edge of the road. Gidday, Alice's father had said and gone into the tumbledown shed on the farm to milk the cows as they were unloaded.

One of the onlookers followed him. 'Let's know if you need any help,' said the man. This was Douglas. He was dark and nuggety, with a sinewy throat rising from his black bush singlet. His hair was crinkly beneath the battered grey felt hat he wore. Nests of hair covered his short strong forearms. When he lit a cigarette, he balanced it for an instant with a delicate flick beneath the tip of his tongue and his top lip before drawing it down into his mouth.

Alice's father managed his farm with care. He's a dreamy bastard, he farms with a textbook in one hand and a spade in the other, the neighbours said to each other, but they were interested. He used electric fences to make the grass go further. His butterfat average inched up, higher than on the farms around about. You might as well talk to Jesus, said his neighbour Niall McNaught, as try to tell my sons how to do that. Niall's voice was without envy. He had enough to go round. His three sons had worked on the land since they left school. Malcolm, the eldest, was married and lived in a house across the paddock from his parents; the second and third boys still lived in the old farmhouse. Alan smiled sleepily at people and worked without saying much. He drinks, Alice's father told her mother, but he's harmless. Douglas was referred to as the baby of the family, although he was twenty-eight.

The entrance to the older McNaught house was by way of a verandah, bordered with curly wooden fretwork. In the morning, it was full of fierce heat, and even the geraniums wilted in the scuffed earth beside the path. In the afternoons, the dogs slept there.

Inside, it was hard to pick that the McNaughts were well-off. Old newspapers and piles of bills were stacked on the sideboards, and ashtrays were emptied only when they were full. In the sitting room, a shabby suite covered in brown moquette was arranged without much thought. The walls were decorated with calendars from the local shops and two ornately framed pictures of Niall's parents, posing formally in their best clothes; his mother wore a long, dark dress with a high collar. An old piano stood beneath these portraits. The McNaughts played it on Saturday nights when friends came to drink beer and sing. Alan played until he passed out, and then Tilly, the mother, took over. They sang 'Roll Out the Barrel', and 'Coming In On a Wing and a Prayer' and 'She'll be Coming Round the Mountain', *when she comes, when she comes, she'll be wearing pink pyjamas when she comes*. Presbyterian they might have been, but they were new people now, they said. They didn't have truck with the old nonsense. 'Well,' Niall said to Alice's father, 'the boys wouldn't hang around for long if we did, would they?' Douglas and Alan slept in the same room they had slept in all their lives, in two of three beds arranged dormitory style, across the passage from their parents' room.

'They've got money all right,' Alice's father said to her mother. If you knew where to look, it wasn't hard to see. A race horse cantered in the front paddock, and two long-finned American cars stood in a garage at the side of the house. Over at Malcolm's new house, his wife, Noelene, had arranged a cabinet full of crystal decanters and Belleek cream lustreware decorated with shamrocks. She hung lace curtains at the windows.

The McNaughts and Alice's parents accepted each others' difference. Tilly of the overflowing ashtrays and ungathered newspapers kept a scrubbed board and an oven that shone like song. Alice's father was crazy about the McNaught boys from the start. They made him feel like one of the people, a real farmer. Alice believes that her parents were happy there. Their marriage, which had appeared frayed and thin, bloomed anew in the McNaughts' benign light.

As for Alice, the McNaughts put up with her.

She thinks of it now in those terms, she can see with hindsight that she was a bumptious, pushy girl with a need to draw attention to herself. She had succeeded at her last school; she resented her new one. The farmers sent their children to boarding school in town if they thought it worth the money, the rest went to Fish Rock High and planned their leaving and marriage. Clover Johnston was one of the exceptions who, if anything, was cleverer than Alice, but made less of it. She was a modest, handsome girl. Her parents farmed at the far end of the district. Alice and Clover became friends, but out of school they were separated by distance.

Tilly was past entertaining teenagers. 'Why don't you go and see Noelene?' she suggested when Alice turned up on her doorstep one afternoon over Easter, looking for company. Tilly's head was tilted to one side, and she was shaking it furiously. 'I got peroxide down my ear to shift the wax,' she explained. 'Makes it fizz, you know. Here, take this bowl of eggs to Noelene, save me a trip.'

Noelene was going to have a baby. Alice found her in the sitting room, embroidering the front of a baby's nightgown. She looked impatient and grown up when Alice arrived.

'What are you going to call the baby?' Alice asked, hoping to engage her attention.

'I can't decide,' said Noelene. 'Do you like Pamela for a girl and Todd for a boy?'

'Awful,' said Alice.

'Charmaine?'

'Blah,' said Alice, preparing to show off. 'How about you call it Homer if it's a boy?'

Noelene looked long-suffering. 'Would you like to hold the ring over my stomach?'

'What for?' said Alice, backing off.

'To find out whether it's going to be a girl or a boy. The last time Tilly did it the ring said it was going to be a girl, but I reckon it's moved too low for that. I'm sure it's a boy.' She was slipping her wedding ring off as she spoke. She picked up a reel of cotton and snapped off a thread, tying it to the ring.

'What do I do?' Alice asked, as Noelene lay down on the sofa.

'Well, you hold it over my stomach and see which way the ring goes. If it turns around it's a girl, up and down it's a boy. Didn't you know that?'

'No.'

'And if it stops in the middle it's a disaster.' Noelene shivered, pulling up her maternity smock to reveal the vast expanse of her stomach. As she lay there, it looked smooth, white and mountainous, then suddenly an oyster-shaped bulge sprouted on its side.

'See, it's the baby's hand,' said Noelene.

Alice felt sick.

'Go on, be quick.'

As Alice picked up the ring, a shadow fell across the door. It was Douglas, Noelene's brother-in-law.

'Well,' he said, 'how's the son and heir?' There was something odd in his voice.

'It's a girl,' said Alice, 'and Noelene's going to call her Guinevere.'

There was a brief pause. 'And slowly answered Arthur from the barge,' Douglas said. In her surprise, Alice nearly dropped the ring.

'It's a load of shit,' said Douglas, turning away. Alice didn't know whether he meant the baby, the ring, or the poem he was quoting from. But once, she realised, he would have gone to Fish Rock High.

'I could have had any of them, you know,' said Noelene when he had gone. She meant the McNaught brothers.

When Alice didn't say anything, Noelene said, 'I have to have a boy before the others catch up. You see?'

'Douglas loves dancing, he goes every fortnight,' said Tilly through a mouthful of pins. She had taken pity on Alice, who was trying to make a dress from some material sent by her aunt. Alice's mother was so busy on the farm, she didn't have time to help.

'Where does he dance?' Alice asked. Public dances were held in the hall, but they were few and far between. Most of the girls from school went; they started at fourteen, so tantalisingly close to maturity by Fish Rock standards. Alice's parents wouldn't hear of her going without them. She had been once with her mother and father and felt like a baby.

'Don't you know about the square dances?' said Tilly. 'The club meets in the hall, it's not an open dance, just about thirty or forty go.' As soon as she had said it, Alice could see Tilly wished she hadn't. She gave Alice a sideways look as if something had just dawned on her.

'You're a big girl,' she said, 'you're growing a helluva big girl. You started a box yet?'

When the Buick next pulled up at the McNaughts' gate, with Douglas at the wheel, Alice was lying in wait. She shot out from behind the cream stand and offered to open the gate for him.

'What brings this on?' he asked, leaning out the car window after she had pulled the gate shut.

'Please, could you give me a lift to the square dancing?'

He sighed, looked out the other window. 'Sure,' he said finally. 'If your parents'll let you.'

That was when Alice began to keep company, of a kind, with Douglas McNaught. He was nearly twice her age. It astonishes her now to think that her parents would let her go with him, but she can see also how it was. They weren't looking at them as two people who might fall in love; they were looking at a kindly, trusted grown up and a child. Nor, for a long time, did Alice think of Douglas as anything other than a means to get her out of the house and down the road. Looking back, she sees herself as truly innocent, despite her brashness. What did he think? Who did he see? These are questions Alice has asked herself since.

Clover, who had several respectable older brothers, was sometimes allowed to go to the dances too. This may have been one of the reasons Alice was permitted to go with Douglas.

One day, Clover took her aside with a look of shock. 'I've heard another word for sex,' she said. Her cousins had told her the word (her brothers would never have said this to her, they were that kind of family, protective towards the women). *Rooting.* That was the word.

They gazed at each other in horror. Pigs rooted in the bush. The connotations were impossibly vulgar, and violent. They knew that sex was a red-hot poker, but they couldn't imagine how they would be burned or blinded. If that was sex, they didn't want it. That week, a girl called Marie, who had left school the year before, said she was dating two men at once and went to the cemetery with one or the other on alternate nights: she was still trying to decide which of them had what she described as the better equipment.

This story got around and filtered back to school. Clover and Alice were open-mouthed with astonishment, while at the same time doubting that it could be true. Over at the McNaughts', Noelene had given birth to a daughter, who she said was just the cutest wee thing, and she'd be trying for another just as soon as her stitches had healed.

When Alice went to the dances, she pitched into the routines, snatching a hand, spinning from the waist, moving onto the next partner: older men with red-veined faces, or Douglas, or one of Clover's older brothers, whoever. They were accompanied by a pianist and a man with an accordion. The caller had slicked-back fair hair and wore a plaid shirt with a neckerchief. He clapped his hands and stamped his foot in time to 'Red River Valley': *Oh we're off to the next in the valley /and you circle to your left and to your right / and you choose your girl from the valley / oh you choose your Red River girl.*

On the way there and back, Douglas hardly said a word. Alice didn't mind, though occasionally she spoke to him. One night, as they drove home between the grassy hills, the moon seemed to float and stop and start, trickling along the sky.

'The moon is a ghostly galleon,' Alice said.

'Jesus. Shit,' he said, his fists bunching around the steering wheel. He was not prepared to lose himself to poetry a second time, she figured.

Each time they got to the McNaughts' gate, opposite the Emerys' farm, Alice jumped out of the car and opened the gate for him; he swept through without an acknowledgement, and she closed it behind him, watching the car's progress over the dewy dust of the track. A kind of happiness had descended on her and the weeks and months that lay between her and the end of school.

That is, until Rhoda Aukett turned up. One square-dance evening, Alice got dressed as usual and went to wait at the mail box. Douglas didn't arrive. She went back inside and rang his house. In her head, she could hear the phone's Morse code signal ringing in the McNaughts' kitchen. Three shorts for an S. Tilly answered after what seemed a long time. 'Didn't he tell you he'd be going straight to the village after milking?' she said, but Alice could tell that she was not surprised.

When she reported that, no, he hadn't told her, Tilly just said, 'He must have forgotten, eh?'

'Won't he be coming back to pick me up?'

Tilly couldn't put it off any longer. 'He's gone to pick up Rhoda. She's staying at the hotel. You know about Rhoda, don't you?'

'Oh, yeah, sure, I know about Rhoda.'

'Well, there, that's all right then.' Tilly sounded relieved.

Alice's mother wandered into the room.

'Douglas running late?'

'A bit. He has to pick up someone called Rhoda.'

'Oh, yes, Rhoda,' she said vaguely, 'I've heard about Rhoda.' It seemed that everyone had heard about Rhoda.

'I'm to wait along the road,' Alice lied. 'He'll be in a hurry when he comes.' She rushed out the door before her mother could ask any more questions.

It was a two-mile walk to Fish Rock. Alice, full of rage, arrived at the dance when it was already nine o'clock and the dance in full swing. She hurried along the darkened main street, passing the drapery where she would soon be working. The women who made the tea sat gossiping in the far corner of the hall. They never danced. Their breasts were encased in shiny satin blouses, and they wore full skirts, but they were not there to dance. The supper plates had been arranged near the slide that separated the kitchen from the dance hall. The zip was coming to the boil. Alice turned it off and filled the urn. At the end of the round, she threw up the shutter and called, in her loudest voice: 'Come and get it', just the way the women did.

There was a flurry in the corner and a ripple of surprise amongst the dancers. Alice stood still and smiled a broad, careful grin.

'Well,' said one of the older women, 'isn't she ever just the little helper?' She said it quite nicely, although it was clear that neither she nor her friends cared for what Alice had done.

Douglas walked towards her, a woman holding onto his arm. She wore a powder-blue crushed-velvet dress. Alice knew at once that he loved this dark and creamy-skinned creature.

'Hi, kid,' he said, 'I didn't expect to see you here.'

That was when she knew he had never really seen her.

He introduced her to Rhoda Aukett, who flashed a dazzling smile. Rhoda didn't appear to mind when Alice climbed into the back of the car to catch a ride home, though Douglas gave a deep scowl in her direction.

Alice later learned that Douglas had met Rhoda in town at the races, where she was a ticket seller on the tote. She had thrown in her job and come to work as a housemaid at the pub in order to be near him. Little by little, Alice got to know her. She would stay out at the farm some weekends, and Tilly would send her over to borrow a cup of sugar or a packet of cigarettes, just the way Alice's parents borrowed from them. Rhoda didn't stay every weekend, and seemed to vanish from sight now and then. Her mother guessed Rhoda was twenty-six or twenty-seven. Quite a while to be on the shelf, she said to her husband. Rhoda carried a spicy fragrance about her as if her skin were impregnated with flower petals. Her breasts were heavy ovals cupped above her tiny waist.

Rhoda did most of the talking, in a soft purring rush, a steady stream of comments about herself, Douglas, the McNaughts. Milking was a painful price for being Douglas's girlfriend, but she had done it when she was a girl, and she supposed she would have to get used to it again when the time came. Men's and cow's shit, it was much the same. Alice would be surprised at what she saw at the pub. Alice didn't know what men were like, oh, you'll never know, you'll never know, she said, and Alice thought, with sudden chilling fear, that she might not and that not knowing might be worse than knowing. The couple who ran the pub were mean with hot water, Rhoda said. Inhaling the spontaneous perfume that surrounded her, Alice wouldn't have thought so, but Rhoda had three baths a day at the weekends, even though it meant saving the water for Douglas when he came in from the shed. *Rhoda Aukett*, she fluttered on, was kind of hard to say, not that it would bother her for long, not when she became Rhoda McNaught. She supposed Alice would be getting married some day too. How did she get along with Noelene? She wasn't too sure that Noelene liked her, but there, she was going to get her nose out of joint a bit, having another woman on the property, Noelene had called her little girl Lorraine, and what did Alice think of that for a name? 'She's probably afraid I'll have the first boy,' Rhoda said. Then she bit her lip as if she had said the wrong thing and something was bothering her. Did Alice want babies when she grew up? Rhoda had asked, changing the subject.

Almost as suddenly as she had arrived, Rhoda Aukett

disappeared. At first Alice didn't notice she had gone, for she no longer visited the McNaughts unless asked to go on a message. One weekend, though, Douglas came over to use the Emerys' phone because theirs was out of order, or that was what he said. Alice wondered why he hadn't gone to Malcolm and Noelene's. Alice heard him tell her father that he would pay for a toll call.

'It's all right, son,' her father said, 'you go right ahead, make as many calls as you want. I know you'll pay me.'

Douglas closed the door and talked for a long time. Alice heard his voice raised, and she leaned her head against the door. 'I'm sorry, I'm sorry, Rhoda, I can't,' he said, and she could hear him crying. It grieved her that Rhoda could be so unforgiving. She couldn't imagine anything bad enough for Rhoda to react like this. It took Alice a while to realise that Rhoda hadn't been to the farm for some weeks, much longer than the usual intervals between calls. Clearly this was no flash point, the quarrel was well established by the time she had got to hear about it.

'She won't be back,' Alice's mother said cryptically. She and her husband looked at each other in a meaningful way.

Soon after that, Douglas came to the house with an odd, almost sly, gleeful look about him, like a boy who has built a tree house that he is sure nobody will find. Could he have a letter sent here?

He and Alice's father went outside and talked. Her father ran his hand through his thinning hair in an anxious way and shook his head once or twice. In the end, she saw him reluctantly agree.

Douglas came in the evenings after milking to check on the arrival of the mail. Alice looked out for a letter from Rhoda. She imagined her handwriting as flowing with untidy loops and an exaggerated incline, like a head held in the hand, a playful smile.

But when the letter came, it was not from Rhoda at all. Alice was there when Douglas picked it up, an official typed envelope sent from Wellington.

'Thanks, mate,' he said to her father. Her father stood awkwardly; it was clear that he wanted to know the contents nearly as much as Douglas. Alice can still see them, the two men standing together, Douglas almost like a son. He turned the letter over in his hands and, for her father's sake, opened it there and then. He took a deep breath and handed it over, his eyes alight. They looked at each other with a mixture of excitement and awe.

'They've taken you,' her father said. 'Oh, good man, I knew they would.'

'I'd better tell the old man,' said Douglas, and he bit his lip in an uncharacteristic boyish gesture. He took out a cigarette and placed it in his mouth without the usual flick.

A week or so later, Douglas appeared, wearing a uniform. Of course, she had learned his secret by then. He had been accepted to join the crack Special Air Service unit as a paratrooper, bound for Malaya to fight the Communists. His uniform was olive-green with a browny-green shirt and tie. On his head, he wore a maroon beret with a winged dagger and the motto 'Who Dares Wins'.

Alice couldn't imagine what the jungle would be like, although now she can. She has stood in the renamed Malaysian jungle and felt the breath of giant butterfly wings against her face, amidst the mingled smells of nutmeg oil and orchids and the lavatory stench of cut durian. The fruit, she was told, can kill a man if it is eaten with alcohol. She has seen a python and a flying frog and spiders that eat birds. Deadly and dangerous and seductive. And, as she has stood there, she has thought of Douglas McNaught.

He had several leaves from the training camp at Waiouru before he embarked. During the last of these, the ailing square dance club held one of its now erratic meetings. Alice had not attended for at least six months, not since Rhoda Aukett first came on the scene. Douglas appeared unexpectedly at the Emerys' doorstep. His official farewell had already taken place, a formal affair with speeches and a special supper on laden trestle tables set out on the hall. Alice's father, with tears in his eyes, had given him a Waterman pen, which he could ill afford. Now here Douglas was, resplendent in his uniform, on the doorstep.

'Feel like a couple of turns, kid?' he asked.

Alice's mother looked up from the bench where she was working, as if she might, for the first time, say something to stop Alice going, then changed her mind. Instead she pressed her lips together.

Farewell was in the air. Even though the club was going into recess, there was a bigger turnout than usual. People came up to say goodbye all over again. Old men, wearing baggy greys and tartan shirts, turned up with the helpers and sat against the wall, just watching. At suppertime, they pumped Douglas's hand, their eyes shining, holding on longer than they needed.

'You gotta knock the bastards out of them trees, son, little devils, knock 'em out,' Alice heard one of them say.

'Give you a tenner for that hat, boy,' said another. Douglas just smiled; it was clear that in his head he had already moved on. He danced with all the women, young and old, bringing the helpers out of their corner. They sang 'Red River Valley' – *from this valley they say you are going / we will miss your bright eyes and sweet smile . . .*

The air outside was cool as they headed for home. The moon was new, and Alice couldn't avoid looking at it through the glass. She turned her money over in her pocket and moved closer to Douglas. When he didn't appear to notice, she moved right up beside him. He shifted slightly in his uniform. A short way up the road, he pulled the Buick over and placed his hand on hers.

What does one say to his daughter now, Alice wonders, remembering. Nothing much. A kiss is a kiss. That is what they did, not much more. When he pressed her against the seat, she whispered, although there was nobody at all in the wide moonlit paddocks who would see or hear them: 'Are you going to root me now?'

'No,' he said and didn't stop kissing her. 'It's all right, I'm not going to give you a baby yet. I'm going to look after you.' He drew her tongue into his mouth, coaxing it with the tip of his, that flickering, darting tongue she had watched, hotter and sweeter than she had imagined, clean of cigarettes since his training had begun. He kissed her throat, down the length of her arm to her fingertips, turned her hands over and kissed the palms and back up into the crooks of her elbows. He slid her blouse down over her shoulders and drew circles round her nipples with his tongue, and all the time he breathed deeply as if drawing the scent of her body into his. She felt as Rhoda Aukett must have felt. She could smell something familiar, flowery and delicate: her body, like Rhoda's must have done, blooming under his touch. He parted her legs and momentarily rested his hand between them.

'Yes,' said Alice.

'No,' he said, replacing her skirt. 'No.'

He switched on the car engine and reached for her hand. 'I won't forget this,' he said.

She believed that, too late, he had chosen her over Rhoda.

Miss Macdonald was pleased with Alice's progress. She had introduced a new idea into the shop. When a new consignment of dresses arrived, she appraised each one carefully. Then she made out a list and rang a number of farmers' wives. 'I've got just the dress here for you,' she told each one. 'Would you like me to send it out on the rural delivery for you to try?'

This new service surprised and pleased the customers. Not a single dress was returned. Miss Macdonald said to Alice one morning that it would be a good idea for her to go into town with her to do some buying at the warehouse. She would get an old friend who had helped her out in the past to keep the shop open.

After they had spent the morning amongst rows of dresses, Miss Macdonald sent her off to look at the shops while she settled the bills. Alice could tell that she was still pleased with her.

Outside, she saw Rhoda Aukett. She was walking along the street, her shoulders slightly bowed. She didn't see Alice as her attention was entirely absorbed by a child, a listless, dreamy-looking boy, perhaps four or five years old. Alice knew at once that it was Rhoda's child. She could not say how she knew, but there was something about the connection between them, and his look of her, that told her. She watched them from a shop doorway, saw the way she turned to him and smiled. Something had worn thin in Rhoda Aukett, but still she smiled, and the child looked back at her with an open trusting face, a face that could still believe that there are reasons for everything and that disappearances are only temporary.

'I saw Rhoda Aukett in town today,' she told her mother when she got home that evening.

'Did she have her kid with her?'

'How did you know?'

She looked at Alice, puzzled. 'Well, Tilly told me. She told everybody when she found out.' Her mother seemed to have forgotten how recently Alice had crossed over that secret divide between schoolgirl and working woman, and how much might still be hidden from her. All the edges were blurred. Clover Johnston's parents were sending Clover off to boarding school for another year. It seemed that Clover faced endless childhood, and Alice was sorry for her.

What she did not ask her mother was whether Tilly knew that Douglas cried when he told Rhoda that she could not bring her child to the farm. For she understood now that this was what was happening the night of the phone call.

One other thing happened before Alice left the drapery shop. Douglas had been gone for more than six months when he sent her a postcard. Alice did not know that the jungle had already claimed him. Not to instant death but to the illness that would persist for the rest of his life. She believes that he did not know how ill he was when he posted the card; she is sure he believed that, back on the farm, where the grass grew in broad swathes and the trees were cropped into hedges and the birds were no more dangerous than a circling hawk, he would recover his health.

His postcard came to the shop, and she guessed that this was another of his small ploys to keep his plans to himself. She realised that he must have had news of her, that she was now working at the drapery and was truly grown up and doing well, and she hoped he had also been told that nobody thought she was difficult any longer. His card said, simply, 'I'm coming home.' That and his name.

Alice has come across a phrase about women's lives that stays with her: *the fraught and endless narrative.* Who am I? Where did I come from? How did I arrive at where I am now? She conducts these interviews with herself. They are not all, or even often, about Douglas McNaught, for a great many other things have happened to her since then. But he is part of the narrative.

Alice remembers a time when postcards were a metaphor for a shorthand account of life: the picture and a dozen words, and you have it all, and, in a way, this was true of Douglas's postcard, although there was no picture and the message was even shorter. But something happened when it came that even now she cannot entirely explain. Miss Macdonald had collected the mail from the post office. Alice was folding a bolt of voile when she brought the card into the shop. Without commenting, she put it down on the counter. Alice read it at a glance. Then she put the material down on the counter and, picking up the card, she walked outside and along the road through the village centre, towards the grassy hills. The narrow valley stretched before her, above her the sky bleached to nothing, around her lay the singing sunlit air of late autumn. Her father might have the son he had wanted. Two farms would become one profitable enterprise. The bloodlines would run cleanly between them. She wanted to squat against the earth, as if pushing out the first child. She smelt the scent of her own desire all over again.

Then she turned around and retraced her steps. She wondered whether his card was a warning to make ready, or whether it was offering her a chance to go. It was one thing to come home when you already knew what lay beyond the valley; it was another thing to stay without the chance of ever leaving. This, too, he might already know.

Besides, there had been Rhoda Aukett.

Alice could tell any of this to Kathryn, but she doesn't. She might tell her that if she had been her daughter her name might have been Catherine spelled with a C and an I, or that her name might not have been that at all. Instead, she tells her that it is difficult to remember much more because she left the valley so soon after she finished school, when a cadetship in broadcasting came up, and she moved south to the city. She has only passed through Fish Rock once or twice since then. She has seen Douglas's grave, and she is sorry about what happened to him. She might, but she does not, tell his daughter that when she rang and said who she was, a shiver like violets shaken before a spring wind had passed through her. She thinks of Kathryn's father as tenderly as she thinks of any man.

HATS

Like turning your hand over, things could go either way with the weather. Six a.m. and the bay is turbulent and green, but at that hour of the morning anything can happen. Standing at the window, just listening, the whole house is a heartbeat. Looking at the bay, the water, the clouds, I think I can hear the busy clink and chatter of the rigging on the boats parked on the hard at the bay, but that can't be right, it's too far away. Oh, you can hear anything, see anything on a morning like this, it's the day of the wedding. Our son's getting married.

There is a stirring in the back rooms; there is so much to do, I will never get done, it's crazy this, but the wedding's to be here, not at her place but mine. I am speaking now of the bride's mother and myself. Well, it's a long story, how the wedding comes to be here instead of there, but that's the way it is. She's bringing the food later in the morning, and there'll be crayfish and scallops like nobody ever had at a wedding before, and mussels of course. They are mussel farmers from the Sounds. They. Well, I mean the bride's parents.

I love our daughter-in-law to be, I really do. You might think I don't mean that, mothers-in-law rarely do, but it's true. Our son's on a win. I want to see him married.

Perhaps they know that. There are times when I think they haven't been so keen. Perhaps they think she could have done better. I don't know. It hasn't been easy, getting this wedding together. But, if you knew him, our son, you'd know she wouldn't settle for anyone else. Anyone *less*. Now there's a mother talking, but I've fallen for it, that same old charm of his, and I'll go on forever, I guess. He puts his arms around me and says, 'Love ya, Ma' and I'll forgive him anything.

It's true. He brings out a softness in me. That and rage. But the anger never lasts for long.

There is no time to go on reflecting about it this morning though. There's the smell of baked meats in the air, I need to open up the house and blow it through, I've got the food warmer to collect from the hire depot, and the tablecloths aren't ready, and I have to set up a place for the presents, and there's his mother, my husband's to be got up, and there're relatives to be greeted, and oh, God, I am so tired. Why didn't anyone tell me I'd be so tired on our son's wedding day, it doesn't seem fair because I want to enjoy it. Oh, by that I mean, I want it to be all right, of course, and I want to do it graciously. We've been at it a bit over this wedding. Them and us. But I want to make sure it goes all right today. They're bringing the food and the flagons of beer; we're providing the waiters and waitresses in starched uniforms, and the champagne. You have to cater for everyone at a wedding.

Eleven a.m. The food hasn't come. The flagons haven't come. She hasn't come. That's the bride's mother. The wedding is at two. I am striding around the house. The furniture is minimal. We've cleared everything back. There's hardly going to be standing room. That's if there ever is a wedding. There is nothing more I can do.

Nothing and everything. If only we had another day. It would have been better if we'd held off another month. The weather would have been better. Not that it's bad, but the breeze is cold. It'll be draughty in the church.

The church, ah, the church. It looks so beautiful. The flowers. They are just amazing. Carnations and irises, low bowls of stocks . . . There are the cars now, all the relatives bearing trays and pots and dishes, straggling up the steps. The food looks wonderful. God, those crays, there're dozens of them. I'm glad they've done the food. I could never have done it so well. And the cake. Our daughter-in-law's aunty has made the cake and it's perfect too.

Everyone's exhausted, it's not just me, they've been up all night. Still, I wish they could have got here a bit sooner, and we all have to get dressed yet. It's cutting things fine. I feel faint, even a little nauseous, as if lights are switching on and off in my brain. She can't be as tired as I am, nobody could be that tired. How am I going to make it through the rest of the day?

'I'd better be getting along,' says the aunt to the bride's mother. 'I've still got to finish off your hat.' The aunt has a knack with things, clothes and cakes, she's the indispensable sort.

Inside me, something freezes. 'Hat,' I say, foolishly, in a loud voice. 'You're wearing a hat?'

There is a silence in the kitchen.

'Well, it's just a little hat,' she says.

'You said you weren't going to wear a hat.' I hear my voice, without an ounce of grace in it, and I don't seem able to stop it. There is an ugliness in the air.

The aunty, her sister, says, 'She needed a hat to finish off the outfit. It wouldn't look right without it.'

41

'But we agreed,' I say. 'You said you couldn't afford a hat, and I said, well, if you're not wearing one, I won't.'

The silence extends around the kitchen. She fumbles a lettuce leaf, suddenly awkward at my bench.

'It's all right,' I say, 'it's nothing.' My face is covered with tears. I walk out, leaving them to finish whipping the cream.

'Where are you going?' my husband says, following at my heels.

'Out. Away.'

'You can't go away.'

'I have to. I'm not going to the wedding.'

'No stop. Don't be silly.' He's really alarmed, I'm right on the edge, and he's right, I might go off at any moment and make things too awful for everyone to endure. At the rate I'm going, there mightn't be any wedding.

'Come into the shed,' he says, speaking softly, like a zookeeper talking down a wild animal. 'You're tired, just tired.'

I follow him. Inside the tool shed I start to cry properly. 'I want a hat,' I say, 'I wanted to wear a hat all along, but I promised her. I promised I wouldn't get a hat.'

'I'll get you a hat. Come along, we'll go into town and buy you a hat.'

'It's too late, the shops will be shut.'

'We could just make it to James Smith's,' he says. But it is too late, I can see that. Even if we broke the speed limit, I'd only have five minutes, it being Saturday. The shops are due to close in half an hour.

'I can't go without a hat. What'll I do?'

'You'll think of something,' he says. 'You always do. Hey, we can do anything, can't we?' He pulls my fists out of my eyes. 'What can we do? We can . . .' He waits for me to join in the refrain with him.

'We can walk on water if we have to,' I chant.

But I'm not sure how I will.

Back in the kitchen everyone is tiptoeing around. 'It looks wonderful,' I say heartily. 'Just great. Don't you think you should be getting along, I mean, if you're going to get dressed?'

They nod. They are not deceived, but they are glad to be excused. They have been afraid to take their leave in my absence.

They are gone, and our son and his best man are dressed, preening in their three-piece suits. Oh, they are so handsome. It calms me, just seeing them. As for him: I want to stroke him. My boy. In a suit. Oh, I'm square, when it all comes down to it. But he's proud of himself too.

'Y'okay, Ma?'

He doesn't know what's been going on, but he sees I'm pale.

'Of course I'm okay,' I say, and for his sake I must be. I must also have a hat.

I ring our daughter. 'What about all those hats you bought when you were into hats?' I ask. I think of the op shops where she has collected feathered toques and funny little cloches. I have a feeling that none of them will suit me. She is so tall and elegant. 'I think they're in the baby's toy box,' she says.

'Have a look,' I command.

'God, I've got to get dressed too.'

I hold grimly onto the phone. She comes back. 'There're three: the black one with three feathers, the sort of burgundy one, and the beige one with the wide brim.'

'That's it, the beige one. I'm sending Dad over for it right now.'

'But Mum.'

'It'll be all right. Well, look, I can try it anyway.'

'But Mum,' – this time she gets it out – 'the baby's been sick on it.'

'How sick?'

'Really sick.'

No one is going to put me off now. I think she is conspiring with the odds to stop me making a fool of myself. I won't let her save me though. 'Dad'll be right over,' I say.

But it's true. The baby has been very sick on the hat. I'm sure our daughter shouldn't have put it back in the toy box like that. I resolve to speak to her at some later date.

In the meantime, there is work to be done. I fill the sink with hot soapy water and get out the scrubbing brush. In a few moments, the sick has gone. I have a soggy felt hat dripping in my hands, but at least it is clean.

The husband and wife team, *available for cocktail, waitressing and barman duties in the privacy of your own home,* has arrived. 'Don't worry about a thing,' they say. 'You just enjoy yourselves, and we'll take care of everything from now on.'

In the clothes drier, the hat whirls around.

Our son has left for the church. Soon we'll have to go too. My husband is resplendent. He wears his father's watch-chain across his waistcoat. His father was a guard on the railways, back in the old days. That watch has started a thousand trains on country railway stations. Sometimes I remonstrate with my husband for wearing it; it doesn't always seem appropriate. Today it is exactly right. The spring in the watch has given up long ago, but the watch will start the wedding on time. Sooner or later.

My hands shake so much, he has to do up the buttons on my Georgia Brown silk dress. 'It's time we were going,' he says tentatively. I know he's thinking about the hat and wondering if he can get me away without it.

But it's dry. Dry and softly drooping around the brim so that it swoops low over my right eye when I put it on. I stare at myself in the mirror, entranced. I feel beautiful. I glow. I love hats. This hat is perfect.

Our son's wife-to-be is late. I don't mind. It gives me time to relax, breathe deeply, smile and wave around the church. Across the aisle, I see her, the mother of the bride. She is not wearing a hat.

Instinctively, I touch the brim of mine. I have shamed her into coming without her hat. I should feel jubilant, but I don't. I feel bad, wonder how to take mine off without drawing attention to myself. But it's impossible. At the door to the church, the priest has said first thing when he sees me, 'Oh, what a beautiful hat.'

I look away, embarrassed. I tell myself I must not think about it. The wedding is about to happen, and we can't repeat it when I'm feeling better, so I've just got to stop thinking about it, the hat on my head.

And then they're there, the two of them coming into the church together, which is what's been arranged, and it's not quite the same old responses, because the priest has said that some of that wouldn't be suitable – he's rather conservative this man, a little disapproving – but they say nice things to each other, making promises to do things as well as they can, and they're so young, so very young, and that's all you can expect from anybody, to do their best, isn't it?

The couple is facing the congregation now. Our daughter stands up at the lectern and reads from the book of Ecclesiastes and then some Keats, *Oh brightest! Thou too late for antique vows,* – and she's pale and self-contained and not showing any signs of things turning over inside her, and so lovely; she and the boy, her brother, look at each other, and it's as if they're the only ones in the church for the moment – *Holy the air, the water, and the fire* – like a conversation just for the two of them, putting aside all their childish grievances, though a few people in the church who haven't done English Lit. look a trifle confused, but it doesn't matter, these two know – *...so let me be thy choir ... thy voice ... thy lute ...* – and then the baby of our son and his new wife cries at the back of the church where he's being held by the aunty, and the spell's broken as the two parents look anxiously after their child. The wind rises in the funnel where the church stands, and a plane roars overhead, and the light shines through the stained-glass window on to the same spot where my father's coffin stood last year, and with all the light and the sound I don't hear any more of the service, I just smile and smile.

It's over. We're forming up to leave. She and I look at each other across the church again. Suddenly, it's all bustle and go, and what none of us have thought about is the way we get out of the church, but there it is, as old as the vows, or so it seems, the rituals of teaming up, like finding your partner for a gavotte, step step step, an arm offered and accepted, she goes with my husband and I go with hers, that's the way it's done. Delicate, light as air, we prepare our entrance to the dance, to the music, but before we do, she and I afford each other one more look, one intimate glance. Hatted and hatless, that's us, blessed are the meek, it's all the same now. We're one, her and me. We're family.

RED BELL

1

A Short Chronicle

From its outward appearance, there is nothing to suggest great change about the supermarket. Believe me, I know that building through and through. I also know the parking lot better than most, not just because I'm so used to manoeuvring into its parked spaces, between the Audis and the Mercedes, or the Mercs, if you like, and the ridiculous SUVs that sound like a sexually transmitted disease, in which young women tote their children around these days. Although that should give you a clue, if you know the place at all, because it wasn't always like that. The lot was more likely to fill with pick-up trucks and dented family wagons, small-nosed cars like my own. I know it so well because a year or so back my dear friend lost her husband, meaning he died, and she was lost to herself, the love and light of her life snuffed out. A month after that, she lost her engagement ring. A thing is just a thing, she said staunchly to her friends, over and again, but her mouth trembled and her hands shook when she said it. The ring was a beautiful antique oval opal, blue fire in its heart, edged with a fine filigree of gold. It stood for all the years she and her husband had been together. More than once, she had recalled the moment when he was a bearded young student, wearing roman sandals and socks, who had asked her humbly whether she would consider him good enough. Of course, she had said, and it was she who swept him off his feet. As she would, she is nothing if not bold. And, of course, there was the music, which he made all his life and for which he became famous. How could a man resist her, or a woman his melody.

But there she was, the ring gone, her finger grown thin as the last months of his illness had ticked by. She had lost it, she thought, somewhere in the supermarket. This is how I came to scour that car park for a week, looking in every crevice and around its kerbs, scuffling through rubbish from cars, old parking tickets, cigarette butts, the whole disgusting detritus.

For all sorts of reasons, then, my relationship with supermarkets feels intimate. When I go inside, there is a turnstile, leading to the fruit and vegetables: the firelight glow of the tomatoes, acid-yellow clumps of lemons, aubergines clad in deep purple, the whole panoply of exuberant edible colour. Sometimes I close my eyes for a second and inhale, as if somehow I can invoke the scent of the past, the rows of citrus trees my father planted up north, the grove of tamarillos that we called tree tomatoes, and the long wires supporting the kiwifruit vines. We used to call them Chinese gooseberries, but only because the plants had come from China in the beginning. Of course, it is inappropriate to call them that now.

There is no smell now, or not of fruit anyway. Many things are wrapped in plastic, and the loose fruit has been chilled, the touch of the sun long gone, the earth dusted from the mushrooms. I have a friend who works in the fruit and vegetable department. We, that is my husband and I, have known him for years. His name is Phan, a man with savage cheekbones and tired eyes, his hair thinning on top. A long time ago, he was a monk in Cambodia, but he disrobed and immigrated to New Zealand. We knew him from his homeland, in the years when we travelled and my husband did his good works in that country torn by landmines, giving comfort to the afflicted. I remember the saffron shimmer of Phan's robes in the heat, the way he held himself, unable to touch me – a woman – while my husband embraced him. And now he is married to a woman who is still back in Cambodia, and they have a daughter.

Phan has been waiting for years to bring his wife to New Zealand, but it is never easy. The people in the Immigration Department aren't always sympathetic to wives like his. So far as they are concerned, they are all a bunch of crooks using sham marriages to get into the country. The documents aren't enough. They want to see photographs and videos of the wedding. I don't like to think of a bunch of bureaucrats sitting at their desks thumbing through the precious albums, watching the videos, not understanding the rattling music or the pageantry of the promenade of friends down a dusty street to summon the bride from her house. Nor will this be enough to satisfy the officials. No, they want DNA samples to prove that the man is the father of his own child, which means that the wife must travel from her village to Phnom Penh, where the sample from their baby can be authenticated. They must have phone records to show how many times the husband has rung his wife. So, he's broke because he's paying for her to travel from place to place and can't afford to phone her every week. Or her phone is broken. Well, that's tough, they can see it's all made up. You cannot believe the things they ask. Even the neighbours are invited to supply letters to say the couple cohabit when the husband returns now and then to Cambodia, in the long years that separate them. What are their friends supposed to do? Stand with their ears pressed against the rough thatch of the walls? I could go on about it, it makes us so furious, and we know that Phan is not the only one treated this way. There are dozens in his situation. Some days I feel like avoiding the fruit and veggies because it's hard to face his misery. But that's impossible because it's the only way into the shop.

At least he can touch me now. We give each other awkward little pats as I stand and sympathise with the latest twist in the saga. He chooses the very best fruit for me. When my friend lost her ring, he and some of the other workers, who are Indian, or Cambodian like him, upended the lettuce bin where people chop the outer leaves off the Icebergs before bagging them. They sorted through every leaf. Once before they had found another woman's ring. That had given great happiness.

That was then. These days, people get impatient when we stand and talk, say EX-*cuse* me in loud nasal voices. I did mention things have changed. It's the film studios along the road that have done it. It's hard to believe that this quiet suburb has become one of the centres of the movie world, but it has. This is the home of *The Lord of the Rings* and all that has followed from that cinematic extravaganza, never mind my friend's beautiful beloved ring. There are studios and workshops and cinema complexes that, should you have the opportunity to glimpse inside as I have once or twice, will reveal a vast empire of glamour, crimson waterfalls of light, Oriental scenes, people dashing around with clipboards in their hands. All of this is hidden behind high timber fences so that only the few can know what's behind them, a sort of false modesty.

But there's not much modesty on show here in the supermarket. If you're local, you need to know your place. There is nothing like testing the ripeness of a cheese and finding the slender fingers of Cate Blanchett alongside yours to inform you that things will never be the same here again. I think she might be nice, but you keep your furtive Kiwi eyes down in situations like this, don't let on you've twigged. Should I have said hullo? Probably not. Friends have reported sightings of Orlando Bloom prowling the aisles, but on this I have yet to score. The lesser mortals – the producers, the directors, the cameramen and women, and assistant camera crews, and PAs to the hierarchy – stride around with a kind of tousled splendour, an impatient swagger that says *we have more important things to do but there it is, we must eat.* I've worked in the screen trade. I confess, for a time, I was not unlike them. These days, I'm on the small side and grey haired. Although I'm invisible, I can pick them at twenty paces.

Something happened just the other day, which brought this sense of dislocation into focus. True, I'd noticed it happening. But the sense that things are so easily displaced, that people land in random situations without exactly knowing how or what will happen next, hadn't before occurred to me with such force. I should have been more alert. There are the earthquakes to the south that have tossed everything and everyone around with reckless disdain, but because the ground here is still, you let down your guard, think things can't happen to me. That is nature, you say, beyond control. You feel fortunate, and guilty too, because you are unhurt. Where you live, everything *looks* the same. Never mind the small tremors.

On this day I'm referring to, the day of the 'incident' as I've come to think of it, I entered the store feeling on top of things and happy, my feet carrying my body around lightly. When I saw Phan, his face was glowing. He had had good news from Immigration. His wife and baby had been granted visas to come to New Zealand. Just visitors' visas, but enough to make him exultant for the moment. He would have to go to Cambodia to fetch them because his wife didn't have the language to enter the country on her own. This would cost him four thousand dollars, but he had worked many extra shifts in order to save the money. All would be well.

I couldn't help asking anxious questions about his preparations. Would his wife have warm clothes for when they arrived and did he have proper heating in the flat he rented? She would be cold, I knew, and I kept asking things like did he have a doctor and did he know about getting the baby immunised. I was mentally summarising the fearfulness of immigration, how frightening it could be, and how alone this woman might feel, even with all the love of Phan to comfort her.

It was he who stood there reassuring me. I was afraid I might have worried him, so I entered back into the spirit of rejoicing. We laughed too loudly and did a high five. A woman wearing a trench-coat and dark glasses said one of those *excuse mes*, and I saw that I was blocking her from the silverbeet, so I smiled and said 'so SO-*ree*'. Besides, I realised I was running on the late side of the day.

I skimmed my trolley past the meat department and along to dairy. That's when I checked my list and saw that I'd left out the red pepper I needed for the ratatouille I was planning for dinner. I parked my trolley neatly at the end of the aisle so that it didn't get in anyone's way, and rushed back the way I'd come from fruit and veggies. When I saw Phan, he grinned as I pointed, mid-flight, at the red peppers. By the time I got to the compartment, he had chosen one. He held it up for me to admire, a sweet red bell pepper, so sensual, so plump in its red sheath that it took my breath away; the kind of object I imagine Georgia O'Keefe might have painted, so suggestive was its cleavage. I held it and paused for a moment to caress its silky exterior – or was it satin? – I couldn't decide, it was just lovely to hold. There was even a freshness about it, as if it hadn't been long picked. It had a faint prickly scent. My father grew these too, and we called them capsicum.

'Must dash,' I said, and by then I was truly late. I scampered back to milk and dairy and dropped the pepper into the trolley, leaving it before glancing off to cereals. It occurred to me at that moment that something was not quite right.

The trolley wasn't in exactly the same position where I'd left it. Or was that the spot? Where had I been when I abandoned the trolley in the first place? Milk and dairy, I told myself. Retrace your steps. Where did you go? The trolley I had thought was mine was half-full, just as mine was when I left it, but only the gleaming red pepper was familiar amongst its contents. It contained tinned food: baked beans and peaches, coconut milk and a packet of sliced bread. I was buying only fruit and vegetables.

A woman picked the pepper out of the trolley with exaggerated care and advanced towards me, holding it in an outstretched hand. She was a large-boned woman, a head taller than me, wearing an office-cleaning uniform. I noticed the hand holding my pepper was calloused.

'Thank you,' I said, taking it from her, 'such a silly thing to do. I'd forgotten where I left my trolley.'

Her face was deeply unfriendly. 'That is my trolley,' she said.

'I know, I know, I'm so sorry.'

She stood, glaring and wordless.

'Thank you,' I repeated. I placed the pepper in my trolley, which I'd now located at the end of the aisle, where I'd left it. I was beginning to feel irritated.

'Why did you do that?' she said.

My head was full of answers as the woman continued to stare me down. Bystanders had begun to stop and watch. An older woman was saying *My, my* in a worried way, wondering what to do. It occurred to me that none of the goods belonged to either of us, or not yet, until we had passed through the checkout, but I sensed there was something smart alecky about saying this that would make matters worse.

'Look, it's sorted now,' I said. My good mood had turned sour.

The woman suddenly turned her back and walked away.

I had thought it was over, but it was not.

A moment or two later, she was back. She walked up to me as close as she could without actually touching me. Her breath was hot on my face. I saw the bitter bruise of anger at the back of her eyes. 'Why would you take someone else's trolley?' she said.

'But I didn't. It was an accident, a mistake.'

'Mistake. People don't make mistakes like that.'

I backed away. She moved after me. I was trembling with the heat of the chicken rotisserie at my back. I had lost all my words, undone by the sudden violence of her look, the tone of her voice. In my head, I heard myself saying: *Cut. Babe, you're out of shot. You're in the wrong location.*

As most of us are, most of the time. We are all lost, at some point or another. Such is the state of our anguish. For it seemed to me, that neither the misappropriation of the trolley, nor the presence of the red bell pepper, could in themselves be the cause of such fierceness, an expression so bruised.

Somebody, I wanted to tell her, has given you bad directions. Try starting the scene over again.

But you know how it is, self-preservation has a way of kicking in.

2

Another day, another place. A week had passed.

I was in the art gallery in Auckland. It is a beautiful gallery with high, soaring spaces. I had been roaming for hours, transfixed. There was a whole room devoted to the Pink and White Terraces, the lost marvel in our history, consumed by the fire and ash of a volcanic eruption. The terraces were buried not far from where I had lived as a young woman. Gone, like the Temple of Artemis or the Colossus of Rhodes, the *theamata* as the Greeks would say, the terraces so lost that nobody knows any more exactly where they are, even though this disappearance happened in a time when records and paintings had been made. I had encountered some people the day before in the hotel where I was staying. I had known one when I was young and he a child. We had spent an hour or more unpacking the past, who knew whom, and how our lives intersected; old ties, histories and sorrows. The meeting had taken me back to another time in my life, when I lived near the place where the terraces stood before they disappeared, before the eruption. I was shaken by this encounter, reminding me of my own metamorphosis from a wild and unhappy creature to a woman with a considered and careful life.

I walked into another tall room, pale-green and white, and stopped before a painting that took my breath away. The painting was called 'Focal Point'. I had not heard of the artist: John Tunnard, from Penzance. This work consisted of softly washed architectural shapes, of precise geometrical design, which vanished at a central point, and that point was marked by a dark intensely red sphere.

I recognised that sphere in an instant.

The flame in an opal, a shining fruit, a heart, a drop of blood: call it what you will.

Beside the painting was an account of the artist's inspiration. It had come from a poem by Cecil Day-Lewis, written in war time: *So shall our time reveal long vistas / of calm and natural growth, / a pattern mysterious yet lucid / for love is the focal point of the pattern / And our heirs shall unfold, / like a cluster of apple blossom in a fine tomorrow.*

That is how it is, I thought to myself. We trace our way through our shifting precarious existence, questioning it over and again, watching out for landmines, sudden explosions, seeking the truth of every moment. There are losses and separations and red beating hearts and flare-ups wherever our gaze rests. Sorrows become wounds, and we each carry the burden of one another.

But there is also love and the fine tomorrows.

2

LONGING

THE HONEY FRAME

When he saw the letter, the professor knew, before his wife handed it to him, that it contained discomforting news. The heat outside was almost beyond endurance, ninety-five Fahrenheit in the shade and still rising. He could smell the trees sizzling as he walked on the path by the river, sensed their exhausted trembling. It was the end of the wild-flower season, and the colours that had so dazzled him throughout the spring had faded, the bright gardens wilted. The high collar and cravat that Frederick's position in life demanded seemed to be choking him. As he entered the shade of the sandstone house, he bowled his hat without ceremony on to the chair in the reception hall and mopped his face.

His wife was waiting, solicitous as ever, ready to take his coat. But she frowned at this display of intemperance. Their house was an orderly one, discreetly furnished and neutral, a cool haven with the blinds half-drawn to keep out the bright sunlight, a house where guests and students alike were greeted with fresh lemonade and soothing words. They had arranged the layout so that the hall opened into their huge music room, where the grand piano stood on its raised platform. Frederick's music students were considered the most polished and well-rehearsed in Perth. Indeed, the best in every respect because the professor accepted only those with natural talent. A student had to pass several tests in order to become his disciple.

'Mail from New Zealand,' his wife said, picking up the envelope from the hall table.

His heart bounced in his chest when he saw the beautiful copperplate handwriting with a slight curl at the end of some letters, perfect in themselves, each word a tiny work of art. He had seen that distinctive handwriting before, the last time perhaps a quarter of a century ago. That envelope had contained an entreaty from a woman, a plea that she be allowed to come to him. The girl, rather, for that is what she was then, little more than a child, had just turned sixteen. Yet she was old enough to marry.

'It contains something else besides a letter,' his wife said. 'An object, a quill perhaps,'

'Hmm,' was all he said. He took the letter, making as if to move to the piano room.

'So, aren't you going to open it?'

'Some childish thing from my brother's boys, no doubt. They're always drawing and doodling, you know how it is.'

'Little Rex must be four or five now.'

'I suppose so. Are you going to get me something cold to drink or must I do it for myself?'

'I'll get it,' she said, offended. As she withdrew from the room, he slipped the letter into his pocket and walked through the music room into his study. When he rejoined his wife, his expression was carefully arranged.

'So, the letter?' she asked, placing a tray beside him.

'As I said, just a drawing.'

'It felt more than that.'

'The children have been collecting odds and ends.'

'Their mother has a neat hand. I didn't remember it so elegant.'

'Really,' he said, his voice sharper than he intended. 'Really.'

'It's a pity your family's so far away,' she remarked after a silence. 'It would be nice if the children could meet their cousins.'

'You'd hate the journey,' he said. 'It's a mighty rough crossing to New Zealand. Wait until there's a railway across the desert.'

'I can't see that happening in my lifetime,' she said.

'They're talking of sending the line further on past Kalgoorlie.' The next day he would be making his annual trip to the gold-rush town, where he would listen to a recital by embarrassed adolescents and choose one of them to study in Perth. Despite his intention to be composed, he heard himself burbling on to his calm auburn-haired wife about the journey to come, about the train that would bear him towards the flaming heart of Australia. His wife merely smiled. He admired her restraint. For the most part, he had grown like her, not the impetuous, half-mad youth who had landed at Fremantle with little more than the ability to read a music score and a packet of pound notes, which his grandfather had slipped him on the sly.

And now, in the dimmed shadows of his home with the heat rising outside, he saw the girl again. 'I'm going for a walk,' he said.

His wife looked at him strangely.

The landscape in which Frederick Fairburn met Esther Gittos was so distant and different that he found it hard to conjure now. The Kaipara Harbour on the western flank of the North Island lay beside a countryside of muted greens and blues, forests lying thick between the many rivers that led to the sea, a wilderness of ash-green mangroves at its edge, their tangled roots emerging from the water, causing the tides to have a still, almost indolent appearance on summer days. When it rained, drops fell like stones skipping the surface of the water. It was a day after rain when the Reverend William Gittos, of the Methodist persuasion, discovered the young man alone in a tent in the bush beside a rough track wide enough to take a bullock dray but not much more. It was hard to know who was the more startled when he lifted the tent flap and saw Frederick reclining on a hammock. The minister was a solemn-looking man with a bushy beard, slightly stained at its tips.

'I'm with the surveyors' team,' Frederick explained.

'Ah, the Great North Road, well, that's certainly needed. It would make my life easier, I'll tell you that.' So they came to explaining one another's presence, the minister telling of the way he travelled by foot around his Māori parish, which stretched to the far reaches of the Kaipara, and the weeks and months he spent away from home performing the Lord's errands, while Frederick related that he was the son of the chief surveyor, but today he had a slight cold, and his father had told him to rest. His tone betrayed a lack of enthusiasm.

'Aren't you happy in your work?' Gittos asked.

Frederick shrugged by way of answer.

'Or perhaps he's not happy with your approach?'

'My father thought it fitting that I followed in his steps.'

'And now he doesn't?'

'I've trained in music. I've been fortunate enough to travel widely in Europe with my grandfather. I studied at the conservatoire in Milan.'

'So now your father is a disappointed man?'

'He thinks music an infatuation rather than a career.' The minister allowed himself the glimmer of a smile. 'We've come to an understanding,' Frederick continued. 'Six months in the bush, and if we're not satisfied with each other then I'll seek work in Auckland.'

'A good meal would set you up. Leave a note for your father and tell him you're with me. He'll know who I am.'

This was the way Frederick came upon the Gittos family. The rain had cleared, and the air was fresh and fine. The mission station was not far from the sea, small waves curdling along the shoreline. He saw a large house built of sturdy timber with several wide verandahs. A garden surrounded the house, and beyond stood an orchard where peaches and figs were ripening and a flock of ducks roamed. And, there, at the heart of the establishment, was Marianne Gittos and her daughters, of whom there were several. The young women and their mother were intent upon building small wooden frames. As they approached the group, Frederick was struck by a humming sound, and he saw that alongside them stood a row of hives and that the singing note was that of the bees.

'This is Mister Fairburn,' the minister announced.

The mother was holding up one of the frames and inspecting its workmanship.

'How do you do? Who did you say, William?' She put her free hand behind one ear.

'I'm afraid my wife is afflicted by deafness,' Gittos said.

One of the daughters leaned over and put her mouth close to her mother's ear. She appeared the youngest. As she shaped the words, her mouth, Frederick observed, was supple and soft and the colour of ripening raspberries.

'Thank you, Esther,' said her father. 'Mister Fairburn will be staying for dinner. You could ask your mother if she will squeeze the neck of a chicken. Or a duck, perhaps, given that Mister Fairburn's father is planning to make a road for us.'

Marianne's shoulders seemed to droop for a moment, as if she had more demands on her for food than she could possibly meet. She turned back towards the beehives and, taking up a feather, moved some bees this way and that before closing the hives. At this, her husband moved back a step or two, appearing surprisingly nervous for a man otherwise so certain of himself, shifting from one foot to another.

'My mother has great skill with bees,' said Esther. 'She's making frames for them to set their honey. It's a new innovation. She hopes to sell honey to the people in Auckland.' She held up the frame and smiled at him through it.

Frederick felt his heart bounce in his chest.

When he thinks back to that day, that is how he will see the Gittos family, as if in a small picture frame, standing there in relief, the mother and father, their five daughters and two sons as well, though it wasn't until later that evening when they were gathered by the piano that he would meet the young men.

When William Gittos suggested that he might play something for them, given that he was of a musical bent, he sat down at their piano and began playing a light Strauss waltz. When he saw some puzzled frowns, he quickly changed to hymns, ending with 'Onward Christian Soldiers', which at the time was quite new. Their voices soared then.

It was Esther, of course, with whom he had fallen in love. She wore her dark hair pulled back from her high forehead and pinned up, although some of it escaped in curly fronds. Her eyes were set wide apart, her cheekbones high. He could tell that she couldn't take her eyes off his face, and he was careful not to return her gaze, in part so that she would try even harder to make his acquaintance though also so that nobody would think ill of him for too frankly observing her beauty.

Night had fallen, and it was agreed that on no account should he try to make his way back through the bush to the survey camp. In the morning, he rose early and went to the kitchen. Already some of the family had risen and were going about their tasks. Across a paddock he could see one of the girls milking a cow. Mrs Gittos was inspecting her beehives. Behind him, Esther spoke.

'My mother's always checking on the hives. My father's terrified of the bees.' She laughed, expecting him to see the joke.

'Do any of you get stung?'

'Only my father. Oh, I can tell you, it's very funny. It keeps him in order.'

'How old are you, Esther?' he said, his voice urgent.

'I'll be sixteen in three months. And you?'

'Twenty-one.'

'Oh, that's perfect.'

'Why perfect?'

She bit her rosy lip and blushed. 'Oh, I don't know. It just seems the right age for a man.'

'On Sunday, I'll be free to visit again. Would you like that?'

She frowned at this. 'But I wouldn't be able to spend time with you on Sunday. It's church, you see, and they would notice if I were missing.'

Frederick took a deep breath. 'You'd meet me alone?' Could it be that Esther was willing to take leaps that he hadn't considered possible? They were standing close to each other.

For a moment, she seemed to hang her head, but when she looked up her eyes were clear and steady. 'You've seen my sisters. None of them have beaus. Nobody dares look at a Gittos girl.' She hesitated, as if waiting for him to take the warning or not, before opening her hands, palms upwards. 'I would like to get to know you, more than anything in the world.'

Frederick closed his eyes, dizzy with her scent. Wild honey, he thought.

In the weeks that followed, as the peaches continued to ripen and the figs darkened and the drowsy bees lumbered in the orchard, they met on Saturday afternoons at half-past two on the dot. It was the earliest his father would release him and the latest part of the day she could take herself off for a walk before the round of chores that occupied the family drew in. It became their time, the half-past two moment. He kissed her on the lips time and again, at first with their mouths pressed shut together, and then on an inward breath, finding themselves in a deeper kind of intimacy that left them both shaken. When he felt her yielding to him in his arms, he had to stop and remind himself that she was still a child, although the urgency of his need was intolerable.

'Essie, I must tell your father that we're planning to get married.'

'He'll say I'm too young.'

'All the same, it won't be long before you're not too young. It'll soon be your birthday.'

She was lying on her stomach on the grass. He picked up the hem of her dress and turned it up above her knees. She lay still, stifling her giggles.

'Hush,' he said, 'they'll hear you.' For they were very quiet on these assignations, keeping their voices almost to whispers.

'There's only my mother here, and you know she can't hear a thing.'

A mottled feather from the duck pen had drifted to the ground nearby. He picked it up and began to stroke the back of her knee with its tip. 'Little bee,' he said.

At which moment, the voice of wrath, the end of his world, his own private doomsday, fell about him. William Gittos and his wife Marianne stood in the orchard, their faces white, William's eyes blazing.

'I may not be able to hear, but I can see,' Marianne said. 'And I can smell an infidel in my presence.'

'You will leave my property,' William said, 'before I kill you.'

'Sir, I was going to tell you,' Frederick stammered, 'I wish to marry your daughter. I am prepared to wait until she is of age. Her honour is mine too.'

'Leave now,' the missionary said. 'I have friends here who will help me tear you limb from limb. If you return, you'll be horse-whipped.' His wife nodded, her lips pulled tight.

When he reflected in years to come, he knew he should have understood how well the Gittos family kept its word. Months later, he answered Esther's letter in person, a letter reminding him that her birthday had been and gone, imploring him to come and rescue her from her family. The oldest of the five sisters opened the door to him. The moment she saw who it was, she screamed. Esther was nowhere to be seen. The sister slammed the door shut.

'Esther,' he shouted and banged the door again. This time the door flew open and Marianne appeared, a riding crop in her hand, seizing his jacket and pulling him inside in one swift hard motion, strong as any man. Then three more of the girls burst in on the scene, all wielding whips, all shouting and screaming. Not a sign of Esther. One of them shouted that Sarah had gone to fetch the law, and all this while they were beating him, the sting of their switches like that of a whole swarm of bees, while he shouted back at them, telling them to stop and he would leave, but they wouldn't. Blood ran down his face and his head felt split open. He looked up from his tormentors and saw Esther standing in the doorway, the back of her hand held to her mouth, her eyes enormous. It is her eyes he will remember, burning like fever.

'Essie,' he cried, leaping to his feet. Summoning all his strength, he tore Marianne's whip from her hands, turning and raising it above her head. She bared her teeth, waiting for the blow.

Esther was walking towards him, her face mask-like, as if in a trance, her hand held out. 'Give me the whip, Frederick,' she said. Her sisters had stilled around them.

'I've come to get you, Essie.'

'Don't hit her. Don't hit my mother,' she said, as if he hadn't spoken.

'Essie,' he said. 'Essie.' He let the whip fall to his side.

'Father said you were already engaged to another girl.'

'Lies,' he said. 'That's a lie. I don't know another girl.'

'Give me the whip,' she said again, and he gave it to her. She handed it to her mother. Seeing that Marianne was about to strike him again, and the sisters were raising their arms again too, he ran straight through a pane of glass, out into the garden, staggering amongst the wallflowers. But men barred his way, proclaiming themselves justices of the peace.

'My God,' he shouted, 'this is a houseful of fiends.' The men arrested him then, and he woke up hours later in the Port Albert prison, a rough place from where there was no escape.

There was more before it was over. More jail and court appearances, and a charge laid for 'being on the premises of the Reverend William Gittos for an unlawful purpose'. The errands of the Lord seemed endless for the minister, who hurried about the court, conferring in grave tones with the men who sat on the bench.

Had Esther written the letter asking him to come for her before or after the lie was told? Nobody could tell him. Or, if they knew, they wouldn't.

An Auckland judge set Frederick free, dismissing the charge. He had shaken his head at the folly of it all. A waste of the court's time. There was no case for Mr Fairburn to answer.

Nonetheless, his family didn't care for a scandal in its midst.

So much for love. He married a rich woman soon after he arrived in Australia. She had made him content enough. When Frederick thought of Esther, he thought that too much happiness was bad for a man.

He stood on the viewing platform at the end of the overnight sleeper taking him to Kalgoorlie. The wide, wild, passionate sky was that bright crimson that heralded dusk in the outback, a colour he loved, reminding him he was still alive. Inside the carriage, men heading for the goldfields were drinking whisky and singing. Later, he would join them, singing along to their bawdy songs. Why not? But as the train swayed and rattled, he stood with his hand in his pocket. He held the envelope against his thigh for just a moment longer before drawing it out. He had read the contents. Just a newspaper clipping, announcing the death of Mrs Gittos. And a dark feather. He drew it across his wrist. He understood that the daughter was sending him a signal. He imagined her alone, her parents dead, her brothers and sisters married. She would be nearly forty now.

He closed his eyes. The sky's dark petals of light hovered behind his lids. The train wheels drummed. As the dusk deepened, he felt a sting of cold on his cheeks. He imagined he caught the scent of honey. He let the clipping go first. Then the feather, floating into the darkness. All the sadness in the world. And yet this, this little shaft of memory, sent to him from a far distance.

MRS DIXON & FRIEND

Bethany was waiting for him on the side of the street. The unexpectedness of it took Peter's breath away. He was used to her being late, but here she was, bright-eyed and early, swinging her handbag backwards and forwards with cheerful disingenuousness, like a girl who knows that if she waits long enough her man will turn up. How right she was, even if he was only her man for a day.

'I thought you'd be waiting inside for me.'

'It's too early for lunch, and it's such a beautiful day. I couldn't resist an extra spot of sun. We'll only have a few more weeks of it.'

And it was a crystal-clear, sparkling day, autumn at its best. If Peter Dixon had been at home on a day like this, he would have looked out and just about seen all the way to the Blue Mountains from his office window. He had forgotten they had days like this in New Zealand. So many times when he had been here in recent years, especially in this small town, they had been wintry and dark.

'You've cut your hair,' he said.

'Yes, at last. Well, you know, coming up forty. I thought it was about time.'

'Forty! You.'

Without meaning to, they had started to drift along the street away from the restaurant, but now he stopped in his tracks.

She laughed. 'It's permissible. It happens. It happened to you.'

'Years ago.'

'Ah, ha. I know. I thought about you when it happened . . .'

'You didn't?'

'Yes, I did. I felt very good about it, very malicious, you know?'

'I can imagine.'

'I thought, oh, God, I bet he's feeling awful.'

'I was.'

'Really?'

'I thought that's what you wanted.'

'Oh, I did too. But it doesn't matter now. Actually, I don't mind being forty. A new stage.'

'So, you got your hair cut, eh? It looks nice, it really does. Did I look a bit shocked? I didn't mean to. I've just never seen you without it long before.'

He wanted to reach out and touch the absence of her hair. What was left was smartly styled, its nut-brown texture springy and vital, flecked with grey. He admired women who let it show, a kind of valour that seemed exciting. Still, it was odd coming across it in Bethany. She had always had the ability to surprise him. Once he had thought her predictable, but he had long understood that this was not true.

They were in a shopping mall with seats and spreading trees and a fountain. It looked like any such modern complex, but it was different because although this was the town he had lived in with Bethany, she had watched its development while he had not. He had gone away because he felt as if nothing would ever change and he was afraid that the sameness would stultify and destroy him. I am being sentimental, he told himself. Underneath, nothing would have changed, and he would still never fit in.

'Shall we sit and watch the fountain?' said Bethany.

'You don't mind?' he asked, as he settled beside her.

'Mind?' Her brow puckered. 'Oh. You mean about us?'

'Fine. I just wondered.'

He saw her involuntary shrug. 'Nobody knows you now. Or, if they do, they've forgotten we were married. It wouldn't interest them any more. Why should it, it's what you wanted.'

So, here they were, and just when she had seemed pleased to see him, they were bickering away already. Across the mall, music boomed suddenly from a record shop as a customer had a stereo demonstrated to him.

'Whatever happened to The Seekers?' asked Bethany, cocking her head. 'I mean, in the end, where did they all go? I remember they reappeared for a while. They looked middle aged, the men anyway. Like all of us.' As she glanced down, he thought that she was boasting a little, knowing that that wasn't how she looked at all, but she had earned the right. 'Then they all disappeared again.'

'I don't know. I haven't thought about them in years. Anyway, they say sixty's the new middle age.'

'Remember that time they were in Auckland?' Bethany said, still intent on The Seekers. Judith Durham was hitting a high note in the shop.

'We didn't go, did we?'

'We couldn't. Your mother said she'd have the children, then Ritchie got measles. It was a big deal.'

He was silent, thinking about Ritchie, the boy they had lost. The boy she had lost, he would think in flashes of anger. And, then again, perhaps it was him. He'd left by then.

'It's all right, it's a good memory,' she said, her voice softening.

'It wasn't such a bad weekend. The Kellys came over and we had a sort of a party and stayed up all night because there wasn't much point in going to bed anyway because of Ritchie being sick. We watched the dawn and the red sky coming up over the hills, and then the rain settled in. Afterwards, when we'd had breakfast, the Kellys went home. Ritchie's fever had passed, so we went to bed and the children slept too. We woke up in the middle of the afternoon, and things had come right. It was kind of like a holiday.'

'So it was. Yes, I remember that. And Julie Felix. Remember how she used to come on the box every Tuesday night? She reminded me of you, with all that long hair of hers, walking down a track. I don't know what sort of track it was. Railway? Wasn't it?'

'I remember the track,' she said, nodding. 'And thinking that it was taking her somewhere. Yes, perhaps, a little like her. I wanted to go along some track, some place. But I never did.'

'You did,' Peter said, his voice thick with emotion. And he was sure he was not wrong. A head had turned in their direction, and an old face that he remembered from long ago blinked in surprise, recognising him, but unable to put a name to his face. The woman turned and walked on. 'Look at you,' he said. 'Look how far you've come. Perhaps further than me.' This cost him an effort.

'Why have you come?' she said then. 'It's not long since you were last here.'

He had been dreading this question. In all the years since he had left, he had only come when there was a crisis, when she was in need. If he were honest with himself and, importantly, with her, this time he had come out of a sense of his own need. At least, he owed it to her to tell her that. She had taken the day off from her job in the hospital laboratory to be with him, as if he must have something important on his mind. Peter didn't appear just for nothing, that is what she would have thought.

He stretched his arms along the back of the seat. Leaves, red and citric yellow, fell in small drifts from the tree above. One settled in her hair. He thought to brush it away, but she appeared not to notice. It sat like a small beneficent offering on her sleek head. Oh, lovely Bethany. Did he really owe her his burdens? he wondered. His journey suddenly looked absurd to him. He had boarded the plane almost on an impulse, booking the flight the night before, the way he had when there was one of those crises. This was a crisis, he told himself, but this time it was his own. On a crisp autumn day, she might be pleased to see him, but he had become incidental in her life, a fragment of her past. There had been another child, a lover who had left her, the death of their own younger son. Now he wanted to tell her his troubles, as if an atonement for his past follies, his desertion. Look, he wanted to tell her, it can happen to anyone. It's happened to me, I've had my comeuppance. Why on earth should she care? Yet the idea had persisted, even on the drive south from the airport, that he was somehow bringing her a gift.

He shivered a little, for even on this brilliant day there was the premonition of snow to come in the months ahead, drifting down from the hills. A light breeze lifted the fallen leaves, turning them on the pebbles inlaid into the concrete paving slabs. Come the winter and a day of sleet, when the new pavement had not been swept and tidied as it was today, it would all look tawdry and ugly, just like any other small town imitating the smartness of cities. With a pang, he visualised Sydney, wondering again whether he should be here at all, what he was doing sitting on a street bench with this woman whom he no longer recognised as the person he had once married, and finding in her a mystery, something seductive that tugged at his heart strings.

She was looking at him, waiting for an answer. As he sought to concentrate, to bring his thoughts back to the moment, he found himself looking at her soft and pliable mouth, remembering its taste.

'It's your birthday next week,' he said. 'April the nineteenth.'

'Clever you. Yes.'

'At Easter. It often fell at Easter.'

'Holy Morning.'

'Is it?'

'So Libby used to say.'

'Has your sister got religion now?' A crass question that he regretted straight away. He had never liked her sister.

'Libby doesn't live here now. It just sounded nice when she said it.'

'So it does.' Her face was turned towards him. The midday light was pure. Bethany's eyes still rested on him, enquiring. There had been a glancing away when she mentioned her sister. It was hard not to wonder what had happened in his absence.

'I want to buy you something,' he said with sudden decision. 'A dress, for your birthday. Yes, you can accept a birthday present. Please. You will? Come on, you know what shops you like. I want to buy it for you now.'

He had pulled her by the hand to her feet, almost roughly, yet in such a way that he hoped would not be obvious. As he propelled her along the street, it was she who was guiding their footsteps as if, in her inability to resist him, she was also abetting him in his intention. It was as though they had agreed to buy the dress from the moment he suggested it.

They stopped in front of a shop. 'I have enough dresses,' she said, as if their ungainly dash along the street was for nothing.

'I want you to have another one. Something you wouldn't buy for yourself.'

'What about our table at the restaurant?'

He looked around the trickle of lunch-time shoppers. 'I reckon they'll keep it. Do they queue for lunch here?'

'I could buy it afterwards. After you've gone.'

'I want to see you buy it.'

'Then it's for you too.'

'Do you mind that?'

She shook her head then, as if sensing he was in trouble, perhaps that he was asking for something smaller and less frightening than what he had come for.

In the shop, the owner hurried forward, a woman with ageing chic, whom he dimly recalled had once owned a much smaller and less well-presented shop in the main street. Since then, she had clearly prospered; the clothing on display was stylish and up to date. A couple of slender, expensive-looking women were selecting clothes for a race meet, choosing their outfits in loud voices. Bethany seemed at ease among them, even though he guessed her clothes, neat as they had become, were seldom purchased here.

'Hullo, Mrs Dixon, how nice to see you,' the woman greeted her. It was a shock to hear her called Mrs Dixon, as if he expected her to have some other name that did not associate them, did not bind them in a multiplicity of acts from which they would never recover, however much they might have told themselves they had. Surprising, too, to see Bethany recognised and greeted as a respected woman of the town.

He had intended ordering events as he would have if buying a dress for another woman – announce their mission, discreetly suggest a price range, stand back and let the women believe they were in charge. As it was, he said nothing. Already Bethany had said that she would look around for a few minutes, and that her friend would wait while she chose a dress.

Again the phrase struck him as curious. Her friend. On reflection, as he watched her flicking through a rack, he decided that he liked it better than husband. How *did* people cope with such referrals from the past?

Bethany had taken a dress from the rack and was looking at it thoughtfully. It was a smoky-grey woollen garment with a cowl neckline and a narrow skirt.

'I'd like to try this on,' she said to the woman. 'What do you think, Peter?'

'Let's see how it looks when it's on.'

'Why don't you take a seat while Mrs Dixon changes?' the woman said, arching an eyebrow. He sat, as Bethany disappeared into a fitting room. He felt precarious and exposed, perched on the light wrought-iron chair in the middle of the showroom. The race-going women were leaving, so at least he had the place to himself.

Bethany took what seemed like an age to change. He tried to imagine her shedding her clothes and wished that he could be there too, that buying the dress gave him the privilege of seeing the transaction through from beginning to end. He could see her struggling among straps and belts, her shoulders and arms erupting out of the top of her undergarments, her breasts bulging across the cutting line of her brassière. Such big, pendulous, pear-shaped breasts they were; his children had suckled them, and he too.

The woman at the counter was busying herself with folding clothes, not looking at him, as if she knew the thoughts that ran through men's heads at moments like this. As if he had ordered a strip-tease. He looked up at the ceiling and whistled softly through his teeth.

Bethany emerged at last, clad in the dress. It fitted her perfectly. 'Do you like it?' she asked, turning slowly in front of him. Underneath the wool her hips pivoted, jutting wide at the edges of her flat stomach. He had pinned those hips beneath him.

'It's lovely on, Mrs Dixon, nice for winter evenings. Lovely for five o'clock.' As if five o'clock were a new discovery in the ordering of time. Bethany, beautiful, in her grey woollen frock.

On a mannequin, he saw a black dress with a high neck and rusty gold and scarlet borders. 'What about the one over there?' he said.

'Don't you like this?' said Bethany with obvious disappointment.

'Yes, but I'd love to see you in that one too.'

'I'm not sure that it's me.'

'Well, you need to be sure, don't you? Have something to compare it with?'

She bit her lip, hesitating, and he thought for a moment that she wouldn't do it, that it was him ruling the roost again and telling her what to do. How could he blame her if she said no?

'All right then, it's worth a try.' She changed very quickly this time, and came out again in the black, gold and scarlet dress.

She was laughing, though at first he couldn't see what was

making her so happy. He saw her watching her reflection, smiled with her, thought of her mouth and the white teeth that troubled her whenever she was pregnant. Once she had let him feel, with the tip of his tongue, the jagged edge of a tooth where the filling had come out. They knew each other, the good and the rotten. You couldn't go much further than that.

'It is me, isn't it?' She whirled around the room, the elegant skirt flaring around her knees, the silk puddling into little bunches of colour, the black displaying the creaminess of her skin. The old, wild, strange Bethany, the one who was different, the one from whom he had had to escape and, however he had chosen to see it otherwise, had never been predictable. She stopped in front of the mirror again, ablaze with excitement. In the glass, she saw his eyes following her, and her own widened as if they'd been caught in the act of love, as if in some sudden, stolen joy, like their long ago rainy 'holiday' Sunday.

'You'll have it then?'

She paused again, sobering, the moment of joy past. 'I don't know that I'd get much wear out of it. But it *is* nice.' She cast a reflective eye towards the grey.

'Have them both,' he said.

'No.' She shook her head firmly. 'I couldn't do that. All right then, I'll take the black.'

Outside, she said, 'I never thought of you buying me a dress.'

'For old times' sake,' he said.

'Yes, for old times,' she echoed, and he knew with sharp and painful clarity that she would probably never wear his present. She might even go back another day for the grey dress, perhaps on layby, for slow and laborious payment.

Along the street, she stopped at a store window full of exotic novelties. 'I'd like to buy something for Jason,' she said. 'Would Patsy mind? Look, a Newton's Cradle. Ritchie and Stephen had one that Nana and Granddad gave them one Christmas. I thought it was an absurd thing to give the children, but they couldn't leave it alone.' Already she was heading into the shop.

Peter looked at the silver balls suspended on their fine filigrees of silver wire and touched them gently, seeing them bouncing off each other, connecting, parting, with riveting rhythmic perfection, coming to rest until they were touched again. Touched, moved, it was much the same.

'I'm not sure when I'll be seeing Jason,' he said. 'Maybe not for a little while.'

Over lunch, he said, carefully so as not to alarm her, not to knock her like the little balls that sprang away from each other, 'It's over, you see, Patsy and me, we've separated.'

'Poor Pete,' she said, holding his wrist as if she were keeping count of his pulse. 'Is it very sad?' If she was surprised she did not show it.

'Enough. We've parted, which is hard, as you know.' He said this to forestall the comfort he had wanted to ask of her. He could see now that it was too much to ask of anyone, and certainly that he would give her nothing by saying, look, it can happen to me, it's not just you, it's me too. I've been punished. Reward and punishment, they were long past.

'I'll miss Jason, of course,' he added. But he didn't know whether that was true. His blond Australian son whined a lot and was never satisfied with anything for long. A pity to have let Bethany spend so much money on her gift, but how could he betray his other child? And to her. He seemed to have made a habit of betraying his children. She would not be pleased to hear him disparage this boy.

'How are Stephen and Abbie?' he asked, partly to change the subject, and partly because he really wanted to know.

Bethany released his arm. 'Stephen's a whole lot better. It's not saying a lot, but he's doing his homework and he should pass his exams. He's civil. I mean, that's progress.' Their son caused her grief.

'I'm really glad. And Abbie?' He knew he spoke too eagerly of the girl, yet of all the children that he and Bethany had had, with this or that person, it was Abbie, not his at all, whom he thought of the most.

'Oh, she's just the same.' Bethany spoke offhandedly, but he had trespassed. He could not have Abbie in exchange for a dress, or a moment of the past, or for any reason at all. He and Bethany had exchanged two useless gifts (for he would keep the cradle for himself, as he suddenly understood was what she expected) and that was where it must stop. Kind Bethany, with slumberous eyes now, in a dim restaurant. She had touched him again, and he turned to her.

She murmured to him, and he had to listen carefully to make sense of what she was saying. 'The nice thing is, if we wanted to, we could, but we don't have to because we can. Isn't that so?'

He knew she was talking of making love, and that although she had made no absolute decisions she had, nonetheless, made his for him. In an hour, maybe two, they would go their own ways, carrying their offerings from each other. There would always be baggage of some sort or another but, as you went along, some of it could be abandoned, replaced if necessary. Wives, too, though friends were harder.

A NEEDLE IN THE HEART

1

The weather was overcast the day Queenie McDavitt took off her bodice at the races. Queenie's real name was Awhina, but her husband had long since renamed her so that people – white people, that is – would remember her name more easily. Her husband was known as Stick because he was a tall beanpole of a man, but it was also an alias for his given name, Robert. He had gone off to place a bet on Sparkling Heels for the next race. There was a queue, and, because the day was heavy and languid, the punters idled around, catching up on news from down the line. Stick wasn't concerned about his wife being on her own at the races, she was a woman who could look after herself. Besides, she had half a dozen of their children and grandchildren in tow. She wouldn't be going far.

This was 1925. Times were hard, but things could only get better, people said. Of course, what they didn't imagine was that things would only get worse and worse.

'I reckon if we got a lucky break and paid the bills, we'd get ahead a bit,' Stick said.

'Perhaps if we just went without for a bit and saved some money,' Queenie said, 'maybe we wouldn't be so darn hard up.'

'What have we got to save anyway?' Stick demanded. They never had anything over, and besides there had been an unexpected doctor's bill this year. The couple lived with several of their children in a steep-roofed three-roomed cottage with a number of flat lean-tos added, not far from the Main Trunk Line that ran through Taumarunui. Stick got work on the maintenance gangs now and then, when his back wasn't playing up.

They ended up going to the races anyway, which Queenie knew they would from the moment he first suggested it. She dressed in her best dark skirt and a white blouse with a ruffle running lengthwise from the collar to the waist, and a maroon coat, covering it with a green plaid shawl that she pinned with a special brooch her father had given her after her mother died at an early age. Her father was a white man from pioneering stock. When he gave her the brooch, he told her, with a good many tears, that it should be hers. He had given it to her mother, even though they had never found a preacher to marry them.

Then he had vanished; she heard he had gone to a sheep station down south. The brooch was oval in shape, made of fine filigree gold with an amethyst set in the centre. The back opened up to reveal a tiny shadowy portrait of her mother, a woman with long lustrous hair and strong bright eyes that burned through the faded image. To finish her outfit, Queenie added a wide-brimmed hat trimmed with fat green roses.

'You'll be too hot,' Stick said.

'You want me to come or not?'

There was no question about that. She'd been up making bacon-and-egg pies and sandwiches half the night before.

She watched Stick, pushing his way through the crowds, and sighed. He had a pound burning a hole in his pocket.

'Give us another quid, old girl,' he'd said.

'I've run out,' she said, although she had one left that she'd hidden in her shoe. Her son Joe tickled her ankle. I know what's making you hobble, Ma. The devil, that boy, although he wasn't a boy anymore, and one you couldn't trust. He was her eldest, once a handsome child, though given to sulking, and now here he was, a married man. He followed his father to place the bet. She wouldn't have bet on Sparkling Heels herself. She'd have gone for Fox Fire, but then who listened to her when it came to horses?

On the blanket beside her, Pearl began to cry. Queenie glanced around, looking for Esme, who was supposed to be in charge of the baby. Her daughter was nowhere to be seen. Queenie pulled a face – she couldn't trust Esme not to wander off for five minutes. She took in the scene as far as she could. The girl could be anywhere among the crowd, although the race track wasn't very big. The ground had been flattened out of a moonscape of felled trees after the railway went through.

Queenie's eyes finally rested on Esme, sitting in the shade of one of the tents making a daisy chain. Like a little kid.

'You tell that Esme to get over here real quick,' she told Lucy, who was ten and one of Mary's children. Mary was second in the family after Joe. 'Tell her I'll give her a clip if she doesn't hurry up.'

'You're supposed to be looking after Pearl,' Queenie said, when Esme came dawdling over. By now she was holding the baby over her shoulder, the practised palm of her hand gently rubbing the baby's back to bring up her wind, but Pearl kept on crying.

Esme took the baby, and Pearl stopped crying almost straight away.

'Just don't go running off and leaving her like that.'

'You were here,' Esme said. She had rippling wavy hair that reminded Queenie of her own mother's, and her eyes were black like Queenie's. Freckles dusted her nose. Esme and Joe, the best looking of the bunch.

'I don't want you hanging around where there's fellas,' said Queenie. 'You keep yourself to yourself. Pearl's your job for the day. D'you know, anything can happen to a baby when it's lying on the ground? I know a baby having a bit of a kick on the grass, and next thing his mother hears him yelling. Well, this kid yells and yells until he's dead, and after he's died a big centipede comes walking out of his ear. You just don't know how quick one of those centipedes can go walking up inside a baby's ear and chew its brains all out.'

'That's horrible,' Esme said. Her eyes filled with quick tears.

Over at the track, the punters were shouting themselves hoarse, and the beating of hooves was shaking the ground where they stood. 'Oh, my God,' yelled a man's voice – there's Fox Fire, she's down,' and then the cry went up that Sparkling Heels was out by a nose, and, would you believe it, that pony had won.

'That'll be the last we see of your father,' Queenie said gloomily, 'now he's got money in his pocket.' Already she could see him in the queue, getting ready for the next race. Esme had put the baby down in her lap, where she lay grizzling again. Queenie took her back. 'I don't know what's the matter with you,' she said. 'You don't seem able to do the simplest thing.'

It made Queenie unhappy, the way Esme was. She was such a beautiful girl, but you couldn't say anything without her taking offence. Esme stretched out, face down on the ground beside her mother and Pearl. Joe came back and said he'd lost ten bob on Fox

Fire but the old man had made five pounds. He'd heard some man had lost a tenner each way on the fallen horse.

'Did your father give back the quid I gave him?'

'He reckons he can turn it into twenty-five.'

'You tell him right now, before he gets to the counter. Go on, do as you're told.'

Joe hesitated but, seeing the look on his mother's face, decided to pursue his father. A shot rang out as Fox Fire was put down, and when that excitement was over a huddle of people began drifting their way, men who were skint like Joe.

'Get some food into you,' Queenie said, holding out a tomato sandwich to Esme with her free hand. 'Come on, you got to eat something.' Esme pulled her hair right down around the sides of her face so that it spread in one dark pool on the blanket. Queenie sighed and touched the living silk of it. The sun was beginning to emerge; Queenie had taken off her shawl, carefully pocketing her brooch, and now she wriggled out of her coat. Joe's wife, Bunty, who'd turned up to join them, held Pearl while she took it off.

A man called Dave Murphy stopped beside the family's picnic, a big man with his stomach tumbling over his belt and a large moustache. He wore a yellow and black suit and his shoes glittered in the dull sunlight. He owned one of the new timber mills in the district. From the mean look on his face and the amount of money he usually jingled in his pockets, Queenie guessed he might be the man who'd lost a tenner each way.

'You're a bit past that sort of caper,' he said.

When Queenie didn't answer, he said, 'I'd have thought you were a bit old for babies. Old Stick still sticking it to you, eh? Still making babies in an old lady?' He laughed loudly at his own wit, at the same time nudging Esme on the ground with his foot.

Queenie said, 'That's enough. This little Pearl is my miracle baby.' The baby had gone to sleep in her arms, and she touched the pale cheek with the back of her finger. They could have as easily called her Lily, but Pearl was what they chose because her paleness and her prettiness had a sheen that made her glow. Queenie had never held a baby this fair in her arms before. Pearl's eyebrows were like silvery smudges, her eyes milky blue, the fine down round her fontanelle white like kitten's fur.

Esme sat up when she felt herself poked in the ribs. She sat staring down between her knees while Dave Murphy looked them all over. Queenie guessed he knew Stick had made a few quid. Dave smelled as if he'd had a few whiskies. He had a way of getting around the liquor ban that was in force in the King Country in those days. Some said he had his own whisky still out in the hills; others said it was amazing what fell off the back of a goods train wagon. Queenie made her voice slow and reasonable, not wanting to aggravate him.

'This little girl is an old woman's magic baby,' she said. 'You remember Magic Man came to town, about a year or so back, and set up in the hall and did his tricks?'

'I heard about him, can't say I saw him.'

'Yes you did. I saw you there, Mister Dave Murphy.'

'Oh, maybe, a busy man like me can't remember everything. Now you mention it, I went down there to haul one of my men back to work. We had to get some timber wagons ready for the night train. Maybe I was there a half-hour.'

'And more. Remember, he did all those handkerchief tricks? Made the handkerchief stretch and tied it up in knots without letting go of the ends. That was pretty clever. And he cut the lady in half. You saw that, didn't you?'

'They do all that stuff with mirrors.'

'There weren't any mirrors there, I walked up and had a look myself. There were no mirrors.'

'Mum, stop it,' said Esme.

'Then, remember, at the end, Magic Man puts the curtain down, and you think the show's all over. Then it comes up again, and he's standing there without a head. His head is sitting on the table beside him. That's a miracle.'

'Hmm. Yes, remarkable, now you come to mention it.'

'A miracle. So, at the end, I went up to him and said, 'Mister Magic Man, I want a new baby because all my babies are pretty well grown up now.'

'Oh, so it was Magic Man who put it there?'

'Now I think you better talk to Stick about that. Nobody puts anything near me except Stick, I tell you. No, I just said to Magic Man, put a spell over me so I can have another baby, and that's what he did. I got what I asked for, my own little jewel.'

'I don't believe a word of it.' Dave stared around angrily, not liking to be taken for a fool. 'What do you make of it, young lady?' he said to Esme.

'I don't know anything about it,' she muttered, the flood of her hair washing over her face.

'Your mother here's a dried-up old lady, wouldn't you say?'

'Nothing dried up about me,' Queenie said.

'Let me see your titties then.'

'You want to see my titties now?' Queenie passed Pearl back to Esme to hold, even though she resisted taking her. Esme held her as if she were a ticking bomb. 'Don't Mum,' she pleaded. Her mother's hands were at the throat of her blouse. She freed one button after another until they were all undone. Dave Murphy stared at the mountain of brown flesh being revealed. The tops of her breasts rippled above the corset that held them in place, hummocks of round honey-gold flesh being revealed.

A group of men was collecting around Dave Murphy. They nudged each other, with sharply indrawn breaths. You could tell they were astonished at their own nerve, standing here and watching. But it was like a spell was cast over them, their eyes riveted on Queenie's cleavage. She slid the blouse off her shoulders and her hands moved to the hooks holding the corset in place.

'No,' shrieked Esme. 'No, no, no.' Mary's girl had gone to fetch Stick and Joe, but Esme was mesmerised and screaming, unable to do anything except sit there clutching Pearl.

The first hook popped undone, the second one.

'Magic,' said Queenie. 'That's what it was.'

Then Joe leapt through a gap between the men, scattering them in all directions, his arms flailing, and Stick, following behind, threw his coat over Queenie just as her sleek breasts tumbled free, covering her long purple nipples an instant before they were seen by the men.

Joe smacked Esme on the side of her face with his open hand. 'You never ought to have let her do that,' he said.

'It wasn't her fault,' said Queenie. 'Here, get up.' She tried to yank her daughter to her feet, seeing the blue bruise already forming on her face.

Stick was more interested in getting Queenie out of it. Making sure his coat was tightly wrapped around her, he began pulling her towards one of the tents to get dressed.

'What about that quid I lent you?' Queenie said, making out she didn't care about all the agitation.

'Forget it,' Stick said. 'Just forget it.'

Joe went to the horses and hitched up their wagon. 'You get that baby out of here,' he said to Esme.

When Esme McDavitt grew up, she had no offers of marriage for a long time. She was made various offers of one kind or another, but she knew none of them would do her any good. Some nights, under the tin roof of the cottage, she ached, wanting things she couldn't have.

Her father and brothers thought she should go up north, try Auckland and see if there was anyone available up there. But Queenie said not to worry about it, a girl's place was at home. She set Esme to some tasks to occupy her time, skills of her own that she had learned in native school when she was a child. Esme surprised her. She sewed the straightest seam you ever saw. It took her only a day and a half to run up a dress, complete with cloth buttons and cuffs.

'People would pay good money for that,' Queenie told Stick.

'Well, let them pay,' he said. 'Get started.' This is what Esme did. She charged modest prices, all that women could pay. A dress cost four shillings, two shillings and sixpence for straight skirts, three shilling for blouses. Sometimes people tried to put it across her, but only got away with it once. She found she liked the business side of things. The money meant she could help her mother out with things Pearl needed for school when she started.

She was riding her bicycle home after delivering a dress, the wind whipping her hair, which she still wore long and untamed. When she reached the railway line, she got off the bike to wheel it over. A group of gangers were sitting smoking on an idling railway jigger pulled in on a loop. Esme pretended not to see them, her foot poised on a pedal, while a train from the south thundered through.

Jim Moffit was riding in the guard van that day, on his way to a job.

Esme never forgot the thrill of it, being singled out by Jim. Perhaps that's what it was, the excitement of being chosen, when so often she had been passed over. He'd seen her standing there beside the tracks. 'Who's that girl?' he asked the men in the van. He told her this later on.

'And what did they say?'

'Just your name. "That's Esme McDavitt," that's what they said.'

'Was that all?'

'Well, it was enough, wasn't it? They knew who you were.'

'Nothing else?'

'Not that I can think of. I said, "Does she live there? Will a letter find her?"'

Jim Moffit wrote:

Dear Mr McDavitt,
I am an Englishman who has been here some three years
now. I have a reasonable education, but times are very bad
back home, even worse than here. I am one of the signallers
who operate the train tablets. I have an offer of a railway
house if I should marry. I am very desirous of making a
closer acquaintance with your daughter Esme, with a view to
marriage. I am thirty-four years old, but I don't see a dozen or
so years making a great deal of difference as I am healthy of body
and mind. I would make her a kind husband.
Yours,
James Moffit.

*

His untamed girl, snatched up from the side of the railway, his clever English head turned in an instant. A bachelor reformed into a husband, all, it seemed, in the twinkling of an eye.

Esme made herself a dusky pink wool dress for her wedding. Before they walked over to the church, her mother pinned her gold filigree brooch on her shoulder. 'Just for today,' she said. 'One day I'll give it to Pearl.'

'I thought you might give it to Mary,' Esme said, surprised that her mother would overlook her eldest daughter.

'Well, you know how it is,' her mother said. 'You know Pearl's our special baby.'

At the last minute, Esme didn't want to go with Jim after all. She hung onto Pearl and cried, trying not to let Jim see her tears. 'You be a good girl for your Ma,' she said.

Jim took her to a hotel in Auckland for their honeymoon. Already, married life was conferring an unexpected grandness.

'Make the most of it,' Jim had said, laughing at her wonder. 'It'll be down to real life once we get home.' Home would be at Ohakune Junction, down south of Taumarunui beneath the volcanic mountain. In a way, she would have liked to go straight there to see the house they had been allocated in Railway Row, the street by the line, but Jim said plenty of time for that.

They travelled on the night train. It was running late, so they had to sit on the platform in the cool darkness for a long time, waiting for it to come. The waiting room was closed until the train pulled in. Esme had told her family to go home to bed: there was no point in everyone being worn out. There didn't seem a lot for her and Jim to say. She realised how little she knew him.

On the way north, he opened up, talking about his job and describing the train tablet system. He worked out of a hut, one of a series along the Main Trunk railway line. He travelled there on goods trains, and at the end of his shift he got picked up and taken home. The tablets were part of the spacing system that set the course of the trains and ensured that there were never two engines on the same stretch of line at once. The numbered tablets were picked up and carried from one section of the line to the other, and only when the tablet, or the 'biscuit' as the men called it, was safely under lock and key at the other end of the section was it safe for the train to proceed. That was when the green light beamed its semaphore message down the line, giving the all clear. With express trains and goods trains rattling past, there was no time for a lapse of attention, no failure of detail that could be allowed.

'I see it's a very important job,' Esme said soberly. They were rushing through another small town. Dawn light was breaking. A deep wide river flowed past them on their left. Stained and grimy miners were gathered near a station, their day ending as others began. Esme felt like them.

'I hold life in these hands,' Jim said, holding out his splayed palms. She shivered, wondering if she were up to the task of supporting Jim in his work. He seemed to read the way she felt. 'Don't worry, we'll be a team. It's going to make a big difference to me, having a wife and comfortable home to come back to at the end of my shift.'

'I'll do my best, Jim.'

'I can teach you things.'

'What sort of things?' she asked, her voice faint. The train wheels beneath her said *click click tschick click click tschik*.

'Wait and see.'

'I left school when I was thirteen. Didn't my father tell you that?'

'Don't worry about all of that right now,' he said. 'It's just you I want.' They still had to get to Auckland, to make love for the first time, to discover who each other really was. She was becoming frightened of him. Then she thought it was just because they were both exhausted and it was taking each of them in funny ways. She wondered if they would go straight to bed when they got to the hotel.

But that wasn't the plan. Jim had arranged a day of sightseeing first, so that she was so tired she hardly remembered what came next.

When she sat at breakfast the next morning, she felt strangely untouched, recalling more of the clean white cotton sheets that had covered her than his body. She had turned to him first thing when she woke. Some mornings at home, Pearl climbed into bed beside her. They would go back to sleep; in cold weather Pearl warming her feet on the backs of Esme's legs. So it was Pearl she looked for when she felt someone in the bed with her, but it was Jim. He kissed her forehead. 'Good morning, Mrs Moffit,' he said. She had felt a weightless sensation, as if she were not really there. Soon after, the housemaid had knocked on the door and delivered cups of tea.

'Milk and sugar everyone?' she'd called.

'Jim, do you take sugar?' Esme said.

'Hush,' he said, when they were on their own again. 'She'll know we're just married.'

While they were waiting for their breakfast to be served,

he pointed out the cutlery on the table. 'Do you see how they set the knives and forks out?' he said. This was how he liked things, everything exactly in place, the knife and fork straight beside the table mats and the bread and butter plates square on the right-hand side of the knife with the small knife pointed straight ahead. A quick learner like her would have no trouble at all.

2

In the morning, after Jim had gone, Esme walked to the window and looked at the mountain, or the place where the mountain should be if the rain was not falling and turning to sleet. Behind her, a thin fire spluttered, spitting sap from wet bark, emitting a smell like incense. It reminded her of the magician she and her mother had met up Taumarunui way when she was still a girl, of the strange soft scent in the air that somehow proclaimed that nothing is real, nothing you ever knew exists. There is only illusion. The whistle of a train sounded through the mist, a long exhalation, a breath, another one. There he goes, she thought, there goes Jim, up the line, the fate of travellers in his hands.

The house in Railway Row was one of twenty-four, twelve on either side of the straight street that ran exactly parallel to the railway lines a few feet away. Tough bush covered the slope above, while flax and toetoe bushes like soft calico flags shivered in the wind alongside the tracks.

Esme gathered up dishes from the table with a snap and a rattle. Jim's irritation had started before breakfast. She knew she wasn't functioning properly. Everything about her felt heavy and tired.

It wasn't as if she hadn't slept; in fact, she'd slept so deeply that when the alarm clock went off she hadn't known where she was.

'Hurry up, will you,' he'd said, razor in his hand as he came into the bedroom bare-chested, his braces hanging in loops over his thighs.

She wanted to say to him, how about you get your own breakfast for once, but she knew that wouldn't do. Though it wasn't as if she didn't work too. On a good week, she could earn almost as much as Jim, not that she mentioned this because it made him angry in a way she couldn't understand. Her dressmaking skills had followed her to Ohakune Junction.

When he did sit down to eat, breakfast didn't please him. He looked as if he were going to cry.

'I'm sorry,' she said. 'I don't know what's come over me.'

'Perhaps you're doing too much,' he said.

'I need something to fill the days,' she said, surprised to hear herself answering back.

'Yes, I suppose you do.' He sighed and folded his napkin, leaving half his food on the plate. 'You should get Pearl to help you more.'

'Pearl? She's only a little kid.' Pearl was asleep in the spare room that was hers when she came for the holidays. It was the room put aside for babies.

'She's ten. Old enough to do a bit around the house. Her mother spoils that girl, and you're just as bad.'

'She's going home in a couple of days.'

She smiled at him then, put her face up for him to kiss, and he seemed restored to good humour, pinching her cheek and looking down fondly at her for a moment before picking up his coat. He glanced out the window at the ugly weather.

'The truth is I could do with a day in bed myself.'

'What would the boss have to say about that?'

'He'd probably say what a lucky devil I was, spending the day under the blankets with a fine-looking woman like you.'

'Jim, he wouldn't.' She felt herself reddening.

'You're the most beautiful girl in the world,' he said.

Once he had gone, she considered cutting a pattern right away instead of washing the dishes. Routine, Jim always said, and she could feel him looking over her shoulder. It put her back in a bad mood, so that she clattered around the kitchen, banging dishes about. You couldn't tell how things were going to turn out. She liked this house. In the front room there were crocheted lace curtains that had taken her months to make. The room was furnished with three wooden-framed armchairs, with red slip covers on the cushions, and a stand-up gramophone. But now, just when everything was finished, Jim was talking about going for promotion, trying to get a job closer to the city. She didn't know how she would fit into a big place.

'What's the matter?' Pearl stood in the doorway in her nightgown.

'Oh, it's you. Go and tell your mother she wants you.' She was surprised at the sharpness of her voice.

'Have I missed breakfast?'

'I've kept you some.'

'I thought you were mad, all the noise you were making.'

'I'm tired. I wouldn't mind if you got dressed and washed the dishes.'

'It's just like home,' Pearl muttered.

'Well, you better get used to it. The holidays are nearly over.'

'I could go to school here.'

'No you can't.'

'You are mad, aren't you?'

Suddenly Esme wanted to cry. She hated Pearl going back to Queenie. She told herself that it was just that she liked having a kid around the place, one of the family. But this morning she wanted to cut out her pattern by herself in peace, with just the sound of the rain coming down.

No, not even that. What she wanted was to sit and work out what was happening; something was going on that she couldn't figure out.

Pearl picked up a dishcloth and swiped it around as if she didn't know what to do with it. Esme bit back a rebuke. My little sister, she said proudly, when she introduced her to folk at the Junction. She still had creamy skin and fair hair. Her teeth were prominent with one tooth much whiter than the others, giving her the appearance of a slightly lopsided rabbit when she smiled. Her talent was singing. She knew all the hymns, and at Christmas she sang a verse of 'Silent Night' on her own at the church:

Round yon Virgin, Mother and Child,

Holy infant so tender and mild

You could hear a ripple around the congregation: her high notes would make crystal shiver. Her singing was the one thing about Pearl that pleased Jim.

When everything was cleared away and the tablecloth folded, Esme laid out the material for the dress she was about to begin, pink linen for the postmistress's wife. Esme would have liked to tell Norma that the colour wouldn't go with her red hair, but Norma was a woman who fancied her own taste. Besides, Norma paid her promptly and liked a chat. Esme laid the pattern on the table and considered it. She could see the sleeves were going to be troublesome; she might have to improvise a bit.

Her sewing machine was a treadle, which meant she could keep both hands free to guide the material while her feet pumped below, going really fast.

'Look,' said Pearl, 'there's a whole lot of men running down to the station.'

'For goodness' sake,' said Esme, and it was at that minute, when emergency sirens were beginning to wail all over the town, that she ran her hand under the speeding needle; it snapped in two, the top shaft entering her thumb as it jerked free of the spindle that held it.

'Oh,' cried Esme, 'oh, oh.' Her hand was covered in a froth of bright blood.

Pearl was at the window, peering out. 'There's been an accident.'

'Well, there's nothing we can do about it.' All the same, she went to the door and opened it, dread in the pit of her stomach. Men in heavy coats were dashing towards a jigger. 'What is it?' she called, but nobody heard her, and in a minute they had disappeared down the line.

'Shut the door and come inside,' she said at last. Her hand still ached where it had been struck by the needle, but the bleeding had stopped. She was sure the needle had gone in, but as there was no sign of it she began to think she had imagined it. The sharp end of the needle was lying on the floor where it had landed. Perhaps the other half had flown across the room and landed in the wood box.

She set to work installing and threading a new needle. The pain in her hand persisted, but when she pressed her thumb, and then her whole hand, she couldn't locate the source of the pain. It occurred to her that the needle might have floated away in her veins.

'Perhaps I should see the doctor,' she said to Pearl.

'Does it hurt?'

'It's better now.' Funny, but as soon as she thought about going to the doctor the pain stopped. She and Jim kept a guinea in a jar on the top shelf of the kitchen in case they needed the doctor; you didn't want to get caught short for emergencies. There might be other needs, more urgent than a stray sewing-machine needle that she couldn't see or find.

And now, some new knowledge entered her, a mysterious unravelling of something so obvious, so already known, that she didn't see how she hadn't worked it out already.

'How would you like to be an aunty?' she said to Pearl.

'Are you and Jim having a baby?'

'Yes, that's right, we are too.'

'I thought you and Jim couldn't have babies.'

'Who said that?'

'I think Mum just wondered. Is Jim pleased?'

'He doesn't know yet.'

'You mean, you told me first?'

'Looks like it, don't tell him I told you.'

Pearl said she'd come down in the holidays and help Esme bath the baby and change its clothes.

'I'd like that,' Esme said.

The rain was clearing, and the hooded mountain began to reveal itself, pointing its ice fingers through the cloud. Just looking at its snow-clad slopes made her shiver. A big knot of people had gathered on the platform, the women emptied out of their houses.

The station master, Alec Grimes, said yes, there'd been a collision on the line, a couple of goods trains. A man had been killed. The Daylight Limited pulled in and wasn't allowed to go any further north, so that now passengers joined with the locals, looking helpless and shaken, while the steam engines panted and hissed on the track.

That evening, very late, Jim came in, white around the mouth. There was a new man in the control hut, a man who was supposed to have finished his training. He was a Māori chap. Probably couldn't read, if you knew the truth of the matter. 'It wasn't my fault,' Jim said, 'even if I was in charge. You can't have eyes in the back of your head. They shouldn't have let that Māori loose. He should never have been allowed the key to the tablets.'

Afterwards, he admitted he shouldn't have said that.

Jim didn't lose his job, although the managers said it was touch and go. He was known as a good worker, perhaps the whole mistake couldn't be laid at his feet. But his chances of promotion had gone for the time being.

When Esme and Jim's son Neil was two years old, she saw Conrad Larsen and fell in love, for the first and only time in her life. All the rest were things, things that just happened, accommodations good and bad, but not love. He was leaning out of a locomotive window as it came into the station, his red cheeks alight from the glow of the firebox he'd been stoking, his navy-blue cap pushed back on his head. Later, she discovered the bald dome beneath the cap, saw the way his head shone in the sunlight. His big gleaming teeth sparkled against the soot where he'd wiped his hand across his mouth.

It happened on a day when she'd had what amounted to a quarrel with her friend Norma. Norma had blue eyes and reddish hair that she wore in tight curls. Esme thought she was a lonely woman. Her daughters had already left home. But since Neil was born, she and Norma had gone past a business relationship and visited each other in their homes, although mostly Esme visited Norma, in her big house with its verandah and trim on the other side of the railway tracks. Neil was at that stage when he was into everything and opening cupboards. She had to watch out for him. Norma liked looking after Neil now and then, and it suited Esme. Jim wasn't sure she should leave him with someone else, even for a little while, but what harm could it do while she walked down to the shops for their meat and a few groceries. She didn't tell Jim about the times when she just went for walks along the paths that led towards the mountain or along the banks of the stream that led to the waterfall. Some days she wondered if she was cut out for motherhood.

It was high summer, and the mountain was stripped of all but its crown of snow and surrounded by a blue haze, the day Esme fell out with Norma. The heat inside the houses had been building since the sun came up.

Norma stood at her bench mincing leftovers from the previous night's roast to make into rissoles. Her eyes were on Neil, seated at the table eating a biscuit. He was a quiet child with a narrow face and slender, curved eyebrows. 'If you like, you could go down and see your mother for the day. Take the morning train down and back on the night train. We'd like that, wouldn't we, little man?'

'I couldn't do that, he'd miss his feed.'

Norma stopped what she was doing. 'You haven't still got that kid on the tit, have you?'

'Just a couple of times a day.'

'That's disgusting,' Norma said, dusting flour off her hands. 'A big boy like that. What does your husband think of that?'

'We'll go and meet your dad,' Esme said, lifting Neil down from the chair, not looking at Norma.

'Not that it's any of my business.'

'No,' said Esme, 'not really.' She fled from the house, gathering up Neil and his toys, as if she had been caught out. Her breasts felt heavy and ripe and shameful. The image of her mother's exposed flesh flashed before her.

'You'll be back,' Norma said, as she paused to open the door. Esme knew then that Norma saw into her, understood that Esme was not really happy in her life, yearned for some kind of freedom that, in some small measure, she offered her.

It was too early for Jim to come home, but she and Neil waited on the platform all the same. Esme heard a goods train's warning whistle and, as it arrived, the sound she loved: the steam belching up while the brakes of the massive machines ground to a halt, the big engine straining like a horse in its stall.

Jim wasn't on the train, but Conrad was.

When she remembers, she thinks how unlikely it was that he would look at her twice. Already she had adopted the ways of an older woman, wearing her hair up in a bun and cheap glasses because she couldn't thread a needle without them.

Still, it was she who saw him first. One of the things she liked was that this time she chose him. When he looked down, she had already said yes.

'Could you look after Neil for an hour?' she asked Norma the next day, as if nothing untoward had happened the day before. She knew what time his train came in. She knew that if she waited on the station he would follow her.

Just like that.

Not, is this all right? Are you sure about this? Nothing of that. Just the two of them on her and Jim's bed. Her hair falling down around her face, her glasses left behind on the kitchen bench, him carrying her through the house, holding her legs around his waist until he could put her down and they could do their business. He had a sweet, oily smell on his skin that she wore all that day.

His hands reached up for her cone-shaped breasts when she swung them above him. She felt him hesitate a moment.

'Steady on,' he said.

'I'm still feeding the baby. I can't get pregnant.'

His mouth then, everywhere.

His chest and arms bulged with muscles. On the ascents when the trains climbed from Waiouru to Tangiwai, through the Junction and on to Raurimu and the great Central Plateau of the island, from Taumarunui up to Frankton Junction, he threw three, perhaps four tons of coal through the fire hole, placing the fuel from corner to corner along the near end of the grate. His wrists were swivelling steel. The arms that held her were like a high fence around her body.

She thought, fleetingly, of the needle that wandered within her. Somewhere, drifting among her blood, the thick red soup of herself, the needle had moved, perhaps entered her heart.

Norma said she'd have Neil at the same time the day after that, but Esme could see that she looked at her oddly. She thought, I look different already.

All through the summer, the geraniums were in a red hot heat around the house, and he kept coming to see her. After the first few days, she stopped asking Norma to mind Neil. She put him to bed in his cot, and hoped he wouldn't wake up. In moments when she tried to behave like a normal person – a person who wasn't frantic with love, a person who mashed potatoes and made gravy and said here you are, here's your tea, dear, and hung out the washing and snapped the napkins when they were dry – she thought that her son would wake and know what she did.

She stopped going to the post office, didn't see Norma anymore.

Queenie sent word that Pearl was coming to stay. She'd seen Jim at the Taumarunui station when he'd gone there on a relieving job, and told him to pass on the message to Esme.

'She can't come now,' Esme cried.

'I thought you liked having her.'

'It's not that I don't want her to come, of course,' Esme said carefully. 'It's just that, well, you know, I'm busy with Neil.'

'One baby's not that much work.'

'Oh, what do you know about housework?' This was what love did to her, it made her bold and reckless in the way she spoke.

'There's no need for that,' Jim said. For an instant, she expected to be hit. And yet, she thought, he couldn't do that, not Jim from Birmingham with his good manners and his kindness. Because, even though he wasn't always happy in himself and he complained about little things, he never did her any harm. Something about his look silenced her. She thought he must be able to sense the permanent swollen ache between her legs that he only made worse when he touched her.

'I guess Pearl could come for a few days.'

'It wouldn't hurt,' he said.

The day before Pearl arrived, she wrapped her legs tightly around Conrad's waist. 'I love you,' she said, running her tongue in the inside of his ear.

'I know,' he said. 'I know that all right.' He pulled her closer to him so that she didn't know where he began and she left off.

Pearl was nearly thirteen. She had grown bosoms and was a head taller since Esme last saw her. She was rounded, and her fair hair spun into ringlets that surrounded her face. She'd sung in the end-of-year concert at school.

'Would you like me to sing my solo?' she asked on the first afternoon of her visit.

'Yes, please,' Esme said, 'of course.' It was twelve-thirty. The train was due in at one.

Early one morning, Pearl sang,
just as the sun was rising
I heard a maid sing in the valley below.
Oh, don't deceive me
Oh, never leave me . . .

At any other time, such pure clarity would have wrung Esme's heart, but before Pearl had finished singing, she said, absently, 'Could you mind Neil for me, d'you think? Just for half an hour.'

'You weren't listening,' Pearl cried.

'Yes, yes I was. Did you get that song off the radio?'

'I hate you. It's true what they say about you, isn't it?'

Esme snatched her wrist and held onto it. 'What do they say about me? What? You just tell me who says what about me. You hear me.'

'Nothing,' Pearl said in a sullen voice. Esme let her arm drop. There was an angry mark where she had twisted Pearl's delicate flesh. 'All right then, I'll look after your rotten baby.'

'Thank you,' Esme said and walked out. She shivered as she hurried to the railway station, wishing she had brought her cardigan. It was autumn now, and all week there had been a hint of frost in the morning. In the blue shadow of the mountain, the cold started early. She stood at the station as she had that first time, only now she felt that people on the platform looked sideways at her, wondering what to expect next.

In fact, nothing much happened. The train came, and Conrad wasn't on it, and as soon as she saw that, she understood what she had already sensed; he wouldn't be there. She would never see him again. There was no real way of knowing this, just the feeling that things had gone too far and something had to change. She glimpsed her reflection in the murky painted window of the station waiting room, in disarray, clutching her arms around herself.

Blindly, she turned and walked away from the station and through the town. Past the butcher's shop, where she should be going to buy some liver and bacon for Jim's tea, and perhaps a sausage for Pearl who wouldn't eat liver. On past the greengrocer's shop, where a quiet patient Chinese woman put apples and spinach in the front window. On beyond the tobacconist's shop, where a group of men glanced at her as she hurried on by.

Nobody greeted her. So it was true then. They knew about her, knew why she stood so brazenly in full sight of everyone, waiting for him.

She set off at a run, along the track beside the Mangawhero, where she used to walk before all this madness began. Further along the stream bed, there was a rocky incline that dropped to a pool. She wanted to lie down in the water and let it freeze her, until she dropped like a stone to the bottom. Would Jim think to look for her there? He might, but she hoped that if he did he would simply leave her there. As winter closed in, perhaps she would float to the surface and be rolled by boulders and glacial ice further down, out to sea or to one of the great lakes, wherever it was the river went. She really didn't care. To love in such an extreme way was to lose her sense and her senses.

Nothing like that's ever going to happen again, she said to herself, and it felt as if she had had an amputation of some kind. She found herself looking at her body as if she could see something missing. She thought about Neil, home alone with Pearl, and how, after a while, the boy would cry for her. Her breasts were leaking milk; she touched herself where her dress was wet and saw herself alone in the bush, a crazy woman with streaming hair, falling blindly across tree stumps and the dried-up grasses of summer. The river bubbled over the stones, shining where the water and the falling light touched them. She saw clouds and bodies floating, waving arms and the star faces of babies in them. Perhaps Pearl could look after her baby; she would soon get into the way of keeping house, the way Esme had. Then she thought that, if that happened, Pearl would be with Jim, and that wouldn't be right.

She turned and walked back towards the town. The sun had dropped away, blood red, followed by the amber light before dusk beneath the mountain top. She began to be afraid of what she would find, and how she would have to face up to Jim's anger if he discovered she'd left Neil with Pearl. *I went for a walk and got lost* was the first story that sprang to mind. If he wasn't home already, might she not gather up Pearl and Neil and catch the train home to Taumarunui? Only the train wasn't due for hours, and he would find them all on the station.

Then she told herself that she had imagined everything. That nobody knew. Conrad had had a day off sick, or his roster had been changed. He'd be on the train the next day. By the time she got to the house, she found herself believing this.

Inside, the kerosene lamp had been lit. Pearl was stoking the fire under Norma's instructions. Norma sat at the table with Neil in her lap, trying to get him to eat some food she'd mashed up for him. There was no sign of Jim.

'I'm sorry,' Esme said to both of them.

'I didn't know where you were,' Pearl said, her tone sour.

'The girl came and got me,' said Norma. 'Thank goodness she's got more brains than I gave her credit.'

'Has Jim been in?' Esme asked.

'Wouldn't be surprised if he was having a drink or two with his mates.'

'Jim doesn't go drinking.' Which was true. Jim wasn't a drinking man: it was one of those things that had recommended him to Queenie.

'Happen he might be now,' Norma said. She stood up, patting the creases in her skirt. 'You know, Esme, it doesn't pay to get your meat where you get your bread.'

'I don't know what you mean.'

'There was a letter came for you. Seeing you hadn't been in for the mail lately, I brought it over when Pearl called me in. My husband said, take it to her, it might be urgent.'

'Thank you,' said Esme again, glancing at the envelope. She didn't recognise the big block letters that spelled her name on the envelope, but she saw the soft glue that held the flap of the envelope in place. She guessed it had been opened.

'Aren't you going to open it?' Norma asked.

Esme crumpled the letter in her hand as if it wasn't important. 'Probably a bill. That's all the mail that ever comes, isn't it?' She opened the door and held it ajar, so that Norma had to walk through.

The letter said:

Dear Esme
You don't know who I am but I think you ought to know a
certain man has been told he will be killed soon unless he takes
some action to stop it happening to him he might have an engine
run over him it will look like an accident I can promise you but
it will happen he has said he will do what he must or rather he
must not.
Yours, a well wisher.

When Esme's next boy was born, she nearly died. The doctor and the nurses at the cottage hospital gave her so much chloroform that if the baby hadn't killed her coming out sideways, the dose almost did.

Esme held her baby close. Already she could tell he was not a placid boy, but every limb seemed so perfect and unblemished she thought he couldn't be real. And this baby had a smell she understood.

'What would you like to call him?' Jim asked.

'What about Philip?' she said tentatively. This was the name of Jim's father, although of course she had never met them. Jim's parents had both died that year, the announcement of their deaths coming by sea mail, in letters edged with black.

'Yes,' said Jim, 'that's a nice idea. You go ahead and call him that.' He stroked the baby's cheek with his forefinger. 'He's a throwback this one,' he said, 'A right little darkie.' Philip had black curls and olive skin.

'One for Mum,' Esme said.

Jim smiled and tickled the baby. It wasn't like Norma had said. He'd never come home drunk. He'd never had a word to say about anything that happened. If anything, he seemed calmer, less willing to find fault with her than he had before.

The year the world went to war, Jim Moffitt said, 'I wish I could go.' He couldn't because he was too old, and he was needed for essential services anyway. Ned, the fifth of Queenie and Stick McDavitt's eight children, said, 'I'm going,' and learned the Māori Battalion song. And Lawrence Tyree, the film projectionist, said, 'I'm glad I can stay here.'

Lawrence had had a hernia operation, which he reckoned would keep him out of the war. He had blond hair and very smooth skin, so much like velvet you'd think he had no beard except for a stain of mottled shadow that appeared at the end of the day. He'd come up to the Junction to live just before the war started and ran the picture theatre on Wednesday and Sunday nights.

'You a shirker?' asked Ned, on his visit to say goodbye before he left for the war. It was half-time at the pictures on Saturday night.

'I'll show you my operation scar if you like.'

'All right,' said Ned, 'I'll put two bob on it there's no scar.'

Everyone squeezed into the foyer to buy lemonade, stood watching as Lawrence began to unbuckle his belt. Someone in the crowd reminded them that there were women and children present.

'Don't bother,' said Ned, 'we don't really want to see it, mate.'

Lawrence shrugged and laughed, as if it were their loss, and caught the florin Ned threw him. After that, there was no more trouble.

'I wish he had shown us,' Pearl said to Esme afterwards.

'You don't want to talk like that,' Esme said. 'People should keep their private parts to themselves.'

So then Pearl asked her, was it true that their mum had shown people her boobs at the races.

'You don't want to listen to gossip,' Esme said. 'There's some people have evil tongues, and if Jim ever heard you say a thing like that he'd make you wash your mouth out with carbolic soap and water.'

'Jim can't make me do anything,' Pearl said, laughing at her. She laughed a lot these days, her lips a big oval around the pushed-out teeth, her tongue darting in the pink cavern of her mouth.

Pearl often stayed at the Junction now. The afternoon Esme had gone away and left her to look after Neil seemed forgotten. Neil was due to start school the following year. Philip was a more challenging child, constantly on the go, a child who said *No!* when he was told to go to bed, and *Why?* when asked to pick up his toys: a wooden truck Queenie had given him for Christmas and two guns from his father. *Bang bang, you're dead*, Philip said, especially to Neil. Esme had her hands full and was pleased to have Pearl around. At fifteen, Pearl had become helpful and willing. She was seeing a boy called Raymond, who was a guard on the railways. He had deep-set eyes and eyelashes like a girl's.

'She's too young to be seeing a boy of eighteen,' Esme said. She had electricity and the phone installed now. People rang through with their sewing orders.

Queenie just sighed on the other end of the line. 'What the heck, he'll be called up any day.'

'I wish she was still in school,' Esme said.

'Oh, school. The authorities are rounding up everyone and

making them stay in schools these days. What's the point of it? Look at you, you're doing all right.'

In the evenings, Esme did Pearl's fair hair up in rags for her. She liked running her fingers through it, her time to relax. She was busier than ever with sewing orders. All the girls were getting married before their sweethearts went away. She wished she felt happier, but at least it was easier to pretend life were normal.

It gave her a shock one night when Jim said, 'I wish I could take you back to the Old Dart.'

'What d'you mean?'

'Home. To England. I could show you the place where I come from.' They were lying in bed, Jim smoking, with an empty tobacco tin perched on his stomach for an ashtray.

'For a holiday? Jim, there's a war on.'

'Well, I know that. But some day I'd like us to go back and live there. Things would be better.'

'What things?' She had thought him settled, even though the hoped-for promotion had never come. It flashed through her mind that Conrad might be back, that he might be trying to see her, and Jim knew about it. 'Don't be silly, Jim. We've got our home here.'

'Oh, I don't suppose you'd want to leave,' he said, with a trace of bitterness.

For a day or two, she found herself afraid and hopeful all over again about Conrad. There was no way of asking anyone, and no sign of him. On his days off, Jim went around in his braces, with grey stubble on his chin. So that was it, England was the pay-off, the price of Philip, and she wasn't going to give him that.

One morning she met Lawrence at the butcher's shop on the

corner of Thames Street when she was choosing calf brains. She had the children with her. Pearl had left again. First she had gone home to see Queenie, who said she could go down to Wellington to be near Raymond while he was training at Trentham, and now she'd gone south. Esme was so angry that Queenie had agreed to this that, for the first time in her life, she and her mother were not speaking.

'I'm going to run the next movie through this afternoon,' Lawrence said. 'It's called *A Star is Born*. Why don't you come over for a preview?'

Esme laughed. 'You'd soon get sick of my kids.'

'I'll take them for you if you like,' the butcher's wife said. 'I'll have finished the accounts by lunchtime.' Joan Stott was a tiny, lively woman who used a cigarette holder. Esme had whipped up some dresses for Joan at short notice when she was going on holiday.

'Well, if you're sure.'

'You could do with a break,' said Joan. 'Your eyes are falling out of your head.'

The movie starred Janet Gaynor; it was about a girl called Esther Blodgett who arrives in Hollywood from the sticks, and learns different ways of walking and talking and making herself up, and gets a new name and becomes a star. A big title came up that showed her destination as being 'the beckoning El Dorado, Metropolis of Make Believe in the California Hills'. Esme didn't know why, but it made her think of Pearl, and she wanted to cry.

The theatre was empty, except for her and Lawrence, who came and sat with her once the film was running through the projection machine. He had to duck back to change the reels, but the rest of the time he sat leaning slightly towards her so that their shoulders touched.

'You like that?' Lawrence asked when it was over. They still sat in the dark.

'I loved it,' she sighed.

He leaned closer, breathing against her neck, like a hot gust of wind. When he ran his finger lightly up and down her bare arm, she didn't stop him.

'What's this then?' he said, his finger paused at a point beneath her elbow.

'What's what?'

He rubbed his thumb and finger together, 'It's something hard.'

'It's my needle,' she said.

'Your *needle*?'

She told him then about the way the needle had broken off and how it was still floating about inside her, how it didn't really hurt, that mostly she'd forgotten all about it, even when she was in the hospital having the boys and should have mentioned it to the doctor. Just sometimes it surfaced in funny places. Perhaps she'd have it taken out if it ever caused any trouble.

'You could be dead by then,' Lawrence said.

'Yes, well, thanks very much.'

'I could show you my scar if you like.'

'No doubt you will anyway,' she said. She reached out and touched the raised red mark on his flat milky-white stomach. It reminded her of her children's stomachs. When he guided her hand further down, beyond the scar, to his busy entertaining penis, she thought, why not? Well, why not? She liked being able to give something to someone. She'd had a nice afternoon.

At home, she looked in the mirror at her smudged face. 'You

fool,' she said and couldn't help laughing, the ridiculous position she'd put herself in, the awkwardness of seats in movie theatres, the way they sprang up behind you when you shifted.

I should leave, she told herself. It's time to get out of here.

But not yet.

Her new baby slipped into the world with hardly a murmur, just a stretch and a wriggle when Esme was standing at the door saying goodbye to Joan Stott, who'd been to collect a dress, as if birth were a frivolous occasion, a good story to be told. Esme hardly had time to lie down on the sofa in the front room. Joan cut the umbilical cord with Esme's pinking shears.

The new baby didn't look like anyone in particular. She had wide eyes, which, when she was older, would assume a slightly startled look. Jim seemed pleased to have a daughter.

'I'd like to call her Janet,' she told Jim before he had a chance to ask. She'd thought about Esther, but it sounded too like her own name, so she settled for Janet.

Dear Esme, wrote Pearl,

I'm having a great time here in Wellington. There's Americans everywhere and they are so good to us girls who are entertaining them. I just love the Marines. You should have seen me down Manners Street the other night wearing one of their caps. Laugh. Me and my friends laughed and laughed. I sing in a club. Give baby Janet a kiss, I'll meet her some day and tell those little brothers of hers to be good boys and do their homework just like their aunty did (ha ha).
Love from your sister Pearl

*

For all her easy delivery, Janet cried a lot. Jim walked her up and down and stayed home some days to help look after the children. His pay was down, so Esme took in more work. She was always tired. Someone had threatened to burn the picture theatre down, and Lawrence had taken himself off because some of the servicemen home on leave were throwing rocks on his roof. Norma and her husband moved on, back up north, which was a relief to Esme. People shifted from this place all the time.

'I'm sorry we didn't get to move away from here,' she said to Jim one evening. She was holding her daughter on her hip with one hand while she put his dinner on the table with the other. 'I expect we should have gone anyway.' She didn't say 'after the accident', although that's what she was thinking. Any number of accidents, if it came to that. It was hard to fathom how their lives had been so pulled apart. She didn't feel exactly responsible. Something had started a long way back, before she could in any way decide for herself how things should have been. Back when she was young. Somewhere in the deep sleep of her early life, in a place she didn't recognise.

'I don't want to leave here,' Jim said, in a mild, alarmed voice. 'This is where I live.'

Things had shifted between them. Before, she had been the one afraid to leave. Before the Depression was over, before the war started, before the movies. Now she wanted to go, but she couldn't see how.

'I thought you'd settle down, now that you've got children.'

No more babies, she resolved. She'd take herself more seriously. Another letter had come. It said, like the song, *I Wonder Who's*

Kissing Her Now. She screwed it up and put it in the fire, but her cheeks burned at the memory of it.

She began to dream every night, bad dreams of wild engines, heaving and grunting like animals in flight. They would disappear, and she would be alone in a clearing. This abandonment was worse because now there was only silence. Cobwebs caught her clothes. When she woke up, she lay in bed panting, trying to brush the threads away from her face.

Later in the war, Esme got a phone call from a woman who ran a boarding house in Hawker Street in Wellington. It was about her sister Pearl, who had been living there. Pearl was in the hospital in Newtown and really sick. It would be as well if Esme could come and see her because the doctors weren't that hopeful. Bad pneumonia, the woman said, in a sombre way.

'I'd better take the train down tonight,' Esme told Jim.

'I should go. You don't know anything about cities.'

'I've been to Auckland. I'll manage, she's my sister.'

He shot her a look then, that later she would think of as pure dislike.

What she would remember were the flags down Cuba Street, like clothes on a washing line outside the People's Palace where she stayed. And all the cars. She counted twenty-five in the street at one time. She looked in the Union Clothing Company for things to take home for Jim and the boys, but decided she could make them just as well. This was while she still thought she was going back. And there was the tram that took her out to Newtown to the big red-brick hospital with the endless corridors.

And collecting Pearl's things from the hospital – not much, because she'd been taken there by ambulance in the night: just a night dress and a gold-plated watch that looked new. Signing her name so that Pearl could be released for burial. She glimpsed Pearl at the undertaker's and said, yes, that was her. That surprising milk sheen of her skin. She had to believe it was Pearl in the coffin. It is her, she told herself, it's Pearl, that's Pearl in there. At the boarding house, clothes to pack, dresses with skirts that would have been billowy in Wellington's winds, she had made some of them herself, and hair combs and make-up, and some bits of jewellery. Esme remembered the brooch then, the one her mother planned to give Pearl, and wondered what would happen to it now. Some packets of cigarettes that she gave to an American who came to the door looking for Pearl because he didn't know she was dead. A few photographs, one of Queenie and Stick, and a couple of Pearl and Raymond taken at the Junction. The next day, Queenie and Stick arrived at Wellington Railway Station, Stick with vacant watery eyes, Queenie hobbling on a cane by this time, older and fatter and tired. Just a touch of gout, she said, nothing to worry about.

Later in the day, Joe and Bunty drove down in their big black Hudson from Taihape where they were share-milking. Joe had a shock of grey hair already. So, there was family there when they buried Pearl. Joe stood close to Esme, and she moved away from him.

The minister who the woman from the boarding house had found said, 'The Lord gave, and the Lord hath taken away; blessed be the name of the Lord.'

'I'm sorry, Esme,' Queenie said. 'It shouldn't have happened to her.'

'It's all right, Mum,' said Esme, who'd done with crying the night before they all arrived. Something had shifted and hardened in her.

'She was just too good for this world,' said Queenie. 'Our magic girl.'

'Yes,' said Esme. 'Magic.' Perhaps Pearl really had been a trick of the light.

'You've got to get on with things,' Joe said, which reminded Esme that she hated him.

'I don't get the connection,' one of Esme's daughters-in-law would say to her one day. 'Is that why you left? Because Pearl died?'

'I suppose so,' Esme said. 'Well, she had something to do with it.'

'But you left the children.'

'I sent for Janet.'

'What about the boys, though? You left the boys.'

Why people leave. There are as many answers as there are people who go, dividing and uncoiling their lives from one another. Esme thought you could drive yourself crazy, thinking about things like this. She did feel things, whatever people thought.

The boys had gone to live with Queenie and Stick for a while because Jim had died before they'd grown up. Then they went to Mary, Esme's older sister, and from there they had gone on to Joe and Bunty's, though nobody mentioned this to Esme at the time. Back and forth, no regular place to call home.

'Yes, it was to do with Pearl,' she said to her daughter-in-law. 'It's hard to explain.'

3

Philip loved the way Petra looked, the strong eyes, her tender, mobile mouth. She wore her hair in a straight, brown bob, her breasts were so small she looked flat-chested some ways she stood, but she had a vitality about her that made him feel at home, as if he were in the presence of someone he had always known. Every time he saw her, he experienced a swoop of joy, one that never went away, even when they were older and things turned to shit now and then, as they were busy making their marks in the world.

They were students when they met. She wore tight skirts with dark sweaters, black stockings and flat-heeled lace-up shoes. When she came towards him in the street, she would have pulled a beret over her hair, a long scarf trailing behind. The year he became engaged to her, Petra was rehearsing *As You Like It* with the university drama school. She was Rosalind. Of course. He was helping to build sets in his spare time.

'My parents will drive you crazy,' she told him when they had chosen the engagement ring. 'I do love them,' she added, a little parenthesis she used from time to time when she spoke of her mother and father. Like an apology. She was an only child. This was a time when young women like Petra were throwing convention out the window. She was a banner-waver like him, a ranter and a raver, hurling herself into causes like ban the bomb and trade unions, and the polemics of poetry; she believed it was all right for her to tell him when she was hot for him.

All the same, she was embarrassed when she said, 'We'll have to have a big wedding. D'you mind?'

'Just as long as you're there,' he'd said, trying to sound resolute.

'They'll want your guest list.'

'I won't have one, just your friends and mine. The rest's up to you.'

'Don't be silly, darling. Your family and all that.'

'No,' he said, 'I don't have any family to ask.'

The Blue Rose China Shop was in a long, elegant room with timber panelling. Margaret Ellis and her husband, Nicholas, a dentist, owned the whole building. Margaret, or Mrs Ellis as she preferred to be called in the shop, was on the phone ordering a dinner set for a special customer, not someone she could hurry, when she spotted a woman turning the Denby Chevron mugs over and pursing her lips at the prices. An older woman, a bit rough around the edges. Her hair was crimped in a fraying ginger perm, and her feet bulged in their shoes.

'Can I help you?' Margaret asked, putting the phone down at last. 'Something for yourself, or a gift? A wedding in the offing, perhaps?'

'My girls are long married,' said the woman, putting a mug down harder than was necessary. 'But I hear you've got one coming up, Mrs Ellis?'

'Yes,' said Margaret, letting the distance in her voice lengthen.

'I saw the engagement in the paper.' The notice in the paper had said: *Mr and Mrs Nicholas Ellis are delighted to announce the forthcoming marriage of their daughter Petra Jean to Philip Moffit of Wellington.* Nothing about Philip's parents.

The woman introduced herself. She was a widow. Her husband used to be in the post office, but he'd passed on a few years back. They'd had hard times in the old days, but she'd learned to count her blessings. Her conversation was more of a continuous monologue than an exchange. She paused when Margaret looked at her wrist watch. 'You reckon that boy Moffit's from Wellington?'

Margaret steadied herself on the edge of the counter as if she'd been caught off balance. 'Our daughter's fiancé?'

'Well, there might be any number of Philip Moffits. But I know that name. Family came from Ohakune way, didn't they?'

'I don't remember Philip mentioning that.' Only she couldn't look the woman in the eye. Petra had told her some brief sketch of his history that he'd given her. The fact was she had no idea. 'We haven't spent a lot of time with him yet. The two young people are studying, you see. Philip's nearly finished his law degree.'

'The law. Young Philip's in the law. Well, my oh my. There's a few things I could tell you about that young man's family I'll bet you don't know. I put a lot of time into his mother, not that Esme gave me thanks, oh no.'

'I'd love to have let her have her say,' Margaret told Nicholas that evening. 'Perhaps I should have.'

'It was probably lies. Gossip.'

'She said she was the postmaster's wife. It sounded pretty convincing. She said, "I suppose he would keep things to himself. Tell you about his dad, did he? Whoever he was?" I asked her to leave then. I told her I was shutting while I went to the bank. So she left.'

'You did the right thing.' All the same, her husband looked as if he had just come across a particularly unpleasant mouthful of decay.

'What's she doing, marrying this boy? We know nothing.'

'It's too late now,' he said. 'We'll have to make the best of it.'

'Darling,' Petra said one evening, soon after this. She and Philip were walking up the hill towards Kelburn, where they shared a flat with four other students. 'Darling, couldn't you come up with an invitation list?'

'We've been through this, ask who you like.' He'd explained already how his mother had gone off with a man called Kevin Pudney and left him and his brother with his father. How none of it had worked out, not for him anyway, until he managed to put it behind him and make it on his own. The going off with Kevin Pudney part was an elaboration, not exactly true, but Kevin had been there when his mother next surfaced in his life.

'My parents just don't understand that you're not going to ask anyone at all. Couldn't you put up with your mother, just for a day?'

'No,' he said. 'No, I couldn't. My mother wrecked everything. My father went to pieces after she left.'

'There might have been two sides to it.'

'Don't you believe that. My father was a saint. It killed him, her leaving him.'

'You said he had cancer.'

'Well, she gave it to him.'

'Oh, for goodness' sake, Philip,' Petra said. 'People don't catch cancer. It's something that grows inside them.'

He walked off ahead of her then, knowing she would follow him. They would say they were sorry to each other, her, then him, in that order.

4

The day of her son's wedding, in the spring of 1964, Esme Pudney got dressed in the small boarding house near the bus station where she was staying in Tauranga. The air was fragrant, scented with citrus blossoms; the gardens full of daffodils and forget-me-nots. She put on a blue silk dress with a hint of pale silver in the weave, liking the way it felt in the soft swathe of colour from the pleats at her hips. She dabbed lavender water between her breasts, powdered her sun freckles. She and Kevin took long summer holidays in their caravan, staying in camping grounds or just near the edge of wildernesses, near lakes and streams. This was after Kevin retired from contract fencing. He was older than her by twelve years. The children were grown up, the two they called their children: Esme's daughter Janet and his girl Marlene, who were pretty much the same age. Marlene had been his youngest, as Janet was hers. He'd been left with Marlene after his wife died. They didn't have much money to come and go on, but when they were chatting to new friends over a barbie, they liked to say they had enough to get by.

Esme left a note for Kevin to say she'd be back on the bus on Sunday evening. It wasn't as if she were afraid of him, it was just that he would have thought her a fool. He couldn't see why she bothered herself about those sons of hers, especially the second one. They'd had them to live for a while, but it was an experiment that didn't work out. He'd given Philip the rounds of the kitchen sink more than once. It wasn't that Philip didn't deserve it, impudent kid that he was, but she did wish Kevin had tried to talk things over with the kid before he let fly. But that was Kevin, a man of action. Like Philip's father, perhaps, although when she remembered Conrad now, there wasn't much she could have told you about him. Where he came from. Who he really was. Not even how old he was. She hadn't asked. If she were honest, it was Jim she really admired. His goodness and the way that he'd stuck to the boys for as long as he could. The way he'd gone on until the end without asking her to say sorry, though, Lord knows, she was.

A crowd of well-wishers had gathered outside the church, the way people did on Saturday afternoons. Esme stood at the back of the crowd, but slightly to one side so she could still get a good view. She'd learned about the wedding from Joe's wife. Bunty called Joe the old bugger and didn't let him get away with much. When Joe heard about the wedding, and how they hadn't been asked, he told his wife to let it go, Philip had moved on from the family long ago. He said this with injury in his voice. How did she think his sister Esme felt, now that was the real rub.

The wedding cars appeared, decorated with ribbons. When the bride stepped out of the car, there was a ripple of surprise. She wasn't wearing bridal white. Instead, she wore a sunflower-yellow satin dress and a wide-brimmed matching hat with a high stitched crown. She carried three lilies, casually, as if they had just been picked from a garden.

Esme was enchanted at once. A performer, a woman of daring.

Petra, an amused, almost mocking smile on her face, looked around, recognising faces, and lifted an ungloved hand. She looked sideways for a moment, turning her head to look straight at Esme. She could see her eyes were looking for some sign that she might know her, so Esme smiled and raised her hand, as if she were a friend. The young woman gave a half smile and took her father's arm.

Inside the church, the organ started to play 'Here Comes the Bride'. The wedding party moved on into the dark church, with its stained-glass windows and the cream freesia favours that lined the pews.

Esme slid into a pew at the back, not that there was much room for the uninvited. She knew Philip wouldn't look past the radiant woman in yellow as she moved up the aisle. She saw him look towards Petra, his curly hair crisply cut, a flower in his buttonhole, his face creased with a wondering smile. Then he turned his back to the congregation and took Petra's hand. Even at the back of the church, Esme could hear his responses, his voice cracking a little with emotion as their vows began.

She wondered for a moment how Philip would manage. Was he up to this, a true golden girl? She felt herself bowled over, so that she had to press her hands tightly together on top of the shelf holding the hymn books. She didn't want strangers to see her crying.

Jim had been playing with the children when she came back from Pearl's funeral. It was raining outside, a solid sleety rain that stung her face. He'd pulled blankets off the beds and draped them over the backs of the kitchen chairs so that they made tents. Neil and Janet were inside the tent with a dish of chopped apple between them. Only Philip stood apart, biting the knuckles of one hand. His eyes, when he looked up and saw her, were huge and incredulous with joy, as if he had never expected to see her again.

'Mummy's back, Mummy's back,' he cried.

This was the moment when she might have lost her resolve. She looked at Jim, and his expression was cool and unfriendly. He had already read her face, and he knew.

'We're having an inside picnic,' Neil said. 'It's good fun playing with Dad.'

Jim said, 'I won't stop you taking the girl. But you're not taking my boys.'

Patient, enduring Jim. With his names on all the children's birth certificates.

'Philip,' she began and stopped, seeing the expression in Jim's eyes.

'They're my boys,' he said.

This was pretty much the last thing of any consequence that he said to her. His head wreathed in steam from the train's engine as he walked back up the platform when she left again, a little bent over already, one of the boys' hands in each of his own. Only the little boy, Philip, looking back and crying, wanting her to come back.

Esme had been on her own for six years when Queenie died. Stick had already gone. It was at Queenie's funeral that Esme met Kevin Pudney.

The way she was living, she took Janet to different farms where she did housekeeping work in return for room and board. Janet, after a patchy, tearful start, was a child who accepted whatever was asked of her. She stayed obediently in farmhouse kitchens, drawing and playing with Plasticine and dolls while her mother worked. Esme had a couple of jobs in the King Country, which meant she got to see her family, and also Neil and Philip now and then. She would have liked to take the boys, but the way she lived there was never enough room for them in the farmhouses where she stayed. Since she left Jim, Esme had set about learning different skills, like making stuffed toys, decorating cakes and arranging flowers. Her employers liked the little unexpected gifts she made for them. A woman with a generous heart, wrote one of her employers. She met some men but, usually, if she dug around a bit, there was a woman somewhere in the background. These years were also taken up with the divorce papers that Jim had served on her, although his death spared her the day in court. It was like a final gift. There were some things she would rather not talk about.

The morning of Queenie's funeral, Esme saw her mother for the last time. The family had taken turns sitting beside her. Not all the family were there. Ned McDavitt had been killed early in the war and, later on, the youngest, Hunter, just before the war was over. One of the sisters lived in Australia. Mary had left Neil and Philip with her husband, who couldn't take time off work to come to the funeral. It was still a big crowd.

At the very last moment, some strangers turned up. They were Māori and, although they said that they knew Queenie had lived as a white woman most of her life, they were related to her and weren't going to let her go without saying goodbye. Kevin, who was their boss, could see that he wasn't going to get them to work for him that day, so he said that he'd drive them over. They were doing a bit of fencing on a hill near Taumarunui.

Esme slipped back into the viewing room one more time, after the unexpected visitors had left to join the mourners heading for the church. She felt shaken by this visit, as if some other corner of her life had been turned over for inspection. There was something she wanted to say to her mother that she couldn't seem to tell her while the others were there. But what she had come to say had dried in her throat. Instead, she let her fingers trail over her mother's cheek. As she was taking her hand away, she felt it touch something hard at the base of Queenie's throat. Leaning over, she looked into the coffin. She saw what she had missed before: the gold brooch with the amethyst glowing in its heart. Perhaps Joe, or Mary, or someone in the family had decided that's where it belonged.

'That was Pearl's,' she said, voicing her indignation in the empty room.

A busy persistent blowfly circled the room.

She reached in and unpinned the brooch and slipped it into her handbag. It felt like the right thing to do.

The wake went on into the evening. The men had had a few drinks by then. Joe, swaggering drunk, kept following her around, wanting to talk to her, as if she wasn't his sister but some loose woman out on her own. In order to get away from him, Esme got talking to Kevin. She explained then how she had three kids, one of them a teenager already.

He said how hard he found it to believe that. He did know what it was like, getting left with a kiddie to raise after his wife died.

'I'm a widow myself,' she said. She hadn't thought of herself like this, but it seemed more or less true, now that Jim had died. She touched the brooch in her pocket. There were some things one simply had to do. Kevin seemed like a gentleman.

Kevin was a great father to Janet. She called him Dad, and she and Marlene were like real sisters. When the boys did come to stay for a bit, he turned out handier with his fists than Esme would have liked. Neil he could tolerate, at least he didn't have ideas above himself. In his eyes, Philip was a cocky little prick, needed knocking into shape. Neil got a job farm labouring when he was fifteen and could leave school. Philip went back to Mary, his aunt. A teacher at the school she sent him to took a fancy to him, and the next thing he was off to boarding school on a scholarship.

'Fancy,' said Esme, 'to think my boy's got brains.'

'They shouldn't give him ideas,' Kevin said. 'Who does he think he is?'

'I wonder where he got them from,' Esme said dreamily, as if she hadn't heard him.

'You ought to know, he's your kid.'

'Yes. Well, so he is.' Her face closed up, shutting him out. They were living in another farmhouse, out the back of beyond. She didn't have to work the way she used to, though she still kept her hand in. There was never any trouble between them except when the subject of Philip came up. After the boy went off to boarding school, she sent ten pounds to Mary to give him every holidays.

After a bit, Mary wrote to her and said she'd better send the money straight to the school because Philip was taking his holidays with his new friends. In the long summer holiday, he'd gone on a tour of the South Island and walked the Milford Track. In winter, he went skiing with a friend's family. They were staying at a lodge at Ohakune Junction. Esme laughed out loud when she heard that. She didn't mention it to Kevin because he wouldn't have got the joke.

She and Kevin and the two girls were happy enough on their own. They moved closer to town so the girls didn't have to travel so far on the bus to school. Both of them did secretarial courses afterwards, and then went off on an overseas trip. They sent cards from Rome and Paris and London. Neil, who had grown into a thin-faced man with quiet ways, got married straight after his twenty-first birthday party; he had a son and a daughter, just eleven months between them, so that, before she knew it, Esme was a grandmother.

These were some of the things Esme Pudney thought about while her son Philip was being married. She understood why she sat anonymously at the back of the church. She wished it wasn't that way, but she didn't see how else things could have worked out. Just as the service was ending, while the triumphant march from the church was forming, she tiptoed past the ushers at the back, out into the spring sunshine.

5

There was a wrap party the night Petra's first movie finished filming. It had been a punishing schedule, up at five each morning, some nights going until ten. There never seemed to be enough time to eat and sleep, but all the time in the world to talk. Everyone was someone's best friend, and sometimes their lover. People told each other outrageous things about themselves. They made dramas out of their own lives, which, whether they were true or not, they knew they would believe from then on. Now suddenly they were all having to say goodbye. Next there might be a stage play, or a television commercial, enough to pay for a few months out of work, Petra had done a couple of those.

Philip, looking across the room at her, could see why they wanted Petra's face. It had a wild vitality that at this moment seemed unbridled. He knew she didn't really want him to be there and, at the same time, that she did, a kind of affirmation that he was part of her life, that he accepted what she did.

At breakfast, the first they had shared since filming began, she had run it past him. 'D'you think we could get the sitter in?' she asked. She had big shadows under her eyes and a trace of make-up at her hairline.

'We've had a lot of sitters lately.' Some nights he needed to go back to his office for work.

She had sat there, blowing the top of her coffee. 'You said . . .' she began.

'Yes,' he said because he didn't want her to remind him of what he had said the previous time the subject of a last-night party at the theatre had come up. 'Is there any way I can get caught up in your brilliant career?' he had asked her, and she'd said, 'Well, come to the fucking party, don't say you weren't asked.' He'd finished up staying home and she hadn't come home until morning.

'Oh, well,' he said, 'the kids are getting used to Debbie.'

'Don't start on me again.'

'I didn't mean it like that,' he said. Debbie was the girl who sat for them. It wasn't as if they were little children any more: a boy and a girl, Jesse and Marigold, twelve and ten.

'I know you work hard, Philip,' she said.

'Yes,' he said because it was true, and he wanted to agree with her and have her back to himself. His life was full of causes. He was a lawyer who believed in helping the poor and giving the underdog a chance. A lot of his clients couldn't afford to pay him properly. He organised food parcels for their families when they were in jail and saw to it that their children went to school. His suits were often rumpled, and he didn't care. In the lunch breaks from court, he and his friends gathered in a café over a bookshop and exchanged case stories. And he took on cases that seemed hopeless; people who were not particularly attractive but might be innocent. You don't have to be good looking to be innocent, he said. As for the money, his father-in-law had paid for the house. It was their wedding present: the title to this house. The house was full of newly delivered furniture and there was a car in the garage.

'I don't want it,' he said at the time. 'I never asked for any of this.'

'Send it back then,' said Petra. 'You can spend the rest of your life chasing lawsuits for the rich and famous and licking boots, or you can accept and do the things you really want to. It's your life.'

'I thought it was ours.'

'I can't change who I am. That's my dowry. Anyone I married would have got the same.'

It had taken some time for him to get over this, causing a bitterness that he later regretted. One day he'd woken up and thought how unfair to Petra he had been, how he needed to recover things before it was too late. He had set out to enjoy the freedom of unexpected wealth. We do our own thing, they told people, we make our own choices. Sometimes it worked and other times it was awful.

At the party, he edged closer to Petra. Someone said, 'I've got this great idea for a movie. It's about a black alien in Harlem being chased by two white aliens.'

'That's such a gross idea,' said Petra, stabbing the air with her cigarette.

Then an actor called Mel wanted to tell them about the most gross experience of *her* life, which was about going to Indonesia and being felt up by a tame orangutan. 'He knew I was a woman,' she said. 'Honestly, can you imagine having a large shaggy ape with his arms around you getting an erection?'

'Easily,' Petra said, and everyone laughed.

'So what's your weird story, Petra?' asked Mel.

'Um.' Petra took a draw on her cigarette and pondered.

Somebody had produced a bottle of Cognac, which was being passed around. A fire had been lit in the grate using bleu de Bresse tubs for kindling. Philip felt his stomach turning over as he waited.

'Philip's mother has a needle floating around in her body that you can actually feel when it gets into her arm.'

'Oh, yuck. How could that be possible? She'd be dead.'

'Apparently it can happen,' Petra said. 'I checked it out when Philip told me about it. It's like bits of shrapnel that soldiers who've been shot at might carry inside them. If it's blunt and hasn't gone into a vein a piece of metal can float around in someone's body for their whole life. It usually builds up a bit of fibroid tissue around it over time.'

'Couldn't it go through your heart?'

'It could, but it wouldn't necessarily kill you – it might just pass through it. Could stuff up your lung though. You can feel it in her arm, can't you, Philip? You can wriggle it around.'

Philip stood up; he felt his face burning with shame.

'Haven't you actually seen it?' asked Mel.

'No, I've never met her.'

'What? Philip, is this true?'

Petra looked up and saw the space where he'd been standing. 'I'd better go,' she said.

Their bed had a big crocheted quilt over it, made with very fine yarn. It had come in the mail after their wedding. Philip said it was old-fashioned, that it wouldn't fit in with their new furniture and the modern décor. Petra left it in a cupboard for a few years and then brought it out. 'I like it,' she said, 'I want to use it.'

'That was my mother you were talking about last night,' Philip said. They were lying under the quilt, around ten o'clock in the morning. The children had made themselves breakfast and switched on the television.

'So what? I mean, really, so what? I've asked you about her often enough, and you just turn your back on it.'

'I did tell you that about her. And look what you made of it, a big drama, a joke.'

'It's not fair to our kids, not knowing anything.'

'Fairness doesn't come into it,' he said and reached out, pulling her close. 'I never knew anything that was fair until I met you.'

'Help me, Philip. I'm over things.'

'What are you over?' He was stifling the panic in his voice.

'Being directed, told what to do.'

'Your work? You could stop.'

'But I don't want to. Sometimes I just don't know what *you* want, that's all.'

'I want you to stay with me,' he said. Simple as that. That was all he wanted.

'Oh,' Petra said. 'That. Well, of course.'

When Uncle Joe died, his son, one of Philip's first cousins, rang to tell him.

'Do you want to come to the funeral with me?' he asked Petra.

'You mean you'll go?' There had been other calls like this over the years, which he had ignored.

'Time I went. We can drive up tonight, stay with your folks.' He'd come to like her family well enough, had forgiven them for buying him. It could have been worse. 'So will you come?'

'Of course. Will she be there?'

'My mother? I don't know, perhaps.'

'Did you like your Uncle Joe?' she asked on the drive north.

Philip shrugged. 'He was a rough bastard but most of them were. I'm told my mother was against me staying there, but it was hardly her choice.'

Petra saw her first, at the other side of the cemetery. 'Who is that woman? I know her face.' She was looking at a plump woman with pink-framed glasses and tinted hair.

'That's her. That's my mother.'

'She was at our wedding.'

'Of course she wasn't.'

'She was. I saw her outside the church.' Petra stood firm.

Everyone was there. Neil and his wife, Janet and her husband, Marlene, who introduced herself icily to Petra as her sister-in-law, well, sort of. There were children everywhere.

They went back to Joe and Bunty's place for the wake. There were sponge cakes and cups of tea and beer laid out on trestle tables under the trees.

'Is it true you're a lawyer?' the relatives kept saying to Philip, in a kind of astonished wonder. 'Well, we'll know where to come next time we land a speeding ticket.' They laughed awkwardly at their own jokes.

'Aren't you on the telly?' Marlene asked Petra. 'Where are your children? You haven't left them at home, surely to goodness?' Philip hadn't wanted them to come; Jesse and Marigold were at home in Wellington with Debbie.

And then there was Esme, who came to the edge of the lawn and stood looking at the gathering and looked away.

'Poor old Mum,' said Marlene. 'It's been hard for her since Dad's been gone.'

Petra could feel Philip stiffening. 'D'you mean Kevin's dead?'

Marlene looked at him with dislike. 'My dad, what's it to you?'

'I'm going over to say hullo,' Petra said to Philip. After a moment, he turned and followed her.

'Hullo,' Esme said. 'I was just going.'

'So are we,' said Petra. 'Can we walk with you?'

The three of them walked abreast, not saying much. 'It's sad about Joe,' Petra said, as they stood by the cars, ready to leave.

Esme's eyes narrowed. 'I needed to see the back of him,' she said.

On the way home, Philip cried, wiping his face with the back of one hand while he drove. 'I don't want to think about her,' he said.

'But you do,' Petra said. 'You never stop. You never have.'

Dear Petra, Esme wrote,

I feel as if I have known you forever. I'm sure lots of people say this to you, because your face is so well known, but this is more than about you being on television. It is something that comes from inside me. It's something that understands why he would have looked towards you for his wife. I was once touched by a magician when I was a girl, and it changed my life forever. There is good magic and bad magic and this man brought some of both kinds to me, but I was never the same afterwards. I know about spells and how they are cast. Some spells can't be broken. I hope to hear from you sometime.

Love from your mother-in-law, Esme.

'I told you she was a liar,' Philip said, 'That's an old yarn of my grandmother's about the magician, it's not her story at all. Something to do with my Aunty Pearl. The one who died.

My grandmother told me she had my aunty after the magician came to town, even though she was old. A kind of miracle. You see, she takes everything as if it were her own.'

'I see what you mean,' Petra said. At the time she was working on another film. She meant to write back to Esme straight away, but it took her awhile to get around to it. When she did, she enclosed pictures of the children. Later, Esme sent her a brooch, a tangled old gold piece of jewellery that needed fixing.

Philip held it in his hand when he saw it, as if weighing it. 'Funny,' he said. 'I never knew she had this. I remember my grandmother wearing it. Well, you are a hit. I'd have thought she'd have given it to Janet.'

'I must write to her.' She was due to go away again.

'Leave it with me,' he said. 'I'll fix it.'

Esme knew he would come. She knew if she waited long enough, lived long enough, that he would come to her. The girl (for that is how she thought of Petra) had her own life. She didn't begrudge her that. She was pleased to get a postcard from her to thank her for the brooch. I'll always treasure it, Petra wrote. The postcard had been sent from Australia where Petra was on tour. Petra was like her, but she'd got lucky: she'd married the right one at the beginning.

Esme's apartment was in the second storey of a block of council flats. She had to climb stairs that were bare and had been pissed on, and she was afraid of some of the young people who hung around there after dark, but the view across rolling country hills was just what she liked, and she had no need to go out at night. Her name was on the waiting list for a ground-floor place, but she didn't care if it didn't happen. Anyone stepping inside her door quickly forgot the ascent through the graffiti in the stairwell. She had turned the flat into a colourful cave, the armchairs covered with peggy-square quilts, the shelves laden with bits and pieces she'd collected along the way, a ruby-red glass a farmer's wife had given her, a blue-and-white ashet from a house where the wife died, a collection of shells that she and Janet and Marlene had collected one holiday at the Mount, pot plants and photographs galore.

'I can get you somewhere better,' Philip said when he came to visit. He had turned up unexpectedly with Jesse and Marigold.

'I wish you'd given me some warning,' she said. 'I'd like to have got food in for them.'

'Don't worry,' he said, 'we've sussed out the fish-and-chip shop. They're going down the road to get some lunch, aren't you kids?'

So they were alone in the flat together.

'They're beautiful,' she said, 'so handsome and tall for their age. So full of self-confidence.'

'They take after their mother.'

'Perhaps,' she said.

'I can afford to get you another place.'

'I don't need another place. I like it here.'

'You can't.' He gestured helplessly.

'What's wrong with this?' She looked around the room, and her eyes travelled on to the hills beyond the window. It was spring, bare trees in the distance were flushed with sweet unfolding buds. 'Pretty as a picture.'

'Did you ever care for my father?' he said, his back to her, as if contemplating what she saw outside. She could tell he knew that he sounded banal, even silly. That he couldn't help himself asking the question, and didn't know a better way of putting it. 'You know, did you love him?'

'Of course,' she said quickly. Too quickly, perhaps. She steadied herself. 'He tried to look after me. It just didn't work out.'

'Look *after* you?'

'Protect me.'

'From what?'

'It's hard to explain. He was a good man.'

He passed his hand over his head. His hair was trimmed neatly, in the centre of his forehead a triangle of hair grew down to a point, his scalp gleaming on either side.

'About Pearl.'

'Well, that was a long time ago,' she said, holding his gaze. 'A sister.' Not my sister, or your sister. That old needle, jostling away with distant pain. She wondered if he would understand. About the old days, about the magic that wasn't so mysterious after all, and about her little Pearl who had come into her life when she was still a child herself, and her bad brother Joe and what he had done to her. And how nothing had ever healed that – and the way her mother tried to make things all right, but they never could be fixed.

'What about her?' he said. 'You left when Pearl died.'

'Do you remember her?' Not answering him.

'Not really.'

'Never mind. Look, that's her in the photograph with her first boyfriend. I think he was killed in the war.'

'She was pretty.'

'Pretty enough. A bit flighty. She could sing. You wouldn't believe how long she could hold a high note.' She might have added something about the way she had tried to look after her, and how when that failed she didn't believe she could look after any of her children. But she stayed silent.

'I see,' he said at last, and from the way he spoke, she wondered what he knew, what he had already worked out for himself, the truth of what she was telling him and not telling him. There was a stamping of feet on the stairs leading up to the apartment as his children returned.

After they had all gone, she lay down on the bed, overtaken by a kind of dizziness. It wasn't new to her. It amazed her that so far she had survived death's steady rhythm, that she had outlived so many people. She heard a car start below. Somewhere in her old aching, bitten heart, she thought, there he goes, my clever boy. He had come to her.

What happened now was not important. She had seen him, and an old remembered happiness stirred within.

3

AWRY

FRAGRANCE RISING

Swimming

The prime minister's towel is green with a narrow pink stripe at either end, a towel chosen by a woman. It lies where he's tossed it aside before stepping into the swimming bath. In his woollen bathing suit, straps taut over his shoulders, he is a black seal slicing through the water, powerful arms plunging, shoulders rearing up and down and up again in a perfect butterfly stroke. Despite all the speed and energy, this is his time for reflecting, a place where there are no secretaries, or bells calling him to the chamber, or papers that can be pushed beneath his nose. This is the place where, in his head at least, he cannot be joined by others.

Not that he is without his spectators. There are people who enjoy the sense of being close to power, who can say that they have seen Mr Gordon Coates himself in his swimming trunks. So near I could almost have touched him, they will say when they return home, for most of them are from the country come to town to take in the sights. And they love him because he is one of them, a country boy who made good. Not an educated man, they will continue, someone like us who didn't stay long at school, but look at the way we get by – like him, we don't need fancy letters after our names, and he has risen right to the top. He has worn a braided jacket and white breeches and shoes with buckles when he went to meet the king. These viewers, who have come to watch the prime minister take his daily constitutional, huddle on the lower path near the water rather than the sheltered gallery, so that when he has finished his swim he must pass them. The Thorndon Baths have a square tower above the dressing rooms and two domed ornamental roofs. Winter is close; there is menace in the wind. You would think that would deter the prime minister, but it seems he swims wet or fine or even when Wellington's southerly is whipping the harbour into a frenzy. The watching men wear trousers that are a little baggy and shiny at the knees, their Sunday best, and high collars beneath their jackets, scarves billowing about them. The women clutch their wraps, legs quivering with cold beneath the new short skirts of the day, woollen cloche hats pulled around their ears.

He lifts his head from the water and, on this fresh morning in late May, he smells a whiff of wood smoke curling from the houses nearby. All of a sudden, there is an ache at the back of his throat and he sees not the blue floor of the swimming pool but the heavy green light that glances through the ebb and flow of the Arapaoa, the slow salt tide between mangrove banks. He catches the fragrance rising from log fires in open paddocks, a fallen macrocarpa perhaps, or old apple trees from the orchards. Beyond the sky-high flames stands a house built close to the ground with low-slung verandahs and creepers winding around the pillars. Across the green lie of land, there is laughter and song on the quiet still air of the Kaipara, telling him his Māori neighbours have risen to begin their day. He stops to listen.

In that moment when he lifts his head, he sees the child,

a little girl with eyes as dark as a zoo panther's hide, although her complexion is pale sepia. She is perhaps five or six years of age, shivering in a ragged yellow cotton frock. She doesn't appear to know where she is. The prime minister is aware that poor children live in this area, but as a rule they stay close to their homes along Sydney and Ascot streets, where the workers' cottages huddle side by side, close enough for the children to hold hands with each other if they reach out the windows. This child looks lost.

There is something wrong here. For a moment, he thinks *It can't be, it isn't her, one of them. How could she have found him?* And then he thinks *Of course not, the child is too young.* He pulls himself up on the edge of the pool, his taste for swimming over, and stands, abruptly shaking water from himself, his moustache showering tiny arcs of dew over his chest as he grabs the towel to wipe his eyes clear. A man steps out, pointing his Box Brownie at the prime minister's large frame.

'No,' he says, holding the towel up and shielding his face. 'Not today.' He recognises the man's peaked cap, worn back to front with a journalist's flamboyance. He has seen the fellow more often than he likes, and it wouldn't surprise him if he were a plant for the Liberals. The pictures he takes of the prime minister have been snapped at the oddest moments, such as when he is dancing in the most gentlemanly fashion with the wife of one his cabinet ministers, the kind of duty he undertakes out of the goodness of his heart, or when he is dining in a restaurant and stops for a cigar between his meat and potatoes and the arrival of dessert. There is a suspicion in his mind that the man wants to make something of a clown of him at least, or a womaniser at worst.

'Mr Coates,' calls out an admirer, holding out a scrap of paper and a pen, 'your autograph, sir.' He brushes past without a second glance. 'Brusque, a man who can be a bit short,' they will say later on. 'He has much on his mind. The economy, it's not in good shape. It's us he will have been thinking of. He just didn't see us that day.'

In the dressing room, he breathes deeply and evenly, trying to recover his composure. He dries himself with care, lifting his balls above his groin as delicately as a girl's dress, dusting the folds with talcum powder. When he is fully dressed, he stands in front of a mirror, adjusting his spotted tie, buttoning his waistcoat, checking the white handkerchief in his pocket, then flicks a tailor-made from the packet in his inside pocket and inhales.

Outside, a sleety rain has begun to fall. The crowd has dispersed. Only the child is standing there, looking at him. Or perhaps just at the space before her, as if trying to discover where she is supposed to be.

'What is it, child?' he asks her. He has daughters of his own. Still she does not speak. On an impulse, he kneels before her.

'You've just come here to live, eh?'

She nods.

'How many days?' He holds up one hand, the fingers splayed, counting them aloud, curling his thumb in his palm then the others, one by one. When he comes to two, the child puts out a hand and clasps them in his.

'Two days, eh? Just two days. Where are you from?'

She shakes her head dumbly.

'What is your name?'

'Janie,' she whispers.

'Janie who?'

'Janie McCaw.' He catches the slight burr in her voice.

'Do you know where you live now, Miss Janie McCaw?'

Again she shakes her head, but he has decided. The name has told him as much as he probably needs to know. There are few Māori here nowadays, although once they had pā sites all over the town.

The child will live in one of the workers' cottages, probably along Ascot Street. There will be a Māori mother, a Scotsman for a father. If her father were Māori, he wouldn't have been given a place to rent. I have a wife and a child, the man will have said, and nobody the wiser about the wife until they moved in. Janie will have set off for school, on this, her second day, and now she has lost her way. Mr Coates has worked all this out as he stands and takes Janie firmly by the hand. There is a cabinet meeting in half an hour, but if he moves quickly he will just have time to return Janie McCaw to her mother. His towel is damp, not soaking, and he wraps it around the child to protect her from the wind. In truth, his curiosity is sparked. He wants to see this mother of whom he already has a picture in his head. Hand in hand now, the two of them walk briskly, or rather Janie trots as she tries to keep up with her protector, back along Tinakori Road. He picks up his pace as he passes his own house, preferring not to be seen. They pass shops and the Shepherd's Arms, where a few men are taking the first drop of the day: a refreshment after work, possibly on the night-cart, which collects the buckets of human faeces. Or perhaps they are bakers who have made the morning's first batch of bread, or railway men. You can't tell one from the other when they are tired and unwashed and banging their fists for a pint, except for the bakers, dusty white with drifting flour. In response to a shouted greeting, Mr Coates touches his hat without a further glance, intent on the task he has set himself. The pair make a sharp left turn, and they have entered Ascot Street.

'Is it here, Janie? D'you think you live in this street?'

The child nods and points. The houses are small and shabby, paint peeling and bubbling in Wellington's salt-laden air, but there is an atmosphere of respectability here as well, lines of washing flapping in the damp air, rows of winter vegetables, cabbages and carrots, the soil dark with recent tilling. Only the house that Janie is pulling the prime minister towards is forlorn and neglected, a blind hanging askew in the window, weeds flourishing in the wasteland of what was once a garden. The family has just arrived, Mr Coates thinks to himself. Soon they will have this place shipshape.

The little girl releases herself from his grip and darts along the path. Before he knows it, she has disappeared into a lean-to washing shed to one side of the building, and next thing a door bangs and she is gone.

This is not good enough. He gives a peremptory knock on what passes for a front door.

Over the fence a woman's head appears. 'Why, Prime Minister, to what do we owe the honour of this visit?'

'I found the child wandering,' he says stiffly, feeling as caught out as if his own wife had appeared out of Premier House these few minutes past. 'Where is the mother?'

'Ah,' says the woman, 'there's no mother there. Just a man called Jock turned up with the kid last week. Dead, he reckons the mother is, taken with flu in the epidemic.'

'I thought the child younger than that.'

'Oh, who can tell, that's his story. She looks after herself.

Which way did you walk, your honour? Past the Shepherd's Arms? I'm surprised you didn't see her old man, or perhaps he's passed out already. Someone will bring him home round dinnertime.'

The prime minister fumbles in his trouser pocket. 'I'd be obliged if you'd keep an eye on her for me.' He presses a pound note into her hand.

He hesitates before stooping to pick up the green and pink-striped towel where it has fallen from Janie McCaw's shoulders onto the path.

Governing

'Hullo, the gang's all here,' the prime minister shouts as he rushes through the cabinet-room door, as if he is exactly on time and waiting for his ministers, not they upon him. He waves a sheaf of papers over his head.

The men gathered at the table look up from their study of the day's order papers, and it's hard for them to suppress smiles behind the wreaths of smoke. This is the way it is: just when things seem gloomy and the books don't balance, Coates bounds in and the serious business of governing the country seems lightened. But this morning he is not in a mood to dally with jokes.

'I have a new idea,' he announces. 'I'm going to introduce a bill that will provide more educational opportunities for young Māoris.'

'That's not scheduled on the order paper,' says Albert Davy, an adviser to the party who, of late, Gordon Coates has begun to look upon with suspicion. He has appeared a stalwart friend in the past, but these days he has a sly air about him, as if he is not quite open. At times he is aggressive in his manner. The night before, he and Coates dined together at Bellamy's. Over pork chops and a whisky or several, Mr Davy had said, in a tone tinged with dislike, that the Right Honourable Prime Minister was playing to the Māori vote to the detriment of the wider population. 'Do you not think,' he had said, 'that if the banks run out of money, your European constituents might have grounds to complain that not enough of the vanishing funds have been spent on them?' This is the very same man who devised the brilliant advertising slogan 'Coats off with Coates', which helped sweep him to victory in the last election.

'I have the support of Sir Maui Pomare,' the prime minister had said then, 'and, on the other side of the house, Sir Apirana Ngata will support me to the utmost, no matter that we are in opposition to each other.'

'That is the trouble,' Davy had replied. 'You have friends in all the wrong places. You're a farmer but you run with Māoris and Red Feds. You've lost your sense of the rest of this country.'

'I'll thank you to keep a civil tongue in your head, Mr Davy,' Coates had said. He had lit a cigar and blown smoke over Davy's roast potatoes. Now he wished he had not.

'I suppose Sir Maui already knows of this,' Davy says evenly, turning to the Minister for Internal Affairs alongside him. 'But the honourable member is Minister for Health, not of education.'

Maui Pomare turns his large handsome head towards the adviser with an expression of contempt. A doctor once, he has spent many years in America. He speaks with a faint twang. 'Health, education, they go hand in hand. Ask any fool that, and he will tell you the obvious: it's not enough for Māori children to be sound in body, though that is surely a beginning, but they'll go nowhere in the Pākehā world without knowledge of its ways.'

'Perhaps Sir Maui has known what you're thinking a lot longer than the rest of us, Prime Minister.'

Coates returns Davy's stare. 'This idea of mine is one I thought of on my way to work,' he says. 'It's to do with the responsibility of parents to ensure that all children attend school on a regular basis, whether they be native schools or otherwise.'

'Then if you have only thought of it this morning, we can't put it through on today's order paper. The bill has to be written.'

Coates shrugs. 'The matter will be raised, the public made aware.' He laughs, runs his hand through his auburn hair. The debating chamber awaits, with its ornate furnishings, lush carpet and green leather chairs. He prepares himself for a performance to the visitors' gallery, where the public watch. The ladies sit in a separate compartment and, even though they have to queue for a ticket in a way that the gentlemen do not, there are always several there, many of them dressed to kill, a fur stole draped casually around shoulders, hats with tilted brims, their mouths red bows. He looks up now and then, aware when one tries to catch his eye.

He will keep his cabinet guessing. He knows the rules as well as they do; whether he will try to break them or not is entirely his business.

Homing In

The green sweep of the trees beside the driveway is what he loves best about Premier House. They are true trees of New Zealand, glossy-leaved, dark and dense and, on a night like this, dripping with fog-strewn cobwebs, shining in the light spilling from the house. When he walks up the drive, he remembers a particular section of land up north that stands apart from the burnt-over earth, with its stumps of scrub where grass has been sown. He owns this piece of land; it's best not to remember that, but it keeps coming back to him, as if in a dream. It's an area of bush so thick that a man could lose himself in a minute if he didn't keep his wits about him. He has planted a kauri tree here in the grounds of his official residence, and one day, a thousand years on, someone will look at it in wonder, marvelling at how it came to grow here in the city.

Premier House, 260 Tinakori Road – the two-storeyed wooden house also known as Ariki Toa – is set above the road. A huge glassed-in verandah on the right shelters the entranceway; beyond is a reception area, bay windows with handsome stained glass and leadlights, twinkling chandeliers. Its grandeur encompasses him. He always knew he had a place in the world. As though this were his destiny.

The children's voices rise to meet him, and then they are throwing themselves at him, one grabbing a hand, another throwing herself at his knees, a flurry of arms and legs. Irirangi – the one on whom he has been allowed to bestow a Māori name, although her skin is as pale as buttermilk, her hair with a hint of auburn gold like his own – and Patricia and Josephine. 'Father, Father,' they cry. 'Where have you been?'

And he's telling them that it's been a busy day at work, and the nanny is saying, 'Quietly girls, quietly, now mind your father,' and in the background one of the older girls, Sheila, he thinks, is at the piano playing something sweet and dreamy – 'Für Elise', perhaps, which is what young girls love to play when they are just getting the hang of music and their fingers are spreading across the keys beyond scales and nursery rhymes. A house full of women: five daughters, the sweet scent of their creamy, freshly washed bodies, and the nanny, who is still young herself, with dark hair and eyes and a flair for fashionable clothes, even if her ankles are not her strong point. He has thought, in passing, of slapping her bottom, just to see what she would do. And, somewhere, somewhere in here beyond the noise and bustle of welcome there is Marge, his pretty English wife with her big blue, adoring eyes.

'Where is she?' he asks the nanny. She looks at him and scowls, and his spirits sink a little. He had forgotten that the nanny is given to moods. Marge has told him that she has been unlucky in love, and that they should be kind to her when she is down. But sometimes he fears she is showing the disapproval Marge would never express, on his wife's behalf. What has he done now?

'Lying down,' says the nanny.

'Is she unwell?'

'It's the Irish in you,' responds the woman, 'all mad. You never stop to think, do you?' The nanny is Scots Presbyterian. She had to think twice about taking on a job in this house, even though they were Protestants. Not the same kind of Protestants as her; the Irish never could be, she said at the time, which had made the prime minister laugh. Now it looks as if nobody is amused.

Marge is coming towards him, her hair all over the place, her cheeks flushed and damp, as if she has indeed been lying in bed, and crying at that. She clutches the *Evening Post*.

'Gordon,' she says, 'how could you?'

There, pictured on the front page: he is walking, hand in hand, with Janie McCaw, out of the Thorndon Baths.

Courting

Perfume. It was Marjorie Cole's scent that had attracted him from the beginning. She had been piteous on the first occasion he met her, a young woman from England who, against all her father's advice and at only sixteen, had come to join her sister and brother-in-law in New Zealand. Her father was a doctor, a man of the world. The thought of this child going to the colonies seemed absurd when she could have a life of comfort at home. But her brother-in-law was sick and, as Marjorie had said to her father, 'Whatever will Babs do among all those Māoris if poor Otter becomes worse?' Her sister had written that they were going to take a small cottage near the sea at a place known as the Kaipara. The weather was good, orchards had been planted, the water teemed with fish. Somewhere Marjorie had read that the first settlers heard the sound of snapper fish crunching the shellfish on the shores of the harbour, and this information she read aloud to her father. The living would be easy.

'What of these Māoris?' her father asked.

'Not many of them,' Marjorie had replied, undaunted. 'On the Kaipara, they have mostly killed each other off.'

Babs and Otter were waiting when her ship sailed into Auckland. The three of them set off with little delay for the Kaipara, travelling by train and ferry to their home near the sea. Marjorie had become uncertain about their venture. On the voyage out, some people who came from the north had told her of the dangers of the Kaipara Harbour entrance, the people who had died. When the ferry rolled and pitched on the last stage of the trip, she thought she might die too.

The small cottage proved to be nothing like an English cottage, more like a shed where a gardener might keep his tools, except a little larger, with a curtain dividing what passed for a bedroom: a double bed on one side and a single bed for her on the other. The travellers had brought a leg of mutton in their provisions and, on that first night, Marjorie put it in the cold oven of the stove and tried to light a fire. Otter had retired to bed, while Babs mopped him down from a fever that had overtaken him on the journey. Outside, in the failing light, a man approached on horseback. Gordon Coates had ridden over from Ruatuna, the family home, when his sister had remarked on the newcomers arriving with their bags and a cabin trunk, heading for the cottage up the road.

'Everything all right?' he called out to the girl standing distractedly in the doorway, running a hand through the waves of her hair. It was so clear that nothing was right that he dismounted and walked over to her. She put her face down so he couldn't see the tears. He put his finger under her chin. She had the bluest eyes of any girl he had ever met. Even though she was in such a dishevelled state, he detected rose water, mixed with the girl's own fresh scent. He had waited for this moment all his life.

Only she was little more than a child. He could see it wouldn't do.

Later, when Otter had died and Babs remarried and gone to Australia, he found Marjorie working behind the perfume counter at Kirkcaldie & Stains, the big department store in Wellington.

No, that isn't quite how it happened. Babs had written him a note to say her sister had gone to the capital. She didn't want to impose on him, and she knew he had affairs of state to attend to, but Marjorie was still a young girl. Perhaps he could look in on her at work. This was before he became prime minister, although such was the force of his delivery in the House, and the changes he had brought about for the poor, that everyone knew of him. He was just about to go to war. When he entered the shop, the doorman tipped his hat to him. The graceful notes of a piano being played on the second floor floated down the stairs. Ladies were making their way to the tearooms, where he knew from past visits there would be tiered stands of cakes and scones and tiny cucumber sandwiches.

The perfume gathered from many gardens now assailed him. Marjorie was absorbed in her task of dabbing scent on the wrist of a customer. When she looked up, she smiled with her pretty rosy mouth, as if she already knew he was there. Her dress draped elegantly from her bustline. The hands that worked their way over the elderly wrist she supported were soft and white, with small shell-shaped nails. He wanted to hold her in his arms. He wanted her to lie in his bed with him. He thought, *This is love*. Although he had taken women in his arms many times, and they had told him they loved him, he had yet to tell a woman he loved her. He thought his heart a cold stone, but now it was not. For a moment he had to steady himself, so dizzy did he feel with emotion, not to mention the persistent drift of jasmine and lavender that suffused the air. Because he was who he was – Mr Coates – the supervisor of the counter agreed, without even raising her eyebrow, that Miss Cole might take an early lunch with her gentleman caller.

'We're apart in years,' Marjorie said, when he blurted out his confession of love. They were not even properly seated.

'Not enough to matter, surely,' he said. 'A dozen or so years. It's neither here nor there.' He had spoken to an attendant as they entered the tearoom, and now, as if by magic, the woman appeared bearing tea and one of the laden silver stands.

'You hardly know me,' she said, as she bit into a cucumber sandwich, shunning the scones with their jam and cream.

'Of course I do,' he said. 'You think I didn't watch out for you up north?'

'I heard you had others to watch out for.'

His face flushed then. 'There's always idle gossip in small towns.'

'Is it not true then?'

'It's in the past,' he said after a pause. 'Whatever it was, it's long ago gone. I would have married by now were that not the case.'

'You're certain of that?'

'I'm bound to the Māori cause in politics,' he said gruffly.

'But not in your heart?'

'Of course it's in my heart. One cannot stand by and watch injustice. I owe an allegiance.'

'To whom, Mr Coates? Who do you owe?'

'The people,' he replied. 'You've seen the Kaipara. I owe the people of the Kaipara.'

Her fingers pleated the sharp edges of the linen cloth in her lap. 'Our home will be there?'

'Eventually,' he said. He spread his hand over hers, sensing her capitulation. 'But for now you will stay here, and – God willing that I should return from this war – one day, I promise you, you'll live in the prime minister's house.'

For her wedding gift, the following week, he bought a dressing table set of amberina perfume bottles, the glass full of reflected yellowish fire. He would have her, and have her, before he sailed. He would leave her with a daughter, but then Gordon Coates often did that to a woman. He would come back to her a hero, and the daughters would keep arriving.

Land

News travels fast in the north. It was always so. On the Kaipara one morning, a flight of fantails flickered around the doorway of the whare of Te Mate Manukau, and then, although he and his wife tried their best to stop it entering, one flew inside. Te Mate Manukau said to his wife, there is trouble in the south. There was bitterness in his voice.

The land above the Ruawai plain seaward of the hill, Ngāti Whātua land, once belonged to the chief, but when his daughter gave birth to the first of her children, he gave it to the man who would be his son-in-law. That was what he believed. The chief continued to believe this when more children were born. He was proud that the man would marry his daughter. The man himself was a chief, a prince among men.

Or so he considered then. He no longer believes that the marriage will take place, although sometimes a lingering hope stirs within him. The fantail entering his house is not a good sign and, since he gave over the land, his thoughts always turn in that direction and how he has come to lose that which was precious to him. The man who would have wed his daughter has changed his mind, had more children already by another woman, and left them behind too, one of them already dead.

His thoughts fly to his grandchildren, who he can see at play not far away. It is simply the death of hope, he thinks then. It is a knowledge being borne to him that what he most desires will never happen.

In the distance, he sees his daughter and, from the way she stands, he sees that she knows something already. Soon enough, he will find out the details for himself. He watches her walk across the paddock, head bowed. When she reaches the river, he calls sharply to her mother.

Her eyes travel the path their daughter has taken. They take in her stance at the edge of the water, up to her knees in the mud, the mangroves closing around her, despair in every line of her body. 'Stop her,' Te Mate commands his wife. His wife can run faster than he can with his stick.

'She'll come back.'

Te Mate is gathering himself, urging his wife on.

'In a minute she will be all right,' she says.

'How can you say that?'

'She knows he is gone. She knew long ago. Don't startle her.'

So it is as he thought, although nobody has told them; it is about the man.

After a time that seems to go on forever, although really it is just a minute or two, their daughter straightens herself, returns the way she went, wiping a mud-stained sleeve across her face. The eldest of her girls runs towards her, pulls at her hand.

Aroha, my darling, my darling, be happy.

It is true, she has thought of slipping into the river, letting it sweep her along out through the mouth of the Kaipara. Of course, her father had been angry. He had given the land. Beautiful land, still clad in bush, tall trees, dark furled ferns, a stand of tōtara.

But what good had his rages done? Gordon wouldn't change his ways. He didn't for her, nor for Annie Ngapo, with whom he has also had children. At the store this morning, the ferryman told her: he is married, it is in the newspaper. The Pākehā girl with a face like whey who stayed here a little while, you know the one I mean? And she knew straight away that it was true, and what she had been told did not surprise her. She had always sensed the ambition in his barrel chest, the one that covered hers so many times, her breasts against his skin. They have known each other since they were children. Through and through. The smell of each other when they lay together. Mussels and eels, whisky and tobacco, their dark mingled musk close to the earth. She could hear the sound of him thinking in the stillest moment.

So, when he asked her that last time they were together, 'What is it that you want?', she had known that he trusted her not to tell him the truth, not to say the words that would have kept him. It was in her power to tear his heart apart, but she didn't. What use was half a heart to her? She didn't say, 'Just you, just you for always,' because that would have been to hold him when he wanted to be set free. Instead she said, 'My darling, my darling, be happy.' And another baby stirred in her womb.

Postscript

Long after, years and years on, when the old people are gone, Gordon will come back to the Kaipara, his power faded, the dances and parties over and also the money, of which there was never as much as one might have thought. He will want to give the land back. When the people say, 'No, it is too late, it cannot be put right now,' he will suggest that one of his daughters marry into the family, so that they will be linked with the land. The daughter herself will seem not to be against this.

But her mother is English. She will say, *it will not do.*

TELL ME THE TRUTH ABOUT LOVE

1

On this blustery Friday afternoon in July, Veronica is able to tell Drew McGuire that she has somewhere else to go after work. She doesn't need to join her colleagues for their weekly social drinks. Thank God it's Friday, but not for her.

'I don't believe you,' says Drew, as they tramp the school's linoleum-floored corridors. 'You can tell me, Vronnie. I know what it's like to be lonely.'

Vronnie. A name he called her when they were young. Nobody uses this name now; it belongs in the dustbin of memories, along with Afro perms and protest movements; Veronica wore maxi skirts and platform soles at the time.

Drew has temporarily rejoined the staff, after an absence of years. He is a thin, fair man, his balding white skull only lightly masked with thread-like hair. Thick spectacles shroud his light-blue eyes. It is his short-sightedness that has caused him to leave the stage.

Drew was an eccentric teacher of English when he first came to the school. The kids liked his accent and his manic gleeful impersonations. People said he was just too good to stay in teaching. Veronica, who loves teaching, could never see the logic in this. She's always liked chalk and scratchy blackboards and the smell of big boys and girls in uniform on wet days. Drew can't wait to be off again when his cataract operation is done. For a while in the nineties, he was in a comedy show on television. He keeps his cell phone on in class to take producers' calls.

Well, yes, Veronica thinks, Drew probably has been lonely, two or three times. She has gathered that Drew is currently unattached. But it is the end of his first marriage that she remembers.

'Truly,' she says, 'I'm going to stay with friends in the country.' It sounds like a Russian novel. She decides not to tell him who she is going to stay with.

'Well, just give me a bell, sweetheart.' He says sweetheart in a deep theatrical way. He and Veronica have arrived at the end of the corridor. Drew stops and fumbles in his pocket for a notebook.

'Have you got a pen on you? I'll give you my number.' Can he be serious? She sees herself as he must, a thickening teacher of history, with straight toffee-coloured hair streaked with grey, half spectacles perched on the end of her nose.

And there is the matter of the past. Surely, he cannot have forgotten the role she played in his life. But perhaps that is her complication, the long view she brings to everything she sees, to the people who reach out to her. More likely he is just thinking that she is someone who might be available. Still, she can't help wondering how well, even, does he remember Maura?

'Now you will ring me,' he fusses, handing her a slip of paper. 'In the old days, we could talk to each other, you and me.' That is not how she recalls it, but at least it is an acknowledgement.

The world is changing all around him, Veronica thinks, and he hasn't noticed. It's like cyberspace hasn't been invented. That's what she likes about history: it's fluid, it changes all the time. Perhaps that's why she remembers all that detail about their lives and re-evaluates it over and again. Some day she hopes she will work it all out. Whereas Drew, she suspects, watching him disappear in the direction of the staffroom, is stuck with a notion of how they were, youthful and unchanged by the passage of time.

Colin was a dark rosy-lipped poet with slim hips and a sweet white smile. His study was a shed in the back garden of the house where Veronica still lives. Handsome young men sat around like acolytes and smoked dope with stringy girls in overalls. Veronica got sick of pulling marijuana plants from between the daisy bushes. The girls talked about menstrual extraction, anger management and recipes for vegetable stew. They walked through the house without knocking. This was Wellington in the days when poets and artists around town still held salons in squalid houses while their wives cooked in woks over broken gas rings. The last of the wild children. By the end of the decade, they would be talking about shares and the falling value of the stock market.

Veronica and Colin's house was almost indecent in its newness, a wooden bungalow on the down side of the road in Highbury, but at least they caught a glimpse of the ocean. Colin was becoming famous; it was the time when he began to think he was invincible. His photograph was in the papers, usually looking hunky and casual, while driving a truck, which is what he did for a part-time job. The *Listener* ran a double-spread feature on him, he often read poems on the Concert Programme in his dark uncultivated voice with its hint of a vee in place of 'th', and a singing intonation. *Real New Zild, but true, a second Baxter, another Glover,* raved one reviewer, not quite what he wanted to hear; he was hanging out with the Black Mountain poets, stylistically, and he thought it was bad for his image. Women rang him late at night. One of his poems was about a Canadian girl with eyes 'like burnt holes in the ice'. More like two piss holes in the snow, said Veronica, who had met the girl. But she said it with a smile because she did trust him, and because she couldn't see that anyone could see much in the girl anyway.

Veronica paid the mortgage but didn't mind, at least not very much, although she would have liked the garden to herself on Sunday afternoons by way of reward. 'My wife, the bank manager's daughter,' Colin said with a laugh. 'I married into the middle classes.' Veronica hated it when he talked like this. Her father was just a bank clerk, she explained, nothing grand. Besides, Colin's references to money management made her feel bossy and difficult. Colin's family were farm labourers. 'Farm labourers never had to worry about mortgages,' he declared, 'they never got them.' The true prole. He and Veronica had met at teachers training college, after Colin finished his degree, but he had flagged teaching before he even started. That bothered Veronica, but by that time they were already married, the glamour couple, the party animals at college, who had taken the plunge as soon as they graduated. At the time, Veronica felt swept off her feet.

'Sometimes I feel like we're drifting,' Veronica told Lewis. Lewis was best man at their wedding and their oldest mutual friend. He was a doctor, setting up his first practice. 'A doctor who can quote Milton and the Book of Common Prayer,' Colin said if asked to describe Lewis. 'Would you believe it?' 'What hath night to do with sleep' was Lewis's favourite quote when they flatted together in university days. But it went back further than that. Lewis had loved words when they were children, living on different sides of the track in the same small town. Perhaps Colin would never have learned anything had it not been for Lewis.

In the early years of Veronica and Colin's marriage, Lewis visited every weekend that he wasn't on duty. Although he rented a beautiful apartment on The Terrace, crammed with treasures from regular travel as the years passed – old maps, African masks, Asian statues – he often preferred to sleep over on their convertible divan than stay at his place alone. 'Lewis is married to us,' Veronica and Colin half joked to each other. There were times when they were hard up – which was most of the time – when they would suddenly have a little money, and Veronica guessed that they had had help again and that it wasn't from her parents.

'Of course you're not drifting,' Lewis said sturdily that afternoon. He and Veronica had been drinking coffee in the kitchen while Colin entertained in the garden. 'You two are the air each other breathe. C'mon, let's see what the blighter's up to.'

And they walked together down the garden, Veronica pleased to have Lewis at her side as they took their place in the group. Nobody appeared to notice their arrival.

At some point, Lewis's visits had become less frequent, she can't remember exactly when, but perhaps for a while without her noticing. 'Jealous,' Colin said when Veronica mentioned it. 'He was always jealous of my friends.'

'He wasn't jealous of me,' Veronica had protested.

'That was different.' He used a tone of exaggerated patience, as if something obvious were escaping her.

What Colin said bothered her. It implied an oddness in Lewis, a failing she couldn't see. 'I'll give him a bell, and he'll turn up, you'll see,' was all Colin said.

Colin hated school teachers' parties. Grown ups playing party games, he snorted. He accompanied Veronica with bad grace; it was a time when it was still not all right to turn up on your own and say your husband was in bed with a cold. Either he went or you stayed home.

When Christmas came around, that year she remembers so clearly, there was nothing for it but beseech him to come. She was due to go on maternity leave, there would be a farewell speech for her. Well, what would she tell them, that he would be there or not? This cost her an effort because of course it was about what people thought, and Colin was fond of saying he didn't care about that.

'Of course I'll come,' he said, putting his arms around her, or as far as her big stomach would allow. 'Whatever made you think I wouldn't?'

This was the party where they met Drew and Maura, newly arrived from Scotland. Drew was due to take up his position in the New Year. You noticed him straight away, dressed in a kilt. He danced with all the staff wives, even Veronica, fox-trotting her around the cleared staffroom at arm's length. He turned games into feats of daring, building a tower of chairs and climbing them, to stand one-legged at the top of the steeple.

'I dare you,' he yelled to the other men. And they did it, the younger men anyway, so that the party turned reckless and chaotic. When Colin's turn came, to Veronica's surprise, he joined in, climbing to the ceiling, where he wobbled uncertainly before collapsing through space, landing heavily on one foot. 'Oh, shit,' he gasped, 'my bloody, bloody ankle.' But he was laughing, and it wasn't broken, only sprained, so that he had to keep it strapped for a month. He would appear at his next reading leaning elegantly on a cane.

Maura never said a word while her husband was performing all these tricks. She sat frozen in a corner and jumped when Veronica spoke to her, responding in a whispering voice. Veronica thought she looked like a margarine sculpture, bland and slightly off-colour. She was a nurse, her specialty nursing children; she thought she would land a job at the hospital quite easily, she said, when prompted.

'Of course I like children,' she said, gulping and looking away from Veronica's swollen stomach. A deep blush flooded her impossibly fair skin when she saw that Veronica noticed. Veronica tried to imagine Maura amongst children's downy heads, bending over them with a sweet, transforming grace. Shy, she decided.

A crowd, including Drew and Maura, ended up at Colin and Veronica's. Colin hobbled around playing the host. He and Drew became friends on the spot.

If Colin went to a party now, he could just get drunk without the games. Except the last time their daughter saw her father he was drinking straight vegetable juice.

During summer, Colin showed Drew around and took him for trips in his battered Bedford van. The van was sky-blue with fluffy white clouds that Colin had painted on the doors. The young people had gone away to follow the sun, or summer jobs. Maura worked at her new job, and Veronica awaited the birth of Freya.

Colin was off work because of his injured ankle. Drew had his almost undivided attention, except in the evenings when Colin wrote late into the night. 'Vronnie, this is the life,' he would say when he came to bed, red-eyed and spent. 'Drew really understands what I'm going through.'

'So, what are you going through?'

'I've got to make some changes. I've got to settle into my own voice. It's all crap, don't you see? I'm sick of the Appalachian bullshit, I need to go back to real meaning. Forget about the kids. It's time I moved on.'

'I see,' said Veronica, longing to sleep, thinking her waters might break at any moment and deny her the luxury. She'd heard variations on this theme before. The poets he knew were old fools and young fools, and women.

'I need to begin again at the beginning.'

'Tomorrow,' she said, closing her eyes.

Colin said he was thinking of getting in touch with Sam Hunt, but he understood Hunt preferred to do his gigs on his own. He might set himself up doing something like that, a tour in the country. Perhaps Drew could go with him and act as his manager, they could do a kind of double act.

'Drew's got a job. He's starting next week at the school.'

'In the holidays, I was thinking.'

'We'll have a baby by then.'

'It's getting the money together to get started,' Colin said gloomily, as if she hadn't spoken.

'I suppose so,' Veronica said.

Veronica found it impossible to explain the way she missed Lewis when he wasn't around. After all, he was Colin's friend first. But Freya brought him back to them, as if he'd never been away. He was almost fatherly towards Freya, the baby who had arrived in the heat of late summer. He visited at the hospital when she was born and distracted the staff with advice bordering on instructions. When she went home, he popped in after surgery just to see how she was doing. He appeared one afternoon while Colin was holding court. A look of surprise and disapproval registered on his face as he looked down the garden from the verandah. Veronica could see him waiting for Colin to give a sign that he had seen him. It didn't come.

Colin stood reading poems aloud to his audience, one hand clutching a sheaf of scruffy papers, the other combing his wavy hair back from his forehead.

Drew sat at the edge of the circle beside the daphne bush, for once appearing a little aloof, perhaps because he was older. Around his head he wore a red-and-blue bandana, a stubble of beard sprouted on his chin.

Lewis leaned on the railing, listening to Colin, his face working.

> *. . . and so I came to where*
> *you slept*
> *touched the dreaming*
> *of your face and knew*
> *your dreams were all of me . . .*

'He's still flogging *Ginger Modern*,' Lewis said.

Colin's very first published poem. Veronica had been proud of it when it appeared, not long after she met him. 'It's for you,' Colin said, as if she might need reassurance that there was nobody else in his life. People looked at her, knowing she was loved by a poet. Like being the mistress of a king or a president.

'I always liked it,' she said.

'Of course,' said Lewis after a pause. His knuckles were white along the edge of the rail. 'Of course, so you should. And who's that chap?' He was referring to Drew. The way Colin recited the poem, he looked as if he were speaking directly to Drew.

'Oh, him, that's Drew McGuire,' Veronica said. 'Trust Colin to show off to the newcomer. He's been quite taken with him.'

'You should take a firm stand,' Lewis said violently.

Veronica was taken aback. Perhaps Lewis really was jealous. She remembers the tremor of the shock she felt, the way something was being said, and not said.

'It's the artist's life, I guess,' Veronica sighed, pushing aside her discomfort. 'He's doing so well, what am I supposed to say? You can't expect him to live just like you, Lewis.' If there was something prissy about the way she said this, she didn't care. Lewis didn't have the right.

Chalk and cheese, the two men used to boast. But the elements were falling apart.

'I get tired of the chip on his shoulder. It's time he grew up.'

Drew stood up on a signal from Colin. He had brought his bagpipes with him.

'You're not going without saying hullo, are you?'

'You tell him from me,' Lewis said as he left, the opening strains of 'Amazing Grace' in his wake.

Veronica and Colin received an unexpected invitation to visit Drew and Maura. To please Drew, Veronica agreed. Now that she had Freya, visiting was like an interruption to the daily flow of happiness that she felt. Freya occupied her night and day. Every fold of her dimpled skin, the beginning of a smile, the extraordinary scent of her, like ripe pears, absorbed her. Her secret little thought: *I don't need history, I've made it.* There is nothing she would not do for this miracle.

The invitation was for Sunday lunch, although Drew called it their 'dinner'. Their flat was a square one-bedroom box with blankets thrown over the shabby armchairs. There was no sign of Maura. 'She's late back from her shift at the hospital,' Drew said. 'I don't expect her to be long.'

He produced some beer from the fridge. Veronica, who was breastfeeding, drank tap water. Drew put on a record, Brailowsky playing Chopin's 'Polonaises' plink plink plink, on and on as the afternoon wore away.

'We wouldn't have come if we'd known Maura was working,' Veronica told Drew, sitting and rocking Freya.

And, later still: 'We would have brought something to eat, something to help out, perhaps we should go now?'

Maura appeared some time after two, not in her nurse's uniform at all. She wore a floral-print dress, which her mother had made her, and a blue cardigan.

As soon as Maura arrived, Veronica saw how she hated them being there. She guessed she was terrified of cooking them a meal. But they were caught, like fish in aspic, until something happened.

Maura refused to be helped. 'You could feed your bairn,' she said when Veronica offered. Her accent was broader than Drew's, he used his for effect in the classroom, she'd heard, to make his students laugh; Maura's slipped through, strong in bad moments, of which there seemed to be many.

The meal was served in the late afternoon, a chicken like Maura herself, pale-skinned and scrawny, blood leaking into the pan juices.

For, Drew said awkwardly farewelling Veronica and Colin at the gate: 'She's wearing her rags today. Sorry.'

Veronica wanted to slap him (for what? Not starting the meal himself? For trying to explain Maura's unhappiness away like this? Probably for inviting them at all). But she was too tired by then, and beginning to feel unwell, to say anything much. The chicken and hard potatoes hadn't agreed with her and, although she didn't know it for another week or so, she was already pregnant with Sam.

'Thank you,' she said instead.

When they were settled in the car and the motor running, she said, 'That was a disaster.'

'You would say that, wouldn't you?'

'Well, they're hard work, those two.'

'I guess he can be a bit of a prick,' Colin said. 'I might have known.' It sounded like her fault, but it wasn't worth an argument. All the same, he seemed to go off Drew for a while.

'Are you getting enough iron?' Lewis asked in a worried way the next time he visited. He wasn't Veronica's doctor, but he fussed over her as if he were. Veronica was already showing her second pregnancy.

Lewis sat at the end of the kitchen table, topping and tailing beans, a tea towel spread over his front to protect his cashmere sweater, his slim hands working with methodical precision at his task.

Colin had rung him. 'Where the hell have you been, mate? C'mon over, we've been missing you.' As he had predicted, Lewis couldn't stay away for long. They had drunk their first bottle of wine; Lewis would stay over for the night. It was impossible to imagine that their friendship would ever be disturbed in any serious way.

Colin said: 'Lewis, you're elected to be Freya's godfather.'

'I thought you didn't believe in that. Religion and superstition, you've said it often enough.'

'Well, this is different. Freya needs a godfather. She needs you.'

Veronica could see the way Colin was casting around for something to give Lewis, an affirmation of their old friendship, a sign that said 'forgive me'. She held her breath, willing Lewis to accept, the old tenderness for them both closing around her heart. She saw them as she did when she first knew them: Lewis, the young doctor, Colin, the scholarship boy still making up his mind what he'd do with his life, two merry, devoted friends.

Lewis gave one of his serious, affable smiles. 'Fine,' he said, 'if it's okay with Veronica.'

None of it would last. This was the evening Drew chose to arrive unannounced, bringing Maura in tow. Veronica was stirring a sauce with her free hand, Freya over her shoulder, when they walked in. Maura was gaunt, her permed hair slicked in greasy ringlets around her head.

'She's missing her mother,' Drew said, as if Maura wasn't there. 'She needs a bit of family life, that's what I told her.'

'But this is just wonderful,' Colin cried. 'At last, my two best friends in the world get to meet each other. They must stay for dinner, mustn't they?'

Veronica saw the way Lewis flinched. Drew had brought a bottle of whisky, which he placed on the table between them.

'Glasses, Vronnie, there's a good lass.' He poured drinks all round, even though the others were drinking wine.

When they had eaten, another difficult meal full of artificial conversation and hesitations, Veronica sat on the sofa and fed Freya. 'D'you want to wind her, Maura? She's been a bit grizzly all day,' Veronica asked, thinking Maura would like that; she nursed children, after all.

'I need a rest from work when I go visiting, thanks very much.' The way she said it offended Veronica. Lewis took the baby instead.

'I'm surprised you're having children so close together, are you just careless?' Maura said, in a small, mean voice that the others weren't meant to hear.

'I think I'm lucky,' Veronica said. 'I like being a mother.'

Maura started to cry. She got up from her chair and went to the bathroom, from where they could hear her sobbing through the wall.

'What did I say, Drew?'

'Just homesickness. I've told her to get over it; she's here now. I tell her she should forget about her mother.' Drew poured more drinks as if he were the host, wanting to hold his place at the centre. Lewis covered his glass.

'You can't just forget about your mother,' remonstrated Veronica, who talked to hers on the phone every day. Maura emerged from the bathroom and sat in the corner of the sitting room, pretending to read Veronica's magazines, but she kept weeping in a noiseless disconcerting way.

'Music, we need some music,' Colin said, casting around. 'We could do with a bit of boogie.' Instead, he dropped on a record that was slow and sentimental.

'Shall we dance?' he asked Veronica.

'I'm tired,' she said, feeling that they were all behaving foolishly and hating the stony-faced way Lewis was looking at Colin.

'I'll dance with you, laddie,' said Drew. 'If our wives won't dance with us, we'll have to make our own fun.'

She could see how truly drunk they both were. Colin never could drink spirits. The two men weren't just jiggling around in the room, they were slow waltzing, Drew taking the lead, even though he was the shorter.

'Perhaps you could think about bringing your mother out for a visit,' Veronica said, trying to ignore the men's antics. What she said seemed kind and reasonable.

But Maura began to wail again, a clear piercing cry that rose to a shriek.

'She needs some treats to look forward to, doesn't she, Lewis?' Veronica plunged on wildly.

'I think Maura needs to go home,' Lewis said, addressing Drew. 'I'm off to bed,' he said turning away.

Before they left, Drew kissed Colin goodbye, lip to lip as if he were a girl. Veronica had never seen two men kissing before, Colin's long blue-ish chin resting in against Drew's white bony one.

Lewis, who had learned to kiss on each cheek when he was in Europe, turned at the door and froze.

'What an exhibitionist,' he said when Drew and Maura were gone.

'It's just acting,' Colin said. His best friend was looking at him with distaste. 'I'll kiss you if you like.'

'Oh, forget it,' Lewis said.

But it shook Colin.

'I'm sorry,' he told them both at breakfast the next morning. 'I'm giving up booze. I need to do some work.'

Veronica invited Lewis over mid-week for his birthday, a celebration they always shared. She didn't think he would come. It'll just be us, she told him, not mentioning Drew and Maura. He said he'd think about it.

He arrived, though, walking in as if nothing had happened. It occurred to Veronica that she and Lewis might be united in an unspoken resolve to keep the friendship alive while the worst passed over. Perhaps, even now, they could all survive.

'Where's Colin?' he asked, picking his way through the kitchen.

'He said he had something to drop off in town. At the radio station, I think.' Colin had given up truck driving. He was on compo because he'd strained his back, and he'd told her it was a great opportunity to focus on his *real* work, and he wouldn't be going back to that stupid job. Lewis didn't seem surprised when she told him this. She didn't say how beside herself she was, because Colin hadn't mentioned any plans for work that would pay the bills.

Although it was his own birthday they were celebrating, Lewis had brought Colin a present, a book of Auden's poems. He wanted to open it straight away. 'I can slip it back inside the wrapping,' he said, impatient as a boy. He was wearing a tweed jacket and a polo-neck sweater. Leaning against the doorway, he looked himself like a poet escaped from the thirties rather than a doctor.

'Where did you say Colin was?' he asked again, holding the book a little away from him. Soon he would need glasses.

'He shouldn't be long.' She slid the oven tray out and peered at the lasagne.

'Will it come when it's picking its nose? What d'you think, Veronica.' She liked the way he called her by her proper name.

'What are you on about, Lewis?'

'Love. Don't you know that poem? "Oh tell me the truth about love." It's a song too.' And then he sang a few lines, his voice musical and lovely. She thought, *I could love him*.

'That's real poetry,' he said with a note of satisfaction. 'Didn't you read Auden at university?'

'I must have,' she said, flustered. Perhaps it was Lewis she was meant to love all along.

They were interrupted by a knock at the door, the imperious rap of someone in a hurry.

The caller was a very young woman called Georgie, whom Veronica recognised as a hairdresser at Fishtails, the salon where she had her hair cut. Veronica had seen her at work, a luscious barley-sugar blonde girl with tanned skin and huge grey eyes. When they opened the door to her, she was full of righteous anger, hands on hips. Her jeans were as tight as a chrysalis skin, a packet of Marlboros stuck out of her black leather coat.

'That friend of yours,' she said, speaking directly to Veronica. 'You'd better come.'

'Who are you talking about?

'Oh, for goodness' sake, you know. The Scotch one.'

'Maura?' Veronica vaguely recalled recommending the salon to Maura when she first arrived. 'Well, I don't know,' Veronica began.

'She's in a daze,' Georgie said. Then her self-confidence deserted her, as if struck by the unlikeliness of what she had done, barging into the house and yelling at two grown-up, serious people. Georgie looked about nineteen. Veronica herself was only twenty-six, but Lewis was older again by some years, as was Colin. The astonishing thing that Veronica would learn about Georgie was that she could touch the end of her nose with the tip of her tongue. Not many people could do that. 'You can't really talk to her,' Georgie was saying. 'I told her not to have another perm, but there it is, her hair'll probably fall out, and she'll blame me. Anyway, there's nothing I can do about that now, I just need to get her out of the salon.'

'She's there now?'

'Won't budge. I took a taxi here. My boss is hopping mad.'

'What actually seems to be the matter?' asked Lewis, using a professional voice. 'What's happened to Maura?'

'She says she's going to kill herself if somebody doesn't come. Her bloke's seeing someone else.'

'Who's her husband seeing?' Lewis's voice was corrosive.

'Oh, I wouldn't know. We're told not to ask things like that, y'know, just listen to the client, what they want to tell you, nothing more.'

'I don't believe it,' Veronica said, 'they've hardly been married five minutes.' When she saw Georgie's raised eyebrows, she said lamely, 'Oh, the pig.' Her mind was racing. All those girls on the lawn. They'd stopped coming lately. Had Drew hit on one of them?

'Perhaps you can't blame him, not really. Well, the way things are between them,' Georgie said.

'What things?'

'They don't do it. She's never done it. She's a virgin. Look, she says she can't go back to their flat on her own.'

'I can't leave Freya,' Veronica said.

'Can you look after her?' Lewis asked Georgie.

'I've got my train to catch. I live in the Hutt.'

'I can run you home later,' Lewis said.

But the problem was resolved by Colin's appearance, although he was wild-eyed and glowering.

'Where are you all going?'

'Out,' said Lewis, throwing him a look of distaste.

Colin's hands fluttered in odd uncertain little movements of assent as he turned away.

'Are you all right, Colin?' Veronica asked, hesitating.

'I'm fine,' he said.

'Come on,' said Lewis, his voice impatient. 'Are we going or not?' He didn't look at Colin. Georgie was looking anxious again.

Veronica sighed as she settled herself into the car. 'One of his moods. Are you sure about Maura and Drew?' she asked Georgie. 'It doesn't make sense. Surely they've tried . . . you know, to have sex.'

'She says she can't screw,' Georgie said. She sat in the front with Lewis, where she had taken her place without deferring to Veronica.

Veronica was taken aback, not so much by the language but the image of violence that screwing Maura evoked. Wasn't desire what kept her and Colin going? She thought so, they'd done a great deal of what Georgie referred to as 'it' (well, how did one quantify the acts of love in a busy marriage?) But she was tired and pregnant, and when she thought about love then, she felt as if she were walking through flannel. She could see that Maura might not be cut out for sex. She leaned her face against the cool glass of the car window and said nothing.

'Pull a right, Lew,' Georgie said.

Veronica cringed in the back seat. Lew. How embarrassing. Glancing sideways at him, Georgie looked as if she were discovering the surface of the moon. She stroked the leather upholstery of her seat.

The woman who cut Veronica's hair was pacing up and down outside Fishtails, waiting for their arrival. The lights inside the shop were turned off, except for a night light. Maura sat alone in a chair, looking straight ahead at her shadow reflected in the mirror, as if there were someone on the other side.

Lewis rolled another chair over and sat down beside her. He spoke to her in a gentle voice. 'It's time to go home, Maura, home to your mum.'

> *A grief that is past, let it pass*
> *Like a leaf in the grass*

Colin left these lines, like a message, on a sheet of paper propped against the coffee pot.

'Isn't the rhyme a bit symmetrical?' Veronica asked, when he came up from his study.

'I didn't write it.'

She hadn't supposed so.

'A Persian poet. Eleventh century. It's straightforward though. Wouldn't you say it was straightforward, Vron?'

Their baby stirred beneath her hand. She was sure it would be a boy this time. Colin wasn't making sense. Whatever this was about, she suddenly didn't want to know, things were messy enough.

When she didn't reply, he said: 'I've got a job at the newspaper. Starting Monday, you can stop worrying.'

Veronica never did find out who Drew was seeing.

Perhaps she could ask him now. But she wouldn't.

Those blank light eyes.

2

When Lewis's BMW rolls peacefully down her driveway, Veronica is as pleased to see him as always. She doesn't chide him about his extravagance. It is such a pleasure just to have someone drive up on a Friday afternoon.

She kneels at the edge of the verandah, nipping tiny spent heads from a patch of sea daisies, hoping to convey that she is not over-eager, that she goes away for weekends in the country quite often. Sitting back on her heels, secateurs in hand, part of her is glad that Lewis knows so little of her movements. It makes her feel independent and slightly mysterious. Another part of her wishes that a man drove up and parked outside her house more often.

'I suppose it's something I miss,' she muses aloud to her women friends. 'It's an effort, though, meeting someone new and interesting.' She knows women who go to singles groups. 'They're just not me,' she says. 'I mean, look, I see all those hairy men's ears in the staffroom. Imagine, well, I can't help it, you see, but fancy getting one's nose caught in all that fuzz.' And she chuckles. She's turning into a character.

When she looks in the mirror, the possibilities are still reflected there, but they are getting clouded in an image of a woman who wears careless make-up and chunky sweaters, and gives papers at in-service training days. 'Kia ora tātou,' she says, 'this afternoon I have a new reading list on the impact of sealers and whalers on the shores of our country.' She will be wearing sensible sneakers.

'The house looks lovely,' Lewis says, bending down to kiss her cheek. How well preserved he looks. His wide shoulders taper down to a firm waistline, his hair is grey and springy. There is something boyishly rumpled about Lewis, in spite of the deepening folds in his cheeks.

'All my own work,' she says. The kitchen is freshly painted, Spanish white walls with dark-green trim around the windows. Early hyacinths bloom in containers on the sills.

He picks around her china, holding up a Clarice Cliff jug.

'Nice. What did it cost?'

They can do this, it's almost like a marriage, the way they talk to each other, even now. China doesn't fascinate him the way it does her, but he knows quality, and he likes the way things are grouped, how they are put together. And where they come from.

'Three hundred at auction.'

'A bargain. Have you packed your toothbrush, then?' Meaning, is she ready to leave.

'Yes, and my hot-water bottle.'

'We do have electric blankets, Veronica.'

'I just like a hot-water bottle on my tummy,'

He groans. 'You've got your cystitis back again.'

'It's better now. You'd think there'd be some rewards for clean living, wouldn't you? I caught a chill when I was on playground duty. Anyway, I'm not coming for a free consultation.'

'Lots of fresh water. No alcohol. No spices.'

'Is it worth coming at all?'

'You'd better. Georgie's expecting you to make up four for dinner.'

'Who's coming?'

He looks uncomfortable. 'You're not the only house guest. His name is Miles.'

'Lewis! Georgie's not matchmaking again?'

'She met him on a course a couple of years back.' His voice is uneasy. Georgie paints in oils, mostly abstracts. 'Miles runs a gallery in Auckland. He's been on a buying trip down here. Georgie must have mentioned him.'

'Of course, I'd forgotten,' Veronica lies. 'Is he gay?' Straight away she regrets the question.

'Probably,' he says, more comfortably. Veronica fumes in silence as she completes her preparations, wishing now that she were staying at home. Of course, Lewis and Georgie are always having people to stay: Georgie's new friends, the ones she has made as she has grown older, or Lewis's students. He teaches part-time at the hospital, the kind of mentor who inspires the young and takes them home to feed and comfort. Hand-fattening, Georgie says. Beautiful creatures, but hungry.

'How are the children?' he asks, studying photographs of her daughter and son.

'Fine. Freya sends her love. She's in love *again*, it seems.' Freya is twenty-three and never seems to settle at things for long. 'And Sam's still in Africa.'

'You miss them?'

'I've never been so free,' she says, collecting her coat. She doesn't mean to sound short, but it's such a stupid meaningless question. She misses her children every day, like an affliction. Some days she doesn't know whether she will resist the temptation to ring them, wherever they are. Not that it's easy to get in touch with her son, a fledgling botanist. She sees him in the hot sun of Africa (had he got this from Lewis, all those African masks he saw on childhood visits?) and remembers the way he burned so easily when he was small. At least there is email, and he lets her know from time to time that he is safe.

Lewis's eyes moisten as he looks at a small framed watercolour, a delicate painting of a lake beneath clouds.

'Remember when you bought this? That weekend we all went to Rotorua and swam under the hot falls?'

'Vaguely.' Veronica is checking her locks. Every evening she inspects them three or four times. It takes time, there are three doors, the back, the front and the garage. Lewis drums his fingers on the table with a gathering impatience.

'I don't take risks. Twelve . . . five, four more to go.'

'We were students, you must remember,' Lewis is saying in the background. It is not the violation itself she is afraid of anymore, not the battering of the body, the penetration, which she can hardly imagine anymore, it is more the loss of solitude, the secret self that old women know. She must have been crazy to say she would spend a weekend in the country with these people. 'You and Colin bought this later in the day, when we wandered into that exhibition.' His irritation with her fussing is palpable.

'So we did. I think you bought it for us actually.'

'Veronica, don't. Please.'

She does remember that day of course, but he doesn't need to know that. They were students then. They were singing and not very sober, that night when they swam at the falls, all three of them skinny-dipping.

'Are we going or what?' She pulls the door too hard behind them.

'I see you've cut the trees,' he says as they climb the path to his car.

'Only thinned. They were blocking the light.'

'What would Colin have said? He was sentimental about trees.'

'Oh, who cares?' she snaps. 'Ask him if you're so keen to know what he thinks.'

He lifts her bag into the boot of the car without answering.

Colin is long gone. He drills wells on the Canterbury Plains and shares a house with his business partner, Nicko. Freya says her father is actually growing rich and careful, and a bit thick around the waist. Nicko makes fantastic lattes for breakfast. He does most of the cooking and keeps the firm's books. Veronica wrinkled her brow at this information. There is something she would have liked to ask Freya, but she didn't.

Veronica has never told Lewis exactly how she and Colin came to part. In fact, she has never told anyone because what happened was so crazy and peculiar.

They had taken a holiday in Gisborne, that small city of swirling beaches and vineyards where the sun rises earlier than on any other city in the world. Although it was a holiday, Colin walked around with a little notebook practising his keen observer's look, snooping on conversations in cafés, hushing Veronica – he was trying his hand at writing for the stage. The newspaper job was long behind him. The children were teenagers when they made what turned out to be Colin and Veronica's last trip together. They decided to stay home, and this, in itself, had undone Veronica. She couldn't believe they wouldn't come. She worked hard on family holidays.

'Let's stay in a motel,' Colin suggested. 'Have a real break. Who needs tents and sand in our lunch anymore?'

In the evenings, Veronica walked through the town on her own. Colin said it was a good time to write up his journal. Sometimes when she returned, she would find him sitting, staring into space. He had had a new book due out in the spring, called *Ginger Modern*, thematically linked poems about an artist who steps out of a post-modern frame into his own reality. They had some spare money. Veronica worked full time again, and Colin usually had some freelance work of one kind or another. Once or twice, he said, well, look, love, you can't just create all the time.

Every evening, Veronica took the same route, dawdling in front of the shops. Cars sped up and down the wide streets, horns honking, girls shrieking. A car stopped one evening while she stood looking into the window of a closed shop, coveting a dress and planning to come back the following day. She felt herself lifted in an instant, scooped up into the vehicle.

A car door slammed shut behind her. Her scream was lost beneath the squeal of tyres. There were three young men, one on each side in the back seat and the driver. They were young dangerous-looking men with dreadlocks and tattooed throats. Beside the driver sat a Rottweiler, the hairs on his ruff standing up.

It is the Rottweiler that will save Veronica.

'So what youse doing out?' asked the grubby youth beside her. The hairiness of his shirt like a pelt against her bare arm, his hand with broken fingernails close to her knee.

'Walking,' she said, her throat dry with terror. 'Just out for a walk.'

'You want a beer, missus?'

'No. But thanks.' *I am too old for this* was her thought. Glancing sideways at the boy's jeans to see whether the dark stretching of his cock had begun, fighting rising nausea. The smell of sour beer, the dirty seat, the dog's fetid breath in her face.

'What's the dog's name?' she asked, keeping her voice as soft and level as she could.

'The Tyrant,' said the driver. From the pride in his voice, she could tell she had taken him unawares.

'Eh, Tyrant.' The Rottweiler subsided, regarding her with curious, friendly eyes. 'Eh, good boy.'

The dog reached forward and licked her face.

'Shit,' said the driver. 'Bloody mongrel. Where you from?'

'Wellington.'

'Walling-ton,' he mimicked her, as if she were the queen in a flowered hat and white gloves taking the Mickey out of them. This was the most dangerous moment, she would think later.

'Why don't we buy him a tin of tucker at the dairy?' She fondled the dog's neck.

'Yeah, why not?' said the driver. Perhaps they had thought she was younger when they picked her up, that they would like her more. Or the driver was just weary of driving around and taking risks. 'We're skint.'

'I could just give you the money.'

'How much?'

Veronica emptied her shoulder bag into her lap, counting notes and loose change, fifty dollars in all.

They had circled the town, back to where they picked her up. 'Have a nice night,' one of them said.

'See you,' she said. The street was as empty as ten minutes before.

She leaned against the window of the frock shop, overwhelmed with such desolation that she thought she would never recover.

A part of her is ashamed, even now. She is ashamed that she did nothing. The next woman might not have been so fortunate, not so able to deal with unruly young men, she might not have liked dogs.

But when she got back to the motel, Colin looked up from his journal, his face furious. 'You're back early,' he said.

'Something happened.'

'Oh, yes.'

She picked up the shiny motel kettle, intending to make tea. 'D'you want to hear?'

'Christ, Veronica, why d'you always interrupt? Just when I'm getting going?'

When she didn't answer, he said: 'Well, what was it then?'

'Nothing.'

In the morning, she said she was going home. She said they should stop living together, there didn't seem to be any point. In her ashamed heart lurked gratitude. Freedom seemed to have come cheap at the price.

Secrets. Veronica has one of her own.

Still, all these years later, she wakes early in the morning and checks locks she knows perfectly well she had secured the night before; in a bookshop one night she hears a young poet reading (for she discovers that a love of poetry is not necessarily forsaken along with the poet): 'she leaves her fingers in the locks' the poet says, it's a phrase that haunts her. It is as if the poem has been written for her. I don't want to be caught unawares, she says . . . I don't take risks.

Although she tells no one about her experience, it is one of those full-stops in her history. A moment she can refer to in all that collection of years that is her life.

When she told Lewis about the separation, he laid the palms of his hands flat down on his desk – she had gone to his rooms to tell him – tears leaking along his nose and into the corner of his mouth. Veronica didn't actually leave Colin. He was the one who moved out. She could have the lot, her middle-class dump. He was lucky to be out of it.

This is not exactly what he told Lewis, sitting in the back bar of De Brett's.

'She needs counselling,' he had said.

'Not Veronica,' said Lewis.

'What about those poems I dedicated to her?' Colin said, head in his hands.

'Well, what about them?'

'I'll have to disown them. Are we still friends?'

'You've got a nerve,' Lewis said. Or this is the version he told Veronica.

By then, Lewis had married Georgie, years before all this happened. It wasn't as if they were all hanging out together by then. But Lewis had never abandoned her.

Veronica leans back on the ivory-coloured leather of the car's upholstery, the dashboard twinkling before her as they join the traffic flow stretching north. The silence between them is not a great way to start the weekend, their usual easy rapport absent.

'He was my friend, too,' Lewis says by way of an ice-breaker.

'I know, I know,' Veronica replies, because something has to be said. They have started this conversation several times over the years, but it never goes anywhere. Really, what Lewis means . . . what they both mean is: *Once we both loved Colin. Only he didn't live up to our expectations.* Which seems callous. As if they are betraying themselves and their own finer feelings.

'Miles isn't gay,' Lewis says, although she hadn't asked. They are waiting at the roundabout for the traffic to clear.

'Miles? Oh, the house guest.'

'Georgie's friend.' His voice is a trifle heavy.

'I wouldn't mind turning over some of my pictures,' Veronica says, glad of the opportunity to steer the conversation in a different direction. 'Perhaps I could talk to this art dealer.'

'I like your pictures the way they are. Oh, this damn traffic.' His fingers drum on the steering wheel. 'Georgie will be waiting for us.'

After her marriage, Georgie's defiant self-confidence seemed to ebb. 'It's lonely being a doctor's wife,' she would complain, her voice puzzled and uncertain.

Lewis would be at his wits' end. 'For God's sake talk to her, will you, Veronica?'

'There's so much responsibility,' Georgie would complain. 'This woman says she's dying of a hernia, the pain's so bad, do you think she'll die?' 'Oh, Veronica, I can't stand how people are in pain, but I don't know whether to call Lewis or not. What's a real emergency?' 'Veronica, we went out to dinner the other night. I'm sure his friends are all laughing at me, all those wives that doctors find in

Fendalton and Khandallah. It's because I'm from Upper Hutt.'

'Veronica, I think I'm too young for him.'

There were times when Veronica thought Georgie might leave Lewis because of all this. She would talk to Georgie with patience and sympathy. Like Maura, whom Georgie had rescued all those years ago, Georgie loved children and didn't have any for a long time. There is a difference though. Lewis and Georgie's marriage was not without heat. But it meandered on and on for years, filled with Lewis's exhausting compassion for his patients, his collection of treasures and their annual travel: Italy, France (all one summer in Arles), the Lake District. Georgie had absorbed a certain amount of knowledge about music and art and food. Indeed, her experiences are broader than Veronica's, although she, too, can afford to travel these days and sometimes does.

And now Georgie has the girls, and Lewis is not on call so often, his practice expanded to include other, younger doctors. At forty, when the subject of children had been dropped as an embarrassing *faux pas* in their presence, Georgie had become pregnant, as if her hormones had suddenly been kick-started. Her life is full in the way Veronica's used to be. The blonde blade of a girl has been replaced by one of those intense older mothers.

She will be waiting for them beside the quiet estuary of the sea where she and Lewis live. There will be pied stilts and herons stalking, high-arched, through the silver-grey skein of water that Georgie looks out upon from her kitchen window, a row of boatsheds, the blue trickle of hilltops on the horizon. A lifestyle property. The two little girls will be reading books in the glowing gold-and-blue room that opens off the kitchen, the table set for dinner, a bottle of wine standing open. During the day, Georgie will have taken two or three calls from her mother, who lives in a rest home. 'What will you have for dinner?' her mother will have asked. 'Have you been out? Who did you see?' Or Georgie's brother may have phoned to ask for money. Georgie tells Veronica about these problems because there is nobody else amongst her friends whom she can tell. 'Although Lewis is so good,' she says wistfully, as if she would have liked to bring a wholesome family to her marriage, like a dowry.

'Miles has arrived,' says Lewis as they sweep into the circular driveway. He makes Miles sound like a present, gift-wrapped and ready. But who is he a present for? And if he is intended for Georgie, why then has she been asked?

'I'm out of control,' Veronica tells herself, 'my fantastical silly mind.' She lives too much in the fabulous clues of history, her own and others. She remembers the first time she stood in front of a class. 'History's not definite,' she had said in a tentative voice. 'It's not all facts and set in concrete. It's more like a jigsaw puzzle or a mystery story, one piece leading to another. We can, each one of us, look at a landscape or a character in history, or even a set of dates, and see something different from what anyone has seen before.'

'Like smelling rats in a dunny,' said a girl in the front row, a supercilious girl with a Roman nose and freckles.

'Quite,' Veronica had said in her young earnest voice, ignoring the way laughter ran around the class, 'the connections and clues are limitless.'

But she has built a career and a lifetime on smelling rats without ever quite finding the source of the smell.

Her place in this family is clear. She has become the aunt, as the children call her, to be dutifully tended. Lewis and Georgie are kind.

The idea of Fauvism, what Georgie describes as 'wild beasts and bright nothingness', has taken hold of her imagination, the words tripping off her tongue. I am at one with the idea of the spirit's journey into the unknown, she tells Miles, while he nods his head up and down and tugs at his beard. He is older than Veronica expected, older than any of them, a man with a big barrel-shaped chest, soft grey hair neatly cut to collar length. He is dressed in a tan raw-silk jacket, a black shirt, his throat bare. A touch tropical for this time of year, but in the firelight he is a graceful energetic figure. He has robust, interesting hands. Yet Veronica sees the way he guards himself, not giving too much of himself away.

'To own a Chagall,' Georgie enthuses, 'what more could there be to life?'

At which Miles frowns and sighs. 'Art may be for the upwardly mobile, but it pains me to say, my dear Georgie, that I think Chagall is out of even your reach. Or my gallery for that matter.'

Georgie flushes, as if caught out at child's play. It's been a while since Veronica last saw her. Her tawny hair is teased up with back-combing. Fine threads of gold nestle in her collar bones, veins throbbing like satin piping in her throat. When she smiles, her upper lip rides a little too high above her teeth, as if she were trying very hard at something.

'Not to own the picture in that way,' she says. 'You don't understand. Just to be able to wake up and look at it. To think about the journey.'

'The journey, oh, yes,' says Miles.

'Surely there's more to art than sales,' Veronica says, defending Georgie.

'That's not what he said,' Georgie replies, her voice sharp.

She has put on music, The Penguin Café's 'Oscar Tango', intense swollen music that makes Veronica's head throb.

She has changed her clothes, something was called for. She leans back, feeling more or less presentable in a grey sweater, more like a tunic, a slender black skirt, long Turkish silver earrings. All the same, she doesn't feel at home in Georgie and Miles's company, more like a detached stranger trying to break into a group without any guidelines as to what will interest them.

Lewis is absorbed in the children from the moment he enters the house. The girls are called Hilary and Aretha. They clutch his legs and demand rides on his back. On a command from her mother, five-year-old Hilary scurries away to bed, but Aretha, two years younger, won't leave. She is still coiled around Lewis's neck when Georgie begins serving dinner.

'She must go to bed. I'd already put them down for the night.'

'Well, there you go, darling child. Mummy says it's time for bed. We'll just have to take you along.' Veronica sees how he is inflamed with love for these girls, all his coolness deserting him.

'I'll come with you,' she offers. 'I'll say goodnight to Hilary.'

From where she is perched on the edge of Hilary's bed, she watches Lewis tuck Aretha into bed, putting her Raggedy Ann down beside her. Lewis would die if anything happened to these kids, she thinks, and shivers.

'Say it, Daddy, say it,' says Aretha. 'The thank you God song.'

'For a lovely day,' he murmurs, 'and what was the other thing I had to say?'

'Now I remember, it's Go-od bless me,' the girls sing along with Lewis.

'Sometimes I worry,' he says, as they return to the dining room.

'I think that I'll be too old to be any use to them when they grow up and I won't have long enough to find out what happens next in their lives. At other times I'm all selfishness and grateful they didn't come earlier. Whatever would Georgie and I be doing with ourselves?'

As she opens the door, Veronica is about to say, 'Pretty much the same as all of us,' but when she sees Georgie and Miles standing side by side, she hesitates and says nothing, momentarily blocking Lewis's entrance into the room. Miles holds a tureen of soup and Georgie has been lifting a ladle from it. It is nothing, Veronica tells herself. A helpful domestic gesture. But their fingers touch.

The meal is simple and to the point: light spinach soup, Basque chicken with a hint of chillies offsetting the peppers and olives, French bread, a fresh green salad, cheeses.

While they are eating, the storm that has threatened all afternoon breaks. Lightning strikes and thunder rolls outside, torrential rain falls straight and flat like an Asian monsoon. The power goes out, and Georgie and Lewis fetch candles, Georgie cursing that the chicken is cooling as they continue their meal in the flickering half dark. They take extra helpings of salad, although Veronica finds it a trifle bitter for her taste. So does Lewis, who says so.

'It's got mustard leaves in it,' says Georgie, defending her territory.

'A minimalist salad,' says Miles.

'Thank you, Miles.'

'An intellectual salad,' says Lewis gloomily. There is another flash of lightning, in which, for an instant, his face is bunched and old.

The moment passes. Instead of art, they lapse into desultory conversation, telling of storms and catastrophes. Miles begins a story about an old woman next to his house (when he still had one, he said, when he was still a married man), who climbed an apple tree in the rain and disappeared. Like Jack climbing the beanstalk and out through a hole in the sky.

Their meal is ending with floating islands, *œufs à la neige*. Almost too rich, Veronica notes, a touch of bravado, perhaps.

'She got stuck in the tree?' Georgie asks, perplexed.

'She dissolved in the rain?' Veronica enters the spirit.

'Fell out of the tree like a ripe apple. As it happened, she'd fallen on my side of the fence – under the hydrangea bush, there all the time.'

'Myocardial arrest,' says Lewis, his tone short. 'I'm going to check that the girls haven't woken up.'

Georgie is still laughing as Lewis leaves the room, her face flushed from wine, her manner careless. She's in love with this man, Veronica sees, observing Georgie's gaze resting on Miles. She knows the way Georgie looks when she is falling in love; she has seen it before, helpless and wide-eyed, a flaring around the nostrils as if she is smelling incense, as she looked when Lewis had knelt at Maura's side in the hairdresser's salon. This cannot be, this terrible wounding of Lewis that is unfolding.

Earlier, she had decided that her modest collection of art wasn't worth discussing with Miles, but now she changes her mind.

'I'm thinking about getting some new pictures,' she says. 'I'd love to look at your catalogues. Have you brought any with you?'

'Of course,' Miles says, switching his gaze away from Georgie. Veronica sees that he understands what Georgie has not, that their looks have been intercepted and translated.

Georgie is abrupt. 'It's getting late. Why don't you talk about it tomorrow?'

'I'd love to,' they chime almost simultaneously.

'After we've brought you breakfast in bed. We like to spoil her,' Georgie tells Miles, as if Veronica needs cosseting.

So Miles and Veronica spend Saturday looking at catalogues and transparencies, in between playing snakes and ladders with the children, waiting for the rain to clear. A drizzle persists, and it is very cold outside. Veronica looks with an appraising eye at Hoteres and Woollastons, an Albrecht that she likes very much, a Spencer Bower that she hovers over, and a host of dazzling others, all artists whom Miles seems to have known in person, to hear him talk; he is full of anecdotes. She puts yellow stickers on pictures she would like to view. She finds one that interests her in particular by an artist she has never heard of, a mysterious upward movement that suggests dancing.

'Influenced by the poem sequence *Ginger Modern*, when it was set to music.'

Veronica draws a sharp breath.

'You know it? A work of genius.'

Georgie is within earshot. She has made a point of not moving out of range all day. Veronica decides not to lie. 'My husband wrote that. Former husband, that is.'

'You were married to Colin?'

'Yes.'

He looks at her with new eyes. 'I knew there was a traumatic divorce.'

'Not really, just a divorce.'

'But it was. Colin never wrote like that again. I met him

afterwards, after you. He told me about it. In the end he gave up. Well, I suppose you know all of that.'

Georgie turns away, as if busying herself with another task.

'It depends on whose version you've heard. Colin didn't stop writing on account of me.'

'How can you be sure of that?'

'I'm not a hostage to Colin's fortune. He stopped writing poems before we parted. He'd turned to journalism.'

'What about *Ginger Modern*? One of the great love poems?'

'An early sequence. He often read from it.'

'So when the poems stopped, you left?'

'You make it sound very obvious.'

'Why are you so fucking calm about this?' Freya had demanded of her mother after the divorce. 'Don't you care?'

Veronica doesn't know. She blames herself for all manner of things – like Freya's boyfriends who come and go, about the physical distance Sam put between them, about her own condition of stasis. She is not sure how any of it has come about, that sudden walk, her refusal to look back. She knows that for most of the time she is content, a woman who has surrounded herself with small treasures and a workload that doesn't leave time for reflection. It is only when she comes here that she is seized by an old restlessness and wonders if she should stop coming.

But, once or twice, she has flicked through old family photographs: Colin, herself and the children, in which she is startled to see herself, body turned slightly away from Colin. That's why history is history, she thinks, we don't see what's happening at the time.

'Perhaps I'm being impertinent,' Miles is saying, 'but Colin mentioned that there was a great love in his past who'd deserted him. It sounded tragic.'

'Oh, love,' she says, in much the same way he had dismissed Georgie's spiritual journey.

'I just assumed. A thousand apologies, Veronica.'

'Accepted.' She feels something closing around her, that old flannelly, bat-wings-in-her-hair sensation.

'All the same, you liked that painting,' he persists.

'A coincidence. I'll look at the rest later,' she says, pushing away his catalogue and yawning. It's not feigned, Veronica really does feel exhausted. Miles puts the catalogue to one side, vexed.

'You two getting along all right?' Lewis asks in passing. He has Aretha on his shoulders and Hilary by the hand. The weather is clearing. 'Who's coming for a walk?'

'All of us,' says Georgie, looking firmly at Miles and Veronica on the sofa.

So they walk, all six of them, through the gathering evening light. The clouds are that dark amber and gold that often follows thunderstorms. The estuary stretches beside them as their boots make rough tracks in the grass. A group of black wading birds, white ruffles under their tails, are slipping the long orange straws of their beaks in and out of the water, as if sipping.

Slipping and sipping. Colin would have liked that. For an instant, Veronica is wistful.

Georgie walks beside Miles, talking animatedly as they slowly draw ahead. The others follow with the children, stumbling as they ford a swampy piece of marshland. The fingers of wind on their cheeks keep them moving. Lewis looks ahead at the two heads bent in conversation. He is not a stupid man, Veronica thinks, he will understand soon enough if he doesn't already. She feels a rush of pity, or something more, for him.

'We should catch up with the others,' she says.

But by now Miles and Georgie are far ahead, having reached a ridge where they stand silhouetted against the evening sky, their figures like dark puppets on the horizon.

'I think the children have just about had enough,' Lewis says. Hilary has been complaining about water in her gumboots. 'Will you tell Georgie, I'm turning back?'

Georgie is startled by Veronica's appearance by her side. Miles is less surprised, as if he had been half expecting her to turn up.

'I suppose I'll have to go too,' Georgie pouts when Veronica explains about the children.

'Perhaps Miles and I can walk on a bit further,' Veronica ventures.

Even Georgie, in this lovelorn girlish way that has overtaken her, understands that for the moment enough is too much. She turns on her heel and stalks off across the paddock. Calling to her family, then breaking into a run and scooping up Hilary to piggyback her, just as Lewis has Aretha on his back. They look like a perfect, laughing, happy family. Veronica feels her heart breaking. Perhaps they will escape this time, but there will be another and another, she supposes, now that Georgie is no longer content.

Miles pockets her hand, almost absent-mindedly, linking his fingers through hers before she can pull away. There is something comforting about the lacy intimacy of their fingers curled up there together . . . like dancing with the man who had danced with the woman who'd danced with a man . . .

'You're not as I might have expected you – had I ever anticipated meeting you,' Miles remarks as they walk on.

'So, what would you have expected?'

'Someone harder.'

'Oh, I'm hard all right.'

'No, you're not. You like rescuing people. As long as it's not yourself.'

'That's presumptuous. Some people shouldn't have to be rescued.'

'Ah, Georgie. I was wondering when we would come to the lecture. Colin said you were a school teacher. A pretty good one, he said.'

'I don't want to hear any more of what Colin thinks of me.'

'Faith is the leap you ask me to take into the darkness . . .' he recites, changing tack.

'Yes, yes,' she says, *'Ginger Modern.* I know it.'

'Well, of course you do. Oh, my God, the scent of those illicit wild flowers in summer, it's all there, so sensual, the lovers drowning in that perfume. The sense of something coming to an end. But of course it must have only been a beginning for you.'

'It was a long time ago.'

'Love, there is always a price . . .'

'Yes,' she says again, her voice sharper than she intends. She brushes her hair from her face.

'He did write it for you, didn't he?'

'You're the one who understands the poem.' A desperate unease has gripped her.

'So who *did* he write it for, Veronica?'

'Oh, who knows? I mean poems are glorious fabrications;

in much the same way as art.' This trips off her tongue, sounding worldly and wise.

'Or history?'

She hesitates. 'Does Lewis know that you know Colin?'

'Colin's never come up in conversation. Should I tell him?'

'Probably not.'

'So where does Lewis fit in?' Miles asks, his tone casual.

'Nowhere. I just wondered.'

Only she has said it first. Lewis. Lewis.

Lewis and Colin, and the wild scents of a summer past.

Colin and Drew.

'Lewis was our oldest friend,' she says stiffly. 'He and I have always taken care of each other.'

'I see.'

And for a startled, awful moment, Veronica realises that he does see, and so, at last, does she. Lewis and Colin had never left each other, at least not until Drew came along.

'Everyone wants to look after Lewis by the sound of it,' Miles says.

'Why do you say that?' Her voice is still rigid in her throat.

'Georgie once told me that she'd saved Lewis's bacon. He'd been jilted. Well, I expect you know all of that.'

'Of course,' she whispers.

Colin and Drew. Not Lewis and Colin anymore. Not even Lewis and Colin and Veronica. Somewhere along the way, had she been the price love had to pay? Why had none of this ever occurred to her?

'*He owes me*, was the way Georgie put it.' Miles, cutting an elegant figure slouching across the paddock beside her, looks straight ahead as he tells her this.

Georgie. Even Georgie knew what she had failed to see. Worse, Georgie has always known everything, from the moment sad Maura wept in the chair of the salon and told her all. Tough little Georgie, coming out of nowhere, full of knowledge. She had known what she was letting herself in for.

Miles speaks kindly, suddenly contrite. 'Some woman Lewis knew I suppose, perhaps she was married, something like that.'

'Yes, something like that. I should go back.' She is thinking, I'll go home tonight. I'll be ill. Or say that Freya needs me, someone will have to take me back.

'I'd like to see you next time I'm in town,' Miles is saying, while the cold air floods her hot face.

They have come to a thicket of pine trees along the knoll and, without Veronica noticing, moved inside a canopy of branches. 'I'd like to make love to you,' he says.

'No,' she says, frightened.

'It might be nice. For both of us.' They stand close together, their breaths foggy in each other's faces. He leans in to kiss her.

'Stop, please stop.' Her legs are trembling, even as she returns his kiss. She sees he has brought her here, certain of where he was going. He will have been here before with Georgie; perhaps even this afternoon he had expected Veronica and Lewis to turn back together.

'Take off your coat,' he says against her ear, his fingers urgent at her buttons. Veronica feels herself already undone. She has been ambushed again. But an old hot remembered flame of desire is licking curiously between her legs. He'll do, she thinks. Like sharing a changing ball, those lollies kids sucked and passed from one to another at school. His silky prick is lying in her hand.

Undressing is a problem in the misty air, trousers that stick to her skin, knickers caught ungracefully round her ankles; he lowers her to the ground quickly so that her white thighs are not visible to him in the waning mauve light. They have done nothing, nothing at all, when he says there is something wrong, something not right. The smell, he says.

Like rotting flesh. They're not on their own.

This, they discover when they draw apart. A human arm lying close to them. Just one discarded arm, not a whole body. Probably a man's, judging by the hairiness and thick spatulate shape of the fingers. It's impossible to tell how it comes to be there, or how it was detached from the rest of itself, if that is how a body might be described in its entirety, although Veronica thinks there is a hint of surgical gauze.

As they restore their clothes, they rehearse this description for Lewis and Georgie. They don't know each other well enough to trust the other one with their lies. 'We were walking under the pine trees,' they will say. Why under the pine trees? And Georgie will know, but won't be able to say. Lewis will guess and will say, at least to Georgie.

All this and more is about to follow.

Rats in the dunny.

In the distance, the house stands alone, shimmering with light and the smoke of wood fire, like a comet's tail. Veronica will stand outside the circle of light as Lewis and Georgie, appalled, draw close to each other.

Later, Georgie will leave Lewis for a time, the children will be miserable, and she will go back to him. Lewis will buy a house in town so that she can have more life of her own; for a short time he will be seen at long lunches with other women, as if to make a point, but none of them will be Veronica.

Veronica thinks she will miss Lewis and Georgie, but she doesn't. At least, not much, after the initial pain of them all going their own way, and they are reduced to sending Christmas emails of good cheer to each other once a year. Some cold words have been exchanged. Lewis had turned away when she confronted him. *Don't come the ingénue, Veronica*, he'd said. *Some people choose to be blind.*

Lewis, her Lewis. Is she a woman who has never truly known love? she will ask herself. And it will come to her, the three of them, her and Colin and Lewis, the time when they were all in love with one another. They might have gone on forever, their magic circle unbroken.

She will have an affair in which she takes much pleasure, with a man who is a little but not ridiculously younger than she is. Desire rekindled cannot be that easily quenched. His skin feels like China roses against hers. He has skinny ribs and a faint foreign smell when she puts her arms around him. It will be her son's idea that the man, a visiting scientist at the Maritime Institute, should visit her. 'Please make him at home while he's over there,' he writes.

Well, Sam.

She will decide, after all, that being on her own is what suits her best. Memory is a fine thing she will say to her friends when they ask her. I am fine by myself.

One night, when the scientist has gone, it occurs to Veronica that Maura is possibly long dead. She wouldn't ask Drew McGuire, and he disappears from the school again not long after his sudden reappearance. She wonders, at intervals, why he had ever come back, like some dark mischief.

Her head is full of old songs, words that won't go away, what they sang in those young days: 'Killing Me Softly', 'Heart of Glass', 'The Story of My Life' . . . with that line about life starting and ending, with who? Someone . . . only her life isn't going to start and end with anyone, or nobody in particular. She begins, very tentatively, to write some poems of her own. She starts:

> *Once in a green time*
> *I began . . .*

The poems will take her far back inside memory. A short history of love or a long history of innocence? She writes on.

She learns that her daughter is about to have a baby, and this interests her as much as love. Or, perhaps, love really is coming her way.

MARVELLOUS EIGHT

When Natalie Soames became a television writer it seemed as if her whole life had changed. Of course, it had been changing for a long time, but up until then the changes had signalled not so much achievement itself but, rather, signs that she was moving closer to her goals. Then one day something happened; it felt like luck.

For years she had asked her Little Theatre group in Mountwood to workshop her plays, but nobody was really interested in local plays, they said. Afterwards, she would say scornfully to reporters who asked her about her early beginnings that they were still into Noël Coward in the provinces. But then she and Monty moved to Wellington on transfer and she met a man at a dinner party given by one of her husband's colleagues. They were civil engineers in a government department. The man said he knew someone who worked in an agency and was sure he could arrange an introduction. She didn't believe it, things like that never happened to young women who had lived most of their lives in Flat Top Road, Mountwood. And even if she did get an introduction, she was sure that if nobody wanted to know in Mountwood, they would want to know even less in Wellington.

But she was wrong. The first person the agency offered her work to was a television producer called Victor. Straight away he rang her up and asked her to come and see him.

'It's great,' Victor said of her script, 'it's the coming thing, women's voices.'

'Is it?' she asked politely. She was interested in Women's Liberation but she wasn't sure whether she was ready to be an expert.

'Look, your work's good. If you can just confront the issues more squarely, I'll make you a household name.' Victor leaned over the desk. He was a man with a high forehead and a mane of fair hair. His eyes were intense. It was said that he was shy with women. You won't get the casting couch treatment from him, the agent had said reassuringly. 'There are women out there who are suffering,' Victor said. 'You know it and I know it. Don't you want to articulate on their behalf?'

'I suppose so.' If she sounded uncertain it was because, until then, it had always seemed wiser to write men as central characters in her plays. But she supposed he was right. Of course she had suffered, still did for that matter. Between them, she and Monty had suffered – over lack of money, broken nights with children, for the small grievances that living amongst the expanses of a new suburb inflicted on people, like loneliness and boredom, and not having a car when they needed it most. In what seemed like the end, they were suffering from not saying enough to one another.

Victor was clearly waiting for more, so she said: 'I didn't *think* I was the only one to blame. Yes, of course I've taken a lot of male-orientated shit.'

'You're smart,' said Victor. 'By the way, I drink.'

'So do I.' It was true, though she had only recently found this out.

'Come to the pub.'

He reminded her of Alec, or Al as he was mostly called, her lover back in Mountwood, but she didn't sleep with Victor. In the year that followed, she was faithful to Al – or Monty. She could never quite decide which of them demanded her loyalty most. For that matter, Victor never asked. Instead, he introduced her to a director called Sonny Emmanuel, and commissioned her to write her first play for television. Sonny had dense dark hair, a beard and a myopic gaze behind his thick glasses. He was saving up to spend a year in a kibbutz, and maybe if he could make enough money he'd take his children too.

Victor loved her play when it was written; everyone in the department was just enchanted, he told her. The play was about a woman who refused to be interviewed with her husband when he went for an important job and she ruined a dinner party with his prospective employers, thus bringing about the downfall of her marriage. *I'm a woman in my own right*, the character said, *I am not a career wife.* Her supportive women friends rejoiced as she looked at the pale dawn of her new freedom. Victor paid Natalie for the script, but there was a problem about production money with the men upstairs. The play made them nervous. 'We'll just have to work on their political education,' Victor said. 'Give it time, we'll do it sooner or later.'

Natalie wrote another play, about a sad love affair between a young woman visiting Wellington on a cruise ship and an ageing artist. Victor loved that too, but in the end there wasn't enough money in the budget for that either. (Far too much OB, luvvie, Sonny told her, and it would ruin it if it were moved inside. Hadn't Victor told her they could only afford three sets, two corners and four minutes of outside broadcast?) 'I'm afraid it's fallen over, Nat,'

Victor boomed over the phone. Still, she could write for their new series in the autumn; that would definitely put her on the map.

He and Sonny were developing the series. The two of them, and various writers, thrashed out ideas in the back bar at De Brett's against the smell of counter lunches. The series, to be called *Marvellous Eight*, was a comedy about a woman counsellor. Each writer was to write one of the eight episodes as a self-contained play, dealing with a day in the counsellor's life.

'I can't write comedy,' Natalie said. 'Anyway, it's sick laughing at counselling, you're laughing at people's problems.'

'Exactly, humour's just grinning at misery.'

'Is that original?'

'Of course it's not. Neither's television. Now write something and don't take yourself so fucking seriously.'

Eventually, she proposed an episode about a woman in her sixties who consulted the counsellor in the hope of finding out how to deal with her children. Her children, in their forties, went to the counsellor so they could work out how to deal with her. Her granddaughters, in their twenties (Natalie had an uneasy feeling that she was shortening the biological timeframe but Victor reckoned they could all just fit into it), were counselled on how to deal with everyone else. Their brother, a cross-dresser, was in training to be a counsellor too. Complications multiplied when the central character took him on as an assistant, unaware that she was counselling all his female relatives.

'Black. Richly comic and very black,' Victor said. 'Whoever is it based on?' They were in the pub.

'It's original,' Natalie said. 'Is that breaking the rules?'

She could have sworn he was nonplussed. 'Actually, what's

done's done, but I thought you might have written about a marriage.'

'I'll tell you when mine gets funny,' she said. She could see now that they had been counting on her. 'Get Sonny to write about his.' She had heard that Sonny had a mistress and that by way of reproach his wife hurled pots and pans at him. She supposed that was why he was going to a kibbutz.

'I can't cope anymore,' Sonny said, 'somebody buy me another beer.'

Mountwood sits, little changed since the summer that started in 1970 and ambled on into a late autumn in 1971. The town is built on a flat plain near the base of a mountain range. Wintry mornings are rigid with ice, summer afternoons simmer like hot honey beneath the sun. On clear nights that sun sets in a bitter bright-pink blaze behind the black hills. A river runs on the outskirts of town, and its edges have been landscaped into a park. The main street is flanked by clothing shops, delicatessens, and miniature department stores. It is dissected by smaller streets, including one that bulges in the middle to form a mall, though the locals call it a 'mawl', and indeed it has become a place where mawling and street violence can happen at any time.

That summer, Natalie and Monty, and Sasha and Jeff, and Dulcie and Al all lived in Mountwood. Some of them were due to leave and some of them are still there and may stay forever. The Flat Top Road subdivision where they all lived had once been farmland. Their quarter-acre sections sat side by side in neat rows. Fast-growing silver-dollar gum trees cast a gentle sheen over the landscape. The gardens bloomed with fruit and vegetables. The women acquired colonial dressers and brought out their grandmothers' china that their mothers had hidden, took contraceptive pills instead of using diaphragms, joined reading circles to counter the effects of television. The men shared transport to work so that the wives could do car pools for kindergarten runs, and Monty and some of the others dug pits in their garages so that they could work under their cars to save money. Natalie can still see Monty's sandy freckled face, frowning and puzzling over a handful of wheel nuts, his spiky hair growing in bunches down his cheeks; like most of the men they knew, he wore sideburns. When he looked up, catching her eye or watching the children, something gleeful flashed behind his eyes.

Over time, the residents of Flat Top Road had begun to prosper. A crowd of them celebrated New Year's Eve together. Dulcie and Al were there. They were older than most of the couples, their children already in high school. It was the first time Natalie had met them properly. Dulcie cornered her to talk about a craft circle she was starting and looked disappointed when Natalie said she wrote.

'That would be difficult to exhibit,' Dulcie said, before moving on.

Behind his wife, Al raised one amused eyebrow.

Later that night, they all danced to The Beatles. None of them would remember afterwards just who danced with whom, but for the rest of the summer they said it was funny the way the heat was getting to them that year. In the winter, Natalie and Sasha began to talk of change. They decided that Mountwood needed livening up. Frequently, they dressed in home-tailored suits and wide-brimmed hats, like other people wore to weddings, and had coffee in the mall tearooms. Sasha said she was going to leave, but Natalie didn't believe her. Jeff was an aerial top-dresser and seemed too rich to leave. Sasha said she was descended from gypsies, and maybe it was true: certainly she was very dark and she had emigrated from England when she was barely twenty, apparently on a whim.

Sasha and Jeff knew Dulcie and Al better than the others did. In an idle lull over coffee, Natalie asked Sasha more about them. Al, she learned, worked as a photographer on the local newspaper, a small daily constantly threatened by takeover. His private passion was growing ferns; he had founded a magazine on the subject, and soon, supported by the conservation movement, he hoped it would become his livelihood. Natalie suggested they all get together again, but Sasha said Dulcie was a bit too brisk for her taste, and Natalie had to agree. Perhaps next summer, Sasha had murmured.

One morning, Natalie rang to arrange a rendezvous, and Jeff answered, sounding bleak and distant when she asked to speak to Sasha. 'Don't be a hypocrite, Natalie. You know she's gone.'

'Don't be silly, where is she?'

'You know,' he said again. 'You really are a bitch, ringing up to gloat.'

But she didn't know. Sasha hadn't told her.

'I thought I knew her,' Natalie told Al, a couple of weeks later. 'Did you know she's living in Auckland?' They had met outside in the car park of the school where Al conducted a night class in horticulture and Natalie attended a creative-writing course run by an English teacher. In private, she thought that she knew more than the teacher. He insisted that her work would never succeed because she had too many characters. Shakespeare had hundreds of characters, she countered. You want me to write to a formula? Life is full of people, that's what it's like, she told him.

'Would you like some coffee?' Al asked, and she thought, why not, well, why not? She couldn't think of anywhere that would be open for coffee at that hour, but still she thought, why not? Her car looked abandoned as they drove off.

'Sasha had a lover all the time,' she told Al wonderingly, as they drove through Mountwood's vacant streets. 'He came down from Auckland and visited her in the afternoons.'

Al shook his head, considering Sasha's defection. Already he had turned the car towards the river.

'I married young, there's never been anyone else since I married Dulcie. Twenty faithful years,' he marvelled to Natalie. She didn't care about his past. He had heavy eyebrows and deeply recessed blue eyes flecked with green. His nose was over-large, his mouth wide and faintly feminine. On field trips hunting for ferns, his arms had turned brown; the backs of his fingers looked like Dutch rusks in a packet.

'You make me feel very young,' he murmured when he had kissed her. He reached for the ignition, the adventure over.

'Wait,' she said.

'I don't want anyone getting hurt,' he said when she slid her hand along the inside of his thigh. 'I don't want any more marriages going under,' he said, like a drowning man.

Then, 'Somebody will see us,' he said, as if it were she who had driven the car there.

'Not like this,' Natalie said, putting her head into his lap.

Nobody had done that to him before.

'I have decided to risk all,' Natalie wrote to Sasha. 'I'm in love with him, and now that the new bridge over the river is finished, Monty has been transferred to Wellington. It doesn't make much difference what I do here. Soon we're going away. What the hell, I'm sure Al will follow me.'

What she didn't describe was the relief it was to leave Mountwood. They had become reckless and foolish, hunting each other out in broad daylight, meeting by the river in lunch hours, at dusk, or on stupid pretexts such as dropping off library books in the middle of the afternoon. When she went home, her mouth was bruised and her clothes stained. Her eyes slid away from Monty's. Most people knew whose cars went where and why. Natalie tried to remind herself that Al did it too, with her, she didn't do it all on her own. In spite of her brave words, it was sapping her energy, the guilt, the arrangements, the excuses, the sheer organisation of it all.

Marvellous Eight is filmed in an Auckland studio that has been converted from a warehouse building. Natalie travels along as part of the team, observing the making of a play, although they have said there might be on-the-spot rewrites. She stays with Sasha, who nowadays lives in a glamorous apartment, part of her settlement from Jeff. That, in itself, suggests a command of her situation that has escaped other friends who have packed up and quit.

Natalie has recently left Monty and she barely makes ends meet. Monty won't give her a thing, he says, and he even wants the children. It is 1974, and men hardly ever get custody, although sometimes Natalie has the impression that her long-suffering mother thinks it wouldn't be a bad idea if they did go to live with him. She is looking after them in Wellington right now.

Certainly, Natalie does not laugh at what she has done. She drinks copious amounts of wine in the evenings and wakes, crying, from deep sleeps. Monty had rung the night before while she and Sasha were having dinner. Her mother had the phone number to ring in case of emergencies, if the children needed her. No doubt she and Monty were in league with each other. 'Come home,' he had said. 'Just come home, everything'll be all right.'

'How can I?' she replied, 'I've got work to do. I have to be here all week.'

'I know. I mean, when you're finished there, come home.'

They have conducted the conversation as if they were still married, and she is just away for a few days.

But Natalie is not ready to go home yet. She doesn't believe she ever will be.

While she is at Sasha's, she sleeps in the spare room where Sasha's son sometimes stays, between boarding school and visiting his father in Mountwood. Sasha's bedroom takes up nearly the top floor of the apartment, and she can see Rangitoto from her window. She shares her king-sized bed from time to time with her new lover. Jewellery, real and paste, tumbles in artful confusion out of a jewellery box onto the dressing table; the scents of frangipani and sweet-pea oils float through the rooms. When Natalie takes a bath, she has first to remove scarlet and citric-yellow glass pebbles from its bottom and lay them around the edge; it is easier to take a shower, but she takes baths because they soothe her and, besides, she has many preparations to make. Lying in the bath, she counts the pebbles: 'He'll meet me, he'll meet me not.' She shaves her legs and under her armpits. When she is dry she smooths lotion all over her skin.

She has arranged to meet Al and stay in a hotel with him for two nights. Today she is moving on from Sasha's place. It has taken weeks to plan. Natalie's anxiety stems not so much from what she is doing but the thought that he will not come, will not be able to get away from Dulcie. It should be easy for him to come to Auckland, but he is such a bad liar she is sure he will mess up his excuses. She harbours, too, a niggling fear that she might get caught. True, she has left Monty, but in the end she would prefer not to be caught out in adultery. The thought of losing her children haunts her. When she has been drinking with Sonny and Victor, she imagines terrible things befalling them.

In the morning, as she prepares to leave Sasha's, solid thick rain falls outside. Sasha eyes Natalie's suitcase.

'You can't carry that thing around all day,' she says. The suitcase is covered with shiny burnt-orange vinyl and stands hip-high. Inside it, there is a new nightdress made of white cotton, sprinkled with blue flowers and a matching brunch coat; the only dinner dress Natalie owns, not black, but an odd shade of purple, currently fashionable, which Natalie fears makes her complexion sallow; a change of day clothes; four pairs of shoes to cover every change in the weather, a large bag of cosmetics, and some extra copies of the *Marvellous Eight* scripts.

'Anyone can see you coming. What will people think?' says Sasha.

Natalie can't see why this concerns Sasha so much. What people think hasn't noticeably bothered her, although they have stayed up half the night talking edgily about their indiscretions. Sasha laughs a lot, and they both drink too much again, and Natalie remembers a moment towards morning when they looked at each other and fell silent. She is too tired to think of what all this means now.

The huge suitcase, salvaged from one of her father's overseas trips, is clearly a mistake. With all her planning, how could she have overlooked something so obvious? All day, while she is in the studio, this foolish, ugly thing will stand in the Green Room, broadcasting her intentions. She has turned down the offer of an expense account hotel. The truth is, she had no idea how to say that she wanted a room with a double bed, not twin.

There is nothing Natalie can do about the suitcase. Sasha, on her way to her new job in a Parnell boutique, kisses her goodbye, looking worried.

'Are you sure you can look after yourself?'

Natalie shrugs, anxious to be on her own. The taxi she orders doesn't come. When she rings the company, they tell her it has already been and nobody came out when they tooted. She says it must have gone to a wrong number. The despatcher is not in a mood to argue. It won't be sent back unless she agrees to wait outside. While she waits, thunder erupts, and she is afraid she is going to be struck by lightning. Rain trickles under the collar of her red plastic mac. When she arrives at the studio, she is half an hour late, her hair is plastered to the sides of her face, her shoes squelching. In the Green Room, she kneels to wrestle with the catches of the suitcase. Under the vinyl, the case is made of cardboard. Water has soaked through a split and collapsed a corner. Sonny Emmanuel stands behind her while she hauls out one of the spare pairs of shoes. 'You're late,' he says, as if she didn't know. 'I can see your tits.'

The studio is like a barn with brick interior walls. Light filters through a skylight in the immense high ceiling. The shadow of the boom is reflected upwards by the studio lights.

'Bleeding hell,' Sonny shouts, 'where's my leading lady?'

'She's in the loo, she's got the trots.' The production secretary is strung out.

'Well, get her out of the bloody loo, tell her I've got a shoot to do. Go and wipe her arse for her, do something, just get her in here.'

By ten o'clock, the leading lady still hasn't appeared. 'We'll do a walk-through. Okay, okay, everybody. Natalie, you be the counsellor, all right?'

'I've never done anything like this,' Natalie protests.

'So you can learn.'

'But I'm the writer, not the actress.' She hears her voice rising, tries to bring it down.

'What are you?' Sonny's eyes are wide, a vein on his forehead stands out like an angry insect. 'Are you the fucking union? Is that what you are? I mean, if you're the union, just sod off! Who needs writers here anyway? I mean, do you know how much per minute it takes to make your crapulous, unfunny little soap opera?'

'I'll do it, Sonny, I'll do it.' I mustn't cry, she thinks

'Okay, good girl, of course you will. Right, stand by everybody, from the top of the scene.' Sonny is suddenly full of false cheer.

Natalie takes up her position at the desk and leans forward, chin resting on her knuckles.

'Great,' says Sonny, 'you look like a counsellor, so help me, even the clothes are right. Very comforting, very bloody pious.'

'They're not,' Natalie starts to say, looking down at the

buttoned-up green blouse, the black jerkin which she had chosen with such care.

'Shut up,' says Sonny, 'just talk to Mick.' Mick is an elfish-looking man, playing the brother in training for counselling. He is wearing a wig and a pink dress.

Natalie picks up the script and begins to read.

NATALIE: So, tell me, what do you think you could bring to your role as a counsellor?

MICK: My soul.

NATALIE: So, what's so special about your soul?

MICK: I can see where others can't.

NATALIE: Tell me what you can see in me. Right now, look at me, hold my gaze, what do you see?

SONNY: Fuck, Nat, this isn't funny. It's supposed to be funny. I thought it was funny when I read it. How could I be so wrong?

MICK: I see a warm, beautiful woman, just like myself.

NATALIE: This is real narcissism, and homophobic as well.

SONNY: You wrote it.

NATALIE: Victor told me to write that. Sonny, I can't do this.

(The actress NATALIE is replacing appears on the set, looking washed out.)

SONNY: Nobody asked you to be Glenda Jackson, ah shit, if you'll pardon the expression, we have an actress on board, welcome darling, for God's sake, don't cry Natalie, I told Victor you'd cry if I let you come on the set ...

Nearly a year has passed since Natalie and Al last saw each other. When she first left Mountwood, she expected him daily.

Her dreams were radiant and carnal. He did meet her once in Wellington, before she left Monty. The reunion hadn't gone well. Looking back, she blamed herself for being too eager. He had gone back to the rules that had been laid down at the beginning. Her declarations of love alarmed him anew. When he returned to Mountwood, he had written: 'I can't leave Dulcie now, you must see how it is for her.' There were the children to think of, he had gone on. He must think of his, even if she did not consider hers (she only just forgave him this). Dulcie had begun menopause. Menopause, Natalie discovered, could last for ten or twelve years.

Yet still he wrote to her, as though she were a listening post in the wilderness. Much later, she would think how unfair that was, as if the unguarded word were less damaging, less compromising than their actions. In fact, they were worse, the words could be revisited, relived, time and again, in secret places. Eventually, his words convinced her that her life was a lie. I have left Monty for good, she wrote to him. Don't think it was on your account, it is what I must do for myself.

This was not the exact truth. Monty had told her one day that if she didn't snap out of herself, he couldn't take any more, and so she had packed, not expecting to leave, but it reached a point where neither would back down and say it was a bad idea. He had wanted her to come back straight away, and then he didn't, and then he turned difficult about property and custody, and she was sure she had done the right thing all along. Natalie told herself she had left him for good. That was what she told Al.

For two weeks, she raced to the post-office drop where she picked up his letters, but nothing came.

Finally, she rang the newspaper office. Al had left. 'Where will

I contact Mr Carter?' she asked, trying to make her voice sound impersonal. As he had been promising, she discovered that the magazine was now his full-time occupation.

She risked more, she rang him at home. Dulcie answered; Natalie hung up. With care, she plotted Dulcie's movements, as she had from the past, the times she went to the supermarket, the classes she was taking this year, the times the women's squash courts were available. It was like living in Mountwood again, without being there. The fourth time she caught him, after nearly a month had passed.

'I can't leave now,' Al said. 'Dulcie and I have put everything into the magazine.'

'You could get something here,' she said, 'you could go part-time here and do the magazine as well.'

'I can't.'

'You mean, she holds the purse strings.'

'Darling, you don't understand. You've got all your life ahead to do the things you want.'

After a while she said, 'Did you ever love me?'

'I do love you.' His voice was weary.

Again, with hindsight, she thinks he might have let it go then. His letters began again. He was responsible too. Was it through vanity that he held onto her? She had read too many novels, she thinks, she was too full of words (though she is no less full of them now), she wanted to believe in romance.

They have arranged to meet during the lunch break by the staircase at Smith and Caughey's at a quarter past noon. Natalie takes the suitcase, deciding on an impulse that he can take it to the hotel during the afternoon, relieving her of its presence in the studio.

Outside, the rain has stopped. Natalie is early, wanting to be there first, to see Al look anxiously for her, his face light up when he catches sight of her.

The perfume counters in the shop are loaded with sample bottles. As she waits, she hesitates, unsure which one to try. Now that she is a writer, Natalie worries about perfume. She has read the unkind things Virginia Woolf said about Katherine Mansfield's scent. From now on, she has vowed to wear only the best, or none at all. A saleswoman offers her a square of blotting paper to spray with samples. She squirts five of the little squares with different perfumes and files them in her handbag. Then, deciding that Nina Ricci can't be wrong, she blasts a tester across her wrists. She resists looking at the store clock until one o'clock has been and long gone.

By the time she gets back to the studio, the actress who plays the brother's grandmother has fallen ill too, and the first actress has had a relapse. A woman who Natalie hasn't seen before is seated opposite the counsellor's chair, and Sonny paces up and down.

'Where the hell have you been?'

'I'm only observing, remember?'

'Oh, yes, I remember, you're just the writer. You smell like piss.'

'It's Nina Ricci.'

'It's probably not her fault. Now, will you sit down? That's Tess; say hullo to her.'

'Hullo,' Natalie says, like an obedient child.

'Are you all right?' asks the woman. Natalie notices Tess's fingers, long and almost stringy, with skin so fine it appears transparent. Tess is small and neat, her cheekbones high, her cap of dark hair fanned with grey above her right ear. A caramel-coloured woollen dress crocheted in a shell pattern skims her hips, ending at least four inches above her knees. Her age could be twenty-five or thirty-five.

'Yes. Thank you.' She likes Tess's voice. 'Sonny's getting up my nose.'

'He gets up everybody's nose when he's working with them. Haven't you worked with him before?'

'Not in the studio. Are you an actress?' Natalie asks.

'No, I play the violin in the symphony orchestra.'

Natalie is bewildered. 'How come you know him so well?'

'Stop talking about me, it's making me embarrassed,' says Sonny.

'He filmed the orchestra, we were playing Bartók.'

'The violins were stunning,' Sonny says. 'Now let's get this show on the road.'

'But why are we doing this, it's pointless?'

'Do you want to run this outfit, Natalie? Do you think you're a director now as well?'

'He's planning his shots,' Tess says, as if she has a lifetime's experience in television. 'It'll help him make up time tomorrow.'

'My nerves are shot now,' Natalie says, with what she perceives as her own grim attempt at humour.

'So are his,' Tess says softly.

Sonny walks over, studying them both. His gaze rests on Natalie. To her surprise, he reaches out and touches her cheek gently. 'There, there,' he says. 'Read the script, you two, okay?'

'Okay.' Tess picks up the script, Sonny returns to the control room, and on his cue they begin to read.

TESS: *(playing MRS OATES, the GRANDMOTHER)* I've been watching my children for signs of improvement.

NATALIE: *(playing the COUNSELLOR)* And how old are the children?

TESS: Forty-nine and forty-three. *(Puts the script down.)* Natalie, that's rich, I like it. My mother's still waiting for me to improve. Are you saying she'll never stop?

NATALIE: Probably not, mine's in total despair, especially now I've left my husband. Should we stick to the script?

TESS: Yes, probably. It's your turn.

NATALIE: Right, um, what strategies have you developed for coping with your family, Mrs Oates?

TESS: I make every day a new day, power of positive thinking, that's what it's all about . . . *(Laughs loudly.) (Note in the script that MRS OATES knits steadily throughout the interview, drawing wool out of a plastic container covered with braided wool.)*

NATALIE: Nice, but what do your daughters think?

TESS: Oh, who cares what they think?

(MRS OATES makes a cat's cradle out of the wool, which TESS simulates very neatly with the plaited woollen belt of her dress.)

TESS: This is a bit of a farce, isn't it? Perhaps if you simply called me Tess, it would seem more natural. We can pretend that's her name anyway.

NATALIE: Her name's Willa in the script.

TESS: Is she a lesbian?

NATALIE: No, it's her grandson who's gay. Well, it looks like he might be.

TESS: Wasn't the writer . . . I mean, did you name her after Cather?

NATALIE: No, I haven't read her work, have you?

SONNY: *(interrupts)* Girls.

TESS: *(reproving)* Women, Sonny, if you don't mind. *(to NATALIE)* Yes, I have.

NATALIE: And are you?

TESS: What? Am I what?

NATALIE: Um ... like Willa?

(A look of surprise flickers across TESS's finely wrought face. She hesitates, undecided as to whether to confide in NATALIE and aware that SONNY is listening. She switches off her microphone and, reaching over, switches off NATALIE's too.)

TESS: Of course not. I'm with Sonny.

NATALIE: You mean *with* Sonny? You're the girlfriend.

TESS: Girlfriend, mistress, I suppose it's got a name. *(She laughs briefly, a sound more suited to the woodwind section, her large eyes luminous.)* I'd even call it love.

NATALIE: You don't look like ... um, well, you're a musician.

TESS: So make sense of it. You're the writer.

NATALIE: Stuff the arts. I could do with a sister.

TESS: You mean you're short of friends right now?

NATALIE: I've got Sasha. Oh, God, I can't go back to Sasha's tonight.

TESS: He didn't come, did he?

NATALIE: How did you know? Was it the suitcase?

TESS: What suitcase?

NATALIE: Never mind. Am I that obvious?

(SONNY picks up a megaphone and shouts at them.)

SONNY: We might as well all go home if you two don't *read*. Tess, will you turn that mike on?

(TESS switches it on.)

TESS: Soon. *(She turns it off again.)* You'll get better, you'll get over today. Well, I don't know what happened, but it looked pretty bad. Things usually get better though, don't you think?

NATALIE: How can you say that? You've got Sonny.
(Wonderingly.) Are you happy? *(TESS's face turns in the direction of where SONNY stands with his headphones on, looks suddenly wistful.)*

TESS: Oh, it was perfect all right. You can laugh, he's a flawed character. There're two sides to Sonny.

NATALIE: Was?

TESS: It's our last day; I'm off to England tomorrow. Probably for good. *(She leans forward in her chair.)* I've got a career, he wants a wife. It came as a shock, I can tell you, after four years of seeing him.

NATALIE: He's got a wife.

TESS: Exactly. *(She hesitates.)* He wants to leave her and marry me. Or something. *(She brushes a strand of hair from her face in an agitated way.)* It's the something I'm not sure about. It's better this way.

NATALIE: I thought he was going to live on a kibbutz. No, don't tell me, he's going to the kibbutz because you won't marry him. Or whatever.

TESS: Something like that.

(NATALIE stands, violently knocking the script aside.)

NATALIE: You're so lucky, you're so goddam lucky.

TESS: Why? Because he wants a wife? Is that what you want people to see? Here comes Natalie, somebody's second wife?

NATALIE: *(sitting down and picking up the script)* Why don't you be the counsellor? I'll be Mrs Oates.

(They switch on their microphones.)

TESS: *(glancing towards SONNY, making sure that he is listening)* You can have him, have Sonny if that's what you want. If you want somebody's husband.

That night they all go to a house in Herne Bay. It is an odd, fussy place with pleated curtains at the windows, Dresden china figurines standing on flimsy mahogany furniture, and salmon-pink carpets that roll fleshily through the rooms. Nobody seems to know who owns it. Afterwards, Natalie's memory of certain events will be hazy, but she does remember that Tess left the house some time during the evening without warning.

Several actresses arrive, including both of those who had been sick earlier in the day, plus a cameraman and other members of the crew, carrying wine and cartons of beer. A party begins, and soon Natalie feels the first mellow haze of wine settling on her brain. Outside, the rain starts again, and somebody says that Mount Ngauruhoe is erupting.

'Why are you going?' she asks Tess, who is dialling the taxi company. 'How can you walk out on him on your last night?'

Tess seems to measure the distance before her eyes, as if it were further than either of them can see. Her fingers pluck at the phone cord as they would an instrument.

'I'm going to get Sonny,' Natalie says. 'You haven't told him you're leaving, have you?' She hates how her words are spinning.

Tess leans forward and kisses her cheek. 'I'm sorry I'm not your sister,' she says.

Sonny is in the middle of a circle of very young actors and actresses in the kitchen. Somebody is cooking paella. 'You can't let her go,' Natalie says, pulling at his sleeve. Nobody takes any notice. There is a whining tension in the air. 'Has anyone seen Victor?' the actress who plays the counsellor asks. Surprised, Natalie looks around the room. Victor is supposed to be in Wellington.

'He won't come here,' the lighting man says.

'For sure.' Agreement rustles around the group.

'Why wouldn't he come here?' Natalie asks, forgetting for a moment that she has to attract Sonny's attention.

There is a brief silence.

'Don't you know, you silly cow?' the actress says. 'They're going to pull the plug on the series. We're folding. Thanks for the useless scripts.'

When she goes back to the doorway, the lights of a taxi are receding through the fog. Natalie has lost her bearings, unable to tell in which direction the city lies. Behind her, people sit on the floor, eating paella off white Wedgwood plates. Sonny comes to the door.

'Come inside.' He puts his arm over her, pinning her against the wall.

'Whose house is this?'

'I don't know.'

'Are we supposed to be here?'

He shrugs. 'It's as good as anywhere.'

'I've got to go,' she says. His breath is on her cheek, his wiry black beard brushes against her face. Behind his glasses, his sad eyes are damp.

'What will you do with your suitcase?' he asks mockingly.

'I've ordered a taxi,' she lies.

'We can send it away,' he says.

'I think I'm coming down with this bug that everyone's got. I think I'm going to be sick.'

'For Christ's sake, don't be sick on the carpet,' he says, releasing her.

She picks up the suitcase from the hallway and walks outside. 'Are you going to be okay?' he calls.

'Was it true? About you and Tess? Or did you both just make it up?'

He follows her out, and she's afraid of what he will do next. But he simply leans over and kisses her cheek. 'Wait in the porch, I'll make sure a cab comes soon.'

Once in the car, she can't remember what address she has given. She thinks they might end up at the hotel she had booked, but the taxi pulls up at Sasha's.

There goes Natalie Soames, people would say, and Al would wish that he was there beside her. Somewhere, years and years later. Like Marius Goring thinking about Moira Shearer in *The Red Shoes*. When the crowd around her dispersed, he would catch up with her. 'Why, how are you?' she would say. As if she had just remembered who he was. 'How are *you*?' he would say longingly, although it was clear that she was wonderful.

This is what she imagined after she got his letter some days later:

My dear,
I was sitting on the roof fixing a sheet of iron that a storm had
dislodged, when I heard a yell. It was Dulcie. She ran outside
before I could climb down to see what the matter was. In her
hand she waved a letter. I knew at once that it was one of yours.
How could I do this to myself? To you? I'd left the letter in the
pocket of my tweed jacket. Dulcie had decided to have it cleaned.
As I scrambled over the roof, Dulcie shouted extracts, so that the
neighbours could hear, and pulled the ladder down. 'Sort that
out,' she yelled, 'get your fancy woman to get you down.' I was
glad that you had left Mountwood. She got in the car then,
revving the engine, and roared off. 'Don't leave me,' I heard

myself yelling. Joan from next door, you know the one I mean, came over, grinning ear to ear, and put the ladder back so I could climb down. 'She's gone to her sister's,' she said. 'She'll be back.' I made a cup of tea and walked out with it to the garden. I saw that the grapevine needed pruning and wondered how I had missed that. I resolved to fix it next year. So it occurred to me that I would stay here, that I couldn't walk away from this crisis, or the next one.

I sent you a telegram, dear, care of Television, Marvellous Eight but the post office returned it. Joan had come over with some casserole for my evening meal. She picked up the phone, because I was feeding the cat at that moment, and they read the telegram back to her, with your name on it. There's no such thing as Section Eight, she said, what's this all about? Marvellous Eight, I said foolishly, the post office got it wrong. 'They've never heard of it,' she said, with that triumph that only neighbours like Joan can muster. I knew she would tell Dulcie.

I hope you weren't too upset when I didn't turn up. Perhaps we can meet some other time.

Yours,

Alec.

P.S. I think my banana palm, the one by the west fence, might fruit next year. I'll send you a case (such optimism), I'm sure they'll be sweet and nutty, just like you. Alec.

Alec. Not Al.

Sweet. Nutty. Nothing there about love.

*

Natalie and Monty are at a Christmas party in Wellington. They have prospered and are growing past middle age. They have had a splendid year. Their lives haven't always been splendid since they began to live with one another again in the spring of that year, in that far-off time, but they have been better than they expected and improving still as the years have passed.

Natalie didn't go back to Monty straight away, and by the time she had begun to consider the possibility he had almost gone off the idea. She sees their lives as tough and grainy then, black and white, like television before colour.

'Why did you go back to him?' her daughter asked once. It is not that her daughter does not care for her father, indeed, they are very close. Rather, she remembers their separation and considers herself damaged by it. Out of such pain and disruption, there has to be a reason, she figures. Why did her mother know her own mind so little? Had she gone back because she was, at heart, simply conventional?

'No,' Natalie had answered at once, somewhat stung. 'It was because I had a second chance to choose. You don't at the beginning when you're young. Or not when I was young. You got swept away by forces beyond your control. But I chose to come back. Actually,' she added, 'that was quite unconventional.'

Sensing scepticism in her daughter's expression, she said, with a flash of anger: 'It was no easier than leaving, what I did.' But that was where they left it. Love was too complicated to explain to one's children, she decided. Choices, she suspects, are as hard-won as ever.

In the wake of *Marvellous Eight*'s collapse, there was little work in the industry for Natalie. Victor didn't return her calls. At first she took a regular job in an office and wrote plays for the stage at night. Later, she found a producer, and the reviews were generally favourable. After a while, she was asked to work for television again.

Victor and Sonny are dead, the industry has changed; Natalie works for independent film companies nowadays, and has as much work as she can handle. The party they are attending is given by a film producer. It is held in the reception area of the studio at ground level, and someone has opened the folding doors so that the room is revealed to the street. Staff and guests sit squeezed up on steps around a staircase amongst life-sized puppets of politicians. At the end of the year, everyone looks tired and drawn, few are glamorous; survivors work hard these days. Most wear stretch Levis and Reeboks, as does Natalie. It is years since she thought of that day of abandonment and loss in Auckland.

Beside her, a young woman asks a question about her work. They fall into conversation. The woman stands out in the crowd, intense and beautiful, with a pale complexion and straight red hair falling to her waist. She wears a short leather skirt, green stockings and yellow shoes that curve up at the toes. The conversation is passing her by, she has come with a cameraman, and people around her are talking shop. She is, she says, a violinist in the Symphony Orchestra.

For a moment, when the violinist tells her this, Natalie is lost for words. Over the years, she has gone to the orchestra many times, watching the musicians as they played, without thinking of Tess. Now, suddenly, she sees Tess's hands clasped on the other side of the table from her. This young woman's hands are just like hers.

Before Natalie can think of anything more to say, there is a diversion in the street. Waiting at the intersection for the lights to change are eight Santa Clauses rollicking around in costume. They are red and loud and call out *ho ho ho* to bystanders. The lights change, and they charge on down the street towards the party. A production secretary rushes out, calling with the offer of a drink.

Chaos and merriment erupt, someone starts to sing 'Jingle Bells', and everyone joins in.

The Santa Clauses cannot stay, they call out again, waving and running down the street.

Monty turns to Natalie, alight with the fun of it. 'How about that? A clutch of Clauses.'

'Oh, well done.' The production secretary has overheard, and already people are calling it out, storing it away in their memories, a clutch of Clauses running down the street on Christmas Eve.

'Marvellous eight,' laughs Natalie, who has been counting. 'Oh, marvellous eight.'

Monty looks at her, puzzled and suddenly guarded.

'There were eight of them,' she says, faltering. 'A marvellous eight.' Only she wishes she hadn't said this, it is something tucked down there in memory where it should have stayed hidden.

Quickly, she turns to introduce the violinist to Monty. He doesn't mind the film crowd these days. His hair is turning white, and he looks like the kind of solid, dependable person in whom people can confide.

The violinist has gone. Across the street, Natalie sees her skipping between the cars, her bright hair like a flag. Then her eye is caught by another snatch of red, another Santa Claus running to catch up with the others; he is having trouble with his beard and stops to adjust it. Nobody else except Monty notices him.

'See,' Monty says, 'there were nine of them.'

Natalie smiles, her heart lifting.

Long ago, she had recognised and been grateful for the way that day had ended, how she had been saved from herself. She can see now that there is always an extra factor, the unknown, the wild card. A letter, an accident, a meeting with a stranger, some quirk of fate that will change the symmetry, deliver people from their expectations.

Monty shakes his head, not wanting to remember that time. But he has seen the evidence, the ninth Santa Claus, the other dimension. It is impossible for her to explain that she has seen it too, and that it was, all of it, all right.

4

AS IT WAS

ALL THE WAY TO SUMMER

On the drive home from the hospital, Annie Pile stared straight through the windscreen, her baby asleep in her arms. She held him as if he were a snake in a basket. The beaten-up light truck rattled and banged over the potholes. All around us, the landscape was steeped in deep-yellow sunlight, shining between the leaves of trees, trickling through the dry kikuyu grass at the edge of the road, nearly blinding Annie's husband, who was driving the truck.

'I had chloroform when I had my operation,' I said. I was wedged between Annie and the passenger door. My parents had hitched me a ride home from the hospital. I'd had pneumonia and then, when I got over that, the doctor said, well, she might as well have her tonsils out and have it over and done with. The hospital was a long way off – more than twenty miles – and, because my parents didn't have a car, they hadn't visited me during the three weeks I was in hospital. My mother had started out to walk one day, but the heat got to her. I was seven, going on eight, at the time.

Nobody in the truck responded, although Annie Pile's husband passed his hand over his straight chunk of hair, as if this in some way signalled acknowledgement.

'I read fourteen books while I was in hospital,' I said. 'My teacher at the hospital said I'll probably go up a class when I get back to school.'

'Make her be quiet, Kurt,' Annie said to her husband. Her hair, as plain as his but fairer, was caught in a pin above her ear, like fencing wire over corn silk. Her mottled cheeks had a raw, chapped appearance; it looked as if someone had made thumb prints on the skin beneath her eyes.

'My wife is so tired,' the man said, with a slight foreign inflection in his voice. 'From having the baby.'

I thought about stroking the baby's finger, to see whether that might make the baby happier, but then I decided it wouldn't work. Instead, I looked at the lush and surprising landscape as we came to the town. In the hedgerows, banana passionfruit hung in ripe canary-yellow clusters. I leaned my head against the cab window, my brown pigtail pressed against the glass. When I shifted, I could feel the imprint of my hair on my cheek, as if my face had been tied to a mooring rope.

We arrived at the gate of the small farm where I lived, and my parents were standing side by side, waiting to welcome me home. My mother was dressed in a pair of dungarees buttoned over a cotton blouse. She was a tiny woman, barely five feet and thin, but so energetic that she seemed to occupy more space. My father was wearing a jacket and tie. His English brogues had a reddish tint in their polished surfaces. He was a tall, lean man, with hollows in his olive cheeks, eyebrows like inverted tyre tracks and a hawkish nose. He had a suitcase beside him, as if he had just arrived home from a journey of his own.

My mother put her arms around me when I got down from the truck, examining me closely, touching my hair and cheek. 'Mattie.

Darling,' she murmured. My father inclined his head towards me, his shoulders stiff.

Kurt climbed down from the truck cab and shook hands with my father. 'A holiday,' he said. 'Nice for some.'

'A few days in Auckland.'

'Oh, well. What did you get up to?'

My father was clearly going to say, *Mind your own damn business*, but remembered just in time that he owed Kurt. 'I saw a couple of musicals.' He drew on a cigarette, holding the smoke in his mouth.

'Gilbert and Sullivan? I heard there was some on.' Kurt's lip curled.

My father released a perfect smoke ring into the still air. '*Cox and Box*. At least there's a good laugh or two in it, not all your Beethoven and high falutin' stuff. My cobber and I had a good laugh all right.'

'Very good. Good for you. We'll be off then.'

'Better have a look at this young 'un of yours. A boy, well, there's something to smile about.'

Annie continued to stare straight ahead of her as if she couldn't see any of them. Her husband looked at her as at a mystery so large and unfathomable that he was afraid of being caught in it. No, worse than that, that he was inside it but couldn't yet understand what had trapped him. He was older than Annie Pile, but in that moment he looked like a fledgling sparrow, young and vulnerable. My mother approached the truck.

'What have you called the baby, Annie?'

'Jonathan.'

'A sound name. He can shorten it if he likes. Names are

important.' She leaned into the truck to peer at the baby, putting out her hand to move the blanket aside a little. Annie snatched the cover back, so that the baby was hidden from view. My mother flushed and straightened. 'Thank you so very much for bringing Mattie home. I hope she was no bother to you, Annie.'

'She needs to hold her tongue more,' Annie said.

'I expect she was excited about coming home.' When Annie didn't reply, my mother said, 'Let me know if there's anything I can do to help.'

As the truck drove away, clouds of red dust billowing behind it, my father glanced down to check that his shoes were not getting dirty. 'Unfriendly sort of a coot. Pile, my Aunty Fanny. He's a Jerry, you know, his name's Pilsener. You know how they change their names, those fellows.'

My mother said, 'Their baby's not right. You can tell.'

'Oh, my Lord,' said my father. 'Well, too bad about that, eh.'

'We're fortunate,' my mother said, and taking my bag in one hand, she took mine with the other, leading me up the path to our two-roomed cottage with the low ceilings. After a moment's hesitation, my father followed her, drew abreast of her.

My mother said contentedly, 'You're home.' She could have been talking to either of us, but I knew her words were directed towards me. For the moment, we were together again, my mother and father and me.

We have different ways to describe things now. We would say that that baby had Down syndrome. We would say that the parents would find joy in their son regardless. But that was then. Our family was momentarily counting their blessings on a bright day beneath a Delft-blue sky, the gorse pods snapping in the heat.

My mother, as you see her in this picture, is so pleased that I am home, and if she is puzzled by my father's absences, she puts it down to the war, that restlessness men get, and lets the matter lie.

We moved north after the war. My father had served in the army as a signaller. He was an Englishman, who couldn't make sense of my mother's relatives, or they didn't understand him – you could take your pick. He dressed differently and spoke 'posh', as my relatives used to say.

'I can't stand it here,' he said when he came back, meaning the house where my mother and I lived with my grandparents. 'We need a bit of an adventure.'

'I don't want an adventure,' my mother said. 'I've got money saved for a house of our own. Why don't you just settle down and get a job like everyone else?'

My father didn't want that. He'd heard about this place up north. Some of his cobbers in the army had talked about it. And they couldn't see themselves settling down in the suburbs.

'We'll live off the land,' he told my mother, his voice passionate in its excitement. 'You'll see, this is no nine-to-five sinecure with nothing to live for except a pension.'

He followed her around for weeks, pleading with her to listen to sense. Then he went away, and when he came back my mother said she'd go. She gave him her post office book with all her savings and told him to add it to the rehab money from the army. 'Just go ahead,' she said, 'buy a place. I'll manage.'

My father loved Alderton from the beginning. My mother loathed it. A lot of people had come out there from China, remnants of the imperial army stationed around Shanghai and Tientsin, at the end of the twenties. They'd emigrated to New Zealand rather than go back to England because they had got used to warmer weather, and they hoped their lives might go on much as they had in China; they planted fruit trees and planned to live off the land. There were some disappointments in store: the living was not as cheap as they expected, and servants were almost impossible to come by. Some of the better-off settlers built big houses; others had to make do with rickety cottages, but they behaved as if they were in palaces anyway. You could step through a crooked door frame into a room full of jade treasures; an ornate silk screen would divide the kitchen from the dining room. A bunch of weather-beaten men and women, getting their hands dirty for the first time, holding parties on the wobbly wooden verandahs of their shacks in the evenings, jitterbugging and drinking gin. They were about as different as you could get from anyone else, around then, at the end of the war. Men like my father and Kurt Pile, as unalike as they were, could be as fanciful or neurotic or sad as they wanted to be, and nobody really cared. The settlers had their own world, and if you were not part of it you were invisible. My father thought he might be able to join it; my mother thought he was deluding himself. He might have been in the army and born in England, but he was from another class of people. Never an officer. They knew.

In the beginning, my parents raised poultry for quick cash, but it took them years to get established. They milked a few cows, separating the cream through their hand-rotated Alfa Laval, and fed the whey to the pigs. Eventually, they planted citrus and tamarillo orchards and filled their garden with cantaloupes, aubergines (or eggplants as they were called then) and capsicums, whatever was rare and exotic at the time, like pepinos with smooth marbled skins and smoky flesh, dragon fruit without the seeds. The trouble was, everything had to be done every day. My mother could accept that, but my father didn't always want to be there. He went away down south when he was supposed to be milking the cows or weeding in the orchard, while she found jobs to keep them going. He often spent days writing letters or just reading. He liked nostalgic books about the English countryside where, it seemed, it was always May and the larks never stopped singing.

My mother took a job for a while, cooking for one of the military wives. The woman, who was called Gloria, wore long beads, and silk scarves as headbands, the knot tied at the back so the ends drifted over her shoulders. She held her tailor-mades in an ivory cigarette-holder, or, when rations ran out, smoked fat rolled lasiandra buds that smelled like Egyptian tobacco as they burned. My mother reported for duty at seven each morning. The cookhouse was at the bottom of the garden of a big house. Gloria had a rope strung from the house to the cookhouse with a bell on my mother's end. When she pulled once, she wanted fresh tea, and when the bell rang twice, she wanted hot toast.

'If I ring three times, it's for an emergency,' Gloria told her friends with a tinkling laugh. 'I know cook will rescue me.'

My mother left for work right after she and my father milked the cows. It was supposed to be my father's job to get me up and send me to school. He simply forgot some days, except to say *stand up straight, girl*. A part of him seemed to think he was still in the army, although you wouldn't have thought so to look at him. On these mornings, his smart clothes were put away in the wardrobe; he dressed in baggy pants held up by braces. He was a smoker too, wreaths of smoke curling around his head as he read on, regardless of anything but the book propped in front of him.

He didn't know how I watched this silent life of his. I discovered what a man's body looked like when I spied him taking a bath. A curtained window divided the cottage from the lean-to containing a tin bath and a copper for heating water and washing clothes. Usually, we had baths one after another, using the same grey suds to save water. One morning, after he had been away for a time, he heated the copper and took an unexpected bath. I raised the curtain, and he was rubbing himself dry in the shadowy room, lit only by a single bulb and the reflection of the flames from the copper fire. When I was a young woman, I saw Oliver Reed in *Women in Love* and I was reminded of my father, that same pale English skin, the colour of potato flesh. He was long and spindly, his chest slightly concave, and yet in the flickering light I found him mysterious and oddly beautiful.

I learned that my father had an army friend called Frank whom he often used to ring up after my mother left for work.

'Tolls please,' he would say nervously after he had rung the exchange. And then, after a pause, 'I want to make a collect call.' He would give the operator a number for down south. 'Eight A, Hunterville.' I can still hear him say it. Short long in Morse code. After a period of negotiation with someone at the other end, punctuated by silences, I would hear his voice, joyful and light, 'Frank, my old mate, how *are* you? Just thought I'd ring for a natter.'

At which point, he would suddenly check to see where I was. 'Hold on a tick, old boy,' he'd say to the person on the other end, looking at me. 'Shouldn't you have gone to school?' Eventually, I got bored with these mornings of idleness and started getting dressed and walking to school on my own, although I was often so late that one of the teachers phoned home and, by chance, caught my mother.

'Why?' she asked my father when she had put the phone down. 'Why can't you do what you say you will?'

'Why do you nag?' His voice had that pleading sound again.

'How can I live with a man who calls me a nag? Why don't you just say shrew and be done with it?'

'Shrew,' he said, testing the word on his tongue and laughing. She didn't laugh with him.

Then she said, 'Look, I know it's hard coming back from the war. I know things happened that I can't understand. Why don't we just have a rest today and we'll do the chores together?'

'What about your job?'

'Oh, that,' she said airily. 'I pulled the bell off the string yesterday and dropped it in the river.'

'You did what? Is this a joke?'

'Not at all.'

'What will they think of us?' He put his hand to his forehead.

'I've got no idea,' she said and laughed. 'They asked for something special for afternoon tea the other day, something sweet and light, chocolate but Oriental, something with a little ginger in it. "All of those things in one dish?" I said. "Well, cook, if you could rattle something up we'll leave it to you," said Madam Gloria. So I took everything I could find in the kitchen and mixed it all up together and iced it and left it to cool, and, when it looked right, I cut it into pieces and served it when the guests came. As I was pouring tea, they were all saying things like, isn't this delicious, and where did you find the recipe, and is this the new cook's doing? So then she said, "Oh, the woman's very good at taking instructions, she can follow a recipe, I'll give her that."'

'You're making this up.' My father was horrified and laughing all at once.

'No, I'm not. So then she said, "I'll get cook to write it down for you," without giving me so much as a look. All right, I thought, all right. And I went back down the path and waited for the bell to ring, and when it did I pulled it so hard it came off in my hand. So I threw it away.'

'In the river?'

'Yes.'

'Then did you go?' I could see he was working out whether this situation could be redeemed.

'No. I waited for her to turn up, trotting down the path in her tatty old silk dress, looking hot and bothered, and she said, "Where's the tea?" and I told her what I thought about her job. I said, "It's much harder to find a cook than to keep one," and I handed her my apron. "You might need this," I said.'

My father looked at her as if he'd seen her for the first time.

'My God,' he said, 'you're a damn fine woman.' He was laughing so hard he could hardly stop. 'We can sell a few more eggs.'

'They'll probably think I poisoned them,' my mother said darkly.

She bought nuts and spices and made the recipe for my father and me. She continued to make it every Christmas time and at birthdays, her wicked ginger treat.

*

One winter, my father's friend Frank came to stay, not exactly with us, although he took his meals at our house. Frank was a much younger man than my father. He had full fresh cheeks and a raspberry-coloured mouth and thick eyelashes. In later life he would turn plump. You could see it then in the softness under his chin. His jacket exuded a grassy smell mixed with cigarette smoke, and bananas, his favourite food. He spent his first few nights at the Homestead, a kind of planters' hotel in the village, with ramshackle accommodation and the only bar in twenty miles. You had to be a house guest to use it. He bought several rounds of gin and tonics for my father as they sat on the verandah and looked down the shimmering stand of gum trees in the valley beyond.

'My cobber bought me a couple of drinks,' my father said, the first night after Frank came north. He giggled and sang. My cobber. These lapses into the vernacular, his way of saying he was a bloke's bloke, sat uneasily inside his English voice, and it irritated my mother. As the ritual at the Homestead persisted over a week or two, it became more than the way he talked that annoyed her, it was something else I didn't understand. She became increasingly silent.

'His money'll run out,' she said.

'He's got a job,' my father said, with triumph.

'Picking lemons?'

'Yes.'

'Maybe you could get one too.'

My father looked alarmed. 'My back would never stand it,' he said.

'Well, then, perhaps I could get a job picking,' she said.

'You'd never reach above the bottom branches,' my father said, but he looked at her with renewed interest.

Frank came to dinner one evening soon after this. He'd moved into a packing shed on a neighbouring orchard, sleeping on a camp stretcher my father had found him. The gin and tonics had run out.

The room in which we ate was narrow, not more than six feet across by about fifteen long, a bench at one end and a coal range on one wall, our gate-legged table, oval when it was folded out, creating a barrier between the kitchen and the other end of the room, where a wooden-backed sofa stood. Seeing it like this, it is not a beautiful room, ugly in fact, its cream walls stained with smoke, red congoleum on the floor. But consider our table, laid with an Irish-linen cloth, heavy silver cutlery, the knives bone-handled, the plates willow pattern. This was my mother's dowry, remnants of another life. The men wore their jackets with ties, my mother a short-sleeved satin sheath dress, in wide horizontal navy-blue and scarlet stripes, with a scooped neckline. I wore a cotton print dress sprinkled with mauve flowers, a gift from my grandmother; it had a Peter Pan collar and short puffed sleeves that ended in bands above my elbows. We were eating the last of the broiler chicken, which my mother had cooked in a slow casserole. But they drank wine, which Frank had brought, out of crystal glasses. Dally plonk, my father said, grinning. Sly grog, my mother retorted, looking at Frank from the corner of her eye.

'I've come north,' Frank said, obviously for her benefit, as he must have already said this to my father, 'because I'm thinking about what to do now the war's over. I don't really want to be a farmer for the rest of my life. My family just took it for granted I'd settle back in Hunterville. But, you know, once you've been away and seen a bit of the world, you can't just accept everything the way it was before.'

'So, you just up and left?' asked my mother.

He shrugged, opening his hands expressively, a surprising gesture, as if to explain how his time in Europe had altered him. 'The cows are dry. It seemed like a good time to get away and sort things out and make a bit of extra money at the same time.'

'You've got your rehab surely?' This was a sore point with my mother. The rehabilitation money for the men who served in the war had got eaten up in this place when it might have gone into something more to her liking.

'I needed someone to talk to,' said Frank, looking at my father. 'Someone who understood. I might go to university, one of the agricultural colleges, something like that.'

'Good idea,' my father said. 'While you're not tied down.' And I thought he looked wistful.

'Perhaps you wouldn't be too tied down to find something for the pot tomorrow,' my mother said. She was serving up pancakes drizzled with golden syrup for dessert.

'Kill another chook,' said my father.

'We've only got four left. Don't you want eggs for breakfast?'

My father looked alarmed.

'I'll pay some board next week,' Frank said.

'But you're not boarding with us,' my mother said. 'You're a guest.'

'Well, if you don't mind me coming over in the evenings, perhaps I could pay for my meals, a regular arrangement.'

'Capital,' said my father. I could see this conversation had been rehearsed.

My mother was a sensible woman. She knew that, if he paid her on a regular basis, she could make it stretch further than my father imagined. 'Ten shillings a week.'

My father looked taken aback and was clearly going to argue for less when she quelled him with a look so sharp it could have cut glass.

'First instalment next Friday all right then?' Frank said.

When they had finished dinner, my father said, 'I'll walk Frank home.'

'Surely he can find his own way now?'

'It's a nice night for a couple of fellas to have a walk and a smoke.'

And so it was, one of those starry nights in the north when, even in winter, it's mild and the air holds the tang of citrus leaves and ripe lemons, and there is a great silence over the shallow hills and valleys. I saw their cigarettes glowing in the dark as they walked off down the road.

This arrangement was all very well, but Friday was still some days away, and so the paying guest had to be fed.

In the morning, my father said to me, 'We're going hunting, Mattie. Get your shoes on.' He'd hardly spoken to me in weeks, not since Frank came. It was not an unfriendly silence, but he thought I should be a girl who sang and danced around. When he did notice me, he wanted to teach me songs, but I was not a singer and a dancer, I was a watcher.

The invitation to go shooting was really a command. We set off across the paddocks, him carrying a shotgun, me tagging along behind. It was still quite early in the morning, the spider webs spotted with dew, light fragmenting off them as the sun rose.

'I miss the Old Dart,' my father said suddenly, as I trailed along. 'You wouldn't imagine it, Mattie, all the people, the streets full of all sorts of them. Merchant bankers, barrow boys, tradesmen, butchers – my goodness, so much meat – and birds in cages hanging in the doorways of houses. There're booksellers, artists, writers . . . I'm reading a book called *The Purple Plain* right now – it's by a man called Bates. Perhaps you're too young to be reading stuff like this, you'll have to ask your mother. Music halls, dancers, poets – *oh, my God, oh, to be in England now.*'

'What's wrong with here?'

'Nothing, dammit, nothing. Don't you listen to a word I say?'

'Well, if there's nothing wrong with here, why do you want to be in England now?'

'It's a line of a poem,' he said almost sullenly. 'And the nothing, that's what's wrong – the nothing of everything. The way people look at you because there's nothing else to look at.'

'Who looks at you?' I mentally scanned my more recent forays into adult territory, trying to work out whether the watcher had been watched.

'Nobody. Here, make yourself useful, learn to hold a gun at the very least.' And he put the rifle in my hands and showed me how to hold it up to my shoulder, although the weight of it was almost too much for me to support. 'Look, we're out to get a pheasant or two for dinner.'

The sun was rising high, and in the golden glow of grass and light I saw something move and my finger squeezed the trigger. A feathered creature rose straight up from the ground and fell back. It was a soft brown hen pheasant. All of a sudden, I was a huntress and a poacher.

Sour fright filled my mouth. I don't have much of a taste for death.

My mother plucked and gutted the two pheasants that we took home (my father shot the second one), her fingers carefully searching for shotgun pellets. She cooked them with rare brilliance, using some of the leftover wine from Frank's visit, and told my father to go out and shoot some more.

Like Frank, my mother got work in the orchards, climbing ladders and picking oranges and lemons with sharp steady snaps of her secateurs. She earned one shilling and sixpence for every case, and she filled them at twice the rate Frank did. She and Frank began to show signs of a camaraderie that hadn't been there before, although the banter was mostly of her making. 'And how many boxes did you fill today?' she would begin. 'Ten, oh my, but then I noticed you picked the lower branches first.' My mother, being small and light and fast, cleaned out the tops of the trees but it was harder work. After a while the orchardists began to pay her a bonus of sixpence a box. By and large it was my mother who paid the bills, while my father worked on our land. His face brightened on the days when she was free to work alongside him.

Sometime around the middle of last century, the climate began to change. I suppose it did everywhere, but the people in Alderton saw it as a sign that their luck had run out. The summers became drier, and droughts set in: in one year, whole orchards wilted and died. At a price, a trucking firm would deliver water, but, without natural rainfall, the settlers were at a loss. They ran hoses from taps, but as most of them relied on water stored in tanks from the winter rains, this soon disappeared, and they had only river water to drink. You could see them toiling up and down the banks of the creeks and river tributaries that meandered through their properties, carrying buckets and pots. Sometimes they just sat among the long grass and aromatic pennyroyal near the waterways, looking lost. We didn't come here for this, you could hear them saying, if not aloud, in their hearts. A few packed up and left.

Others installed pumps, or built reservoirs in their backyards that filled with brackish dirty water, unfit for drinking but temporarily they provided water for the gardens. My father and Frank built a reservoir behind our house: it needed the two of them to pour the concrete. Frank had thick, wide shoulders that he bared to the sun. His fair skin burned easily, so that for days he walked around looking raw and stripped, but he kept trudging steadily to and fro between the mounds of cement and sand. He'd been up north a couple of years by this stage. There didn't seem any pretence that he would go back south. He was still a big man, but he'd got harder, the edges of his flesh more crisply defined. My father took many breaks, stopping to smoke in the shade of the gum trees, torrents of coughing hurtling out of his lungs. My mother, observing the slow progress of the reservoir, picked up a shovel and carried concrete too, straining against its weight.

This summer held little for me. I had turned ten, and my friend Jocelyn had gone away for the long holiday. Sometimes in the holidays, I would go south on the train to stay with my aunt, but for one reason or another I couldn't go that year. One afternoon, I stood under a gum tree with my father, wishing the day would end because then it would be tomorrow and I could start doing nothing all over again, and it might turn out better than today. Frank saw my father watching him and came over.

'There must be easier ways than this to find water,' he said.

'Tell me,' my father said, wearily, leaning on his shovel.

He hadn't shaved for days, and his face looked gaunt and grey, the worse for the cloudy film of cement.

'There was an old codger down Hunterville way used to be able to divine water; you know, find it in the ground to show where to sink a well.' Reaching out, he pulled a slim branch from a young gum tree, choosing one with a forked stem. He took out his pocket knife and started whittling a three-pronged Y-shaped twig.

'See,' Frank explained, 'the old joker turns the stick with the long piece pointing upwards and he holds the sides, one in each hand.' He demonstrated how to hold it, curling his fingers right around the two prongs, his thumbs pointing away at either side. 'Then he walks along, and when he comes to the place where there's water, down where you can't see, the stick begins to turn, pointing out where the water is.'

'Just like that?'

'Well, I saw what he did a couple of times when I was a kid. He's gone now, long dead that old joker.' He threw the stick aside. 'I tried and tried but I never could make it turn. Wood's wood.'

'I've heard of that, now I come to think of it,' my father said. 'A dowser.' He picked up the stick and, holding it the way Frank had shown him, began walking through the paddock.

'You have to *think* water. Go on mate, you've got to concentrate – you think water, water.'

'Jesus, that's all I think of.' My father was going to throw the stick aside in disgust, but my mother had just come down the paddock and she wanted to try too.

'Go for it,' Frank said, 'you could make money out of it, a trick like that. Not that the old joker ever had much – probably spent it all on the boozer. He was a funny old bandicoot.'

My mother was solemnly pacing along, holding the stick upwards. 'How will I know?' she called out.

'They reckon you know, that you can't stop the thing once it starts. Reckon it's got a mind all of its own.'

'Ah,' she said after a while, 'I don't believe all that sort of baloney. It would have been a trick you saw.'

'There mightn't be any water under this piece of dirt,' Frank said, not unreasonably. 'Maybe some people who've got the knack can find water, but only if there's water there to start with.' He sounded huffy, as if my mother had called him a liar.

Nobody had offered the stick to me. When they started work again, I picked it up, held it in my hands the way the others had done and walked slowly past the hen house and along the hedge line.

At first nothing happened. Then something began to stir. Like some live creature struggling to get out of my hands. I thought *water water*, as if I were thirsty, and the twig curled down towards the earth. It's almost impossible to describe what something as strong as this feels like in your hands: something bucking, like riding horses bareback, stronger than the kick of a gun. I think now it was more like a sexual tension, not something children are supposed to have. By the time I was grown and married, this ability to locate underground springs had all but vanished. I looked up and saw Frank, gone to take a pee, watching me behind veiled eyes.

I wanted to say, *It's a secret*, but I could tell that it wasn't going to stay one, and besides, what was I doing, watching him about his private business?

'I can do it,' I said, returning to my parents. 'I can make the twig bend.'

'I reckon she's a little witch,' said Frank, who had rejoined the group.

'You're fibbing, Mattie.' My mother looked furious.

'No, I'm not,' I replied hotly, wanting to prove myself now.

'Show us,' my father said.

'Don't encourage her,' my mother said. But, egged on by my father and Frank, I began to show them how easy it was. My mother watched for a moment and then turned away, as if I were behaving badly.

When the reservoir was finished, a sudden storm erupted, a timely opening of the skies that caused flash floods and slips on the dry land, and then the summer went back to being the same as before: bone-dry, sere heat, blindingly bright. Frogs gathered in dozens at the freshly filled reservoir, sheltering from the relentless sun. I put on my bathing suit and swam with them, allowing them to cling to my legs with their tiny pulpy hands. I let them use me as a floating log, a dozen or more sitting on me while I floated on the scummy surface of the water.

'Funny kid,' Frank said to my mother, thinking I couldn't hear him.

'You just leave her alone. Leave my kid out of it,' my mother said.

'Out of what?' Frank said lazily.

'Just stick to what you're good at, whatever that is,' my mother snapped, turning on him, as if her careful mask had slipped away. I remember that his face was flushed that evening, in a way it often was of late. He had made other friends at the village, and he didn't eat at our place every night, hadn't done for a long time, although he was always there at the weekend when he couldn't find someone to gain him entrance to the Homestead bar.

There was, if I look at this now, a certain raffish charm about the way we lived. In our own way, we were eccentric settlers too, depending on fruit and produce and self-sustainment. A delicate father with a taste for the good life. The devoted friend. The child all but abandoned to the natural world. The nurturing but over-burdened mother. But then, in the same way, there is the question of my mother's life.

There was a day when I went looking for her. I had come in from visiting Jocelyn. Jocelyn, the same age as me, was a head taller and confident in everything she did. She always put her hand up in class, even when she didn't know the answers, as if by a bright and engaging manner she could convince those around her, and the teachers in particular, that she was clever. I often knew the answers when she failed to provide them, but I preferred to write them down, so that, puzzlingly to her, I often succeeded by examination in those subjects at which she had appeared to shine in class.

There was, between our mothers, a wary kind of friendship. Jocelyn's mother, Viv, who had once been a school teacher, prided herself on knowing everyone.

'I'm not going to let all that gung-ho nonsense get in the way of things,' she said, referring to the China hands. She was a meaty woman, who wore her hair rolled up at the bottom, pinned at the sides with clips. 'I like making myself useful to people.' Ingratiating, my father said unkindly, but my mother was happy to have another woman to talk to now and then, and pleased there was some place I could visit. The settlers' children kept to themselves.

If my mother was careful to keep a slight distance between herself and Viv, it was possibly because she detected a willingness to pass on information about others. Or, you could say, Viv was a gossip. On a day when I went looking for my mother, Viv had issued an invitation for me to go swimming with Jocelyn. I called out to my mother several times. I was sure she wasn't far away because a pot was simmering quietly on the stove. Yet there was something abandoned about the place that made me panic when she didn't answer. I rushed outside, calling and calling again.

She must have been there all the time because suddenly, as if from nowhere, she said, 'Yes, what is it?'

She was standing among the pale shapes of the blue gum trees, quite still. Absorbed into them, like a branch, or a group of leaves suspended in the motionless air.

When I went towards her, she was smiling, pleased, I think, that she had so easily vanished from view. I felt afraid and alone, as if she had been spirited away. But she came towards me, calling cheerfully for me to take a billy of eggs from her as if nothing had happened.

This is not to suggest that my mother was other than a vital presence in our household, or that she was wilfully disappearing before our eyes. It was just that she had developed a certain aloofness, especially towards the men in her household. Not towards me, not as a rule. She and I had dialogues of our own, role-playing the characters on the radio serials. 'You can pretend I'm Delia,' she would say, and start vamping among the tamarillos. The fruit had drum-smooth red skin, the insides held black seeds and rouge-coloured flesh and, to me, a tainted, bitter taste. She clipped and slid the fruit, clipped and slid it, into a bulging pouched apron. 'You can kiss me if you're quick, but nobody must know, least of all your wife,' she'd say, in a la di da voice.

'My wife no longer cares who I kiss,' I'd say.

'Ah yes, but she does, that's half the pleasure,' my mother would breathe. 'We have our little secrets.'

'How about we might sail away in a boat together,' I might say.

She would snort. 'Is that the best you can do?' The question was meant for me, not the character. When we held these sultry improbable conversations, you'd swear, catching a glimpse of her hard at work in the orchards, that she were a man, with her overalls and close-cropped hair. I think now that my mother was in despair and that being still, being invisible, was her way of hiding it from me.

One night, when Frank wasn't there, after I was supposed to have gone to bed, I got up and found them, my mother and my father, dancing cheek to cheek on the ugly congoleum floor. The radio was playing 'Smoke Gets in Your Eyes' and, when we got to the bit about your heart being on fire, I saw that my mother was crying.

I crept away without being seen. I could never tell how things would be between them.

Frank came around and said that a military chap, a Wing Commander Thorne, had heard that I could divine water and, as he was about to put down a well, could I come over and check it out. My mother was out at the time. I remember my father looking doubtful.

'He'll pay,' said Frank.

'An air force wallah, eh? Must be one of the new lot. You'd better put on some tidy clothes,' my father said, warming to the idea. I could see he was pleased to be asked. Like the shooting expedition, he didn't ask me whether I wanted to go or not.

'Suppose Mattie can't do it?' my father said, as we walked down the broad dusty avenues towards Hubert Thorne's house.

'She will,' Frank said confidently. 'You can tell she's a natural.'

'But we don't know if she really found water. We didn't put a well down.' (As it happened, my father had wanted to, and Frank had urged him and my mother to throw caution to the winds and sink a bore, but on this one matter my mother stood absolutely firm. I think part of her was afraid that I might lose my new-found aura of magic.)

'I can tell you,' said Frank, 'what that girl does wouldn't happen unless there was water there at the end of the stick.'

Quite a crowd had gathered round. All the wing commander's family was there, including Maisie, who went to St Cuthbert's, and her brother Cecil, who was at King's in Auckland, and some of the neighbours, along with the well driller and a man who worked for him. Wing Commander Thorne had one languid eye and one that looked at you straight. That lazy eye didn't hide the impatience of his manner.

The well driller had already put down a test bore and not struck water. 'If he puts down another dud, I won't be able to carry on. Too costly. Can she do it or not?' he demanded.

The well driller was looking surly. 'I've got it worked out now,' he said to my father. He could tell by his calculations from the river flow, beyond the rise, which way the water would go. You didn't always get it right first time. He looked at me with a mixture of contempt and misgiving. I could tell how I worried him, a kid in a tartan skirt with straps over the shoulders of her white blouse.

'She can do it,' my father said in a blithe way.

I felt an urgent sense of excitement, as if I were about to throw off my inhibitions and become a performer after all.

I was offered a twig that someone had pulled from a tree, but I turned it down, preferring to choose one of my own. I took my time getting it ready, holding it out and measuring it with my eye, although that wasn't really necessary. I knew when I could get a twig to work. All the same, I was nervous. It was one thing to feel that wild thing in my hand, but I didn't know any more than my father whether there would be water below. The twig turning was something that happened to me, rather than because I made it happen.

I walked around with an earnest expression, clasping the twig and pacing slowly about. At first nothing happened. I heard Maisie and Cecil start to giggle. But I thought *water* and then the twig bent sideways, away from me, so that I had to follow where it was leading. At a certain point, the twig pulled inexorably down towards the earth.

Someone started to clap, probably Frank, but others joined in. I walked left to right and right to left, and the twig pulled only at the one place – five yards from where the well driller had reckoned on putting the well down.

'I don't reckon it's there,' he said. 'You don't know if this kid's a fake.'

'It always turns in the same place,' said Frank.

'Put a blindfold on her,' the man said.

'Excellent idea,' said the wing commander. He spoke to my father. 'How about it, old chap? Will you tie your handkerchief around the lass's eyes?'

A flicker of concern passed over my father's face, as if he realised that things had gone far enough. 'It's all right,' I said, 'you can do it.' Because by now I knew that whatever force was pulling the twig, it would happen anyway.

And it did.

They sank the bore in the place I showed them. We waited around for a while as the well driller began his work, not expecting anything to happen soon. But the water was near the surface, buckets of beautiful clear water gushing out in a steady stream. Wing Commander Thorne gave my father five pounds for his trouble in bringing me over. 'Buy the little lass a new dress,' he said, which was an expression, more than a reflection on what I was wearing. Cecil and Maisie took up a game of croquet they'd been playing before I came, as if nothing unusual had occurred.

When my mother heard about it, she said, 'You won't be doing that again.' She was in a towering white-lipped rage and didn't speak to my father for days. Frank was banned for nearly a fortnight.

'She's not a circus kid,' she said later when she'd recovered.

'I know,' my father said, looking embarrassed. 'But for that much money.' Already there had been several offers for my services. He glanced sideways at me. 'She could go away to school.'

'No,' said my mother so fiercely that my father and I jumped. 'No, Mattie stays here. With me.'

Viv visited my mother unexpectedly one day. She had come with a special request. Just as a favour to her, could I look for water down at the Piles' place. Annie and Kurt, the ones who had the baby that was different.

My mother said, 'She doesn't do it for anyone.'

'Well,' Viv said, 'Annie is in a bad way. That place is dried right up, and Kurt's so busy looking after her and the child, I don't know what's to become of them. My husband bought them a tank of water because things were so dry they couldn't so much as make a cup of tea. But we can't afford to be doing that all the time. Anyway, Annie just takes baths – it's as if she doesn't know how to save water, or anything, these days. It wouldn't be so bad if she washed a few clothes now and then. The thing is, Kurt got all the pipes and everything a few years back, but they never decided where to put the bore down.'

'We owe them a favour,' my father said.

'Well.' My mother looked undecided. 'If Mattie agrees. If we kept it to ourselves.'

'Of course,' Viv said.

'No money changes hands.'

My father looked disappointed, but seeing he was the one wanting to be helpful, he nodded in agreement.

Things were just as bad at the Piles' house as Viv had described them. She led us into the house before Kurt had time to stop her. Perhaps Viv really did want my father to understand the situation, thought it best to let him know. Annie was surrounded by an indescribable chaos of unwashed clothing and dirty dishes. The forlorn baby, Jonathan, had grown into an unsteady child, with a filthy napkin falling from his waist. The beds were not just unmade; the mattresses were soiled and full of holes. The only thing of quality was a piano, a rosewood baby grand that shone with a strange wild lustre in the squalor of the house. Viv told us Kurt played in the evenings; depending on which way the wind was blowing, she heard the music spilling through the blue gums that divided their boundary lines. (No, this is fanciful; Viv didn't speak like this, but it's how I've come to hear the story of that music, which was often spoken of in the district.) Annie was expecting another child. She appeared not to recognise me, and although she followed us out when we went to look for water, she wandered back inside almost straight away, looking distracted. Viv, Kurt and my father were my only audience.

Not that I found anything. I don't know whether there was water there or not, but while I walked around the place, the twig felt dead in my hands, as lifeless and still as if it were all a silly game. Like Delia and Dr Paul. I wasn't a miracle child after all.

Word got around of course. My self-importance ebbed away. At school, people fell silent in my presence, as if I were some sort of charlatan to be avoided at all costs. After I'd moved away from a group, I'd hear them starting to talk again. I stopped being Jocelyn's friend, and she had a birthday party to which I was not invited. I stayed home and watched the settlers' daughters walking to the party carrying gifts. After the birthday, Jocelyn started talking to me again and I was invited over as if nothing had happened, but I didn't go.

Frank said I needed a manager and he could have told my parents the conditions weren't right at that place. If he'd been there, he'd have advised against me going on a tom-fool errand like that.

Annie Pile's health got worse. Her sister, Petal, came from down south to stay for a while. Early one morning, Viv arrived at our house and introduced Petal.

'I was the baby of the family,' Petal said self-deprecatingly. 'They'd kind of run out of names.' There were eleven siblings: Annie was number eight, three above Petal, who was a bright-eyed woman in her late twenties. Short, not unshapely, in a heavy-breasted, big-beamed way, she was so different from Annie that it was hard to think of them as related. She had lovely neat ankles beneath her flowered cotton skirt. It was Viv, of course, who had sent for Petal, because somebody had to do something about Annie. Viv knew that Petal was a nurse. She was a single woman, good at her work; the hospital where she worked had agreed to take her back when she'd finished looking after her sister.

The purpose of this second visit from Viv soon emerged. Petal needed someone to help clean up the Piles' place – it was beyond her on her own, what with having to look after Annie and Jonathan at the same time. With the new baby due any day, she was working against the clock. Naturally, she would pay my mother.

'I don't do cleaning work,' my mother said. I could see her glaring at Viv, as if to say, why can't you do it? Surely this was charity again, of the worst kind.

'I told Petal you'd done some housekeeping,' Viv said, apologetically.

My mother began to shape her refusal, then changed her mind. I guess she was thinking, as my father had before, that the Piles had helped out once. And there was the matter of the well that I had failed to deliver. Perhaps there was something, too, about Petal's open, friendly smile that my mother liked. She said she'd be right over.

Here is another dinner party. My mother and father and Frank and Petal and me. My mother has cooked chicken in cider, with green capsicums and apples. She has made the cider herself. There is a dessert to follow, light sponge floating on lemon cream.

Kurt has been invited to the meal but has chosen to stay home and play his lonely broken chords of Beethoven, spilling them on the fragrant night air of Alderton City. Annie has gone away, probably for good. Their children, Jonathan and a new and wholesome baby called Derek, are being taken care of by another of the sisters, who will end up keeping them. Soon Kurt will move to Auckland, where he and his wife and children will live under different roofs, but at least they will see each other from time to time, and then, slowly, less and less. My mother will know about all this because Petal will tell her when they meet, which will be often in the years ahead.

Something has been decided before this meal takes place. I don't know exactly who decided, but an event is all set to happen. Frank and Petal are going away to get married. This dinner is their farewell. At the end of it, my father proposes a toast.

'To Frank and Petal, good health.' His voice quavers and, this time, it is he who has the burnish of tears in his eyes.

After Frank and Petal had gone, my mother fell ill for many months. She'd had boils, a sign of overwork and distress and perhaps something lacking in her diet. One erupted on the back of her head and turned into a carbuncle, a boil with several heads. She walked up and down all night, taking my father's cigarettes and smoking incessantly. Sometimes she tried to lie down, but that was worse than standing, keeping her swollen, poisoned head upright. My father called the doctor, a man known for strong drink and occasional incoherence. He wiped his eyes with the back of his hand as if he didn't believe what he saw, then reached inside his bag and took out a scalpel. Hold still, he told her, and lanced the thing open.

It got worse instead of better. By the time Viv came around and arranged for her to go to hospital, the thing had thirteen heads, each like living putrid creatures with existences of their own. My mother nearly died in the hospital. I went south to live with my aunt for a while. It was not unlike Annie Pile's situation, only my mother did recover. In time, I went back home, changed and less wayward.

Frank and Petal visited as often as they could. They had four children in quick succession, and there were times when they couldn't get away from the farm. Frank bought out the farm next door to his family home in Hunterville, and developed a big herd. Later, my parents shifted away from the north and lived closer to them, although that was a matter of chance rather than design. Sometimes they all went away for their holidays together.

There was a particular day I remember, not long before I met my husband. I was working as an advertising copywriter for the radio station in the town where we now lived. There was a lake near our house. My father had a row boat that I used to mess around in some weekends. I had gone on liking the outdoors, even though my head was absorbed with men. I had long since stopped divining water, as if a certain energy in me had been subverted.

I didn't know that Frank and Petal had come for a visit. I had worked overtime at the station and, afterwards, I cycled straight to the lake, thinking that I would row out a little way, or perhaps along the shoreline. But when I got to the lake, I found that the boat was already in use. My father was rowing Frank vigorously out away from the shore.

It was a calm, golden afternoon, willows trailing in the lake, small fish leaping. There was a tart smell of autumn in the air.

I watched the boat and saw my father rest on the oars in a patch of sunlight. He and Frank exchanged some banter. My father's face wore a look of such sweet peace that it has stayed with me forever.

Late that afternoon, when everyone had returned to the house, they got me to take their photograph together on Frank's camera. My mother doesn't look like her old farm self; she has changed and become suburban, in a way she had wanted to be all those years before. She wears a knee-length tweed skirt, a cream Viyella blouse, a jumper and a scarf fixed with a brooch my father gave her one birthday – a little pearl on a spiralling gold wire – and sensible, comfortable shoes. Her hair has grown longer to cover an appalling scar. Petal wears an acrylic powder-blue pantsuit with beige ankle socks and black slip-ons. The men wear jackets, but their shirts are open at the throat. This is more or less how they will go on looking for another thirty or so years, all of them growing stouter except for my father, who will grow thinner and fade away first.

There they are, the four of them: my mother and father and Frank and Petal.

SILVER-TONGUED

A few years ago, I met a young man who, had I been a younger woman, I might have considered to be romantically inclined towards me. As it was, he was looking for someone to listen to his troubles. He chose me because I had told him a dramatic story in a bar in Banff, about a night when I raced across a darkened countryside in a state of blind panic, totally lost in a place I knew well. Looking for and continually missing the road that would have led me to the side of a woman I loved, who was dying. Although this happened on the other side of the world from Canada, I think he was struck by the immediacy of the way I told the story.

'You tell this as if it happened quite recently,' he said.

'Well, it's ten days ago now.'

'Ten days.' He looked as if he had been stung, as if something had brushed past that was too close for comfort – all the intimations of mortality that people entertain when they are in some sort of difficulties of their own. I was with a group of writers who had just swum under the stars at an elegant resort spa, where the sudden presence of an uninhibited group was clearly viewed by the other bathers as an intrusion. We were hot and rosy and flushed with steam and the conversations that happen when new friendships are developing. Let's have a drink, we all said to each other, but by the time we found a bar open we'd all gone off the idea and drank coffee instead, knowing we would keep ourselves awake, but needing to be alert because we had so many revelations to make to each other. Much later in the evening, the young man and I walked back to where we were staying, arm in arm in the starlight, peeling away from the others in the group. He was dark with stealthy fingers that rested on my inner arm. We had been told to watch out for rutting elks that might charge us if they were disturbed. Elks have rights over humans in Banff. They walk down the middle of the streets while motorists wait, and they walk through gardens and backyards.

The previous week, I had been on another tour, back home in New Zealand. In case this sounds like coincidence, I should say that this is how writers earn much of their keep: they go from one place to another, talking about their work to whoever will listen, while booksellers stand behind a little table and exhort the audience to buy books. It's not as bad as it sounds. Some of the best days of my life have been spent in halls and libraries and rooms set aside in old country pubs, talking to people who love books the way I do. I would go even if it were not a necessity, although, that once, I would rather have just sat with my aunt. I had been sent a message that she was ill and didn't have long to live.

This was no ordinary aunt, if such a person exists. I mean, she wasn't someone else's mother – she had no children of her own – and I've often thought of her as another mother of my own. That's what I would call her when I spoke at her funeral. Of course, I felt the pull of needing to be in two places at once. But I had a new book out and I'd promised my publishers I would go on this tour. And there was a real coincidence, one of those elements of random chance that seem so significant they are like an omen, an instruction in themselves. The tour was of the Waikato, where Flo had lived for most of her life, and where I, from time to time, had lived too. That green heart of dairy country, full of pastel-coloured cows with contemplative eyes. All the venues, except one at the end, were within driving distance of the cottage hospital where my aunt was being nursed. It had been arranged that I would drive a rented car from one place to another, before flying on to the last town. There was a serendipity about all of this, and the idea of calling off the tour didn't really arise.

I began with a visit to the hospital. As I arrived, I heard Flo's voice, frail and yet fierce, echoing down the corridor. She cried, *Come and get me, come and get me* in an incessant high drone. Her cloudy eyes didn't recognise me straight away, although there was a hint of their old blackness beneath the cataracts.

When she did, she said, more calmly, 'You've come for me then.'

'I've come to see you.'

'Just to see me?'

'Hush,' I said, 'it'll be all right. I love you.'

She turned her head the other way. 'Love. Don't talk to me about love,' she said.

I thought then that I had always just been coming and going in my aunt's life; I was never permanent. Yet, for as long as I could remember, she had been waiting for me. But at least I came back, whenever I could. In those last days before she died, she would wake with a start from bouts of laboured breathing, and I would say 'I'm here.'

'I'm here,' she would mimic, and yet there was something easier about her breathing every time she realised I really was there beside her.

On that first evening, the night nurse said she needed morphine. 'Personally, I think the pain relief that's been offered her is too light,' she said. Every time we tried to turn Flo, she screamed: *Please please leave me leave me please leave me.*

'What can we do about it?' I asked the nurse. I liked this young woman; she was very small and neat in her movements, almost as if she were a dancer, which I later learned she had trained to be until her ankles lost their shape.

'Get a doctor,' she said. 'You're the next of kin, if you say she needs a doctor, we can call one.'

'Do it,' I said.

The doctor, a young Indian man, took one look and then drew me outside and into the corridor. 'As much as she needs,' he said, 'as much as it takes. But you must tell her.'

I went in and sat beside her and said, 'Flo, can you hear me? The doctor says morphine.'

Her eyes widened. 'Morphine?' she breathed, as if being offered a love potion. She must have known its power: she had nursed more than one patient towards their last seductive inhalation.

Only this morphine was neither inhaled nor injected but rather drops placed on her tongue. 'Bitter,' said Flo. It reminded me of one of her sayings. 'Life's had a few bitter pills, but you get by.' She slept for a while. When she woke, the morphine had begun to wear off and it was time for her to be turned again.

Please. No, not that.

And then I understood: it was at the height of each turn, the moment before her body pivoted down, that she began to scream and her free arm to flap wildly. When I caught it in my own, it was like a cold old fish flipper. 'You're afraid of falling, aren't you?' I said.

And she agreed that, yes, she was and that, if I held her hand, she wouldn't fall. It was much the same as walking over a height: that sense of relinquishing control, fear of abandonment. I suffer from that too.

I said to the nurse, who was called Joy, 'How long do you think this will take? I mean, I don't want to see her go on suffering like this.'

Joy gave me a careful, serious scrutiny. 'Do you mean,' she said eventually, 'do people go on with their lives, or keep vigils like our grandmothers did?'

'Yes, something like that. I want to be here when she needs me.'

'I think you're doing the best you can,' she said. 'I can't tell you when it will happen exactly. Death's no flash in the pan for the old. It needs a lead-up, a preparation time that says it's done when it's ready, not when it's convenient.'

'Like baking?'

'I guess that's a way of looking at it.'

'That's Flo,' I said, 'she was a terrific cook. You should have tried her orange loaf.'

I saw Joy look at my aunt in a new, less clinical way, as if she could see beyond the helpless creature she had become to someone younger, more vital – a glimpse perhaps of the person I still saw.

'You should get some rest and do whatever it is you have to do,' she said.

Early the next morning, as dawn was breaking, I heard Flo again before I saw her, only this time she was singing. *Look for the silver lining / Whene'er a cloud appears in the blue / Remember, somewhere, the sun is shining / And so the right thing to do is make it shine for you.* Her room looked out on a grove of orange trees; I could see rabbits skipping beneath them.

After I had seen Flo, heard her singing and spoken quietly with her, I drove north to give a lunchtime reading of my work and, when that was over, I drove back again. The colourful Waikato landscape is like a sky banner: it should be trailing itself behind a helicopter. The grass has the shimmer of Thai silk. On good days, like the ones that followed me through most of that week, the buttercup yellow of the sun shines out of an electric-blue sky. Then there's the way the gardens grow there like tornadoes of colour. But there's an unpredictability about it, too – the way passing clouds can turn the landscape black, and the night so dark that starlight is not always enough to show the way.

I decided to stay on in the town for as long as I could. I took a room at the edge of the park, overlooking the thermal spa resort. I was struck, just a week or so later, by the way the Earth is connected, when I found myself in another thermal town on the opposite side of the world. This one, near the hospital, used to be the haunt of fashionable people early in the twentieth century. They had built pavilions and a tea kiosk called Cadman House. I have a white china teapot stand, with a picture of the teahouse drawn in worn gold gilt, which I bought for a dollar in a second-hand shop. In the picture, a woman in a long full skirt is playing tennis on a court in front of the kiosk. This was just what Flo would have loved: it was like the beginning of her own life and my mother's, and their sisters' as well.

That afternoon, Flo and I talked for almost the last time. Mostly we spoke about old times when I used to come by train from up north, and she'd come to meet me, and also about the time I'd lived with her after I left school, the way I'd driven her crazy when I was a teenager, and how things pass.

'Through my journey of life, I've simply liked to help people,' she said. And in a way that was true. There was nothing grudging about what she remembered that afternoon.

'I should be getting along,' she said, as if she were visiting me. 'Theo will be waiting for me.' She began to knead my thumb between her own and her forefinger, with a strong clawing intensity.

'I reckon it's time you went to him,' I said. 'Forty years. You've kept him waiting long enough.'

'He'll be there.'

'What will you say to him?'

'What time's the quinella?' She gave a gentle snicker of pleasure.

Towards five in the evening, something altered: she slipped into unconsciousness and her breathing became shallower. At times, I thought she had stopped altogether. I didn't call anyone because I believed this was it, the moment she had waited for, when I would be with her, and she would simply let go.

Only she didn't die, she went on living for several more days, drifting in and out of sleep. In the mornings when I went back, she had begun to shout, wails of grief echoing through the corridors of the small hospital. 'Do not go gentle into that good night,' I said grimly to myself.

It seemed that it was only the beginning.

What followed for me was a kind of dreamtime, a compulsion to keep going that I still can't explain. Driving, speaking, coming back in the middle of the night to be with my aunt. What did I say to people I met? So you want to be a writer. Well, you must learn to live with yourself, however difficult that might be at times, because you're on your own in this job, you need to make space in your life, settle on your priorities. A writer's life is not spent in an

ivory tower. Learn to accept that real life is full of interruptions.
You have children? Yes, of course, many of us do. Write for fifteen
minutes a day – it's better than nothing at all. No, I agree this is
not about craft and style, but it's about how to survive, which is
the best I can tell you right now. Can I guarantee this recipe for
success? No, no, of course not. Nothing is certain. Forgive me,
I have to leave now.

Not all my vigils were alone. (What had Joy seen in me that
made her so sure I would keep watch, as my grandmother might
have done?) I got to know others on the staff – Betty and June,
I remember in particular. They were both capable women; unlike
Joy, they nursed part time and worked at home on their farms.
They chatted about their lives and families and asked me what it
was like to be well known, to be in the newspapers. I said that,
when it all came down to it, it was pretty much like other people's
lives; certainly, the big important things were, like birth and
death. They said, yes, they could see that, and wasn't it strange how
everyone was interested in much the same things. She was so proud
of you, they said, looking down at Flo's inert body. It's as well she
had you.

As well as these nurses, there was my aunt's neighbour, who had
lived close by for several years, a middle-aged woman called
Pamela, with dark hair swept up in frosted peaks and beautiful
casual country clothes. She organised speakers for the Lyceum
Club and was on the National Party branch committee. I could see
why my aunt would have got along with her, although the unease
between me and Pamela was palpable. I was the sort of woman she
could never trust. I saw her eyeing my appearance and comparing
it with her own. Mostly I wore a loose-fitting roll-neck pullover

made of fine Merino wool, black pants and a gaily coloured blue and yellow scarf, which I didn't change from day to day because I was travelling light and fast. For my part there may have been some element of jealousy present because it was clear that, in some ways, Pamela knew Flo better than I did. She had shopped for her, cut her toenails, intimate things like that. And she'd collected the mail for Flo every day, which meant she knew exactly how often I wrote.

When conscious, Flo looked at me with a certain malice.

'And where have you been?' she said each time, glaring through one half-closed eye.

'I was just out for a while. You knew I'd come.'

'I'm here,' she'd say in her mimicking, piping voice.

'Oooh,' Pamela said on an indrawn breath, on one of these afternoons.

'Don't be upset,' said Joy, who had arrived with a damp flannel for me to wipe Flo's face. 'This isn't the Flo you know; she's left.' I knew what she meant, but Pamela looked bewildered.

'I think I'll go home for a shower,' she said.

'What a good idea,' I said, trying not to sound too eager for her to leave.

Joy lingered in the room, looking at objects taken from Flo's house. Pamela had brought them there, some weeks before, as a kind of sad reassurance to Flo that living in a hospital room was like being at home. Not that I disapproved – I would have done the same thing myself, had I been around to do it. There were bits of pretty porcelain china with floral motifs and a little silver-rimmed vase with a hand-painted Egyptian scene on it that Flo had been given for her twenty-first birthday. But there could never be enough in that room to explain what Flo was really like, had been like for ninety years of life. Joy studied Flo and Theo's wedding photograph. 'How pretty she was. What a stylish, vivacious-looking woman,' she remarked.

'She reminded me of the queen,' I said.

'Really?'

I couldn't help elaborating. 'I met the queen once,' I said. 'The tips of her gloves stuck out beyond her fingers, so I simply had to wriggle the soft white kid. From the look in her eyes, I realised I'd held on longer than I should. But I wanted to say, you're like my Aunt Flo. I didn't, of course, because she might have taken it as rudeness, or too personal.'

'She might have taken it as a compliment.'

'I doubt it. Or if she had, she would have said nothing. They say she never acknowledges compliments, simply accepts them as of right. Or, she might have said, "Why? Why do you think this?" and I would have had to explain that her skin was of a similar texture and she wore her hats at much the same angle. Although, when she was young, Flo wore her hats much more rakishly than the queen. I could have told her that, when Flo smiled in unguarded moments, the dour look she had often melted away. Like hers.'

'What did you really do?'

'Oh, I smiled nervously, like most people do, and made a funny, awkward curtsey, the way we were taught to at school when we won a prize.'

'If I'd gone on to be a dancer, I might have got to meet the queen too,' Joy said.

'You met Flo instead,' I said with a laugh, but when I looked at Joy's face, I saw how thoughtless I had been – she did have a sense of loss, which she had hoped I might acknowledge.

To cover the discomfort between us, I set out to describe my aunt's house, the one Theo built for her at the end of the Depression when the building trade was slow and it gave his men work. He could still afford to buy Flo a diamond ring, if not as big as the Ritz, at least the Nottingham Castle Hotel. The house was expansive, flowing out in all directions from the central heat of the kitchen. There were several places where you could be by yourself: the formal sitting-room, used only on Sundays; the large closed-in sun porch; the small pretty bedroom that I occupied when I was there; Flo and Theo's own bedroom with its dark dresser and a fat mattress on the bed, which Flo never changed in the forty years she was a widow; the dining room with a copper coal scuttle gleaming on the hearth, and Theo's miniature spirits collection lining the head-high shelves on the walls. Yet, in spite of its generous proportions and spaciousness, it was a dark house. For a start, the walls were all stained-timber panelling, and then Flo kept the brown holland blinds three-quarters drawn in every room – all day, every day, until it was time to close them right up again at night.

Theo wasn't young when he married Flo, and she made him wait. She said she'd marry him, and then she changed her mind. For a while, after he'd built the house, his own mother and father lived in it, so she was not its first mistress, and I think that might have had something to do with the trouble between her and Theo later on. Certainly the parents weren't happy either when she changed her mind for a second time and said she'd marry him after all.

All this thinking on Flo's part took some years. She was, perhaps, thinking about and remembering Wilf Morton.

*

My mother told me about Wilf Morton and Flo. The family lived on my grandfather's sheep station, one of the big prosperous runs of the 1900s. As well as my mother, the youngest, there was Helena, the beautiful, frail daughter, Monica, the clever one, and Flo, the funny, laughing girl, at least when she was a child. My mother had been irrepressible and cheeky and was sometimes slapped by her big sisters for bad behaviour. She rewarded them by watching everything they did, especially when they brought young men to stay at the farm. Later, she paid them back by giving birth to me while they remained childless. Not that they saw it that way, they envied but never disliked her. I brought my mother status she never anticipated in those days when her sisters shouted and pleaded with her to leave them alone and mind her own business.

Wilf Morton was Flo's fiancé, and he stayed on and off at the farm for years, without showing any sign of setting the day for a wedding. Other young men who stayed at the house lent a hand with the stock, took their turn in the shearing sheds, trying out their hands as fleecos, collecting up the wool as it peeled off the sheeps' backs, dragging it away in preparation for storing it in the presses.

Not Wilf.

Wilf was always playing tennis. He stayed around the house wearing whites, the extravagant cuffs of his trousers turned up so they wouldn't brush against the grass. His hair looked as if it were permed, his eyebrows beneath a long white forehead were dark and straight as pencil lead; on the little finger of his left hand he wore a signet ring inset with a grape-coloured garnet. Even if you couldn't see the ring, you could tell he was flashy by the way the men in the family looked at him. Beside him, Flo looked a trifle plain, although she wore the most fashionable clothes of any of the sisters, and she was the one with a dimple in her chin. She also got engaged to Wilf, although her father didn't approve of the match, said he didn't feel he knew enough about the man and, since she was a girl who liked nice things, would love be enough? But the fact was when he was around Flo shone as if lit within, and when he wasn't there she was withdrawn and miserable, refusing to take part in conversation at dinner. This led my grandmother to say to her one day, when Wilf had been absent for a week or more and nobody was sure where he was, 'Really Flo, I'll be pleased when you're married and out of it.' This was an unusually sharp rebuke for her to give Flo, whom my mother suspected was her favourite child.

The next day, all Flo's sulks – as her mother had started calling these black moods – had disappeared. Wilf arrived back at the farm driving a new Model T Ford and bringing with him two men and a boy. The men were very well dressed, the younger man with his hat pushed back on his head so that the brim tilted upwards. He walked around the farm with his arms folded and an inscrutable look on his face, while the other man linked his fingers in front of his chest and made jokes. The boy with them was different from the boys on the farm. He wore his shirt open down his chest and put a hand on one hip and crossed his legs, pointing his foot like a dancer. Wilf tousled his hair and said, 'You're a real little bounder, aren't you?'

As usual, Flo's face glowed at the sight of Wilf. She must have known he was coming because she was dressed up in a pretty flapper dress with a long straight line to the knee and below that a band from which fell several straight pleats. She wore white stockings and strapped shoes.

What were these men doing at the farm? They didn't say immediately, although it emerged that one was a stock and station agent and the other a man from the bank. They were planning to foreclose on the farm, but that was a common enough story in the years that followed. What mattered was why Wilf Morton was with them.

'I'm going to spend the summer teaching this young man to play tennis,' he said, indicating the boy, whose name was Ralph. Ralph had an almost grown-up sister called Annabelle, who would be home from finishing school soon, and their father, the bank manager, was keen that they improve their athletic skills. Wilf had been offered a live-in job coaching them. Wilf smiled around the table when he told the family this.

It was clear that this was the first time Flo had heard about the arrangement. 'Does this mean you'll be going away?' she asked.

Wilf looked sideways at her. 'Well, I guess so. I mean, I can't teach Ralph and Annabelle here, can I?'

'So you're going to live at their place?'

There was a long silence while everyone examined their plates for a last speck of gravy. The rat, my mother said, when she recounted this. He knew my grandfather was going under and he'd found himself a better prospect. Not that she could see it, poor foolish Flo. My mother had a strong sisterly affection for her, but her later position in the family had given her a sort of second sight about her sisters, as if she had become the wise adult.

'For a while,' Wilf said. 'It's a job.' He sent one of his wide disarming smiles in the bank manager's direction.

Flo put her napkin to her mouth, as if she were going to be sick, and stood up.

'Flo,' said her mother. 'Manners.'

'I thought you'd be pleased,' said Wilf.

Anyone looking around that room would have known that the person who was most pleased was my grandfather. His own grief and sense of betrayal would come later, when he learned what the visit was really about and how the bank manager and his adviser were calculating the number of wool bales left in the shed that he couldn't pay anyone to take away. Flo walked out of the room without a backward glance and stayed in her room for several hours. She drew the curtains, and when Wilf went to her door and called her she didn't come out.

'Flo,' he said, 'I'm off now. Aren't you going to say goodbye?'

When she didn't answer, he said, 'All right then. All right.'

The Model T roared into life, and some muted goodbyes were called.

'Just leave her,' my grandmother said. 'Let her alone.'

It was an odd sort of a business, my mother said when she related this.

I went to live with Flo and Theo after I left school, so I could get an office job – good skills for life. I learned to type and write letters for an accounting firm, and gained a working knowledge of how to handle money. I had money of my own to buy clothes and make-up, which gave me a happy feeling of independence.

Theo said, when it was suggested I live there, that it would be a good thing for Flo. 'She's become a bit unstuck,' he told my mother, scratching his thin, sandy hair. He didn't say this in front of Flo, of course. My mother had gone down to talk the idea over with the pair of them. I think she was worried about me going there, but Flo had written and suggested it, and my parents were at a loss to know what to do with me, an awkward girl, described as 'having brains', who refused to take up any of the standard careers open to girls in those days.

Theo had a strong builder's face, with lips worn thin by the elements, clamped around the twenty or thirty tailor-mades he smoked a day. He recited his Masonic pledges in the bath behind closed doors and visited his mother at her house along the road every other evening. The two houses were at each end of a long street in a town that was rich in memorials, sparse in trees, with three hotels and a railway station straddling its main artery.

I liked it all well enough in the beginning. My aunt was enraptured by my presence, as if now she had me all to herself, and I really lived with her. She planned my meals with care and made my favourite foods, and worried about who I would marry. Although I was only sixteen, she had her eye on a man called Tommy Harrison. He was a persistent, lugubrious boy, who wore a brown hat when he came to town on Fridays, the important day of the week when farmers attended to their business. His father was a rich farmer, and Flo set her heart on my making a match of it with him, as if I could somehow rescue the family fortunes, however belatedly. Tommy called at the office to drop off the farm accounts on a regular basis and asked me to dances in a whisper, as he handed over the invoices. I could see his palms sweating. I went once or twice, but found excuses after that.

At the same time my aunt was doting on me, I was learning other things.

I thought Flo was happily married. I thought she had everything a woman could want. But when I went to live with her, rather than just being there on holiday, I found out things were different.

Some of the problems, at least, appeared to revolve around Theo's mother, now a widow, at that house at the end of the street. Theo would say he was just popping in to see his Ma on the way home, and then he'd stop on until eight o'clock or so, while the dinner Flo cooked him ruined in the oven. Often his mother would feed him the food that Flo brought her at the weekends. Theo's mother had been moved sideways from her expectations when Flo took over her house, and she wasn't going to let the matter rest. She was used to laying claim to her son. Theo worshipped her; it was a common male problem of wanting to spend his life between two women, only this wasn't about a wife and a mistress. There would be quarrels when Theo came home late, and silences that lasted between them for days, until Flo relented.

'I suppose I'd better call in on the old bid,' she'd say in her most vicious voice. 'Are you coming with me? You'll give me an excuse to get away.' Flo would often visit her mother-in-law at the weekend, when I couldn't plead work.

We always set off for his mother's house laden with cakes and casseroles that Flo made in preparation for her visits. I can see now that food was Flo's vocabulary for an inner life, a way of saying, at best, that she truly cared for you or, at least, that she was making a peace offering.

'She tarts herself up, that girl does,' Theo's mother said to Flo one day when I'd gone on a visit. She usually spoke of me in the third person. I was wearing my latest acquisition, a pair of wheel-shaped clip-on earrings made of blue feathers with diamanté centres.

'Don't speak like that,' Flo said. 'She's like a daughter to me.' I felt her edge her chair protectively towards mine.

'Well, really, I do beg your pardon,' said the mother-in-law, snorting. She had a lined face like a small old berry, very pale and dusty with powder.

'I'll put your cakes away,' Flo said. She clattered tins as she got them out of a kitchen cupboard and banged the lids as she shut them. She draped a clean tea towel over the enamel casserole dish she had stood on the bench. From the way her lips were pressed together it was clear Flo wasn't planning any more conversation.

'You're so kind to me,' her mother-in-law said in an exaggerated way. 'What's in the casserole today?' You could tell the way she really wanted to know: an old greedy expression glanced across her face.

'Chicken.'

'You sure you haven't put liquor in it? I thought I tasted liquor in the last one you brought.'

'I wouldn't waste booze on you.'

'I thought I smelled it. I go to church you know,' she said, turning to me.

I nodded without speaking, thinking that anything I said would be wrong.

'A pity you don't have a Frigidaire,' Flo snapped. 'This food won't last five minutes in the heat.

'Oh, well, who's a spoilt girl? We know you have the best of everything.'

'Theo'd buy you one in a flash,' said Flo. 'You know you only have to snap your fingers and you can have what you like.'

'I'm too old to be filling up the house with expensive contraptions like that. Tell that girl to help you more.'

'We're getting out of here,' Flo said ominously. She snatched up her bag and pulled her cardigan off the back of the chair.

'Feathers and paint make a little girl just what she ain't,' the older woman said, as we were leaving. 'I guess she's better than nothing.' She slammed the door shut as if she thought Flo might hit her.

But Flo was staring straight ahead as she marched down the street with me at her heels, and I saw that there were tears glistening in her eyes. 'I've had a few bitter pills in my time,' she said, as though her jaw were aching, 'but that really has to be the limit.'

The barren daughter-in-law. The childless woman. I see now I was her trophy child, her daughter for the moment.

Of course she had wanted children. Once when I was visiting, we chatted about people we'd known in the town.

'What became of Tommy Harrison?' I asked. My children were playing in the garden where we could watch them. The sun was melting out of the sky, and I thought the children should come in and put on more sun block, but Flo said, 'Oh, leave them, the sun's good for them,' the way she said, 'Oh leave the young people alone, let them smoke,' though she didn't herself and I think would have hated it if I did.

'Tommy Harrison? Oh, he's around. Full of himself.'

'I could have told you that.'

'Well, never mind. I'm glad you didn't marry him.'

'Why? You were keen enough at the time.'

'He didn't have any children. You might have ended up the same as me.'

'Oh, Flo,' I said. I didn't know whether I wanted this conversation to go on, but this was the moment she had chosen to tell me. About the missed periods for a month or two, and the heavy swelling of her breasts, all the hope that followed her around and then the stains in her panties, a day of cramps, and it was over every time. And how this happened not once but often – endless farewells in the bathroom.

'Oh, well,' she said, and I knew what she would say next, 'You know, there've been a few bitter pills. We were too old, Theo and me. I don't know what I was thinking of, that he could give me kids. Don't you think those children of yours should come in out of the sun?'

'Yes,' I said, relieved.

She had a sliver of snot on her lip that she wiped away with the back of her hand.

'Hay fever,' she said.

Not everything in that house was darkness, but when it came, it fell swiftly. Flo and Theo loved the races and dressed up whenever there was a weekend race meeting. This went on for years, until suddenly Flo wanted a change, and they stopped. But they'd decorated their lavatory like one of those joke toilets, with pictures of racehorses, dozens of them, especially of the famous Phar Lap, whose heart, it was discovered when he died, weighed a whole fourteen pounds.

And, deep in the house, there was a wide passage with a recess, which was like Flo's throne room. A low seat made of plaited leather on a carved wooden frame sat beside a highly polished mahogany table. On the table stood three objects: a brass box containing photographs of the family, several of me as an infant and of the farm where she grew up; a swirling cloudy-green

Crown Devon jug, kept filled with flowers (hydrangeas were her favourite); and the telephone. Flo sat on the low seat and talked on the phone for hours, either to her older sisters, or to her best friend, Glad Dean, with whom she'd nursed in the tuberculosis sanatorium during the war.

One evening, when I was talking on the phone, I let one of my new silver bracelets rest on the table. When Flo called out that dinner was ready, I swung around from the table, scraping the bracelet along the surface, leaving a deep gouge behind.

'You stupid cow,' Flo shouted at me. 'Stupid, stupid, stupid.'

And then she didn't speak to me for a week. Theo slunk around the house, not speaking either.

As Theo was taking his lunchbox out of Flo's Frigidaire one morning, I said, 'I'm sorry, Uncle Theo.' Flo was taking a bath, and the door to the bathroom was firmly closed. Suddenly, the big sprawling house seemed too small for the three of us, and I had been thinking that if things didn't improve soon I should probably pack up and go back up north to my parents. I felt joyless and as stupid as Flo had accused me of being. I had thought that Theo liked me living with them, but now I felt unwelcome. He gazed past me as if I wasn't there.

'About the table. I didn't mean to do it.'

He shook his head as if to clear it. 'What about the table?'

'About the scratch.'

'I don't know what you're talking about.' He was a bulky man, a bit big around the ears, with a small fold of fat between the base of his head and the beginning of his neck. He put his arm around me with an awkward little squeeze. 'C'mon little tart, you're doing all right.' That was what he called me, his pet name.

It was Friday when this happened. In the evening he came home very late.

'Been at our mother's, have we?' Flo said, without looking up from the bench. His dinner was like a mud cake on the plate.

'No, as a matter of fact, I havven been to Ma's.' He stumbled down the passage to the bedroom.

I thought she would stay in the kitchen, but she followed him, telling him to speak to her. 'Well, just say something will you,' she shouted.

His voice when he answered was too low to hear, but I heard hers, full of contempt. 'You're drunk. Think again.'

Then she said something else I didn't hear.

'It's not my fault,' he said.

So any number of things could have been going on in that house, and the scratch on the table was beginning to seem like the least of them.

Flo kept up her silence for another week. She spoke to neither Theo nor me, not even the pass-the-butter stuff. Flo would rather suffer and eat dry bread than ask.

Then, as suddenly as all this had started, she was herself again. She resumed the preparation of my favourite foods and was seemingly peaceful, at least with me, until I left at the end of the year to go to another job further south, which my parents had arranged. In the week before my departure, Flo moved back inside herself, although not in the same furious way she had before. It was more as if she were resigned to something that, again, she could not control.

*

Less than a year after I left, Theo complained one morning of not feeling well. He went to the doctor and discovered he was dying. He fought a brief battle, which hardly seemed like a fight, with a rapid-moving cancer that had started in his prostate. Shortly after, his heart stopped beating. Just like that, without the ceremony of goodbyes.

The day after the funeral, Helena, the beautiful sickly sister, arrived at Flo's house with all her bags and said she'd come to stay a few weeks.

'You don't need to. I can manage,' Flo told her.

'I doubt it,' Helena said. She stayed for twenty years, until she, too, died. After Theo's death, Flo took a job in the county office, keeping minutes for all the council meetings. She had talents nobody had ever guessed. In the evenings, she went home and cooked Helena's meals, and although Helena talked in a lively fashion whenever I was there, I never heard Flo speak to her directly.

Once Theo had gone – a builder one day, a man dead and buried a month later – Flo discovered him, as if he had been the love of her life. I think this was one of those fictions that becomes truth. A reconstruction. People believe what they want, I told my audiences on that tour, while Flo was at the hospital. You can say what you like about the boundaries between life and art, but people decide what they believe and that's that.

Which I suppose is what Flo did, what kept her going, through the years with Helena and the years beyond that.

Flo's poor old rotting hulk had a stale smell hovering over it that no amount of bathing and attention would remove. She breathed in shallow puffs beneath an oxygen mask, not appearing to know or hear us.

I was due to appear on a panel of writers in the town of Cambridge, nearly an hour's drive away from the hospital. I was ready to move on. The driving to and from to the hospital had taken a toll. I spoke in a kind of dream when I stood up in front of an audience. In my head, I knew Flo must die soon, but how long is soon? I was going abroad, and in a day or so there would be nothing for it, I would have to say my own goodbye. I was to go to Gisborne the next day, the last stage of my journey, and then home.

'I'll stay with Flo,' Pamela said when I explained the situation. I could see how reproachfully she looked at me. I had changed into clothes more suitable for an evening gathering, a long dark skirt with a fuchsia-coloured jacket.

'I'll see if I can get a later flight tomorrow,' I said. 'I'll stay in Cambridge tonight and come back first thing in the morning.' Putting it off.

I met the group of writers in Cambridge and checked into the room next to Davina Worth, a playwright. She writes monologues for solo voices, some of which she performs herself. She's got clear green eyes and dark hair streaked with grey that falls from a centre parting. She's a great person to be around, a formidable presence on stage. I began to think that I should not have worried about coming, as she and the poet who was there too would be enough in themselves. I saw the way Davina looked at me. 'What have you been doing to yourself?'

I tried to explain, told her how I might still have to go back to the hospital that night. I'd rung and spoken to Joy, and she'd been non-committal when I asked how Flo was.

'You'd tell me if she got worse, wouldn't you?'

'Yes,' she agreed.

'Promise?'

'I do, yes, I promise.'

'You're driving yourself nuts,' Davina said when I relayed this conversation to her. 'You're going to Canada next week, stop doing this to yourself.'

The booksellers sold fifty-seven copies of our books that evening in Cambridge. 'Well done,' they said and gave us our cheques for our appearance fees.

'I should go back to the hospital,' I said.

'You're exhausted,' said Davina. 'You need to come out with us. When did you last eat?'

She and the poet and I ended up in a café, a reckless kind of place, full of celebrating Cambridge horse breeders having a night out because someone had sold a horse for a million dollars. I can't remember what I ate, but I drank two glasses of wine and laughed a lot. Davina told us a story about when she'd done some training in Australia for the theatre, and she'd rehearsed Ophelia. No matter how hard she tried, she couldn't find her way into the character, which didn't surprise me. Davina is too much of an extrovert, too thoroughly optimistic about life. 'I couldn't get it right. I said to the director, this Englishman with his broad Midlands accent, I said, "Barney, what am I going to do?" And Barney just threw his hands in the air and said, "I don't *know*, perhaps you should think of yourself as a cross between a piece of jasmine and a booterfly."'

This struck me as so funny, I laughed until I cried, that terrible cracking-up sort of laughter that isn't about humour, it's painful and uncontrollable. The others looked at me with concern. When I recovered myself, I said abruptly, 'I'll ring the hospital.'

My phone was out of battery. 'I'll phone from the motel when I get back,' I said.

Davina said, 'You needed to do this tonight. What you've been doing is too hard on you. You have to stop.'

The motelier had stayed up for me. 'I've got a message for you. It's about a relative of yours. I'm sorry, it's bad news. She's not expected to live through the night.'

'I'm away,' I said to Davina.

'I'll come with you.'

'No, you won't. I'm going to sleep at the hospital.'

'Shall I let the organisers know you're not going to Gisborne tomorrow?'

'I don't know,' I said. 'I'll let tomorrow take care of itself.'

I set out into the dark Waikato night.

Five or six kilometres out of town, the emergency petrol light came on. Slowly, and very carefully, I turned and drove back to town. Everything had turned into a terrible slow-motion drama.

The first petrol station I came to was self-service only at that hour of the night. The young man behind the steel grille wouldn't come out for me.

'My aunt is dying,' I said.

'That's what they all say.' He had a cold, lunar face with shadows under his eyes. I couldn't get the bowser to work.

'Please,' I said, crying and shaking the grille. 'Please, Flo's dying.'

'I'm under orders.' He was eating a steaming pie out of a wrapper.

'I said, I won't hurt you. I gave a talk in the town tonight.'

He didn't even answer me.

I drove further up the town. Further away, in the opposite

direction from Flo, I found another petrol station and was able to fill the car. An hour had passed since I set out. Then I turned the car into a racing boat of a vehicle, opening her out on the long straight roads as if she were under sail with the wind behind her. Was it the wine? Confusion? Terror at not, in the end, being where I had said I would be? Not being there.

And where have you been?

I'm here, Flo, I'm here in the middle of a dark road, and my eyes are blinded by tears, and I cannot see the familiar landmarks.

I had missed a vital turn-off, and suddenly I was spinning again in the opposite direction from where I was supposed to be going. I reversed, tried to retrace my route, found I had gone in a loop and was heading towards the nearby city of Hamilton, down the motorway with no off-ramp for several kilometres. I came to a roundabout, slowed, understood at last where I was, and set off again. Two hours. The car flying – a hundred and twenty on the clock, a hundred and thirty, a hundred and forty. I remembered Flo ringing me one evening, after she had driven her ancient Mini Minor into a ditch somewhere around here. It had floated in the water, rocking gently until someone pulled her back to safety. Her car worked again when it was dried out, but the council officer wouldn't give Flo her licence when it came up for renewal at the end of the year. 'You'd think after all those years I worked for them, they'd have more respect,' she said at the time. 'Young whippersnappers.'

A hundred and sixty. I had never driven this fast before. I started to sing to keep myself awake. During the previous winter, I had taught a creative-writing class. On the last day, my students had sung a waiata, a song of respect and thanks, the one that goes

Te aroha, Te whakapono, Me te rangimārie, Tātou tātou e, and that is what I sang. It means, roughly speaking, love, faith, peace, for all of us. I don't know whether she would have liked it, but I thought that if I sang it and sang it, it would sustain me somehow and take me to where she was, and I would, after all, be *there*. That when she said, 'And where have you been?' I would say, *I'm here*.

And then I was there, and at the front of the little country hospital in a pool of light, clustered on the verandah, I saw a knot of women standing, and I knew that I was too late, that it had already happened.

Pamela came forward to embrace me, but I pushed her away.

'She went at seven minutes after midnight.' It was twelve fifteen, and frost was gathering under the trees outside the hospital.

I walked down the corridor without looking at any of them. I didn't say I was sorry I hadn't been there.

'I'm here, Flo,' I said. But she was not going to reply, not ever. My poor wounded old starfish, her hands together, fingers pointed towards me, poor old fish, stranded for good.

I shouted at her. 'Why didn't you wait?'

I tore some flowers out of a vase and strewed them around her. When I came through and joined the others, somebody said, 'We'll get you a cup of tea.' They looked frightened of me. Even Joy.

I told them I didn't want any damn tea and walked out of the hospital and got into the car. Nobody tried to stop me, though I think now they probably should. I drove very slowly, as if I were a blind person who'd been allowed out on the road. When I got back to the motel, I found I'd locked my keys inside my room. I banged on Davina's door, but she didn't hear me. It was three o'clock in the morning. I thought I should sleep in the car, but then I thought I was a grown up now, the next in line to die, one of the old people, so I rang the motelier's emergency bell.

I left, headed for Gisborne in the morning and, when I got there, I talked again. About writing. About the imagination. Don't be constrained by the truth, I said.

Some days after that, we sang 'Sheep May Safely Graze' at Flo's funeral, and the next day I flew to Canada.

The Sylvia Hotel at English Bay in Vancouver seemed the most perfect hotel in the world. It was covered with ivy; the interiors had dark old beams and rich stained-glass windows. I slept in a bed of such deep comfort in a large airy room that, when I woke up late in the afternoon, I was happy and felt free. I walked along to a shopping centre and bought a face mask from a cosmetics supermarket, complete with an open cool bin of products that looked as if they should have been in a delicatessen. The face mask was made from shiitake mushrooms and came in a pottle, resting on ice inside another little container. Elsewhere, I bought an umbrella and a Vancouver newspaper. I went back to the Sylvia Hotel and put the mask on my face. It seemed as if flesh was being drawn to the surface. Afterwards, I felt totally cleansed, as if I were making myself over into a new person. I sat and watched the sea and ate a chicken breast stuffed with ginger and grapefruit.

On the flight from Calgary, my plane flew into the eye of the sun, its bright glare leaning through the window. I sat beside the young man I'd met up with in Banff. We had reached that stage of intimacy that insisted (or he did anyway) that we sit together on aeroplanes in order to continue, uninterrupted, the story of our lives. A seemingly endless narrative. I remember the feeling of being dazzled by the sunlight.

Flo flew in an aeroplane only once in her life, the only time she left New Zealand. She and a group of her friends from the council decided to go to Rarotonga for a holiday. As she went to the departure lounge, her foot caught in the escalator and she fell down and knocked her head. She went on with the journey because she was with her friends, but she didn't like it, didn't have a good time. Give me good old New Zealand any day, was all she said about it. Fear of falling. One way or another.

Once, in the town where my parents and I lived when I was young, my mother ran into Wilf Morton. She was standing in the hardware shop and heard a voice asking for a pound of nails. She knew him straight away, she said, even though his hair was iron grey and he was standing with his back to her. It was something about the way he spoke, as if asking for a pound of nails were a favour he was bestowing on the shopkeeper.

I only knew about this at the time because I heard my mother telling my father in a low angry voice that evening. But later on, I could see it very clearly. I have a photograph of Wilf, which was tucked in an envelope inside one of the recipe books that I salvaged from Flo's house, his name written on the back in pencil.

'I said to him, "What are you doing here, Wilf Morton?"'

'And what did he say?' my father asked, with unusual animation. He enjoyed stories in which my mother's family came out worse than he did, not that Wilf Morton had ever been family.

'He lives here,' my mother spat.

'Oh, Gawd, that's serious,' my father said.

'On the other side of the inlet.'

'Well, I suppose that's not so bad. You can keep your eyes skinned when you go to town.'

'Why should I have to cross the road to avoid that man?'

'Fair enough,' my father said. 'Did he say what he was up to?'

'He said he was retired.'

'Retired from what?'

'Exactly,' said my mother. 'That's what I said to him – "And what are you retired from, Wilf?" He didn't answer me, just smirked.'

I reminded my mother of this once, when we were talking about family matters and the interminable question of why Flo was like she was. (This surfaced when Flo had been irascible or silent on our visits, especially in the days when Helena lived with her.) I'd heard the bones of the story about Wilf leaving Flo once before.

'Oh, that Wilf Morton.' My mother shrugged in the oblique sort of way her family had.

'What made him so dreadful? Apart from leaving her.'

'There were some things missing,' she said.

'You mean he stole things?'

'Something like that.' They didn't go into details either in that family. A trinket, a farm, a heart – my mother could have meant any of those things. A sense of honour, perhaps; we might think it misplaced nowadays.

I had been asleep. The young man had kindly placed a pillow against me. I looked down on a tapestry of forests and lakes beginning to cloud with ice. Soon we would be in Winnipeg. The young man had quickened my senses, but I was old enough to know that what seems romantic on the outside can be a substitute for grief, and I was grateful to have gone on in the world long enough to understand that. Later, we would send signals from afar, messages through mutual friends, invitations to book launches that were impossible for the other to attend, things like that, not the conspiracies of the heart that letters and emails involved. I've known any number of silver-tongued men, but I think my aunt only knew one.

I sat in the Sylvia Hotel and watched the sea. Some of this story hadn't happened then, but in a few days it would. The young man I would meet in Banff, he was as dangerous as an elk. He was going to meet up with his wife later on the tour. He was nursing one of those harsh little secrets that men have, the kind that are common enough, but will tear lives apart. I've made several generalisations about men here: by and large, I think they're not bad, which is one of those sweeping assertions that don't get as much press as the other sort. Let me say here that I think Theo was as decent and kind a man as it was possible to meet. I knew nothing unpleasant about him, nor have I heard anything since to alter my opinion of him. It was just that he lacked judgment in some aspects of his life, that he was helplessly in love with his wife and that he was undeniably homely.

You could say people bring it on themselves, but I'm not sure it's true; one will be absent from a marriage – there in the flesh, but absent in themselves. And then it's too late. You can tell from looking at some couples, even in photos, that one person's eyes have slid outside the frame. I have a picture of a group of us writers who went on that tour, and the young man from Banff is there with his wife. On that day, he is in the marriage still (although not for much longer), but his eyes are following the exit signs.

I came across a quote written by a young Frenchman in the

seventeenth century. I've kept it for so long I don't know how I found it. It's copied down in my handwriting on a brown scrap of paper, brittle with age:

L'absence est à l'amour ce qu'est au feu le vent.

Absence is to love what wind is to fire.

SILKS

When I think of love and how things began for us, I think of a house by a lake and us lying in bed with our skin like twin silks sliding together. I remember the venetian blind and the slats of light that shone through, moonlight but also sunlight, because that was the way it was: we were in that bed night and day. That was the time, too, or thereabouts, when I began a kind of worship for a writer who lived by lakes and made love with a man in a room where the slatted blind made stripes on the soft and shining light of his back.

The writer, a Frenchwoman called Marguerite Duras, was born in Vietnam, a girl who made love with a man of another colour, a woman who lived outside the pale. That was like me, only I married the man I was in love with, when I was young. Who knew whether it would last? That was the question they all asked, the good Presbyterian men and women who were my aunts and uncles, on the day that I married. We married, my husband and I, in a church with flax-lined walls, while a thunderstorm broke overhead and the rain poured down, and nobody could hear the promises we made. As I say, I was very young. My waist was twenty-two inches in circumference. I had thick, dark hair. The art of love came easily to me. I worked in a library and read French writers, and Duras was another love, a passion that went hand in hand with the discoveries of the flesh that I was making. In my lunch-hours I rushed home. My husband would be there before me. We would make love and go back to work. It was an exhausting life.

Duras led us to Hanoi, but this was many years later. Close to fifty, in fact. We could look back and say fifty years of married drama and laugh, but it held the ring of truth and remembered fires, the silky fire of sex, the fiery nights when we broke things, a couple of black ragers in our worst moments.

It was not the first time we had been to Vietnam. We were no strangers to the East, but we hadn't been to Hanoi. I had followed Duras around the world, stalked her ghost: to Saigon (which is how I think of Ho Chi Minh City because Saigon sounds wilder, tougher, more glamorous, I suppose); to Chợ Lớn, where she had spent her afternoons in the bed of her Chinese lover when she was supposed to be at school, and along the Mekong River in a flat-bottomed barge in search of her house (which we never found); and to Neauphle-le-Château, the French town where her house stands abandoned beside the still dark pool that is another reflection of what I call my inner life. I had leant my face against her windowpane, looked at the scuff marks her feet had made on the skirting boards of her kitchen. And I had been to her plain grave in Paris, marked with the stark initials: M.D. Just that. But I had not been to Hanoi, where, for a brief time, her widowed mother ran a boarding house beside a lake. My own mother had worked in a boarding house. You will see how it comes together, her life and mine, though sometimes this interest can be misunderstood. Are you an alcoholic? I was once asked by a journalist. Of course I said no, because I am a woman of good reputation and live in a small country. I had written an account of my life, and the journalist thought it incomplete. They always want to know more than you want to tell them. They want a scandal, of course. Duras was an alcoholic. She drank herself into comas. I have never done that. For a time, I drank too much. That isn't the same thing at all.

My husband met me in Bangkok Airport. He had been to Phnom Penh, where he worked as a volunteer for one of the aid organisations. As he has grown older, he has become more and more interested in saving the world. He does good works and changes lives. I can't be like him. I find it hard to visit slums, to work alongside the halt and lame, without assuming the zealous smile of a person offering charity. The heat gets to me, and the begging for money, and the children for whom good works will never be enough, the despairing women. And, if I'm honest, I find it hard to get along with the aid workers, who seem to me either rampantly Christian or else escapees from some other reality, jittery with cheap alcohol and casual sex, blazing-eyed and reckless. They're not all like that, but enough to make me wary. The more time I spend with them, the more determinedly ordinary I become. Judgemental in my way, as the aunts and uncles at my shoulder, a prim elderly woman with frangipani stuck awkwardly behind my ear. My husband doesn't look out of place. He seems part of the landscape. He sits on the side of filthy streets and eats what's offered to him while he talks to the people who live there.

As soon as I saw him at the airport, I thought, *He doesn't look well, something's not right.* He was pale and wandering in his speech. Although we had planned our meeting carefully, he had confused the times and gone to wait at the airport many hours before my plane from Auckland was due in Bangkok. My luggage was the last off the carousel, and by the time I came through the gates he was hysterical about my whereabouts, and security guards had to restrain him from rushing through the incoming passengers to find me. But when he did see me, he didn't seem pleased, almost as if I were a stranger. We prepared to board the plane for Hanoi, although, even as we did so, I thought it a terrible idea. If there was something wrong, perhaps we should stay in Bangkok. We passed through check-in and relinquished our luggage, so it was too late to turn back. My husband asked me to find a chair so he could take a rest on the way to the gate lounge. I said, 'Do you think you're well enough to go on this flight?'

He said that of course he was, which is what I should have expected. He doesn't give in easily. Before he left Phnom Penh, some friends had taken him to a noodle shop to eat lunch. It was dirty, he said, but he didn't want to offend them. He may blend into the landscape, but he tries to be careful, particularly as he had come home to me once before with an illness that had developed in the tropics and took him close to death. Perhaps, he thought, he had eaten something at the noodle shop. Whatever it was, it would soon pass.

We arrived at night, and the airport was utter chaos: hundreds jostling together, some coming, others going, taxi drivers looking for work, pushing people out of their way. Our driver found us, the board bearing our names held high above the heads of the crowd, and some time later we were being driven towards Hanoi, or so far as I knew. The road fell quiet, and a dark countryside rolled alongside us. We crossed a river and a bridge that seemed to stretch into infinity; I sensed the water beneath us.

'I think we're crossing the Red River,' I said, expecting my husband to be excited. He had wanted to see this river, which is also known as Mother River, for such a long time. 'This must be Thăng Long Bridge.' He had done so much research, knew all the facts and figures about this extraordinary feat of engineering and about the two villages that lay beneath its spans. He didn't answer me, and I felt irritated. I thought he could have made a little effort.

We drove on and on, and we could have been anywhere, being taken far away from our destination. There was no way of knowing or of asking the silent driver, who spoke no English. There was hardly a light to be discerned in the black landscape, and this was something I would learn, that the Vietnamese use electricity sparingly and utter darkness is not unusual. When, at last, the glimmer of a city shone before us, my husband slid sideways onto my lap, resting his head there until we arrived at our hotel.

'I'll let you check in,' he said, handing me his passport. This was something he had never done before.

I had been travelling for many hours. I gave my husband some Lomotil from our first-aid supplies to cure his stomach upset, then lay down in the Sunway Hotel and slept until morning, hoping that he would do the same. The sheets were made of exquisitely fine, white cotton.

He was worse in the morning, but still I thought it would pass. I went to breakfast. The dining room of the hotel was restful, like that of a French inn. The walls were covered with vivid Vietnamese artworks that, although colourful, didn't detract from the cool white-and-green ambience of the room. I ate some dragon fruit and melon and a little muesli. I walked along the street, a shabby crowded avenue in the Old Quarter, slung low with the great burden of electrical wires, just as when the war was on, although nearly thirty years had passed. I walked nearly to the end of the street until I came to the Opera House, then became alarmed that I wouldn't be able to find my way back and my husband would be alone and frightened and more ill. At that moment, perhaps, I understood that things could be serious and that, actually, I was trying to walk away from the situation. I went back to the hotel. He looked dreadful. He didn't want a doctor, but we agreed that if he wasn't any better by three o'clock, I would call for one. But it was two o'clock when I went to the reception desk. 'Help me, please,' I said. 'My husband is sick.'

'We'll get a taxi for you, Madam, and send you to a clinic,' the woman said.

But no, I said, no, he needs a doctor to come to him; and very soon one did, a young woman, with an attendant following her, and a short time after that an ambulance was summoned, and my husband was carried on a stretcher with an oxygen mask over his face through the lobby of the Sunway Hotel, and a siren was shrieking above us, and through the window I saw the thousands of motorbikes that clog the streets of the city fanning out about us. I had dropped everything, thrown some valuables in the safe and fled.

At the clinic, he was isolated from others coming and going, though I sat beside him and laughed and made jokes. I was given a gown and mask to wear. I said things like, 'Here I am in Hanoi, looking after you, I'm pretending to be Hot Lips Houlihan', and pushed my mouth out to make it fat.

'Wrong war,' he said. 'Wrong country.' He didn't have much to say after that. Before I met him, my husband had been a pilot in the air force. I said, 'Buck up, old chap.' I sang a line or two of 'The Bells of Hell Go Ting-a-ling-a-ling'. Nothing made him laugh. I still didn't believe there was much that a quick shot of antibiotic wouldn't cure. A young French doctor came and went, his face grave. Hours passed. My husband seemed worse. 'We think he has cholera,' the French doctor said. I stopped joking.

Outside, night had fallen. The doctor said, 'You realise your husband is very ill?' Dazed, I said, 'Yes, no, yes I do,' and started to cry. He looked at me wearily as if I were misbehaving. 'We're going to send your husband to a hospital where he'll be more comfortable. You'll need to check it out with your insurance company.'

But night was hours ahead of us in New Zealand, and when I tried to phone the insurance company there was nothing but a voice message giving the times that the company was open. The woman behind the desk at the clinic had an impassive Vietnamese expression. She explained that, if my insurance company could not confirm our policy, I must pay for my husband's treatment for that afternoon. Could I please hand over my credit card? The cost was five-thousand dollars, or thereabouts.

In my haste to leave the hotel, I had brought only one of the two cards we carried, and it did not have enough money on it. I cried again, I may have shouted, but none of it made any difference. In the background, my husband was a strange grey-paste colour, and tubes and drips were poking out from all over him. I said that I would talk to my twenty-four-hour bank service, and I did. In the end, the credit was authorised. As we left the clinic, we reached the street in the midst of Hanoi, its street vendors and crowds, the bright lights of open shops, the cascades of silk in front of them. An ambulance waited for us. My husband was carried by four men holding his wheelchair, but before he could be boarded he projected a wild, vile green plume of vomit that spread over everyone within reach. Green rain. Shrill cries of horror erupted from the passers-by. Those carrying my husband turned and began to carry him back into the clinic.

'Put him in the ambulance,' I screamed. 'Please get him to the hospital.'

But it seemed that first he must be made clean, so the whole process began all over again. Midnight had passed by the time the ambulance left the city. We drove, again through silence. The Vietnamese had put up their shutters, lain down to sleep. The motorbikes that choked the streets earlier had disappeared. The lights had gone out except for the tiny flickers of fires peppering the pavements, illuminating the shadows of late workers bending over their pots. The ambulance progressed very slowly. We seemed to be moving far away from the city centre. I had no idea what direction we were taking. I saw the shapes of buildings through the gloom, so I knew that we must still be within the confines of the city. Days had passed since I left home, and already a day had gone since I had eaten the cloudy flesh of the dragon fruit at the hotel.

We reached the hospital, a stark building, concrete and totally without charm. A team of nurses rushed to my husband's side, and, as suddenly as we had entered the fluorescent-lit space of the hospital, he had disappeared. The place seemed otherwise deserted, except for a man behind a big desk. 'You will now show me your passport,' he said.

I showed it to him.

'You will now give me your husband's passport.' He took it from me.

'Can I have it back, please?' I asked.

He shook his head with impatience. 'Not until he leaves the hospital. They tell me your papers for the insurance are not in order. You will now give me five-hundred dollars.'

'American?'

'Yes.'

'I don't have that much money on me,' I said.

'Show me how much.'

I opened my wallet and turned it out on the counter; a little over three hundred dollars fell out, perhaps another fifty in smaller notes. He picked through them. 'I have to have some money to get back to my hotel,' I said. 'I have no idea where I am.'

'Three hundred will do,' he said.

'I want to see my husband.'

'That is not possible. The doctor will come.'

I waited in a vestibule with couches covered in brown faux leather. While I waited, a woman I soon discovered was American came to the desk. Her husband had just been admitted with a heart problem. He, too, had gone to intensive care.

'But this is preposterous,' she said loudly to the man at the desk. 'He's had a murmur like this before, he doesn't *need* intensive care. In the morning, I'll take him to Bangkok, see a proper doctor. Tell them to take him out of there.' The man spread his hands in a gesture that said, 'This is not my problem.' My eyes met his, and for a moment something like sympathy passed between us. At least I hadn't told him what to do.

The woman introduced herself to me. Her name was Irene. She had just come to Hanoi with her husband, who was to work in one of the banks. I have never quite understood American women. When I travel, I find them often generous and funny and warm, but they have a brittle edge that threatens to snap if they are crossed.

'Hey, seems you're a bit stranded,' Irene said, when we had exchanged a few words, and she gave me her card. 'If you're still on your own tomorrow night, we could go out and play a bit, what d'you think? Don't worry about your husband, he'll be fine. At least these doctors know how to fix tummy bugs.'

A Vietnamese doctor appeared and introduced himself to me.

'Your husband is now in isolation,' he said.

'Has he got cholera?'

'No. It is not cholera.'

'What is wrong with him?'

'He has rotavirus. Very infectious disease.'

A virus, I thought. 'It's not serious, then?'

'Oh, yes, it is serious.'

'He won't die, will he?'

'Oh, maybe. His kidneys do not work now. He is, how do you say, dehydrated. He should have seen a doctor much more early.'

'Tonight? My husband might die tonight?'

'Prob'ly.'

'I must see him.'

'Not possible. Now he is in isolation. You go home now.'

'Where? Show me where he is.'

After a while, he relented and took me in a lift to another floor. I was led through a door that had to be unlocked from the other side by some nurses. After that, there was another locked door, and through a window, in a bare cell, I saw my husband lying naked on a stripped-down bed. He appeared barely conscious.

'I'll stay here.'

'No, you cannot stay here. You must leave now.'

A nurse took my arm. She led me back to the lift and accompanied me to the ground floor. 'You must go.'

I shouted at her. 'I'm not going anywhere. I'll sleep here.'

She shrugged and made a face at the man behind the desk. I lay down on the concrete floor. The nurse left, and I was by myself. I sobbed then, as if I would never stop. All the old fretted and worn seams of love that had stretched but never parted were laid out before me. My husband was dying, and I was alone in a city where I had never been, lying on a concrete floor. Each of us was alone.

The man at the desk came over to me. 'You may lie on a bed that is in the next room,' he said. 'It is for emergencies. If an emergency comes, you must get out of the bed.'

And this small act of kindness had its effect. My behaviour was pointless and ridiculous. I took my mobile phone and worked out how to dial our children's numbers with the country code added in. But it seemed they had turned off their phones for the night. I figured that it must be about half-past five in the morning. I have a friend who sleeps badly and lives alone. I called her. I said, 'Find my children. Please.'

Our daughter rang me. 'Mum,' she said. 'Mum. Don't let my father die.'

Our son rang me. 'Mum,' he said. 'Mum.' He was crying.

The man at the desk came into the room a short while later. He said, 'Your ambassador is coming.'

My daughter had rung the night desk at Foreign Affairs and explained that her father was dying in a hospital in Hanoi. The man had agreed, with some scepticism, to check it out. But the people from the embassy who arrived in a large Jeep at the door of the hospital were not sceptical. They were kind and practical and had brought a translator with them, and some food and bottles of mineral water and dry ginger ale. I had never been more pleased to see people from my own country. A while later, I left the hospital with them. I was told a senior doctor would see me in a few hours. They took me back to the hotel in the city, promising to fetch me when I had had time to shower and eat breakfast, talk to my insurance company and perhaps sleep a little. All of which I did, except the last. But before I did anything else, I wrote a long letter to my husband, in which I told him what had happened since we left Bangkok, because I was certain he wouldn't remember and I thought it unlikely the nurses would have the language to tell him where he was or how he had got there or why he couldn't see me. I told him, too, how much I loved him, how he must fight to get well because, if he didn't, I wasn't sure that I could go on. Although this seemed like blackmail, it was better than saying goodbye in a letter. I needed him to help me go on with my life, I said. It was as simple as that. Once before he had nearly died, but he had got better, and he could do it again.

I saw the senior doctor, an older man, impatient with people like me. His job was to make people better, not talk to the relatives. The translator from the embassy sat with me, but the doctor did command some stilted formal English. He interrogated me. 'Do you wash your hands properly?'

'Yes,' I said.

'When you go to the lavatory?'

'But of course.'

'Rotavirus comes from dirty food that is contaminated with excrement. You need to be more careful.'

'But I haven't given my husband his dinner for more than two weeks,' I said.

So then I had to explain my journey, where I had come from, how my husband and I had met in Bangkok, how I had expected him to be happy when he saw me but he wasn't. I made it into a little drama, waved my hands about, and he allowed himself a small smile before his expression closed again.

'Your husband will be here for quite some time,' he said. 'We will do what we can to make him well. Now I must see the next wife.'

The next wife was Irene, who had grown angrier since I saw her the night before, and a new wife waited behind her, a dark Portuguese woman who was stranded and almost without language. She was weeping in a silent persistent way, unchecked snot covering her lip. This was Maria, whose husband had fallen down some steps on a cruise ship and hit his head. Smash, she said, smash.

The translator took me to the clinic where I had been the day before. Now that the insurance company had cleared our policy I could get my money back. The clinic wanted to give me the money in dongs, Vietnamese currency. Fourteen million. In the end a deal was struck, and I got the five-thousand dollars in hundred-dollar bills.

'You must make sure the safe is locked very hard,' said the translator.

So began my life in the Sunway Hotel. A woman who ate dinner in the Allanté Restaurant most nights of the week and came to know the waiters by their names. The food was excellent, both Vietnamese and French. It's difficult to recall what the dishes were, although I would eat them over and over again as a way of passing the time, of doing what I must in order to keep going, and yet it's hard to remember. I know that there was food cooked with nuoc mam and ginger and lemongrass, as well as bœuf bourguignon and crème brûlée. The house wine was Luis Buñuel rosé, named for the Spanish movie director who had taken up with Mexico and made films about violent sex, religion and ecstasy. As rosés go it was all right. The problem was how to order more than two glasses without drawing attention to myself. It was wildly expensive, but I had handfuls of hundred-dollar bills in my safe, and I didn't really care. After dinner, I moved downstairs to the jazz bar and listened to a trio of musicians. I got to know their repertoire as well as I knew the menu and have as easily forgotten it, but while I listened to them I could drink another glass of Luis Buñuel.

I was a woman who was driven across the city of Hanoi in a taxi four times each day, return journeys made once in the morning and once in the afternoon, to find out how my husband was doing, because I couldn't ring up and ask. Nobody had the language to answer me. When I arrived at the hospital, I made my way to intensive care and waited for a doctor to see me, sometimes the Vietnamese doctor who got angry when he had to talk to me again, sometimes French doctors who were kinder on the whole. None of them would allow me into the room to see my husband, although I was allowed to peer through the glass. I talked to the other wives. Irene's husband had taken a turn for the worse, but then so had Maria's. The fizz had completely gone out of Irene, she was surly and tired. Maria crossed herself incessantly and cried.

'It's really a case of whose husband is going to die first, isn't it?' Irene said.

When I was not being driven to the hospital and back, I walked the streets and lakesides of the city. There are hundreds of lakes, but, when I came to Hoàn Kiếm, I was certain I had found the one I was looking for, the lake where Duras's mother had run the boarding house, a location where Duras had suffered a great trauma as a child. I say location because Duras was also a film-maker so, as I read her, my mind was making pictures. A red bridge led to a temple near the shore. I was constantly surprised by the redness of things in Vietnam. A pavilion that, from afar, appeared the size of a chimney, had been built in the centre of Hoàn Kiếm in honour of a fifteenth-century Vietnamese hero: his magical sword was said to have been eaten by a gold tortoise. Hoàn Kiếm means Lake of the Restored Sword. On the shoreline stood a row of French colonial villas, and I decided there and then that this was exactly where the boarding house was, or had been. I had thought there was a red bridge in Duras's story, but when I go back to her text there is no sign of one. I had begun to feel impatient with Duras, that she had led me into unimaginable danger, and I had almost had enough of her. I crossed the red bridge and came to the temple and lit some incense for my husband, then I sat and watched the surface of the lake. In the green days of love, when we were young, he and I had sat on the steps of our apartment and watched the dark light of night falling across that other lake.

One afternoon, when I arrived at the hospital, a second American woman, the wife of another man who worked in the city, had set up camp at the entrance to intensive care. This woman, who was called Stacey, was very bad news, crazy and out of control, far worse than I had been. She was so thin she looked as though she might break in half. I have no idea what was really wrong with her husband because her language was peppered with lengthy bursts of unintelligible medical terminology. From the drift of it, I supposed that, like Irene's husband, it must be something to do with his heart. Both Stacey's parents were doctors, and she was on her mobile calling them in New York, as they diagnosed her husband's condition and told her what treatment he needed. She crouched on the floor, skinny backside in the air, shouting the names of drugs as she wrote them down on a pad in front of her. 'These doctors,' she screamed, 'they have no idea what they're doing. Mommy. I have to stop them.' Two French doctors appeared and tried to calm her down. The Vietnamese doctor, the one I tried not to irritate, was watching, his expression implacable. He was not easy to appease. I had learnt to keep quite still in his presence, not to speak loudly or move my hands about quickly. A week of my vigil had now passed, and I had been allowed in to see my husband for just one minute. I thought he had recognised me. He was surrounded by tiny Vietnamese nurses with hands like the wings of dragonflies, and it seemed that he knew them better, in that minute, than he did me. But then I was wearing a mask and gown.

Irene and Maria and I looked at one another while Stacey raved on. 'Pouf,' said Maria and turned away. She appeared not to have changed her clothes for several days. She was still wearing the same elegant dark garments she had on when I first met her, only now they were soiled and shabby, and her hair was matted around the sides of her face. Irene was trying to get her husband to Bangkok, but their paperwork wasn't in order, which had confounded her, and, besides that, Bangkok Airport was closed because of political riots.

Irene, looking at Stacey, said: 'Well, that sure as shit isn't going to get her anywhere.' We looked at one another again, for once with real recognition. The survivors. So far.

At the embassy I had struck up one of those surprising spontaneous friendships that would carry on beyond the moment, past Hanoi. Anne lived by the West Lake in a tower block of diplomatic apartments. The rooms were cool and beautifully furnished, with pictures by New Zealand artists on the wall and books by New Zealand writers on the shelves. I ate with her and her husband some evenings on their balcony overlooking the lake, and near to Trúc Bạc, which John McCain famously parachuted into after he'd been shot down during the Vietnam War. Anne had begun to take me in hand. She had taught me how to say *xin chào* (hullo) and *cảm ơn bạn* (thank you), both very useful phrases. *Xin chào, cảm ơn bạn*, I said, endlessly smiling. What else could I say? Nobody would accept my Western tips, which were not permitted in communist Vietnam. Hullo and thank you got me a long way. Anne sent me to look at cathedrals, showed me about the city, took me to restaurants I wouldn't have found on my own. I had promised the staff at the embassy that I wouldn't walk out alone at night, and I had no real wish to do so.

Once night fell, I wanted to stay in the Sunway Hotel and eat and listen to jazz. Oh, yes, and drink Luis Buñuel rosé. Anne had lent me a novel by Joan Didion, one that captured a familiar tone in her writing: a lone woman in a deserted tropical hotel, drinking bourbon and waiting for something to happen, before someone gets killed by secret agents. Often there are jacaranda petals floating on a swimming pool filled with dirty water, and riots in the distance. There was no swimming pool at the Sunway, but, yes, one night, two Americans went up in the lift at the same time as I did. They were dressed in beautiful suits, wore expensive watches, sported crisp handkerchiefs in their breast pockets. The older of the two, a big man, had shining silver hair, not a strand out of place. The younger one, shorter, tubbier, said, 'So if there's nothing doing here, what happens next?' The older one said, 'We go down to Saigon and see what we can stir up there.'

It was as if I were invisible. Later, in the jazz bar, I saw an Asian man dressed with even more exquisite care – silk socks, gold-framed spectacles – sitting reading a newspaper. I thought, he's going to meet with those men from upstairs. And, after a while, the older one did come down. The Asian man produced two very large cigars and, from his pocket, a guillotine cutter that sat snugly in the palm of his hand. He squeezed his hand shut and opened it with a look of satisfaction on what I supposed was a perfect cut before offering it to the American and repeating the ritual. They sat with little conversation between them. After some time had passed, the second, younger American appeared, took his seat and accepted the ritual of the cigar, though he looked pale at the prospect.

Of course, I wanted to stay and hear what I could, but there are only so many glasses of Luis Buñuel one can drink, and so many times you can listen to a jazz trio when they have completed their repertoire for the third time, without being observed. The Asian man had become aware of my presence.

The younger American reminded me of someone. Not Didion,

I thought, Graham Greene. *The Quiet American*. There's trouble brewing here.

Trouble lurked everywhere, if you let it find you. I took a taxi to the Temple of Literature in the heart of Hanoi. The taxi driver charged me five times the fare I knew I should pay. When I remonstrated, he pushed me out of his taxi and came around to where I stood, clutching the side of the car, demanding the money. I gave it to him but also wrote the number of the taxi in my notebook as it disappeared down a boulevard.

The temple I had come to visit was built in honour of literature, a university begun in the year 1076. Five courtyards lie behind thick stone walls, filled with flowers and ancient trees and white-robed monks gliding through the shadows. As I walked in the temple grounds, I thought how the concept of temples built to honour words was so different from where I came from. I have made a temple in my head for words for as long as I can remember. They have preoccupied me when I should have been doing other things. Cuckoos and crickets, spring crocuses, they have darted and bloomed in my brain. I've put them down on paper, fought them and rearranged them and regretted them. Sometimes, when we were careless, my husband and I, words stood in the way of love, those wrongly chosen, spoken in haste, shouted, as if we were killing each other.

As I am drawn to words so, too, I have a passion for synchronicity, numbers and apparently random events that fall into unexpected order. A strange thing had happened at the embassy the day before. One of the women who worked there asked me what part of my city I lived in, back home in New Zealand. When I told her, she said, 'I've got a friend who lives in that suburb. What street?'

I told her. She said, 'That's the street where my friends live. What number?'

The house turned out to be two doors away from mine. In fact it was a house where my husband and I once lived, a place where we were not always happy and words could turn as sour as milk on a hot day.

Now, in the Temple of Literature, some other words flooded back, ones that I'd forgotten for years: I bind myself unto this day. I stood still and listened to the refrain. Not writers' words or the cruel barbs of the past. Nothing to do with Hanoi.

I bind unto myself the power
Of the great love of cherubim;
The sweet 'Well done' in judgment hour ...

It goes on for many verses. St Patrick's Lorica. My father's family was Irish. What I knew was just this: I was bound each day to the hospital where my husband lay and words for the moment seemed neither here nor there.

At the hotel, I reported the taxi driver. Almost as soon as I had done this, I regretted it. What did it matter? I had my dollars. The head of the taxi company came to the hotel, gave me back my money, apologised and bowed. I said, 'I don't want him to get into serious trouble. I expect he has a family who depend on him. Don't make him lose his job.' The head of the taxi company bowed again.

I told someone at the embassy what had happened. 'He'll be all right, won't he?' I asked.

The woman looked at me and shrugged. 'He's probably been taken into the forest and shot.'

I said, 'You don't mean that.' She didn't reply.

I don't know what happened to the man. But I looked at

myself in the mirror that night, Western and virtuous and deadly. Jacaranda petals on the surface of the pool.

I blame myself. That is a fact, and it doesn't go away. In the hospital, Stacey was still crouched on the floor outside intensive care, still babbling into her phone, banging her free fist up and down on the concrete. She saw me and stood up, switching off the phone. 'Do you believe it,' she screamed. 'I've told these jerks in there what to do, and they're not listening to me. My daddy knows what they should be giving him.'

'They may not have that specific drug,' I said.

'It wouldn't matter if they did, they're too stupid to know what to do.'

'Perhaps they know more than you think,' I said. I saw the Vietnamese doctor looking at me, his gaze calm and level. 'Would you like to come in and see your husband?' he said. 'You could give him a little food.'

I put on my mask and gown. 'Does this mean he's going to get well?'

'In time,' he said. 'Soon he will go to another ward.'

I fed my husband small spoonfuls of rice porridge. I met Anne for lunch. We went to the Green Tangerine, a restaurant in an old French building with a mysterious staircase to an upper landing. We took a table in the courtyard; for dessert we ate *citron givré*, a tangerine carefully hollowed out and refilled with the flesh mixed with cream and liqueur. The soft substance, the tart mixture of flavours combined like shots, as if we were drinking hard liquor. I began to feel drowsy. Anne said, 'About that money you've got in your safe?'

'Yes?'

'Perhaps it's time you bought yourself some treats. How about we go down Silk Street this afternoon?'

So we resorted to Pho Hàng Gai, Rue de la Soie, the street lined with silk shops. I picked up handfuls of different silk, holding them to my face, and in some I thought I detected the scent of skin like warm honey on the tongue, though it may have been that of food cooking at the back of the shop or incense burning. It didn't matter. If I closed my eyes for a moment, I was overcome with a young woman's ardour, could see the golden sheen on the back of my husband, my beloved, the play of light and dark, and I thought, M.D., you haven't abandoned me. I was wrong to doubt. I ordered jackets and skirts and pants. I went on doing this for several days, the sweet cool fabrics slithering between my fingers, like the touch of my lover, while hundred-dollar bills drifted away.

I left the three wives behind me at intensive care. No, I think Irene rescued her husband the same day my husband was moved to another room, one where I could make short visits and talk to him. Irene and her husband were returning to America. Stacey may still be in Hanoi, perhaps strapped to a chair somewhere, out in a forest. I could have spared her a backwards glance, but I didn't. But I did put my arm around Maria, awkwardly, because we were strangers, only there was nobody else and she was on her own. 'He was a good man, my husband,' she said, or that's what I understood her words to mean. His body was being taken away.

Another week passed. We talked a little during my visits, but not about much. My husband couldn't imagine the places I'd been visiting. I watched as the tiny beautiful hovering nurses tenderly massaged him. I saw that they liked him, and I wanted him back for myself. Early one morning, I made my forty-first taxi ride across the city. I met with a French nurse, who was accompanying us back to New Zealand. Four seats were booked for our party at the front of the plane – one for the nurse, one for an oxygen tank, one for my husband, and me. We boarded an ambulance, and my husband caught brief glimpses of the city as we drove through it. We passed over the long bridge spanning the vast river that I'd detected the night we arrived.

'Is that the Red River?' he asked. When the nurse said yes, he turned his head, and I saw he had tears in his eyes.

'Well, then, I've seen it,' he said. 'The Red River.'

Tạm biệt, I said under my breath. Goodbye. Goodbye, Red River, red bridge, red country.

I took his hand, our two skins crumpled together. Old silks.

STIPPLED

Jill has lived two doors along from a particular house on the hill for forty-five years without once visiting it. It is not that she is unneighbourly; she greets the people who now live there when she sees them. If they needed help, she would offer it. Sometimes she stands on the road below when she is out for a walk and admires the additions that have been made to the house, the way it is extended to twice the height it was when she lived there, the extra flight of steps, some smart new windows. With its increased height, she believes it will catch some sun, like a tree reaching up to light, which it never used to do.

It was the lack of sunlight that was her undoing when it was her house. Well, that and the steepness of steps and the squalor when she and Jack and the children first moved in. Jack and Jill are not their real names, but they will do for now. A woman had lived there when the house was still owned by the state; she had been there for several decades while the house collapsed around her, the matchwood lining untreated, the rickety kitchen cupboards still filled with the remnants of her last meals when they bought the house. It was what they could afford when they came to the city, a house the state wanted to dispose of because it was such a ruin and, as the area had become fashionable, state houses no longer had a place in this street.

Besides, Jack could look at planes coming in and out of the aerodrome not far away; when he was younger he had been a pilot in the air force. And there was the sea to look at, he reminded her, the gleaming vastness of the ocean lying in the distance. Never mind that when the wind howled, and it often did in this windy city perched on the edge of the sea, the roof rattled and shook as if it were about to fly away.

They toiled in that house, cleaning it up, adding to it, laying carpets and fresh curtains at the windows. One would think Jill might have been happy, but she wasn't. She was in a constant state of despair, crying and throwing plates when things all became too much. Their house in the provinces had had sunlight and a garden; the children fretted and fell ill too often.

'It'll be all right, love,' Jack said time and again, and each time she apologised for her discontent. His crinkly black hair was showing threads of grey. Things would get better, she promised. The house looked great, she would assure him, he had worked so hard, it wasn't that she didn't appreciate it. During the day, when he was away at work, Jill wrote plays for radio. They paid well and, with the extra she brought in, they could fit out a new kitchen; they had friends over, she tried to think of it as home. Jack was a person who cared for other people in his job as a teacher. She knew it wasn't fair that he had to come home to caring for her while she behaved like an invalid. But he was worried too; their boy was boisterous and had begun playing on the street, their quiet reflective daughter had nowhere to go except her bedroom, next to the alcove where her mother's typewriter clacked far into the night as she took on more and more work.

A long, curving path was carved into the hillside above street level. It led to the house of an old couple called Hettie and Roland, so close yet only partially visible because of the angle of the terrain. They had lived on the hill for even longer than the tenant who had died in the room where Jack and Jill slept. One day, Jill encountered Hettie on the pathway.

'Come in, I need a visitor,' Hettie had cried. 'Do come in for a cup of tea. Or a glass of brandy, or whatever you fancy.' Jill had followed her along the path and up the stairs, built at a gentle gradient.

Hettie slipped a key from a ledge behind a bush, near the back door. 'I keep Roland locked up,' Hettie said with a chuckle. Jill wasn't sure whether she meant it or not. The husband was there as it turned out; Jill was to discover he always was.

'I hear you scribble a bit,' he said when they had been introduced. 'So they tell me.' She supposed he was referring to the neighbours. As she was learning, the neighbours here seemed to keep up a constant murmuring dialogue to one another.

'I'm a writer, yes.'

He snorted. 'I wouldn't want my wife doing that. Getting her name put around.'

Still, he talked pleasantly enough about the weather and the government (he didn't ask her about her politics, only contemplated his own. He was hoping they would soon be rid of the lefties when the election came around). All the while, Hettie was clattering around in the kitchen making a pot of tea, which was cooling by the time she finally poured it, having refused Jill's offer of help. There was no sign of a brandy.

Hettie and Roland's house seemed like everything that Jill and Jack's was not. Morning sunlight fell through the dining-room window and into the sun porch and the front room where Roland sat day after day, his ancient legs swaddled in a blanket. The rooms were stuffed with furniture that would have been expensive when it was new. A gas fire glowed in a grate, with an old-fashioned fireplace surround made of mauve tiles, stippled with white flecks. Outside lay a large neglected garden. The astonishing view of the sea and mountains stretched endlessly before them, exposed on the cliff top to both the north and to the south. It was difficult to believe that a house so different to theirs could be so close, within calling distance of one another, just a house in between.

'You can have it when we've finished with it,' Hettie said cheerfully one day. She liked having Jill call in. Nobody else came these days.

Roland hunkered down in his chair. He had been a banker in his day; he intimated that he had made some good investments. 'I'm not leaving here,' he said.

'Well, you just might have to,' Hettie said in a chirpy voice and laughed. Her white hair straddled her face, and her nose dripped. Jill thought there was something odd about her response, though she couldn't put her finger on it. 'Our son doesn't want it. We've just the one son,' she told Jill. 'That's right, isn't it Roland?'

'Just one,' he said and winced.

'I can never remember. Sometimes I think we had more.' Her voice was wistful.

'That's enough, Hettie,' Roland said.

'Such beautiful children you have, Jill,' she said, as if she hadn't heard him.

'I'd be choosing who I sold my house to,' Roland said, his lip curling. He might be chair-bound, but his mind still crackled. 'If I ever did. I don't think you'd be able to afford this one.' He fixed Jill with a cool, appraising stare. It seemed that her visits didn't please him, he had taken against her for some reason she couldn't discern. He saw her and Jack as new people, and poor at that. Who else would have bought the dump along the path? Or perhaps it was simply that he saw Hettie as she had become and was ashamed that Jill saw it too, for she could hardly have missed the way things were.

'I'll let you know if the house ever goes on the market,' he said, his voice crisp. She saw herself then, in his eyes an opportunist come to get the better of them, two old people falling apart. That must be the problem. Her face was hot, it wasn't as if she had asked, the conversation belonged to them. Yet he must have seen how she looked around her with longing.

It was the last time Jill visited them.

Someone, another neighbour, told Jill that Hettie had been found wandering downtown in her nightie. Apparently, it was Hettie who needed locking up, not that this surprised Jill.

And then, without a word to anyone, Hettie and Roland were gone. Jill heard this when she was buying bread at the local shop on the corner. She supposed that the son, whom she had never met, had come and taken them away. The house was being rented out. Or that's what she was told. Later, she saw a death notice in the paper for Hettie, but it seemed Roland was still alive.

Four years had passed since she and Jack had come to live on the hill.

When the phone rang one evening, Jill answered. It was Mark, the son of Hettie and Roland. This was the first time she had heard his name. He was ringing, he said, for the honour of his family name. Only that day, he had learned that Jack and Jill had been told that, when his parents' house was up for sale, they would be told.

'I thought it was rented out,' Jill said.

'That didn't work out.'

Jill's heart was racing. 'So we could buy it?'

'Well, not exactly. We've had an offer for it. The sale closes tomorrow.'

'So – what exactly is the point of you ringing me?'

'As I mentioned, our honour.' His voice was impatient, as if this might be a concept she wouldn't understand. 'My father thought you ought to be told; I gather he'd made some sort of a promise to you. Well, we lived in that place for a long time. It's where I grew up. We knew the people all around.'

'The neighbours, yes.'

'My parents had a good name in that street.'

'Of course,' Jill said. 'But the house is still on the market until tomorrow?'

'Technically, yes, that's the case. But really it's gone.'

'So it's still possible to make a higher offer than the one you have?'

'It's in the hands of the land agent,' Mark said. 'Really, it's out of my hands.' He named the land agent and hung up before Jill could speak again.

When she told Jack, his face darkened. 'The prick,' he said. 'He didn't want us to have it.' Jill hadn't realised that he wanted the house too. He'd never said when she had gone on about it. 'You've dreamed about that house, haven't you? I know, love, I know.'

'It must be standing empty,' she said. 'All the time, and we didn't know.'

'Shall we go and look at it anyway? We could break in.' Jack was like that, a man of good works who, underneath it, was a law unto himself. 'Just so we could have it for an evening.'

'Actually, we mightn't have to break in,' Jill said. 'I know where there might be a key.'

The children had reached an age when you could take your eyes off them for a little while. They called out to them to mind themselves for half an hour.

Just as Jill guessed, the spare key to the house was tucked away on the ledge, where she had seen Hettie retrieve it years before. It was a very still evening, a winter chill in the air as if there might be a frost in the morning.

A floorboard creaked as they entered the house. 'Must be Roland,' Jack said, making Jill give a muffled scream. He was good at that, conjuring up small frights out of nothing, his way of joking.

But the house was empty, stripped of every single thing that had made it Hettie and Roland's place. The rooms seemed to roll on, one after the other, making the house much larger than they had believed it. It wasn't a grand place, not a mansion like some of the old houses in the city, although it had high, white ornate ceilings of an earlier time. There was just something about the space and lightness of the house that entered one, now that it had been stripped bare to its essential self. The electricity was turned off at the mains, but a box of matches remained on the stippled hearth, perhaps so the land agent could demonstrate the fire. Jack lit a match and tried the gas flame; it sprang into life, and within minutes the room was glowing with its heat.

There were leadlights in the windows, and a big bay window where Jill could see herself curled up reading a book.

'Look at this,' Jack called, and she went through to the bathroom where he stood admiring a dark-pink bath and wash-stand, quality Shanks porcelain. 'You don't see that every day.'

'That would have to go.'

'You vandal, no way.'

'We can't have a pink bath.'

'Yes, we can.' Jack caressed its rim lovingly. 'Beautiful.'

Outside, night was falling and the sweet and dreaming sky began to fill with a huge new moon that frisked past the windows. Jack began to sing 'I See the Moon', and Jill joined in, belting out the song in the house that wasn't theirs, sitting by the radiant fire. Planes coming into land floated past the window. Sometimes, Jack explained, they would fly in from the north, depending on which way the wind was blowing. This one was flying into the wind that was coming from the south; when there was a northerly wind, they would fly in over the sea.

'The children,' Jill said dreamily. 'We'd better go.' Already she could see the house filled with their books and the things Jack liked to collect: model aeroplanes, sets of scales, goofy notices.

'You'd be happy in this house,' Jack said, a statement, not a question. They had turned off the gas, taking one last tour. At the window of the main bedroom, Jack stopped. 'Kōwhai,' he said. 'I've been looking for somewhere to plant a tree. I'll put it beneath this window, and I'll live long enough to lie in bed and watch the tūī coming in the spring and hear them sing.' So he didn't need to tell her how he felt about the house.

As they replaced the key, Jack said, 'Whatever the offer is, tell the land agent we'll go higher.'

'We can't afford to do that,' Jill said.

'We can't afford not to.'

'We haven't any money.'

'Well, just make it up,' he said. 'It'll turn up.'

They stood on the moon-flooded lawn for another long moment. A large ngaio tree overlooked it, a trickle of shadows falling through its leaves. It is a lawn where both their children will dance at their weddings; Jill will surround it with white roses when their daughter marries, dappled light, stippled light, trickling through the tree branches. One day, Jill will look at the tree in wonder. 'Everyone I've loved has stood beneath this tree,' she will say to whoever is listening, although that's probably nobody because all around her is laughter and chatter, but it will be true: her parents, all but one of her aunts, her and Jack's children, and their children too, and the friends of her childhood, who have never abandoned her, will all have come here and been happy. This will be years and years later, and the house will have grown in size, added onto here and there, though much will remain the same. Like the bath. And, by then, Jack will have seen and heard his tūī sing in the kōwhai tree he plants, its blossom hard on the windowpane, the birds opening their throats full throttle.

'You can't do that,' the land agent said when Jill walked into his office the next day. 'That house is sold.' He was a thin man with unnaturally high colour in his cheeks, which rose even higher as his agitation increased. He wore a checked shirt beneath a tweed jacket and a tie made of a ropey fabric.

'No, it's not.'

'I tell you, I have a deal.'

'But the deal is not signed.'

'You're guessing.'

'No, I'm not,' Jill said. 'The vendor rang me last night. Now, listen to me, here is our offer, it's better than the one you have. At this very moment, our lawyer is arranging the finance. You can't deny your client the best possible price. It would be' – and here she paused with a moment of inward glee – 'dishonourable.'

'My people may outbid you.'

'Then we will go higher again.' Her recklessness thrilled her, her lies rolling off her tongue.

'Have you got a house to sell?'

'Yes.' At least that was true.

'If you place your sale in my hands, perhaps I could consider the whole matter.'

'Done,' Jill said, as if there were no further question, and held out her hand. His was clammy, but he took hers anyway.

The light and shade of their lives. It all happened in that house. There was no turning back to their old ways, or not for long. They learned to get over things, to forgive. The house two doors along became a bad dream, a place of sorrows. So near and yet so close to disaster had they come.

When Jill thought about the perils they had encountered, she shivered and put her arms around herself. Or Jack, when he was near.

The odd thing that happened, as if odd was not already enough, was that the people who wanted to buy Hettie and Roland's house in the first place were not disappointed at all when they discovered they could buy Jack and Jill's instead, and so for a while they became neighbours, until they moved on. Jill thought she should visit them but found she couldn't. That was when it began, her resistance to walking back along that path. *That path.* There are some paths you can't turn back on, or you will die. It was enough to see the white wall of the old place from her bedroom window, that is, until the kōwhai tree had grown up in front of it so that in her head it no longer existed.

Storms still battered their new house, as with the old one, but they felt safe in a way they had not done before, the timber frame sturdy enough to resist those gales that thundered in from the north and the south and sometimes within.

Not long after they moved into the house, she met another neighbour at the store, an old man who had known Hettie and Roland. Recently, he had visited Roland in the nursing home where he now lived. 'He asked how things were going over your way,' he said. 'He asked how the Māori outfit was treating his house.'

Jill doesn't tell Jack this.

Why? Because it doesn't matter.

They are who they are, and it's their house now.

As they get older and still busier, Jill and Jack will travel abroad, often together, sometimes alone. But, whenever she leaves the house, Jill will walk around it, saying goodbye. *Goodbye, goodbye, house, I'll be back,* she will tell it. And it will be waiting there for her, as if she had never been away, ready to enfold her. A poet friend of hers will write a sequence of poems about *her* house, and there is a phrase in one of them that Jill thinks of often – *thou house* – like a prayer, an incantation.

The steps will become more difficult for Jack to negotiate, as Jill supposes must have happened to Roland. She has almost forgotten the existence of the people who went before, though, when a door creaks, Jack might still say, *Hullo, Roland* or *Go home, Hettie*. He will sit in the sun in the long, still days of summer and watch the aeroplanes fly past, reliving the days when he had taken to the skies. He will wear a look of contentment, his eyes following Jill around. 'I'm so happy,' he will say.

One evening, Jill will come home late. Jack will forget that he is old, and he will go racing down the steps to meet her.

Jack will fall down and break his crown, and that will be the end of that.

Jill will not go tumbling after, but her heart will tumble on its own, over and over again, so bruised she thinks it will never recover.

She will stand at the window on nights when the moon is rising and the lights of aeroplanes trail fire across the dark sea as they come in to land. She will turn and look back to the stippled fireplace and see the two of them, merry as thieves, making the house their own.

They will not know any of this on the night of the dancing firelight and the big tender moon.

They will not know.

ACKNOWLEDGEMENTS

From *Mrs Dixon & Friend*, Heinemann, 1982: 'Mrs Dixon & Friend'

From *Unsuitable Friends*, Century Hutchinson, 1988: 'Hats'

From *The Foreign Woman*, Vintage, 1993: 'Circling to Your Left', 'Marvellous Eight'

From *The Best of Fiona Kidman's Short Stories*, Vintage, 1998: 'Tell Me the Truth about Love'

From *A Needle in the Heart*, Vintage, 2002: 'A Needle in the Heart', 'All the Way to Summer', 'Silver-Tongued'

From *The Trouble with Fire*, Vintage, 2011: 'Fragrance Rising', 'Silks'

New and previously uncollected: 'Red Bell' (a shorter version appeared in the *Warwick Review* UK), 'The Honey Frame' (first appeared in *takahē* magazine), 'Stippled'

'Tell Me the Truth about Love' is a poem by W.H. Auden.

Extract from the untitled poem 'written on seeing the Four Freedoms section' by Cecil Day-Lewis reprinted by permission of Peters Fraser & Dunlop (www.petersfraserdunlop.com) on behalf of the Estate of C. Day-Lewis.

The song referred to in 'All the Way to Summer' is *Smoke Gets in Your Eyes* (Harbach/Kern).

Look for the silver lining / Whene'er a cloud appears in the blue / Remember, somewhere, the sun is shining / And so the right thing to do is make it shine for you comes from 'Look for the Silver Lining' (Kern/De Sylva) © Universal Music Publishing. Reproduced by kind permission of Universal Music Publishing.

The poem referred to in 'Stippled' is from *House Poems*, no 15, by Rachel McAlpine.

Seven Lives on Seven Rivers by Dick Scott provided inspiration and information for the stories 'The Honey Frame' and 'Fragrance Rising'.

'Do not go gentle into that good night' is a poem by Dylan Thomas.

The picture on page 343 is reproduced with kind permission of Motueka Public Library.

The author thanks Louisa Kasza and Harriet Allan for their wise and perceptive editing, and for their friendly support for the work.

THE INFINITE AIR

The tale of the glamorous and pioneering woman known as 'the Garbo of the Skies'.

1909. In Rotorua, New Zealand, Nellie Batten pins a picture of legendary pilot Louis Blériot above the cot of her newborn daughter, Jean.

1934. Jean Batten climbs into the cockpit of her Gipsy Moth, aiming to beat Amy Johnson's solo flight record from England to Australia.

Spurred on by her mother in the face of this huge challenge, Miss Batten joins the ranks of the great early aviators, thanks to her superb navigation skills, persuasive character and unerring instinct for self-promotion. But it is a life that will know both triumph and tragedy, as her glittering success and exhilarating flights cannot last forever . . .

'A fascinating read' *Red Magazine*

'The extraordinary story of an extraordinary woman' *Irish Times*

'A gripping historical read' *Woman's Own*

PAPERBACK 9781910709085

EBOOK 9781910709115

SONGS FROM THE VIOLET CAFÉ

New Zealand, 1943. Violet Trench crosses Lake Rotorua with a small boy, Wing Lee, but rows back alone.

Twenty years later, the same body of water is the scene of an event that will have lasting repercussions for Violet and her employees at the café she now runs on the lake shore. The lives of these young people will diverge, their paths to independence taking them as far apart as Cambodia and the USA, but Violet's influence will continue to mark both those who leave and those who stay behind.

'Readers are in good hands; like all Kidman's writing, it is engaging and captivating' *The Lady*

'Kidman, a poet, is a beautiful writer' *The Times*

PAPERBACK 9781910709177

EBOOK 9781910709191

ALL DAY AT THE MOVIES

'Plumes of flame pierced the night sky, curling and licking and caressing the hurrying clouds, and there was nothing anyone could do except watch the crop burn . . .'

In 1952, war widow Irene Sandle takes up work in New Zealand's tobacco fields, hoping to build a new life for herself and her daughter. But this bold act of female self-sufficiency triggers a sequence of events whose repercussions are still felt, long after Irene's death. Against a backdrop of immense social and political change, Irene's four children lead disparate lives, and learn how far family ties can bind – or be lost forever.

With unflinching honesty and characteristic compassion, Fiona Kidman deftly exposes the fragility of even the closest human relationships, as she weaves together the narratives of a family and its changing fortunes across fifty years and three generations.

'A sweeping saga of a fascinating life and an entertaining insight into the early days of aviation' *Historical Novel Society*

'A thrilling tale of adventure and heartbreak – Kidman has triumphantly brought this inspirational heroine to life' *The Lady*

PAPERBACK 9781910709344

EBOOK 9781910709382

THIS MORTAL BOY

'The offender is not one of ours. It is unfortunate that we got this undesirable from his homeland.'

Auckland, October 1955. If young Paddy Black sings to himself he can almost see himself back home in Belfast. Yet, less than two years after sailing across the globe in search of a better life, here he stands in a prison cell awaiting trial for murder. He pulled a knife at the jukebox that night, but should his actions lead him to the gallows? As his desperate mother waits on, Paddy must face a judge and jury unlikely to favour an outsider, as a wave of moral panic sweeps the island nation.

Fiona Kidman's powerful novel explores the controversial topic of the death penalty with characteristic empathy and a probing eye for injustice.

'A universal and honest book ... an intimate portrait of one family over time, trying to reach back to the past for some fragment of understanding' *San Francisco Book Review*

'A truly gifted writer. She explores the subtleties of human interaction and family with a deft and insightful hand' *Trip Fiction*

PAPERBACK 9781910709580

EBOOK 9781910709597

Printed in the USA
CPSIA information can be obtained
at www.ICGtesting.com
JSHW030801170124
55522JS00003B/3

9 781913 547646